The Book of
Longer Short Stories

The Book of

LONGER SHORT STORIES

Selected and Introduced by
JAMES MICHIE

STEIN AND DAY/*Publishers*/New York

First published in the United States of America in 1975
Copyright © 1974 by The Bodley Head
All rights reserved
Printed in the United States of America
Stein and Day/*Publishers*/ Scarborough House,
Briarcliff Manor, N.Y. 10510

Library of Congress Cataloging in Publication Data

Michie, James, comp.
　The book of longer short stories.

　London ed. published under title: Book of longer
short stories, 1900-1974.
　　CONTENTS: Hudson, W. H. El Ombú.—Conrad, J. The
secret sharer.—Moore, G. Albert Nobbs. [etc.]
　　　1. Short stories, English. 2. English fiction—
20th century. I. Title.
PZ1.M579Bo3　[PR1309.S5]　　823'.01　　74-26613
ISBN 0-8128-1786-9

Contents

The Book of
Longer Short Stories

Introduction

What is a 'longer' short story? The answer, here, is one of between ten and twenty thousand words, longer than a short story usually is, but shorter than what is uneasily called a novella. In this anthology the stories are by British authors and were written in this century.

The traditional short story has a history of about a hundred years, and still survives healthily while its original patron, the weekly literary magazine, has given up the ghost. For economic reasons it has tended to be on the short side: at its best as fine as the best of Saki, at its worst as blatant as the worst of O. Henry, but usually, because of limits of space, dependent on an arresting opening or a shock ending, a bizarre situation, verbal wit, and emotions that, inevitably, come close to sentimentality or cynicism. Not many authors have been able to afford to write to any length they please; yet creative impulse has often refused to trim or stretch itself to the needs of the market-place. Some of the best stories of this century have been of an awkward size and lie, undiscovered except by critics and devotees, in a Collected Works. Most of the stories I have chosen will, I suspect, be unfamiliar to the average lover of literature.

By its very nature the 'longer' story is capable of greater depth than the short one. It does not have to begin with a 'bang': it can afford, like a Chekhov play, a leisurely, even deceptively ordinary opening, during which the time-bombs are cunningly fused and planted. It has enough time, in fact, to suggest time. It has enough room,

too, to adorn bare anecdote with the attractions of setting
and of character explored rather than sketched. None of
these stories relies purely upon 'point'; all of them leave
behind them more enduring and less definable reverbera-
tions – a sense of weather, the feel of a place, the memory
of a gesture, the mystery, not to be shaken off, of a personality (even of the narrator himself), quite apart from
the mere fact of what actually happens. Indeed, what fails
to happen may turn out to be the important thing.

A word of explanation for those who will look in vain
for a story by Kipling. Most of Kipling's best stories were
written before 1900 and sprang from his experience of
India; he wrote good stories after that, but not one of over
ten thousand words which seems to me representative of
his full power, and for that reason I have not given him
a place.

The following twelve stories simply represent my own
passionate preferences. Reviewing them after several read-
ings, I am struck by the fact that nine are set outside
England, four take place in or near a hotel, in four there
is a heavy fall of snow, in two a young honeymoon couple
are the central figures, the titles of two feature the word
'Mexican' and of two others the name of a tree. Such odd
coincidences, though they may reflect some unconscious
quirk of choice on my part, and though it may be amusing
to point them out, are no more significant than a red wig
being used in two different plays. In making this selection,
if I have had any criterion in mind it has been originality –
that mysterious amalgam of creative spontaneity and dis-
ciplined habit which makes imitation impossible and
parody self-defeating. On that I rest my case.

El Ombú, the first story, fittingly belongs to the oldest
tradition of story-telling – the camp-fire yarn. Through
the mouth of the old man, Nicandro, we are told the
bloody and ill-starred history of the men and women who
once lived in the now ruined house by the *ombú* tree, in
the Argentine pampas. Hudson catches to perfection the
sing-song style of the ancient gaucho, who has no doubt

told his tale many times but whose undulled grief only serves to sharpen his art. Leisurely but intense, veering but never losing track, rising and falling with the different remembered emotions, its pastoral flourishes strangely embellishing the three violent deaths and the pitiable madness that are its theme, the voice of the narrator holds one tranced in a sort of primitive subjection. Nicandro says that he was born in 1798; Hudson elsewhere mentions that he heard the story in the late 1860s from just such an old man, and made notes at the time. Over thirty years later he wrote it down. What other twentieth-century writer could have produced such a glowingly authentic 'antique'?

The Secret Sharer was also based on a true incident, one which Conrad heard of during his early years at sea. The plot – unlike that of *El Ombú* – can be told in a few words. The narrator, a young captain fresh to his command and feeling a stranger on board, discovers a seaman of about his own age clinging exhausted to a ladder at the ship's side during the night: he has, it turns out, under provocation killed a member of the crew of another ship and escaped. Intuitively, the captain recognises decency in the other face and finds himself, against all his professional instincts, hiding the man in his cabin; and finds too, disconcertingly, under the tension of the petty manoeuvres he has to devise to avoid detection, that he has come to regard the runaway as a fellow stranger, almost as his other self. In the end the 'secret sharer', with the connivance of his protector, slips over the side, to swim for it. We do not know what happens to him. We never learn the name of the narrator and we scarcely remember the name of the fugitive. We are left with a mystery that somehow persists in pointing back towards ourselves: 'It was, in the night, as though I had been faced by my own reflection in the depths of a sombre and immense mirror.'

The atmosphere of conspiracy and claustrophobia, the whispering in the darkness, the contrasting shock of normal noises on board, the insomniac anxiety in the midst of the sleepy waters of the Gulf of Siam, are evoked with eerie power. Conrad called *The Secret Sharer* one of his 'Calm-pieces' in opposition, for instance, to *Typhoon*; but the turbulence that lies at the heart of it breathes as violently as the 'eye' of any actual hurricane.

Albert Nobbs is an extraordinary work, not nearly as well known as it ought to be, for George Moore's books are little read nowadays. The subject is extraordinary – the experiences of a woman who spent her life disguised as a waiter in a Dublin hotel – but just as extraordinary is the fact that the author could handle it with such uncomplicated tenderness. But perhaps that is not so strange as it seems: Moore belonged to a generation unbothered by the discoveries of Freud and the struggle for women's rights, and he can tell the story of Albert Nobbs, 'neither man nor woman, just a perhapser', without the sexual or social self-consciousness which would surely have embarrassed it had it been attempted by a 'realist' writer forty years younger and more 'aware'. Albert's plight is described with a restrained compassion that makes it the equal of Moore's other moving account of a woman's hard life, *Esther Waters*. The technical skill, concealed rather than displayed, is remarkable. There is a story within a story, and the shift from one narrator to another goes almost unnoticed; although there are two characters who can be called, according to circumstances, either 'he' or 'she', the choice between them is always subtly right and not once is the reader confused; there are no quotation marks for speech, but there is never any doubt who is speaking; the long paragraph is used without strain and with effortless clarity. In conversation Moore was notoriously egotistical, yet *Albert Nobbs* could only have been accomplished by a writer long dedicated to observation and self-effacement.

The Black Dog and *The Almond Tree* both seem to me to be peculiarly and attractively English. One a winter-, the other a summer-piece, they are full of weather and earth, and in each the self-renewing beauty of the countryside softens the ugliness of the human self-destruction that occurs. Lizzie drowned in the pool under the hornbeam-tree, and Arthur lying in the snow beside the hawthorn-bush, are corpses, like those in pre-Raphaelite paintings, that we can bear to look upon. Both stories have a poetic, slightly eccentric ('mannered' would be quite the wrong word) style that is the mark of an author who works not so much against as regardless of fashion. In a very English way, too, the unspoken is as important as the explicit. In *The Black Dog*, once Gerald and Orianda have swum the river naked we know instinctively that they will never become lovers. In *The Almond Tree*, the unspoken is even more significant because the unhappy marriage is 'projected' through the memory of a boy, and everything is therefore slightly, and exactly rightly, out of focus: the blur has the paradoxical effect of intensifying the child's certainty of insight into the pain of the adult world.

The Dead is a justly famous story; indeed there is no other story of its length that I admire more. For the first forty pages there is nothing to suggest that it is anything more profound than a domestic *genre* painting of a middle-class Dublin musical party; but so brilliant is the brush-work that one would have been perfectly satisfied if it had remained merely that. Then, in the last half-dozen pages, the 'time-bomb' explodes: the evening is transformed by the invisible figure of Michael Furey, everything has to be looked at again through the spectacles of memory and mortality. Michael Furey does not 'count' in the story except in so far as Gabriel Conroy cannot make love to his wife that night because of him. The title is not *The Dead Youth*. He is a representative ghost, faint but infinitely powerful, a reminder that the dead, like the snowflakes that fall universally in the last sentence, are everywhere, softly, present among the gatherings of the living.

Aldous Huxley was a very uneven short story writer, but in the collection entitled *Little Mexican* he was at his happiest, in both senses of the word, and it is because of this seductive quality that I have included the story of that name. It is written with an infectious relish that makes it, above everything, enjoyable. Elsewhere Huxley's satire often fails for lack of real hatred, just as his essays in emotion often fail for lack of real conviction; in *Little Mexican* there is no target, no effort, no comment. 'Mr Oosselay' (as urbane an observer as 'Herr Issyvoo' in a better known context) bathes his Italian scene in the light of such serene irony that he and his fellow players, each with his faintly theatrical air – the author in his outsize 'artist's' hat, Fabio 'like a soldier on the stage', the old Count with his white moustaches and imperial 'in the grand Risorgimento manner' – seem like picnickers on some Illyrian lawn. It is a halcyon, but not an escapist region: truth does not hurt here, yet it is still hard for all that. Fabio and his wife, the old Count and his Colombella and the offstage Lucio act out their ancient comedy, and, when the curtain comes down on the old man's final wink, one cannot help feeling that all is for the best, even if it is in the wickedest of possible worlds. Even the destruction of the Tiepolos, which were described with such exquisite gusto, arouses nothing more than a fatalistic, half-delicious shrug of the shoulders.

When I hear Somerset Maugham dismissed as a mere 'anecdotalist' concerned with surfaces, I think of Renoir's retort to the man who criticised Monet for being nothing but 'an eye': 'Yes, but what an eye!' Maugham's best book, in the opinion of many, is *Ashenden*, which was based on his own experiences as a British agent during the 1914–18 war. Which is the best of the 'Ashenden' stories? Eric Ambler had said that if the question were polled *The Hairless Mexican* would probably receive the most votes. It would certainly get mine.

From the first to the last sentence – both equally unforgettable – the action of the story compels complete attention. Before the Hairless Mexican makes his appearance, we are already consumed with curiosity to meet him. The words of R., Ashenden's chief, are a potent appetiser: 'He hasn't had the advantages of a public-school education.... The tears will run down his face when he hears

Gounod's "Ave Maria" on the gramophone, but if you insult his dignity he'll shoot you like a dog.' From the moment he enters, wigged and scented, with his bright red nails and his iron handshake, we are in the grip of a fascination. His short absences from the narrative fill us with impatience for his return. When he does return, his entrances are invariably sudden and unnerving. He steals every scene as effortlessly as he takes the money from Ashenden at piquet.

What on earth are we to make of General Manuel Carmona – we, like Ashenden, pale, conventional people by comparison? For all his experience as an observer of men, Ashenden is out of his depth with this life-enhancing professional killer. At first, he finds the Mexican's flamboyance 'very much to his taste'. Later, when Ashenden's nerves are under strain, he becomes 'that chattering, hideous and fantastic creature'. He can display 'a feline elegance, even something of beauty'. He may be 'absurd', but he is 'not a man to be trifled with'. In the end he is, with a ghastly literalness, 'a bloody fool'. Yet even the knowledge brought by the denouement does not help us to decide finally about him. That verdict of 'bloody fool' surely expresses, as well as dismay and horror, an exasperated sort of affection.

The Man Who Loved Islands was written near the end of Lawrence's life, when disease was making his irritable genius more edgy than ever. It is slightly flawed by exasperation – by an antipathy towards all the characters, by a hatred almost of life itself (an element in Lawrence that was always lurking underneath his celebrations of natural instinct); in places it is careless and repetitious; yet it has its full share of the marvellous vatic quality that belongs to the best of the late poems and stories. Whether or not it was aimed at Compton Mackenzie, who had bought two small Channel Islands in the 1920s, is unimportant; the fact that the island-lover in the story is a writer who shops in Bond Street is, in my opinion, a mistaken lapse into the particular. It is a universal fable, not a local satire. It shows 'how tiny it [an island] has to be before you can presume to fill it with your own personality'. It is about man's need of society and his simultaneous craving for solitude, a dilemma that haunted Lawrence all his wandering, unattached life. The three islands – the familiar fairy-tale 'test of three' – are successive trials of the Master's ability to live with other people, with a woman, and, finally, with himself. They are, of course, really the same test. He fails because his motives are life-denying, death-inclined. The punitive snows of oblivion at the end may be gentler than the old flames of hell, but Lawrence is preaching a fierce sermon all the same, with 'No man is an island' as its text.

Episode at Gastein appeals to me because of its hauntingly 'negative' quality – and I mean 'negative' in a far from derogatory sense. Ludwig de Broda is the negative man *par excellence*. At forty he may be youthful in appearance, but he is backward-looking: when his old friends from Vienna greet him in the hotel with cries of 'Der Bobby!' the nickname rings grimly out of date. Recently he has stopped believing in the reality of his own name; he feels 'spectral'. He has been toying with the idea of finding a wife, and when he meets Laure in Bad Gastein, it occurs to him that she may fit the bill. In spite of her genuine 'orange' hair, she is not much more vivid than he. The bright snows and dark firs of the resort, reminiscent of a photographic negative, are the setting for his bloodless courtship and equally bloodless flirtation with suicide. Inside the discreet, silent hotel, with its glass walls and huge mirrors, the characters drift like fish in an aquarium, while, beyond, the mountain torrent suggests the passion – for life or for death – that de Broda is incapable of. Even the mineral water he drinks mocks him with the ebullience he lacks.

We observe what fails to happen during de Broda's holiday as if through glass, with a sort of avid detachment. We are not sorry for him because he is so sorry for himself. He is too self-concerned to see the truth: that it is not youth, as he thinks, that he needs, but courage. The two big tears that he sheds at the end only go to swell 'the other water' – the water not only of the warm bath, but of the snows and torrents of Wildbad Gastein that enclose this story with their elemental cold.

Graham Greene's and William Trevor's stories share a central situation: a young, ill-matched honeymoon couple arrive at a hotel abroad and are deliberately haunted by another, older couple. Whether the attempt to interfere is benevolent or predatory, it raises the same shadowy, sardonic question: can the wrongly married be either rescued or wrecked by outsiders? does intervention make any difference at all? Both stories conjure up a memorable atmosphere of place: the same odour of sexual unhappiness hangs about out-of-season Antibes in the mistral and the corridors of the squalid Slieve Gashal Hotel in Galway in summer. Both authors confidently walk the wire between laughter and tears. In *The Grass Widows*, the impersonal, straight-faced tone of the narrative makes the humour even funnier and the sadness correspondingly sadder. Despite the grotesqueries of Mr Doyle and the hilarious horrors of his establishment, the emotion we feel at the end is entirely tragic. In *May We Borrow Your Husband?*, on the other hand, the narrator declares himself: he is an ironic, middle-aged novelist and a minor actor in the events he describes; but for that very reason his comments need not be accorded the full weight of truth. If, he says, the young bride whose husband is being seduced by two homosexuals 'recognised the situation it would be a tragedy; if she were ignorant it was a comedy ... it was in the end a comedy ... a farce even'. The reader has licence to demur. Trevor's story is a tragedy because we cannot readily imagine Daphne Jackson avoiding the doom of Mrs Angusthorpe. If Greene's is a farce rather than a tragicomedy, it can only be because there is something about Poopy (her single dirty joke perhaps?) that allows us to picture her escaping one day from her

15

inevitable disillusion as hopefully as she arrived, with brand-new luggage.

These two stories seem to me models of how to solve the eternal problem of where exactly an author should place himself to best effect in relation to his characters and his readers. If he plays God, he cannot allow himself a single cough in the direction of his audience. If he is a voyeur in a cupboard, how does he eat, sleep and see enough of the action to relate it? In *The Grass Widows* the creator never intrudes, in *May We Borrow Your Husband?* he never clumsily tries to conceal himself. In their different ways they exemplify supreme artistic tact.

JAMES MICHIE

W. H. HUDSON

El Ombú

This history of a house that had been was told in the
shade, one summer's day, by Nicandro, that old man to
whom we all loved to listen, since he could remember and
properly narrate the life of every person he had known in
his native place, near to the lake of Chascomus, on the
southern pampas of Buenos Ayres.

I

In all this district, though you should go twenty leagues
to this way and that, you will not find a tree as big as this
ombú, standing solitary, where there is no house; therefore it is known to all as 'the ombú', as if but one existed;
and the name of all this estate, which is now ownerless and
ruined, is El Ombú. From one of the higher branches, if
you can climb, you will see the lake of Chascomus, two
thirds of a league away, from shore to shore, and the village on its banks. Even smaller things will you see on a
clear day; perhaps a red line moving across the water – a
flock of flamingos flying in their usual way. A great tree
standing alone, with no house near it; only the old brick
foundations of a house, so overgrown with grass and weeds
that you have to look closely to find them. When I am out
with my flock in the summer time, I often come here to
sit in the shade. It is near the main road; travellers, droves
of cattle, the diligence, and bullock-carts pass in sight.
Sometimes, at noon, I find a traveller resting in the shade,
and if he is not sleeping we talk and he tells me the news
of that great world my eyes have never seen. They say

that sorrow and at last ruin comes upon the house on whose roof the shadow of the ombú tree falls; and on that house which now is not, the shadow of this tree came every summer day when the sun was low. They say, too, that those who sit much in the ombú shade become crazed. Perhaps, sir, the bone of my skull is thicker than in most men, since I have been accustomed to sit here all my life, and though now an old man I have not yet lost my reason. It is true that evil fortune came to the old house in the end; but into every door sorrow must enter – sorrow and death that comes to all men; and every house must fall at last.

Do you hear the mangangá, the carpenter bee, in the foliage over our heads? Look at him, like a ball of shining gold among the green leaves, suspended in one place, humming loudly! Ah, señor, the years that are gone, the people that have lived and died, speak to me thus audibly when I am sitting here by myself. These are memories; but there are other things that come back to us from the past; I mean ghosts. Sometimes, at midnight, the whole tree, from its great roots to its topmost leaves, is seen from a distance shining like white fire. What is that fire, seen of so many, which does not scorch the leaves? And, sometimes, when a traveller lies down here to sleep the siesta, he hears sounds of footsteps coming and going, and noises of dogs and fowls, and of children shouting and laughing, and voices of people talking; but when he starts up and listens, the sounds grow faint, and seem at last to pass away into the tree with a low murmur as of wind among the leaves.

As a small boy, from the time when I was able, at the age of about six years, to climb on to a pony and ride, I knew this tree. It was then what it is now; five men with their arms stretched to their utmost length could hardly encircle it. And the house stood there, where you see a bed of nettles – a long, low house, built of bricks, when there were few brick houses in this district, with a thatched roof.

The last owner was just touching on old age. Not that he looked aged; on the contrary, he looked what he was, a man among men, a head taller than most, with the strength of an ox; but the wind had blown a little sprinkling of white ashes into his great beard and his hair, which grew to his shoulders like the mane of a black horse. That was Don Santos Ugarte, known to all men in this district as the White Horse, on account of the whiteness of his skin where most men look dark; also because of that proud temper and air of authority which he had. And for still another reason – the number of children in this neighbourhood of which he was said to be the father. In all houses, for many leagues around, the children were taught to reverence him, calling him 'uncle', and when he appeared they would run and, dropping on their knees before him, cry out, '*Bendición, mi tío*.' He would give them his blessing; then, after tweaking a nose and pinching an ear or two, he would flourish his whip over their heads to signify that he had done with them, and that they must quickly get out of his way.

These were children of the wind, as the saying is, and the desire of his heart was for a legitimate son, an Ugarte by name, who would come after him at El Ombú, as he had come after his father. But though he had married thrice, there was no son born, and no child. Some thought it a mystery that one with so many sons should yet be without a son. The mystery, friend, was only for those who fail to remember that such things are not determined by ourselves. We often say that He who is about us is too great to concern Himself with our small affairs. There are so many of us; and how shall He, seated on His throne at so great a distance, know all that passes in His dominions! But Santos was no ordinary person, and He who was greater than Santos had doubtless had His attention drawn to this man; and had considered the matter, and had said, 'You shall not have your desire; for though you are a devout man, one who gives freely of his goods to the church and My poor, I am not wholly satisfied with you.'

And so it came to pass that he had no son and heir.

His first two wives had died, so it was said, because of his bitterness against them. I only knew the third – Doña Mericie, a silent, sad woman, who was of less account than any servant, or any slave in the house. And I, a simple boy, what could I know of the secrets of her heart? Nothing! I only saw her pale and silent and miserable, and because her eyes followed me, I feared her, and tried always to keep out of her way. But one morning, when I came to El Ombú and went into the kitchen, I found her there alone, and before I could escape she caught me in her arms, and lifting me off my feet strained me against her breast, crying, '*Hijo de mi alma*,' and I knew not what beside; and calling God's blessing on me, she covered my face with kisses. Then all at once, hearing Santo's voice without, she dropped me and remained like a woman of stone, staring at the door with scared eyes.

She, too, died in a little while, and her disappearance made no difference in the house, and if Santos wore a black band on his arm, it was because custom demanded it and not because he mourned for her in his heart.

2

That silent ghost of a woman being gone, no one could say of him that he was hard; nor could anything be said against him except that he was not a saint, in spite of his name. But, sir, we do not look for saints among strong men, who live in the saddle, and are at the head of big establishments. If there was one who was a father to the poor it was Santos; therefore he was loved by many, and only those who had done him an injury or had crossed him in any way had reason to fear and hate him. But let me now relate what I, a boy of ten, witnessed one day in the year 1808. This will show you what the man's temper was; and his courage, and the strength of his wrists.

It was his custom to pay a visit every two or three months to a monastery at a distance of half a day's journey from El Ombú.

He was greatly esteemed by the friars, and whenever he went to see them he had a led horse to carry his presents to the Brothers; — a side of fat beef, a sucking-pig or two, a couple of lambs, when they were in season, a few fat turkeys and ducks, a bunch of big partridges, a brace or two of armadillos, the breast and wings of a fat ostrich; and in summer, a dozen ostriches' eggs, and I know not what besides.

One evening I was at El Ombú, and was just starting for home, when Santos saw me, and cried out, 'Get off and let your horse go, Nicandro. I am going to the monastery to-morrow, and you shall ride the laden horse, and save me the trouble of leading it. You will be like a little bird perched on his back and he will not feel your few ounces' weight. You can sleep on a sheepskin in the kitchen, and get up an hour before daybreak.'

The stars were still shining when we set out on our journey the next morning, in the month of June, and when we crossed the river Sanborombón at sunrise the earth was all white with hoar frost. At noon, we arrived at our destination, and were received by the friars, who embraced and kissed Santos on both cheeks, and took charge of our horses. After breakfast in the kitchen, the day being now warm and pleasant, we went and sat out of doors to sip maté and smoke, and for an hour or longer the conversation between Santos and the Brothers had been going on when, all at once, a youth appeared coming at a fast gallop towards the gate, shouting as he came, 'Los Ingléses! Los Ingléses!' We all jumped up and ran to the gate, and climbing up by the posts and bars, saw at a distance of less than half a league to the east a great army of men marching in the direction of Buenos Ayres. We could see that the foremost part of the army had come to a halt on the banks of a stream which flows past the monastery and empties itself into the Plata, two leagues further east. The army was all composed of infantry, but a great many persons on horseback could be seen following it, and these, the young man said, were neighbours

who had come out to look at the English invaders; and he
also said that the soldiers, on arriving at the stream, had
begun to throw away their blankets, and that the people
were picking them up. Santos, hearing this, said he would
go and join the crowd, and mounting his horse and followed by me, and by two of the Brothers, who said they
wished to get a few baskets for the monastery, he set out
at a gallop for the stream.

Arrived at the spot, we found that the English, not
satisfied with the ford, which had a very muddy bottom,
had made a new crossing-place for themselves by cutting
down the bank on both sides, and that numbers of
blankets had been folded and laid in the bed of the
stream where it was about twenty-five yards wide. Hundreds of blankets were also being thrown away, and the
people were picking them up and loading their horses
with them. Santos at once threw himself into the crowd
and gathered about a dozen blankets, the best he could
find, for the friars; then he gathered a few for himself
and ordered me to fasten them on the back of my horse.

The soldiers, seeing us scrambling for the blankets,
were much amused; but when one man among us cried
out, 'These people must be mad to throw their blankets
away in cold weather – perhaps their red jackets will keep
them warm when they lie down tonight' – there was one
soldier who understood, and could speak Spanish, and he
replied, 'No, sirs, we have no further need of blankets.
When we next sleep it will be in the best beds in the
capital.' Then Santos shouted back, 'That, sirs, will perhaps be a sleep from which some of you will never awake.'
That speech attracted their attention to Santos, and the
soldier who had spoken before returned, 'There are not
many men like you in these parts, therefore what you say
does not alarm us.' Then they looked at the friars fasten-
ing the blankets Santos had given them on to their horses,
and seeing that they wore heavy iron spurs strapped on
their bare feet, they shouted with laughter, and the one

who talked with us cried out, 'We are sorry, good Brothers, that we have not boots as well as blankets to give you.'

But our business was now done, and bidding good-bye to the friars, we set out on our return journey, Santos saying that we should be at home before midnight.

It was past the middle of the afternoon, we having ridden about six leagues, when we spied at a distance ahead a great number of mounted men scattered about the plain, some standing still, others galloping this way or that.

'*El pato! El pato!*' cried Santos with excitement. 'Come, boy, let us go and watch the battle while it is near, and when it is passed on we will go our way. Urging his horse to a gallop, I following, we came to where the men were struggling for the ball, and stood for a while looking on. But it was not in him to remain a mere spectator for long; never did he see a cattle-marking, or parting, or races, or a dance, or any game, and above all games el Pato, but he must have a part in it. Very soon he dismounted to throw off some of the heaviest parts of his horsegear, and ordering me to take them up on my horse and follow him, he rode in among the players.

About forty or fifty men had gathered at the spot, and were sitting quietly on their horses in a wide circle, waiting to see the result of a struggle for the pato between three men who had hold of the ball. They were strong men, well mounted, each resolved to carry off the prize from the others. Sir, when I think of that sight, and remember that the game is no longer played because of the Tyrant who forbade it, I am ready to cry out that there are no longer men on these plains where I first saw the light! How they tugged and strained and sweated, almost dragging each other out of the saddle, their trained horses leaning away, digging their hoofs into the turf, as when they resist the shock of a lassoed animal, when the lasso stiffens and the pull comes! One of the men was a big, powerful mulatto, and the by-standers, thinking the victory would be his, were only waiting to see him wrest the ball from the others to rush upon and try to deprive him of it before he could escape from the crowd.

Santos refused to stand inactive, for was there not a fourth handle to the ball to be grasped by another fighter? Spurring his horse into the group, he very soon succeeded in getting hold of the disengaged handle. A cry of resentment at this action on the part of a stranger went up from some of those who were looking on, mixed with applause at his daring from others, while the three men who had been fighting against each other, each one for himself, now perceived that they had a common enemy. Excited as they were by the struggle, they could not but be startled at the stranger's appearance – that huge man on a big horse, so white-skinned and long-haired, with a black beard, that came down over his breast, and who showed them, when he threw back his poncho, the knife that was like a sword and the big brass-barrelled pistol worn at his waist. Very soon after he joined in the fray all four men came to the earth. But they did not fall together, and the last to go down was Santos, who would not be dragged off his horse, and in the end horse and man came down on the top of the others. In coming down, two of the men had lost their hold of the ball; last of all, the big mulatto, to save himself from being crushed under the falling horse, was forced to let go, and in his rage at being beaten he whipped out his long knife against the stranger. Santos, too quick for him, dealt him a blow on the forehead with the heavy silver handle of his whip, dropping him stunned to the ground. Of the four, Santos alone had so far escaped injury, and rising and remounting, the ball still in his hand, he rode out from among them, the crowd opening on each side to make room for him.

Now in the crowd there was one tall, imposing-looking man, wearing a white poncho, many silver ornaments, and a long knife in an embossed silver sheath; his horse, too, which was white as milk, was covered with silver trappings. This man alone raised his voice. 'Friends and comrades,' he cried, 'is this to be the finish? If this stranger is permitted to carry the pato away, it will not be because of his stronger wrist and better horse, but because he carries firearms. Comrades, what do you say?'

But there was no answer. They had seen the power and resolution of the man, and though they were many they preferred to let him go in peace. Then the man on a white horse, with a scowl of anger and contempt, turned from them and began following us at a distance of about fifty yards. Whenever Santos turned back to come to close quarters with him, he retired, only to turn and follow us again as soon as Santos resumed his course. In this way we rode till sunset. Santos was grave, but calm; I, being so young, was in constant terror. 'Oh, uncle,' I whispered, 'for the love of God fire your pistol at this man and kill him, so that he may not kill us!'

Santos laughed. 'Fool of a boy,' he replied, 'do you not know that he wants me to fire at him! He knows that I could not hit him at this distance, and that after discharging my pistol we should be equal, man to man, and knife to knife; and who knows then which would kill the other? God knows best, since He knows everything, and He has put it into my heart not to fire.'

When it grew dark we rode slower, and the man then lessened the distance between us. We could hear the chink-chink of his silver trappings, and when I looked back I could see a white misty form following us like a ghost. Then, all at once, there came a noise of hoofs and a whistling sound of something thrown, and Santos' horse plunged and reared and kicked, then stood still trembling with terror. His hind legs were entangled in the bolas which had been thrown. With a curse Santos threw himself off, and, drawing his knife, cut the thong which bound the animal's legs, and remounting we went on as before, the white figure still following us.

At length, about midnight, the Sanborombón was reached, at the ford where we had crossed in the morning, where it was about forty yards wide, and the water only high as the surcingle in the deepest parts.

'Let your heart be glad, Nicandro!' said Santos, as we went down into the water; 'for our time is come now, and be careful to do as I bid you.'

We crossed slowly, and coming out on the south side, Santos quietly dropped off his horse, and, speaking in a low voice, ordered me to ride slowly on with the two horses and wait for him in the road. He said that the man who followed would not see him crouching under the bank, and thinking it safe would cross over, only to receive the charge fired at a few yards' distance.

That was an anxious interval that followed, I waiting alone, scarcely daring to breathe, staring into the darkness in fear of that white figure that was like a ghost, listening for the pistol shot. My prayer to heaven was to direct the bullet in its course, so that it might go to that terrible man's heart, and we be delivered from him. But there was no shot, and no sound except a faint chink of silver and sound of hoof-beats that came to my ears after a time, and soon ceased to be heard. The man, perhaps, had some suspicion of the other's plan and had given up the chase and gone away.

Nothing more do I remember of that journey which ended at El Ombú at cock-crow, except that at one spot Santos fastened a thong round my waist and bound me before and behind to the saddle to prevent my falling from my horse every time I went to sleep.

3

Remember, señor, that I have spoken of things that passed when I was small. The memories of that time are few and scattered, like the fragments of tiles and bricks and rusty iron which one may find half-buried among the weeds, where the house once stood. Fragments that once formed part of the building. Certain events, some faces, and some voices, I remember, but I cannot say the year. Nor can I say how many years had gone by after Doña Mericie's death, and after my journey to the monastery. Perhaps they were few, perhaps many. Invasions had come, wars with a foreigner and with the savage, and Independence, and many things had happened at a distance. He, Santos Ugarte, was older, I know, greyer, when that great misfortune and calamity came to one whom God had created so strong, so brave, so noble. And all on account of a slave, a youth born at El Ombú, who had been preferred above the others by his master. For, as it is said, we breed crows to pick our eyes out. But I will say nothing against that poor youth, who was the cause of the disaster, for it was not wholly his fault. Part of the fault was in Santos – his indomitable temper and his violence. And perhaps, too, the time was come when He who rules over all men had said, 'You have raised your voice and have ridden over others long enough. Look, Santos! I shall set My foot upon you, and you shall be like a wild pumpkin at the end of summer, when it is dryer and more brittle than an empty egg-shell.'

Remember that there were slaves in those days, also that there was a law fixing every man's price, old or young, so that if any slave went, money in hand, to his master and offered him the price of his liberty, from that moment he became a free man. It mattered not that his master wished not to sell him. So just was the law.

Of his slaves Santos was accustomed to say, 'These are my children, and serve because they love me, not because they are slaves; and if I were to offer his freedom to any one among them, he would refuse to take it.' He saw their faces, not their hearts.

His favourite was Meliton, black but well favoured, and though but a youth, he had authority over the others, and dressed well, and rode his master's best horses, and had horses of his own. But it was never said of him that he gained that eminence by means of flattery and a tongue cunning to frame lies. On the contrary, he was loved by all, even by those he was set above, because of his goodness of heart and a sweet and gay disposition. He was one of those who can do almost anything better than others; whatever his master wanted done, whether it was to ride a

27

race, or break a horse, or throw a lasso, or make a bridle, or whip, or surcingle, or play on a guitar, or sing, or dance, it was Meliton, Meliton. There was no one like him.

Now this youth cherished a secret ambition in his heart, and saved, and saved his money; and at length one day he came with a handful of silver and gold to Santos, and said, 'Master, here is the price of my freedom, take it and count it, and see that it is right, and let me remain at El Ombú to serve you henceforth without payment. But I shall no longer be a slave.'

Santos took the money into his hand, and spoke, 'It was for this then that you saved, even the money I gave you to spend and to run with, and the money you made by selling the animals I gave you – you saved it for this! Ingrate, with a heart blacker than your skin! Take back the money, and go from my presence, and never cross my path again if you wish for a long life.' And with that he hurled the handful of silver and gold into the young man's face with such force that he was cut and bruised with the coins and well nigh stunned. He went back staggering to his horse, and mounting, rode away, sobbing like a child, the blood running from his face.

He soon left this neighbourhood and went to live at Las Vivoras, on the Vecino river, south of Dolores, and there made good use of his freedom, buying fat animals for the market; and for a space of two years he prospered, and every man, rich or poor, was his friend. Nevertheless he was not happy, for his heart was loyal and he loved his old master, who had been a father to him, and desired above all things to be forgiven. And, at length, hoping that Santos had outlived his resentment and would be pleased to see him again, he one day came to El Ombú and asked to see the master.

The old man came out of the house and greeted him jovially. 'Ha, Meliton,' he cried with a laugh, 'you have returned in spite of my warning. Come down from your horse and let me take your hand once more.'

The other, glad to think he was forgiven, alighted, and

advancing, put out his hand. Santos took it in his, only to crush it with so powerful a grip that the young man cried out aloud, and blinded with tears of pain he did not see that his master had the big brass pistol in his left hand, and did not know that his last moment had come. He fell with a bullet in his heart.

Look, señor, where I am pointing, twenty yards or so from the edge of the shadow of the ombú, do you see a dark green weed with a yellow flower on a tall stem growing on the short, dry grass? It was just there, on the very spot where the yellow flower is, that poor Meliton fell, and was left lying, covered with blood, until noon the next day. For no person dared take up the corpse until the Alcalde had been informed of the matter and had come to inquire into it.

Santos had mounted his horse and gone away without a word, taking the road to Buenos Ayres. He had done that for which he would have to pay dearly; for a life is a life, whether the skin be black or white, and no man can slay another deliberately, in cold blood, and escape the penalty. The law is no respecter of persons, and when he who commits such a deed is a man of substance, he must expect that advocates and judges, with all those who take up his cause, will bleed him well before they procure him a pardon.

Ugarte cared nothing for that, he had been as good as his word, and the devil in his heart was satisfied. Only he would not wait at his estancia to be taken, nor would he go and give himself up to the authorities, who would then have to place him in confinement, and it would be many months before his liberation. That would be like suffocation to him; to such a man a prison is like a tomb. No, he would go to Buenos Ayres and embark for Montevideo, and from that place he would put the matter in motion, and wait there until it was all settled and he was free to return to El Ombú.

Dead Meliton was taken away and buried in consecrated ground at Chascomus. Rain fell, and washed away the red stains on the ground. In the spring, the swallows returned and built their nests under the eaves; but Ugarte came not back, nor did any certain tidings of him reach us. It was said, I know not whether truly or not, that the advocate who defended him, and the judge of first instance who had the case before him, had quarrelled about the division of the reward, and both being rich, proud persons, they had allowed themselves to forget the old man waiting there month after month for his pardon, which never came to him.

Better for him if he never heard of the ruin which had fallen on El Ombú during his long exile. There was no one in authority: the slaves, left to themselves, went away, and there was no person to restrain them. As for the cattle and horses, they were blown away like thistle-down, and everyone was free to pasture his herds and flocks on the land.

The house for a time was in charge of some person placed there by the authorities, but little by little it was emptied of its contents; and at last it was abandoned, and for a long time no one could be found to live in it on account of the ghosts.

4

There was living at that time, a few leagues from El Ombú, one Valerio de la Cueva, a poor man, whose all consisted of a small flock of three or four hundred sheep and a few horses. He had been allowed to make a small rancho, a mere hut, to shelter himself and his wife Donata and their one child, a boy named Bruno; and to pay for the grass his few sheep consumed he assisted in the work at the estancia house. This poor man, hearing of El Ombú, where he could have house and ground for nothing, offered himself as occupant, and in time came with wife and child and his small flock, and all the furniture he possessed – a bed, two or three chairs, a pot and kettle, and perhaps a few other things. Such poverty El Ombú had not known, but all others had feared to inhabit such a place on account of its evil name, so that it was left for Valerio, who was a stranger in the district.

Tell me, señor, have you ever in your life met with a man, who was perhaps poor, or even clothed in rags, and who yet, when you had looked at and conversed with him, has caused you to say: Here is one who is like no other man in the world? Perhaps on rising and going out, on some clear morning in summer, he looked at the sun when it rose, and perceived an angel sitting in it, and as he gazed, something from that being fell upon and passed into and remained with him. Such a man was Valerio. I have known no other like him.

'Come, friend Nicandro,' he would say, 'let us sit down in the shade and smoke our cigarettes, and talk of our animals. Here are no politics under this old ombú, no ambitions and intrigues and animosities – no bitterness except in these green leaves. They are our laurels – the leaves of the ombú. Happy Nicandro, who never knew the life of cities! I wish that I, too, had seen the light on these quiet plains, under a thatched roof. Once I wore fine clothes and gold ornaments, and lived in a great house where there were many servants to wait on me. But happy I have never been. Every flower I plucked changed into a nettle to sting my hand. Perhaps that maleficent one, who has pursued me all my days, seeing me now so humbled and one with the poor, has left me and gone away. Yes, I am poor, and this frayed garment that covers me will I press to my lips because it does not shine with silk and gold embroidery. And this poverty which I have found will I cherish, and bequeath it as a precious thing to my child when I die. For with it is peace.'

The peace did not last long; for when misfortune has singled out a man for its prey, it will follow him to the end, and he shall not escape from it though he mount up to the clouds like the falcon, or thrust himself deep down into the earth like the armadillo.

Valerio had been two years at El Ombú when there came an Indian invasion on the southern frontier. There was no force to oppose it; the two hundred men stationed at the Guardia del Azul had been besieged by a part of the invaders in the fort, while the larger number of the savages were sweeping away the cattle and horses from the country all round. An urgent order came to the commander at Chascomus to send a contingent of forty men from the department; and I, then a young man of twenty, who had seen no service, was cited to appear at the Comandancia, in readiness to march. There I found that Valerio had also been cited, and from that moment we were together. Two days later we were at the Azul, the Indians having retired with their booty; and when all the contingents from the various departments had come in, the commander, one Colonel Barboza, set out with about six hundred men in pursuit.

It was known that in their retreat the Indians had broken up their force into several parties, and that these had taken different directions, and it was thought that these bodies would re-unite after a time, and that the larger number would return to their territory by way of Trinqué Lauquén, about seventy-five leagues west of Azul. Our Colonel's plan was to go quickly to this point and wait the arrival of the Indians. It was impossible that they, burdened with the thousands of cattle they had collected, could move fast, while we were burdened with nothing, the only animals we drove before us being our horses. These numbered about five thousand, but many were unbroken mares, to be used as food. Nothing but mare's flesh did we have to eat.

It was the depth of winter, and worse weather I have never known. In this desert I first beheld that whiteness called snow, when the rain flies like cotton-down before the wind, filling the air and whitening the whole earth. All day and every day our clothes were wet, and there was no shelter from the wind and rain at night, nor could we make fires with the soaked grass and reeds, and wood there was none, so that we were compelled to eat our mare's flesh uncooked.

Three weeks were passed in this misery, waiting for the Indians and seeking for them, with the hills of Gaumini now before us in the south, and now on our left hand; and still no sight and no sign of the enemy. It seemed as if the earth had opened and swallowed him up. Our Colonel was in despair, and we now began to hope that he would lead us back to the Azul.

In these circumstances one of the men, who was thinly clad and had been suffering from a cough, dropped from his horse, and it was then seen that he was likely to die, and that in any case he would have to be left behind. Finding that there was no hope for him, he begged that those who were with him would remember, when they were at home again, that he had perished in the desert and that his soul was suffering in purgatory, and that they would give something to the priests to procure him ease. When asked by his officer to say who his relations were and where they lived, he replied that he had no one belonging to him. He said that he had spent many years in captivity among the Indians at the Salinas Grandes, and that on his return he had failed to find any one of his relations living in the district where he had been born. In answer to further questions, he said that he had been carried away when a small boy, that the Indians on that occasion had invaded the Christian country in the depth of winter, and on their retreat, instead of returning to their own homes, they had gone east, towards the sea coast, and had encamped on a plain by a small stream called Curumamuel, at Los Tres Arroyos, where there was firewood and sweet water, and good grass for the cattle, and where they found many Indians, mostly women and children, who had gone thither to await their coming; and at that spot they had remained until the spring.

The poor man died that night, and we gathered stones and piled them on his body so that the foxes and caranchos should not devour him.

At break of day next morning we were on horseback marching at a gallop toward sunrise, for our Colonel had determined to look for the Indians at that distant spot near the sea where they had hidden themselves from their pursuers so many years before. The distance was about seventy leagues, and the journey took us about nine days. And at long last, in a deep valley near the sea, the enemy was discovered by our scouts, and we marched by night until we were within less than a league of their encampment, and could see their fires. We rested there for four hours, eating raw flesh and sleeping. Then every man was ordered to mount his best horse, and we were disposed in a half-moon, so that the free horses could easily be driven before us. The Colonel, sitting on his horse, addressed us. 'Boys,' he said, 'you have suffered much, but now the victory is in our hands, and you shall not lose the reward. All the captives you take, and all the thousands of horses and cattle we succeed in recovering, shall be sold by public auction on our return, and the proceeds divided among you.'

He then gave the order, and we moved quietly on for a space of half a league, and coming to the edge of the valley saw it all black with cattle before us, and the Indians sleeping in their camp; and just when the sun rose from the sea and God's light came over the earth, with a great shout we charged upon them. In a moment the multitude of cattle, struck with panic, began rushing away, bellowing in all directions, shaking the earth beneath their hoofs. Our troop of horses, urged on by our yells, were soon in the encampment, and the savages, rushing hither and thither, trying to save themselves, were shot and speared and cut down by swords. One desire was in all our hearts, one cry on all lips – kill! kill! kill! Such a slaughter had not been known for a long time, and birds and foxes and armadillos must have grown fat on the flesh of the heathen we left for them. But we killed only the men, and few escaped; the women and children we made captive.

Two days we spent in collecting the scattered cattle and horses, numbering about ten thousand; then with our spoil we set out on our return and arrived at the Azul at the end of August. On the following day the force was broken up into the separate contingents of which it was composed, and each in its turn was sent to the Colonel's house to be paid. The Chascomus contingent was the last to go up, and on presenting ourselves, each man received two months' soldier's pay, after which Colonel Barboza came out and thanked us for our services, and ordered us to give up our arms at the fort and go back to our district, every man to his own house.

'We have spent some cold nights in the desert together, neighbour Nicandro,' said Valerio, laughing, 'but we have fared well – on raw horse flesh; and now to make it better we have received money. Why, look, with all this money I shall be able to buy a pair of new shoes for Bruno. Brave little man! I can see him toddling about among the cardoon thistles, searching for hens' eggs for his mother, and getting his poor little feet full of thorns. If there should be any change left he shall certainly have some sugar-plums.'

But the others on coming to the fort began to complain loudly of the treatment they had received, when Valerio, rebuking them, told them to act like men and tell the Colonel that they were not satisfied, or else hold their peace.

'Will you, Valerio, be our spokesman?' they cried, and he consenting, they all took up their arms again and followed him back to the Colonel's house.

Barboza listened attentively to what was said and replied that our demands were just. The captives and cattle, he said, had been placed in charge of an officer appointed by the authorities and would be sold publicly in a few days. Let them now return to the fort and give up their arms, and leave Valerio with him to assist in drawing up a formal demand for their share of the spoil.

We then retired once more, giving *vivas* to our Colonel. But no sooner had we given up our arms at the fort than we were sharply ordered to saddle our horses and take our departure. I rode out with the others, but seeing that Valerio did not overtake us I went back to look for him.

35

This was what had happened. Left alone in his enemy's hands, Barboza had his arms taken from him, then ordered his men to carry him out to the patio and flay him alive. The men hesitated to obey so cruel a command, and this gave Valerio time to speak. 'My Colonel,' he said, 'you put a hard task on these poor men, and my hide when taken will be of no value to you or to them. Bid them lance me or draw a knife across my throat, and I will laud your clemency.'

'You shall not lose your hide nor die,' returned the Colonel, 'for I admire your courage. Take him, boys, and stake him out, and give him two hundred lashes; then throw him into the road so that it may be known that his rebellious conduct has been punished.'

This order was obeyed, and out upon the road he was thrown. A compassionate storekeeper belonging to the place saw him lying there insensible, the carrion-hawks attracted by his naked bleeding body hovering about him; and this good man took him and was ministering to him when I found him. He was lying, face down, on a pile of rugs, racked with pains, and all night long his sufferings were terrible; nevertheless, when morning came, he insisted on setting out at once on our journey to Chascomus. When his pain was greatest and caused him to cry out, the cry, when he saw my face, would turn to a laugh. 'You are too tender-hearted for this world we live in,' he would say. 'Think nothing of this, Nicandro. I have tasted man's justice and mercy before now. Let us talk of pleasanter things. Do you know that it is the first of September to-day? Spring has come back, though we hardly notice it yet in this cold southern country. It has been winter, winter with us, and no warmth of sun or fire, and no flowers and no birds' song. But our faces are towards the north now; in a few days we shall sit again in the shade of the old ombú, all our toil and suffering over, to listen to the mangangá humming among the leaves and to the call of the yellow ventevéo. And better than all, little Bruno will come to us with his hands full of scarlet verbenas. Perhaps in a few years' time you, too, will be a father, Nicandro, and will know what it is to hear a child's prattle. Come, we have rested long enough, and have many leagues to ride!'

The leagues were sixty by the road, but something was gained by leaving it, and it was easier for Valerio when the horses trod on the turf. To gallop or to trot was impossible, and even walking I had to keep at his side to support him with my arm; for his back was all one everbleeding wound, and his hands were powerless, and all his joints swollen and inflamed as a result of his having been stretched out on the stakes. Five days we travelled, and day by day and night by night he grew feebler, but he would not rest; so long as the light lasted he would be on the road; and as we slowly pressed on, I supporting him, he would groan with pain and then laugh and begin to talk of the journey's end and of the joy of seeing wife and child again.

It was afternoon on the fifth day when we arrived. The sight of the ombú which we had had for hours before us, strongly excited him; he begged me, almost with tears, to urge the horses to a gallop, but it would have killed him, and I would not do it.

No person saw our approach, but the door stood open, and when we had walked our horses to within about twenty yards we heard Bruno's voice prattling to his mother. Then suddenly Valerio slipped from the saddle before I could jump down to assist him, and staggered on for a few paces towards the door. Running to his side I heard his cry – 'Donata! Bruno! let my eyes see you! one kiss!' Only then his wife heard, and running out to us, saw him sink, and with one last gasp expire in my arms.

Strange and terrible scenes have I witnessed, but never a sadder one than this! Tell me, señor, are these things told in books, – does the world know them?

Valerio was dead. He who was so brave, so generous even in his poverty, of so noble a spirit, yet so gentle; whose words were sweeter than honey to me. Of what his loss was to others – to that poor woman who was the mother of his one child, his little Bruno – I speak not. There are things about which we must be silent, or say only, turning our eyes up: Has He forgotten us! Does He know? But to me the loss was greater than all losses: for he was my friend, the man I loved above all men, who was more to me than any other, even than Santos Ugarte, whose face I should see no more.

For he, too, was dead.

And now I have once more mentioned the name of that man, who was once so great in this district, let me, before proceeding with the history of El Ombú, tell you his end. I heard of it by chance long after he had been placed under the ground.

It was the old man's custom in that house, on the other side of the Rio de la Plata where he was obliged to live, to go down every day to the waterside. Long hours would he spend there, sitting on the rocks, always with his face towards Buenos Ayres. He was waiting, waiting for the pardon which would, perhaps, in God's good time, come to him from that forgetful place. He was thinking of El Ombú; for what was life to him away from it, in that strange country? And that unsatisfied desire, and perhaps remorse, had, they say, made his face terrible to look at, for it was like the face of a dead man who had died with wide-open eyes.

One day some boatmen on the beach noticed that he was seated on the rocks far out and that when the tide rose he made no movement to escape from the water. They saw him sitting waist-deep in the sea, and when they rescued him from his perilous position and brought him to the shore, he stared at them like a great white owl and talked in a strange way.

'It is very cold and very dark,' he said, 'and I cannot see your faces, but perhaps you know me. I am Santos Ugarte, of El Ombú. I have had a great misfortune, friends. To-day in my anger I killed a poor youth whom I loved like a son – my poor boy Meliton! Why did he

despise my warning and put himself in my way! But I will
say no more about that. After killing him I rode away with
the intention of going to Buenos Ayres, but on the road I
repented of my deed and turned back. I said that with my
own hands I would take him up and carry him in, and call
my neighbours together to watch with me by his poor
body. But, sirs, the night overtook me and the Sanborombón is swollen with rains, as you no doubt know, and in
swimming it I lost my horse. I do not know if he was
drowned. Let me have a fresh horse, friends, and show
me the way to El Ombú, and God will reward you.'

In that delusion he remained till the end, a few days
later, when he died. May his soul rest in peace!

5

Señor, when I am here and remember these things, I
sometimes say to myself: Why, old man, do you come to
this tree to sit for an hour in the shade, since there is not
on all these plains a sadder or more bitter place? My
answer is, To one who has lived long, there is no house
and no spot of ground, overgrown with grass and weeds,
where a house once stood and where men have lived, that
is not equally sad. For this sadness is in us, in a memory
of other days which follows us into all places. But for the
child there is no past: he is born into the world light-
hearted like a bird; for him gladness is everywhere.

That is how it was with little Bruno, too young to feel
the loss of a father or to remember him long. It was her
great love of this child which enabled Donata to live
through so terrible a calamity. She never quitted El
Ombú. An embargo had been placed on the estancia so
that it could not be sold, and she was not disturbed in her
possession of the house. She now shared it with an old
married couple, who, being poor and having a few animals,
were glad of a place to live in rent free. The man, whose
name was Pascual, took care of Donata's flock and the
few cows and horses she owned along with his own. He
was a simple, good-tempered old man, whose only fault

was indolence, and a love of the bottle, and of play. But that mattered little, for when he gambled he invariably lost, through not being sober, so that when he had any money it was quickly gone.

Old Pascual first put Bruno on a horse and taught him to ride after the flock, and to do a hundred things. The boy was like his father, of a beautiful countenance, and black curling hair, and eyes as lively as a bird's. It was not strange that Donata loved him as no mother ever loved a son, but as he grew up a perpetual anxiety was in her heart lest he should hear the story of his father's death and the cause of it. For she was wise in this; she knew that the most dangerous of all passions is that of revenge, since when it enters into the heart all others, good or bad, are driven out, and all ties and interests and all the words that can be uttered are powerless to restrain a man; and the end is ruin. Many times she spoke of this to me, begging me with tears never to speak of my dead friend to Bruno, lest he should discover the truth, and that fatal rage should enter into his heart.

It had been Donata's custom, every day since Valerio's death, to take a pitcher of water, fresh from the well, and pour it out on the ground, on the spot where he had sunk down and expired, without that sight of wife and child, that one kiss, for which he had cried. Who can say what caused her to do such a thing? A great grief is like a delirium, and sometimes gives us strange thoughts, and makes us act like demented persons. It may have been because of the appearance of the dead face as she first saw it, dry and white as ashes, the baked black lips, the look of thirst that would give everything for a drink of cold water; and that which she had done in the days of anguish, of delirium, she had continued to do.

The spot where the water was poured each day being but a few yards from the door of the house was of a dryness and hardness of fire-baked bricks, trodden hard by the feet of I know not how many generations of men, and by hoofs of horses ridden every day to the door. But after a long time of watering a little green began to appear in the one spot; and the green was of a creeping plant with small round malva-like leaves, and little white flowers like porcelain shirt buttons. It spread and thickened, and was like a soft green carpet about two yards long placed on that dry ground, and it was of an emerald greenness all the year round, even in the hot weather when the grass was dead and dry and the plains were in colour like a faded yellow rag.

When Bruno was a boy of fourteen I went one day to help him in making a sheepfold, and when our work was finished in the afternoon we went to the house to sip maté. Before going in, on coming to that green patch, Bruno cried out, 'Have you ever seen so verdant a spot as this, Nicandro, so soft and cool a spot to lie down on when one is hot and tired?' He then threw himself down full length upon it, and, lying at ease on his back, he looked up at Donata, who came out to us, and spoke laughingly, 'Ah, little mother of my soul! A thousand times have I asked you why you poured water every day on this spot and you would not tell me. Now I have found out. It was all to make me a soft cool spot to lie on when I come back tired and hot from work. Look! is it not like a soft bed with a green and white velvet coverlid; bring water now, mother mine, and pour it on my hot, dusty face.'

She laughed, too, poor woman, but I could see the tears in her eyes – the tears which she was always so careful to hide from him.

All this I remember as if it had happened yesterday; I can see and hear it all – Donata's laugh and the tears in her eyes which Bruno could not see. I remember it so well because this was almost the last time I saw her before I was compelled to go away, for my absence was long. But before I speak of that change let me tell you of something that happened about two years before at El Ombú, which brought a new happiness into that poor widow's life.

It happened that among those that had no right to be on the land, but came and settled there because there was no one to forbid them, there was a man named Sanchez, who had built himself a small rancho about half a league from the old house, and kept a flock of sheep. He was a widower with one child, a little girl named Monica. This Sanchez, although poor, was not a good man, and had no tenderness in his heart. He was a gambler, always away from his rancho, leaving the flock to be taken care of by poor little Monica. In winter it was cruel, for then the sheep travel most, and most of all on cold, rough days; and she without a dog to help her, barefooted on the thistle-grown land, often in terror at the sight of cattle, would be compelled to spend the whole day out of doors. More than once on a winter evening in bad weather I have found her trying to drive the sheep home in the face of the rain, crying with misery. It hurt me all the more because she had a pretty face: no person could fail to see its beauty, though she was in rags and her black hair in a tangle, like the mane of a horse that has been feeding among the burrs. At such times I have taken her up on my saddle and driven her flock home for her, and have said to myself: Poor lamb without a mother, if you were mine I would seat you on the horns of the moon; but, unhappy one! he whom you call father is without compassion.

At length, Sanchez, finding himself without money, just when strangers from all places were coming to Chascomus to witness a great race, and anxious not to lose this chance of large winnings, sold his sheep, having nothing of more value to dispose of. But instead of winning he lost, and then leaving Monica in a neighbour's house he went away, promising to return for her in a few days. But he did not return, and it was believed by everybody that he had abandoned the child.

It was then that Donata offered to take her and be a mother to the orphan, and I can say, señor, that the poor child's own mother, who was dead, could not have treated her more tenderly or loved her more. And the pretty one had now been Donata's little daughter and Bruno's play-mate two years when I was called away, and I saw them not again and heard no tidings of them for a space of five years – the five longest years of my life.

6

I went away because men were wanted for the army, and I was taken. I was away, I have said, five years, and the five would have been ten, and the ten twenty, supposing that life had lasted, but for a lance wound in my thigh, which made me a lame man for the rest of my life. That was the reason of my discharge and happy escape from that purgatory. Once back in these plains where I first saw heaven's light, I said in my heart: I can no longer spring light as a bird on to the back of an unbroken animal and laugh at his efforts to shake me off; nor can I throw a lasso on a running horse or bull and, digging my heel in the ground, pit my strength against his; nor can I ever be what I have been in any work or game on horseback or on foot; nevertheless, this lameness, and all I have lost through it, is a small price to pay for my deliverance.

But this is not the history of my life; let me remember that I speak only of those who have lived at El Ombú in my time, in the old house which no longer exists.

There had been no changes when I returned, except those five years had made Bruno almost a man, and more than ever like his father, except that he never had that I-know-not-what something to love in the eyes which made Valerio different from all men. Donata was the same, but older. Grey hair had come to her in her affliction; now her hair which should have been black was all white – but she was more at peace, for Bruno was good to her, and as a widow's only son was exempt from military service. There was something else to make her happy. Those two, who were everything to her, could not grow up under one roof and not love; now she could look with confidence to a union between them, and there would be no separation. But even so, that old fear she had so often spoken of to me in former days was never absent from her heart.

Bruno was now away most of the time, working as a

cattle drover, his ambition being, Donata informed me, to make money so as to buy everything needed for the house.

I had been back, living in that poor rancho, half a league from El Ombú, where I first saw the light, for the best part of a year, when Bruno, who had been away with his employer buying cattle in the south, one day appeared at my place. He had not been to El Ombú, and was silent and strange in his manner, and when we were alone together I said to him, 'What has happened to you, Bruno, that you have the face of a stranger and speak in an unaccustomed tone to your friend?'

He answered, 'Because you, Nicandro, have treated me like a child, concealing from me that which you ought to have told me long ago, instead of leaving me to learn it by accident from a stranger.'

It has come, I said to myself, for I knew what he meant: then I spoke of his mother.

'Ah, yes,' he said with bitterness, 'I know now why she pours water fresh from the well every day on that spot of ground near the door. Do you, Nicandro, think that water will ever wash away that old stain and memory? A man who is a man must in such a thing obey, not a mother's wish, nor any woman, but that something which speaks in his heart.'

'Let no such thought dwell in you to make you mad,' I replied. 'Look, Bruno, my friend's son and my friend, leave it to God who is above us, and who considers and remembers all evil deeds that men do, and desires not that anyone should take the sword out of His hand.'

'Who is He – this God you talk of?' he answered. 'Have you seen or spoken with Him that you tell me what His mind is in this matter? I have only this voice to tell me how a man should act in such a case,' and he smote his breast; then overcome with a passion of grief he covered his face with his hands and wept.

Vainly I begged him not to lose himself, telling him what the effect of his attempt, whether he succeeded or failed, would be on Donata and on Monica – it would break those poor women's hearts. I spoke, too, of things I had witnessed in my five years' service; the cruel sentences from which there was no appeal, the torments, the horrible deaths so often inflicted. For these evils there was no remedy on earth: and he, a poor, ignorant boy, what would he do but dash himself to pieces against that tower of brass!

He replied that within that brazen tower there was a heart full of blood; and with that he went away, only asking me as a favour not to tell his mother of this visit to me.

Some ten days later she had a message from him, brought from the capital by a traveller going to the south. Bruno sent word that he was going to Las Mulitas, a place fifty leagues west of Buenos Ayres, to work on an estancia there, and would be absent some months.

Why had he gone thither? Because he had heard that General Barboza – for that man was now a General – owned a tract of land at that place, which the Government had given him as a reward for his services on the southern frontier; and that he had recently returned from the northern provinces to Buenos Ayres and was now staying at this estancia at Las Mulitas.

Donata knew nothing of his secret motives, but his absence filled her with anxiety; and when at length she fell ill I resolved to go in search of the poor youth and try to persuade him to return to El Ombú. But at Las Mulitas I heard that he was no longer there. All strangers had been taken for the army in the frontier department, and Bruno, in spite of his passport, had been forced to go.

When I returned to El Ombú with this sad news Donata resolved at once to go to the capital and try to obtain his release. She was ill, and it was a long journey for her to perform on horseback, but she had friends to go with and take care of her. In the end she succeeded in seeing the President, and throwing herself on her knees before him, and with tears in her eyes, implored him to let her have her son back.

He listened to her, and gave her a paper to take to the

War Office. There it was found that Bruno had been sent to El Rosario, and an order was despatched for his immediate release. But when the order reached its destination the unhappy boy had deserted.

That was the last that Donata ever heard of her son. She guessed why he had gone, and knew as well as if I had told her that he had found out the secret so long hidden from him. Still, being his mother, she would not abandon hope; she struggled to live. Never did I come into her presence but I saw in her face a question which she dared not put in words. If, it said, you have heard, if you know, when and how his life ended, tell me now before I go. But it also said, If you know, do not tell me so that I and Monica may go on hoping together to the end.

'I know, Nicandro,' she would say, 'that if Bruno returns he will not be the same – the son I have lost. For in that one thing he is not like his father. Could another be like Valerio? No misfortune and no injustice could change that heart, or turn his sweetness sour. In that freshness and gaiety of temper he was like a child, and Bruno as a child was like him. My son! my son! where are you? God of my soul, grant that he may yet come to me, though his life be now darkened with some terrible passion, though his poor hands be stained with blood, so that my eyes may see him again before I go!'

But he came not, and she died without seeing him.

7

If Monica, left alone in the house with old Pascual and his wife, had been disposed to listen to those who were attracted by her face she might have found a protector worthy of her. There were men of substance among those who came for her. But it mattered nothing to her whether they had land and cattle or not, or what their appearance was, and how they were dressed. Hers was a faithful heart. And she looked for Bruno's return, not with that poor half-despairing hope which had been Donata's, and had failed to keep her alive, but with a hope that sustained

and made her able to support the months and years of
waiting. She looked for his coming as the night-watcher
for the dawn. On summer afternoons, when the heat of
the day was over, she would take her sewing outside the
gate and sit there by the hour, where her sight commanded
the road to the north. From that side he would certainly
come. On dark rainy nights a lantern would be hung on
the wall lest he, coming at a late hour, should miss the
house in the dark. Glad, she was not, nor lively; she was
pale and thin, and those dark eyes that looked too large
because of her thinness were the eyes of one who had beheld grief. But with it all there was a serenity, an air of
one whose tears, held back, would all be shed at the
proper time, when he returned. And he would, perhaps,
come to-day, or, if not to-day, then to-morrow, or perhaps
the day after, as God willed.

Nearly three years had passed by since Donata's death
when, one afternoon, I rode to El Ombú, and on approaching the house spied a saddled horse, which had got loose
going away at a trot. I went after, and caught, and led it
back, and then saw that its owner was a traveller, an old
soldier, who with or without the permission of the people
of the house was lying down and asleep in the shade of
the ombú.

There had lately been a battle in the northern part of
the province, and the defeated force had broken up, and
the men carrying their arms had scattered themselves all
over the country. This veteran was one of them.

He did not wake when I led the horse up and shouted
to him. He was a man about fifty to sixty years old, grey-
haired, with many scars of sword and lance wounds on his
sun-blackened face and hands. His carbine was leaning
against the tree a yard or two away, but he had not un-
buckled his sword, and what now attracted my attention
as I sat on my horse regarding him was the way in which
he clutched the hilt and shook the weapon until it rattled
in its scabbard. His was an agitated sleep; the sweat stood
in big drops on his face, he ground his teeth and moaned,

47

and muttered words which I could not catch.

At length, dismounting, I called to him again, then shouted in his ear, and finally shook him by the shoulder. Then he woke with a start, and struggling up to a sitting position, and staring at me like one demented, he exclaimed, 'What has happened?'

When I told him about his horse he was silent, and sitting there with eyes cast down passed his hand repeatedly across his forehead. Never in any man's face had I seen misery compared to his. 'Pardon me, friend,' he spoke at last. 'My ears were so full of sounds you do not hear that I paid little attention to what you were saying.'

'Perhaps the great heat of the day has overcome you,' I said. 'Or maybe you are suffering from some malady caused by an old wound received in fight.'

'Yes, an incurable malady,' he returned, gloomily. 'Have you, friend, been in the army?'

'Five years had I served when a wound which made me lame for life delivered me from that hell.'

'I have served thirty,' he returned, 'perhaps more. I know that I was very young when I was taken, and I remember that a woman I called mother wept to see me go. That any eyes should have shed tears for me! Shall I now in that place in the South where I was born find one who remembers my name? I look not for it! I have no one but this' – and here he touched his sword.

After an interval, he continued, 'We say, friend, that in the army we can do no wrong, since all responsibility rests with those who are over us; that our most cruel and sanguinary deeds are no more a sin or crime than is the shedding of the blood of cattle, or of Indians who are not Christians, and are therefore of no more account than cattle in God's sight. We say, too, that once we have become accustomed to kill, not men only, but even those who are powerless to defend themselves – the weak and the innocent – we think nothing of it, and have no compunction nor remorse. If this be so, why does He, the One who is above, torment me before my time? Is it just?

Listen: no sooner do I close my eyes than sleep brings to me that most terrible experience a man can have – to be in the midst of a conflict and powerless. The bugles call: there is a movement everywhere of masses of men, foot and horse, and every face has on it the look of one who is doomed. There is a murmur of talking all round me, the officers are shouting and waving their swords; I strive in vain to catch the word of command: I do not know what is happening; it is all confusion, a gloom of smoke and dust, a roar of guns, a great noise and shouting of the enemy charging through us. And I am helpless. I wake, and slowly the noise and terrible scene fade from my mind, only to return when sleep again overcomes me. What repose, what refreshment can I know! Sleep, they say, is a friend to everyone, and makes all equal, the rich and the poor, the guilty and the innocent; they say, too, that this forgetfulness is like a draught of cold water to the thirsty man. But what shall I say of sleep? Often with this blade would I have delivered myself from its torture but for the fear that there may be after death something even worse than this dream.'

After an interval of silence, seeing that he had recovered from his agitation, I invited him to go with me to the house. 'I see smoke issuing from the kitchen,' I said, 'let us go in so that you may refresh yourself with maté before resuming your journey.'

We went in and found the old people boiling the kettle; and in a little while Monica came in and sat with us. Never did she greet one without that light which was like sunshine in her dark eyes; words were not needed to tell me of the gratitude and friendliness she felt toward me, for she was not one to forget the past. I remember that she looked well that day in her white dress with a red flower. Had not Bruno said that he liked to see her in white, and that a flower on her bosom or in her hair was an ornament that gave her most grace? And Bruno might arrive at any moment. But the sight of that grey-haired veteran in his soiled and frayed uniform, and with his clanking sword and his dark scarred face, greatly disturbed her. I noticed that she grew paler and could scarcely keep her eyes off his face while he talked.

While sipping his maté he told us of fights he had been in, of long marches and sufferings in desert places, and of some of the former men he had served under. Among them he, by chance, named General Barboza.

Monica, I knew, had never heard of that man, and on this account I feared not to speak of him. It had, I said, been reported, I knew not whether truthfully or not, that Barboza was dead.

'On that point I can satisfy you,' he returned, 'since I was serving with him, when his life came to an end in the province of San Luis about two years ago. He was at the head of nineteen hundred men when it happened, and the whole force was filled with amazement at the event. Not that they regretted his loss; on the contrary, his own followers feared and were glad to be delivered from him. He exceeded most commanders in ferocity, and was accustomed to say scoffingly to his prisoners that he would not have gunpowder wasted on them. That was not a thing to complain of, but he was capable of treating his own men as he treated a spy or a prisoner of war. Many a one have I seen put to death with a blunted knife, he, Barboza, looking on, smoking a cigarette. It was the manner of his death that startled us, for never had man been seen to perish in such a way.

'It happened on this march, about a month before the end, that a soldier named Bracamonte went one day at noon to deliver a letter from his captain to the General. Barboza was sitting in his shirt sleeves in his tent when the letter was handed to him, but just when he put out his hand to take it the man made an attempt to stab him. The General, throwing himself back, escaped the blow, then instantly sprang like a tiger upon his assailant, and seizing him by the wrist wrenched the weapon out of his hand only to strike it quick as lightning into the poor fool's throat. No sooner was he down than the General

bending over him, before drawing out the weapon, called
to those who had run to his assistance to get him a
tumbler. When, tumbler in hand, he lifted himself up and
looked upon them, they say that his face was of the whiteness of iron made white in the furnace, and that his eyes
were like two flames. He was mad with rage, and cried out
with a loud voice, "Thus, in the presence of the army do I
serve the wretch who thought to shed my blood!" Then
with a furious gesture he threw down and shattered the
reddened glass, and bade them take the dead man outside
the camp and leave him stripped to the vultures.

'Thus ended the episode, but from that day it was
noticed by those about him that a change had come over
the General. If, friend, you have served with, or have even
seen him, you know the man he was – tall and well-formed,
blue-eyed and fair, like an Englishman, endowed with a
strength, endurance and resolution that was a wonder to
everyone: he was like an eagle among birds, – that great
bird that has no weakness and no mercy, whose cry fills
all creatures with dismay, whose pleasure it is to tear his
victim's flesh with his crooked talons. But now some secret
malady had fallen on him which took away all his mighty
strength; the colour of his face changed to sickly paleness,
and he bent forward and swayed this way and that in the
saddle as he rode like a drunken man, and this strange
weakness increased day by day. It was said in the army
that the blood of the man he had killed had poisoned him.
The doctors who accompanied us in this march could not
cure him, and their failure so angered him against them
that they began to fear for their own safety. They now
said that he could not be properly treated in camp, but
must withdraw to some town where a different system
could be followed; but this he refused to do.

'Now it happened that we had an old soldier with us
who was a curandero. He was a native of Santa Fé, and
was famed for his cures in his own department; but having had the misfortune to kill a man, he was arrested and
condemned to serve ten years in the army. This person

now informed some of the officers that he would undertake to cure the General, and Barboza, hearing of it, sent for and questioned him. The curandero informed him that his malady was one which the doctors could not cure. It was a failure of a natural heat of the blood, and only by means of animal heat, not by drugs, could health be recovered. In a grave case the usual remedy of putting the feet and legs in the body of some living animal opened for the purpose would not be sufficient. Some very large beast should be procured and the patient placed bodily in it.

'The General agreed to submit himself to this treatment; the doctors dared not interfere, and men were sent out in quest of a large animal. We were then encamped on a wide sandy plain in San Luis, and as we were without tents we were suffering much from the great heat and the dust-laden winds. But in this spot the General had grown worse, so that he could no longer sit on his horse, and here we had to wait for his improvement.

'In due time a very big bull was brought in and fastened to a stake in the middle of the camp. A space, fifty or sixty yards round, was marked out and roped round, and ponchos hung on the rope to form a curtain so that what was being done should not be witnessed by the army. But a great curiosity and anxiety took possession of the entire force, and when the bull was thrown down and his agonizing bellowings were heard, from all sides officers and men began to move toward that fatal spot. It had been noised about that the cure would be almost instantaneous, and many were prepared to greet the reappearance of the General with a loud cheer.

'Then very suddenly, almost before the bellowings had ceased, shrieks were heard from the enclosure, and in a moment, while we all stood staring and wondering, out rushed the General stark naked, reddened with that bath of warm blood he had been in, a sword which he had hastily snatched up in his hand. Leaping over the barrier, he stood still for an instant, then catching sight of the great mass of men before him he flew at them, yelling and whirling his sword round so that it looked like a shining wheel in the sun. The men seeing that he was raving mad fled before him, and for a space of a hundred yards or more he pursued them; then that superhuman energy was ended; the sword flew from his hand, he staggered, and fell prostrate on the earth. For some minutes no one ventured to approach him, but he never stirred, and at length, when examined, was found to be dead.'

The soldier had finished his story, and though I had many questions to ask I asked none, for I saw Monica's distress, and that she had gone white even to the lips at the terrible things the man had related. But now he had ended, and would soon depart, for the sun was getting low.

He rolled up and lighted a cigarette, and was about to rise from the bench, when he said, 'One thing I forgot to mention about the soldier Bracamonte, who attempted to assassinate the General. After he had been carried out and stripped for the vultures, a paper was found sewn up in the lining of his tunic, which proved to be his passport, for it contained his right description. It said that he was a native of this department of Chascomus, so that you may have heard of him. His name was Bruno de la Cueva.'

Would that he had not spoken those last words! Never, though I live to be a hundred, shall I forget that terrible scream that came from Monica's lips before she fell senseless to the floor!

As I raised her in my arms, the soldier turned and said, 'She is subject to fits?'

'No,' I replied, 'that Bruno, of whose death we have now heard for the first time, was of this house.'

'It was destiny that led me to this place,' he said, 'or perhaps that God who is ever against me; but you, friend, are my witness that I crossed not this threshold with a drawn weapon in my hand.' And with these words he took his departure, and from that day to this I have never again beheld his face.

She opened her eyes at last, but the wings of my heart

drooped when I saw them, since it was easy to see that she had lost her reason; but whether that calamity or the grief she would have known is greatest who can say? Some have died of pure grief – did it not kill Donata in the end? – but the crazed may live many years. We sometimes think it would be better if they were dead; but not in all cases – not, señor, in this.

She lived on here with the old people, for from the first she was quiet and docile as a child. Finally an order came from a person in authority at Chascomus for those who were in the house to quit it. It was going to be pulled down for the sake of the material which was required for a building in the village. Pascual died about that time, and the widow, now old and infirm, went to live with some poor relations at Chascomus and took Monica with her. When the old woman died Monica remained with these people: she lives with them to this day. But she is free to come and go at will, and is known to all in the village as *la loca del Ombú*. They are kind to her, for her story is known to them, and God has put compassion in their hearts.

To see her you would hardly believe that she is the Monica I have told you of, whom I knew as a little one, running bare-footed after her father's flock. For she has grey hairs and wrinkles now. As you ride to Chascomus from this point you will see, on approaching the lake, a very high bank on your left hand, covered with a growth of tall fennel, hoarhound, and cardoon thistle. There on most days you will find her, sitting on the bank in the shade of the tall fennel bushes, looking across the water. She watches for the flamingos. There are many of those great birds on the lake, and they go in flocks, and when they rise and travel across the water, flying low, their scarlet wings may be seen at a great distance. And every time she catches sight of a flock moving like a red line across the lake she cries out with delight. That is her one happiness – her life. And she is the last of all those who have lived in my time at El Ombú.

JOSEPH CONRAD

The Secret Sharer

I

On my right hand there were lines of fishing-stakes resembling a mysterious system of half-submerged bamboo fences, incomprehensible in its division of the domain of tropical fishes, and crazy of aspect as if abandoned for ever by some nomad tribe of fishermen now gone to the other end of the ocean; for there was no sign of human habitation as far as the eye could reach. To the left a group of barren islets, suggesting ruins of stone walls, towers, and blockhouses, had its foundations set in a blue sea that itself looked solid, so still and stable did it lie below my feet; even the track of light from the westering sun shone smoothly, without that animated glitter which tells of an imperceptible ripple. And when I turned my head to take a parting glance at the tug which had just left us anchored outside the bar, I saw the straight line of the flat shore joined to the stable sea, edge to edge, with a perfect and unmarked closeness, in one levelled floor half brown, half blue under the enormous dome of the sky. Corresponding in their insignificance to the islets of the sea, two small clumps of trees, one on each side of the only fault in the impeccable joint, marked the mouth of the river Meinam we had just left on the first preparatory stage of our homeward journey; and, far back on the inland level, a larger and loftier mass, the grove surrounding the great Paknam pagoda, was the only thing on which the eye could rest from the vain task of exploring the monotonous sweep of the horizon. Here and there gleams as of a few scattered pieces of silver marked the windings of the great river; and on the nearest of them, just within the bar, the tug steaming right into the land became lost to my sight, hull and funnel and masts, as though the impassive earth had swallowed her up without an effort, without a tremor. My eye followed the light cloud of her smoke, now here, now there, about the plain, according to the devious curves of the stream, but always fainter and farther away, till I lost it at last behind the mitre-shaped hill of the great pagoda. And then I was left alone with my ship, anchored at the head of the Gulf of Siam.

She floated at the starting-point of a long journey, very still in an immense stillness, the shadows of her spars flung far to the eastward by the setting sun. At that moment I was alone on her decks. There was not a sound in her – and around us nothing moved, nothing lived, not a canoe on the water, not a bird in the air, not a cloud in the sky. In this breathless pause at the threshold of a long passage we seemed to be measuring our fitness for a long and arduous enterprise, the appointed task of both our existences to be carried out, far from all human eyes, with only sky and sea for spectators and for judges.

There must have been some glare in the air to interfere with one's sight, because it was only just before the sun left us that my roaming eyes made out beyond the highest ridge of the principal islet of the group something which did away with the solemnity of perfect solitude. The tide of darkness flowed on swiftly; and with tropical suddenness a swarm of stars came out above the shadowy earth, while I lingered yet, my hand resting lightly on my ship's rail as if on the shoulder of a trusted friend. But, with all that multitude of celestial bodies staring down at one, the comfort of quiet communion with her was gone for good. And there were also disturbing sounds by this time – voices, footsteps forward; the steward flitted along the main-deck, a busily ministering spirit; a hand-bell tinkled urgently under the poop-deck. . . .

I found my two officers waiting for me near the supper

table, in the lighted cuddy. We sat down at once, and as I helped the chief mate, I said:

'Are you aware that there is a ship anchored inside the islands? I saw her mastheads above the ridge as the sun went down.'

He raised sharply his simple face, overcharged by a terrible growth of whisker, and emitted his usual ejaculations: 'Bless my soul, sir! You don't say so!'

My second mate was a round-cheeked, silent young man, grave beyond his years, I thought; but as our eyes happened to meet I detected a slight quiver on his lips. I looked down at once. It was not my part to encourage sneering on board my ship. It must be said, too, that I knew very little of my officers. In consequence of certain events of no particular significance, except to myself, I had been appointed to the command only a fortnight before. Neither did I know much of the hands forward. All these people had been together for eighteen months or so, and my position was that of the only stranger on board. I mention this because it has some bearing on what is to follow. But what I felt most was my being a stranger to the ship; and if all the truth must be told, I was somewhat of a stranger to myself. The youngest man on board (barring the second mate), and untried as yet by a position of the fullest responsibility, I was willing to take the adequacy of the others for granted. They had simply to be equal to their tasks; but I wondered how far I should turn out faithful to that ideal conception of one's own personality every man sets up for himself secretly.

Meantime the chief mate, with an almost visible effect of collaboration on the part of his round eyes and frightful whiskers, was trying to evolve a theory of the anchored ship. His dominant trait was to take all things into earnest consideration. He was of a painstaking turn of mind. As he used to say, he 'liked to account to himself' for practically everything that came in his way, down to a miserable scorpion he had found in his cabin a week before.

The why and the wherefore of that scorpion – how it got on board and came to select his room rather than the pantry (which was a dark place and more what a scorpion would be partial to), and how on earth it managed to drown itself in the inkwell of his writing-desk – had exercised him infinitely. The ship within the islands was much more easily accounted for; and just as we were about to rise from table he made his pronouncement. She was, he doubted not, a ship from home lately arrived. Probably she drew too much water to cross the bar except at the top of spring tides. Therefore she went into that natural harbour to wait for a few days in preference to remaining in an open roadstead.

'That's so,' confirmed the second mate, suddenly, in his slightly hoarse voice. 'She draws over twenty feet. She's the Liverpool ship *Sephora* with a cargo of coal. Hundred and twenty-three days from Cardiff.'

We looked at him in surprise.

'The tugboat skipper told me when he came on board for your letters, sir,' explained the young man. 'He expects to take her up the river the day after tomorrow.'

After thus overwhelming us with the extent of his information he slipped out of the cabin. The mate observed regretfully that he 'could not account for that young fellow's whims.' What prevented him telling us all about it at once, he wanted to know.

I detained him as he was making a move. For the last two days the crew had had plenty of hard work, and the night before they had very little sleep. I felt painfully that I – a stranger – was doing something unusual when I directed him to let all hands turn in without setting an anchor-watch. I proposed to keep on deck myself till one o'clock or thereabouts. I would get the second mate to relieve me at that hour.

'He will turn out the cook and the steward at four,' I concluded, 'and then give you a call. Of course at the slightest sign of any sort of wind we'll have the hands up and make a start at once.'

He concealed his astonishment. 'Very well, sir.' Outside the cuddy he put his head in the second mate's door to inform him of my unheard-of caprice to take a five hours' anchor-watch on myself. I heard the other raise his voice incredulously — 'What? The captain himself?' Then a few more murmurs, a door closed, then another. A few moments later I went on deck.

My strangeness, which had made me sleepless, had prompted that unconventional arrangement, as if I had expected in those solitary hours of the night to get on terms with the ship of which I knew nothing, manned by men of whom I knew very little more. Fast alongside a wharf, littered like any ship in port with a tangle of unrelated things, invaded by unrelated shore people, I had hardly seen her yet properly. Now, as she lay cleared for sea, the stretch of her main-deck seemed to me very fine under the stars. Very fine, very roomy for her size, and very inviting. I descended the poop and paced the waist, my mind picturing to myself the coming passage through the Malay Archipelago, down the Indian Ocean, and up the Atlantic. All its phases were familiar enough to me, every characteristic, all the alternatives which were likely to face me on the high seas — everything! ... except the novel responsibility of command. But I took heart from the reasonable thought that the ship was like other ships, the men like other men, and that the sea was not likely to keep any special surprises expressly for my discomfiture.

Arrived at that comforting conclusion, I bethought myself of a cigar and went below to get it. All was still down there. Everybody at the after end of the ship was sleeping profoundly. I came out again on the quarter-deck, agreeably at ease in my sleeping-suit on that warm breathless night, barefooted, a glowing cigar in my teeth, and, going forward, I was met by the profound silence of the fore end of the ship. Only as I passed the door of the forecastle I heard a deep, quiet, trustful sigh of some sleeper inside. And suddenly I rejoiced in the great security of the sea as compared with the unrest of the land, in my choice of that untempted life presenting no disquieting problems, invested with an elementary moral beauty by the absolute straightforwardness of its appeal and by the singleness of its purpose.

The riding-light in the fore-rigging burned with a clear, untroubled, as if symbolic, flame, confident and bright in the mysterious shades of the night. Passing on my way aft along the other side of the ship, I observed that the rope side-ladder, put over, no doubt, for the master of the tug when he came to fetch away our letters, had not been hauled in as it should have been. I became annoyed at this, for exactitude in small matters is the very soul of discipline. Then I reflected that I had myself peremptorily dismissed my officers from duty, and by my own act had prevented the anchor-watch being formally set and things properly attended to. I asked myself whether it was wise ever to interfere with the established routine of duties even from the kindest of motives. My action might have made me appear eccentric. Goodness only knew how that absurdly whiskered mate would 'account' for my conduct, and what the whole ship thought of that informality of their new captain. I was vexed with myself.

Not from compunction certainly, but, as it were mechanically, I proceeded to get the ladder in myself. Now a side-ladder of that sort is a light affair and comes in easily, yet my vigorous tug, which should have brought it flying on board, merely recoiled upon my body in a totally unexpected jerk. What the devil! . . . I was so astounded by the immovableness of that ladder that I remained stock-still, trying to account for it to myself like that imbecile mate of mine. In the end, of course, I put my head over the rail.

The side of the ship made an opaque belt of shadow on the darkling glassy shimmer of the sea. But I saw at once something elongated and pale floating very close to the ladder. Before I could form a guess a faint flash of phosphorescent light, which seemed to issue suddenly from the naked body of a man, flickered in the sleeping water with the elusive, silent play of summer lightning in a night sky. With a gasp I saw revealed to my stare a pair of feet, the long legs, a broad livid back immersed right up to the neck in a greenish cadaverous glow. One hand, awash, clutched the bottom rung of the ladder. He was complete but for the head. A headless corpse! The cigar dropped out of my gaping mouth with a tiny plop and a short hiss quite audible in the absolute stillness of all things under heaven. At that I suppose he raised up his face, a dimly pale oval in the shadow of the ship's side. But even then I could only barely make out down there the shape of his black-haired head. However, it was enough for the horrid, frost-bound sensation which had gripped me about the chest to pass off. The moment of vain exclamations was past, too. I only climbed on the spare spar and leaned over the rail as far as I could, to bring my eyes nearer to that mystery floating alongside.

As he hung by the ladder, like a resting swimmer, the sea-lightning played about his limbs at every stir; and he appeared in it ghastly, silvery, fish-like. He remained as mute as a fish, too. He made no motion to get out of the water, either. It was inconceivable that he should not attempt to come on board, and strangely troubling to suspect that perhaps he did not want to. And my first words were prompted by just that troubled incertitude.

'What's the matter?' I asked in my ordinary tone, speaking down to the face upturned exactly under mine.

'Cramp,' it answered, no louder. Then slightly anxious, 'I say, no need to call any one.'

'I was not going to,' I said.

'Are you alone on deck?'

'Yes.'

I had somehow the impression that he was on the point of letting go the ladder to swim away beyond my ken – mysterious as he came. But, for the moment, this being appearing as if he had risen from the bottom of the sea (it was certainly the nearest land to the ship) wanted only to know the time. I told him. And he, down there, tentatively:

'I suppose your captain's turned in?'

'I am sure he isn't,' I said.

He seemed to struggle with himself, for I heard something like the low, bitter murmur of doubt. 'What's the good?' His next words came out with a hesitating effort.

'Look here, my man. Could you call him out quietly?'

I thought the time had come to declare myself.

'I am the captain.'

I heard a 'By Jove!' whispered at the level of the water. The phosphorescence flashed in the swirl of the water all about his limbs, his other hand seized the ladder.

'My name's Leggatt.'

The voice was calm and resolute. A good voice. The self-possession of that man had somehow induced a corresponding state in myself. It was very quietly that I remarked:

'You must be a good swimmer.'

'Yes. I've been in the water practically since nine o'clock. The question for me now is whether I am to let go this ladder and go on swimming till I sink from exhaustion, or – to come on board here.'

I felt this was no mere formula of desperate speech, but a real alternative in the view of a strong soul. I should have gathered from this that he was young; indeed, it is only the young who are ever confronted by such clear issues. But at the time it was pure intuition on my part. A mysterious communication was established already between us two – in the face of that silent, darkened tropical sea. I was young, too; young enough to make no comment. The man in the water began suddenly to climb up the ladder, and I hastened away from the rail to fetch some clothes.

Before entering the cabin I stood still, listening in the lobby at the foot of the stairs. A faint snore came through the closed door of the chief mate's room. The second mate's door was on the hook, but the darkness in there was absolutely soundless. He, too, was young and could sleep like a stone. Remained the steward, but he was not likely to wake up before he was called. I got a sleeping-suit out of my room and, coming back on deck, saw the naked man from the sea sitting on the main-hatch, glimmering white in the darkness, his elbows on his knees and his head in his hands. In a moment he had concealed his damp body in a sleeping-suit of the same grey-stripe pattern as the one I was wearing and followed me like my double on the poop. Together we moved right aft, barefooted, silent.

'What is it?' I asked in a deadened voice, taking the lighted lamp out of the binnacle, and raising it to his face.

'An ugly business.'

He had rather regular features; a good mouth; light eyes under somewhat heavy, dark eyebrows; a smooth, square forehead; no growth on his cheeks; a small, brown moustache, and a well-shaped, round chin. His expression was concentrated, meditative, under the inspecting light of the lamp I held up to his face; such as a man thinking hard in solitude might wear. My sleeping-suit was just right for his size. A well-knit young fellow of twenty-five at most. He caught his lower lip with the edge of white, even teeth.

'Yes,' I said, replacing the lamp in the binnacle. The warm, heavy tropical night closed upon his head again.

'There's a ship over there,' he murmured.

'Yes, I know. The *Sephora*. Did you know of us?'

'Hadn't the slightest idea. I am the mate of her—' He paused and corrected himself. 'I should say I *was*.'

'Aha! Something wrong?'

'Yes. Very wrong indeed. I've killed a man.'

'What do you mean? Just now?'

'No, on the passage. Weeks ago. Thirty-nine south. When I say a man—'

'Fit of temper,' I suggested, confidently.

The shadowy, dark head, like mine, seemed to nod imperceptibly above the ghostly grey of my sleeping-suit.

63

It was, in the night, as though I had been faced by my own reflection in the depths of a sombre and immense mirror.

'A pretty thing to have to own up to for a Conway boy,' murmured my double, distinctly.

'You're a Conway boy?'

'I am,' he said, as if startled. Then, slowly . . . 'Perhaps you too—'

It was so; but being a couple of years older I had left before he joined. After a quick interchange of dates a silence fell; and I thought suddenly of my absurd mate with his terrific whiskers and the 'Bless my soul – you don't say so' type of intellect. My double gave me an inkling of his thoughts by saying: 'My father's a parson in Norfolk. Do you see me before a judge and jury on that charge? For myself I can't see the necessity. There are fellows that an angel from heaven— And I am not that. He was one of those creatures that are just simmering all the time with a silly sort of wickedness. Miserable devils that have no business to live at all. He wouldn't do his duty and wouldn't let anybody else do theirs. But what's the good of talking! You know well enough the sort of ill-conditioned snarling cur—'

He appealed to me as if our experiences had been as identical as our clothes. And I knew well enough the pestiferous danger of such a character where there are no means of legal repression. And I knew well enough also that my double there was no homicidal ruffian. I did not think of asking him for details, and he told me the story roughly in brusque, disconnected sentences. I needed no more. I saw it all going on as though I were myself inside that other sleeping-suit.

'It happened while we were setting a reefed foresail, at dusk. Reefed foresail! You understand the sort of weather. The only sail we had left to keep the ship running; so you may guess what it had been like for days. Anxious sort of job, that. He gave me some of his cursed insolence at the sheet. I tell you I was overdone with this terrific weather that seemed to have no end to it. Terrific, I tell you – and a deep ship. I believe the fellow himself was half crazed with funk. It was no time for gentlemanly reproof, so I turned round and felled him like an ox. He up and at me. We closed just as an awful sea made for the ship. All hands saw it coming and took to the rigging, but I had him by the throat, and went on shaking him like a rat, the men above us yelling, "Look out! look out!" Then a crash as if the sky had fallen on my head. They say that for over ten minutes hardly anything was to be seen of the ship – just the three masts and a bit of the forecastle head and of the poop all awash driving along in a smother of foam. It was a miracle that they found us, jammed together behind the forebits. It's clear that I meant business, because I was holding him by the throat still when they picked us up. He was black in the face. It was too much for them. It seems they rushed us aft together, gripped as we were, screaming "Murder!" like a lot of lunatics, and broke into the cuddy. And the ship running for her life, touch and go all the time, any minute her last in a sea fit to turn your hair grey only a-looking at it. I understand that the skipper, too, started raving like the rest of them. The man had been deprived of sleep for more than a week, and to have this sprung on him at the height of a furious gale nearly drove him out of his mind. I wonder they didn't fling me overboard after getting the carcass of their precious ship-mate out of my fingers. They had rather a job to separate us, I've been told. A sufficiently fierce story to make an old judge and a respectable jury sit up a bit. The first thing I heard when I came to myself was the maddening howling of that endless gale, and on that the voice of the old man. He was hanging on to my bunk, staring into my face out of his sou'wester.

' "Mr Leggatt, you have killed a man. You can act no longer as chief mate of this ship." '

His care to subdue his voice made it sound monotonous. He rested a hand on the end of the skylight to steady himself with, and all that time did not stir a limb, so far as I could see. 'Nice little tale for a quiet tea-party,' he concluded in the same tone.

One of my hands, too, rested on the end of the skylight; neither did I stir a limb, so far as I knew. We stood less than a foot from each other. It occurred to me that if old 'Bless my soul – you don't say so' were to put his head up the companion and catch sight of us, he would think he was seeing double, or imagine himself come upon a scene of weird witchcraft; the strange captain having a quiet confabulation by the wheel with his own grey ghost. I became very much concerned to prevent anything of the sort. I heard the other's soothing undertone.

'My father's a parson in Norfolk,' it said. Evidently he had forgotten he had told me this important fact before. Truly a nice little tale.

'You had better slip down into my stateroom now,' I said, moving off stealthily. My double followed my movements; our bare feet made no sound; I let him in, closed the door with care, and, after giving a call to the second mate, returned on deck for my relief.

'Not much sign of any wind yet,' I remarked when he approached.

'No, sir. Not much,' he assented, sleepily, in his hoarse voice, with just enough deference, no more, and barely suppressing a yawn.

'Well, that's all you have to look out for. You have got your orders.'

'Yes, sir.'

I paced a turn or two on the poop and saw him take up his position face forward with his elbow in the ratlines of the mizzen-rigging before I went below. The mate's faint snoring was still going on peacefully. The cuddy lamp was burning over the table on which stood a vase with flowers, a polite attention from the ship's provision merchant – the last flowers we should see for the next three months at the very least. Two bunches of bananas hung from the beam symmetrically, one on each side of the rudder-casing. Everything was as before in the ship – except that two of her captain's sleeping-suits were simultaneously in use, one motionless in the cuddy, the other keeping very still in the captain's stateroom.

It must be explained here that my cabin had the form of the capital letter L, the door being within the angle and opening into the short part of the letter. A couch was to the left, the bed-place to the right; my writing-desk and the chronometers' table faced the door. But any one opening it, unless he stepped right inside, had no view of what I call the long (or vertical) part of the letter. It contained some lockers surmounted by a bookcase; and a few clothes, a thick jacket or two, caps, oilskin coat, and such like, hung on hooks. There was at the bottom of that part a door opening into my bath-room, which could be entered also directly from the saloon. But that way was never used.

The mysterious arrival had discovered the advantage of this particular shape. Entering my room, lighted strongly by a big bulkhead lamp swung on gimbals above my writing-desk, I did not see him anywhere till he stepped out quietly from behind the coats hung in the recessed part.

'I heard somebody moving about, and went in there at once,' he whispered.

I, too, spoke under my breath.

'Nobody is likely to come in here without knocking and getting permission.'

He nodded. His face was thin and the sunburn faded, as though he had been ill. And no wonder. He had been, I heard presently, kept under arrest in his cabin for nearly seven weeks. But there was nothing sickly in his eyes or in his expression. He was not a bit like me, really; yet, as we stood leaning over my bed-place, whispering side by side, with our dark heads together and our backs to the door, anybody bold enough to open it stealthily would have been treated to the uncanny sight of a double captain busy talking in whispers with his other self.

'But all this doesn't tell me how you came to hang on

to our side-ladder,' I inquired, in the hardly audible murmurs we used, after he had told me something more of the proceedings on board the *Sephora* once the bad weather was over.

'When we sighted Java Head I had had time to think all those matters out several times over. I had six weeks of doing nothing else, and with only an hour or so every evening for a tramp on the quarter-deck.'

He whispered, his arms folded on the side of my bedplace, staring through the open port. And I could imagine perfectly the manner of this thinking out – a stubborn if not a steadfast operation; something of which I should have been perfectly incapable.

'I reckoned it would be dark before we closed with the land,' he continued, so low that I had to strain my hearing, near as we were to each other, shoulder touching shoulder almost. 'So I asked to speak to the old man. He always seemed very sick when he came to see me – as if he could not look me in the face. You know, that foresail saved the ship. She was too deep to have run long under bare poles. And it was I that managed to set it for him. Anyway, he came. When I had him in my cabin – he stood by the door looking at me as if I had the halter round my neck already – I asked him right away to leave my cabin door unlocked at night while the ship was going through Sunda Straits. There would be the Java coast within two or three miles, off Angier Point. I wanted nothing more. I've had a prize for swimming my second year in the Conway.'

'I can believe it,' I breathed out.

'God only knows why they locked me in every night. To see some of their faces you'd have thought they were afraid I'd go about at night strangling people. Am I a murdering brute? Do I look it? By Jove! if I had been he wouldn't have trusted himself like that into my room. You'll say I might have chucked him aside and bolted out, there and then – it was dark already. Well, no. And for the same reason I wouldn't think of trying to smash the door. There would have been a rush to stop me at the noise, and I did not mean to get into a confounded scrimmage. Somebody else might have got killed — for I would not have broken out only to get chucked back, and I did not want any more of that work. He refused, looking more sick than ever. He was afraid of the men, and also of that old second mate of his who had been sailing with him for years — a grey-headed old humbug; and his steward, too, had been with him devil knows how long — seventeen years or more — a dogmatic sort of loafer who hated me like poison, just because I was the chief mate. No chief mate ever made more than one voyage in the *Sephora*, you know. Those two old chaps ran the ship. Devil only knows what the skipper wasn't afraid of (all his nerve went to pieces altogether in that hellish spell of bad weather we had) — of what the law would do to him — of his wife, perhaps. Oh, yes! she's on board. Though I don't think she would have meddled. She would have been only too glad to have me out of the ship in any way. The "brand of Cain" business, don't you see. That's all right. I was ready enough to go off wandering on the face of the earth — and that was price enough to pay for an Abel of that sort. Anyhow, he wouldn't listen to me. "This thing must take its course. I represent the law here." He was shaking like a leaf. "So you won't?" "No!" "Then I hope you will be able to sleep on that," I said, and turned my back on him. "I wonder that *you* can," cries he, and locks the door.

'Well, after that, I couldn't. Not very well. That was three weeks ago. We had a slow passage through the Java Sea; drifted about Carimata for ten days. When we anchored here they thought, I suppose, it was all right. The nearest land (and that's five miles) is the ship's destination; the consul would soon set about catching me; and there would have been no object in bolting to these islets there. I don't suppose there's a drop of water on them. I don't know how it was, but to-night that steward, after bringing me my supper, went out to let me eat it, and left the door unlocked. And I ate it – all there was, too. After I had finished I strolled out on the quarter-deck. I don't know that I meant to do anything. A breath of fresh air was all I wanted, I believe. Then a sudden temptation came over me. I kicked off my slippers and was in the water before I had made up my mind fairly. Somebody heard the splash and they raised an awful hullabaloo. "He's gone! Lower the boats! He's committed suicide! No, he's swimming." Certainly I was swimming. It's not so easy for a swimmer like me to commit suicide by drowning. I landed on the nearest islet before the boat left the ship's side. I heard them pulling about in the dark, hailing, and so on, but after a bit they gave up. Everything quieted down and the anchorage became as still as death. I sat down on a stone and began to think. I felt certain they would start searching for me at daylight. There was no place to hide on those stony things – and if there had been, what would have been the good? But now I was clear of that ship, I was not going back. So after a while I took off all my clothes, tied them up in a bundle with a stone inside, and dropped them in the deep water on the outer side of that islet. That was suicide enough for me. Let them think what they liked, but I didn't mean to drown myself. I meant to swim till I sank – but that's not the same thing. I struck out for another of these little islands, and it was from that one that I first saw your riding-light. Something to swim for. I went on easily, and on the way I came upon a flat rock a foot or two above water. In the daytime, I dare say, you might make it out with a glass from your poop. I scrambled up on it and rested myself for a bit. Then I made another start. That last spell must have been over a mile.'

His whisper was getting fainter and fainter, and all the time he stared straight out through the port-hole, in which there was not even a star to be seen. I had not interrupted him. There was something that made comment impossible in his narrative, or perhaps in himself; a sort of feeling, a quality, which I can't find a name for. And when he ceased, all I found was a futile whisper: 'So you swam for our light?'

'Yes – straight for it. It was something to swim for. I couldn't see any stars low down because the coast was in the way, and I couldn't see the land, either. The water was like glass. One might have been swimming in a confounded thousand-feet deep cistern with no place for scrambling out anywhere; but what I didn't like was the notion of swimming round and round like a crazed bullock before I gave out; and as I didn't mean to go back . . . No. Do you see me being hauled back, stark naked, off one of these little islands by the scruff of the neck and fighting like a wild beast? Somebody would have got killed for certain, and I did not want any of that. So I went on. Then your ladder—'

'Why didn't you hail the ship?' I asked, a little louder.

He touched my shoulder lightly. Lazy footsteps came right over our heads and stopped. The second mate had crossed from the other side of the poop and might have been hanging over the rail, for all we knew.

'He couldn't hear us talking – could he?' My double breathed into my very ear, anxiously.

His anxiety was an answer, a sufficient answer, to the question I had put to him. An answer containing all the difficulty of that situation. I closed the port-hole quietly, to make sure. A louder word might have been overheard.

'Who's that?' he whispered then.

'My second mate. But I don't know much more of the fellow than you do.'

And I told him a little about myself. I had been appointed to take charge while I least expected anything of the sort, not quite a fortnight ago. I didn't know either the ship or the people. Hadn't had the time in port to look about me or size anybody up. And as to the crew, all they knew was that I was appointed to take the ship home. For the rest, I was almost as much of a stranger on board as himself, I said. And at the moment I felt it most acutely. I felt that it would take very little to make me a suspect person in the eyes of the ship's company.

He had turned about meantime; and we, the two strangers in the ship, faced each other in identical attitudes.

'Your ladder—' he murmured, after a silence. 'Who'd have thought of finding a ladder hanging over at night in a ship anchored out here! I felt just then a very unpleasant faintness. After the life I've been leading for nine weeks, anybody would have got out of condition. I wasn't capable of swimming round as far as your rudder-chains. And, lo and behold! there was a ladder to get hold of. After I gripped it I said to myself, "What's the good?" When I saw a man's head looking over I thought I would swim away presently and leave him shouting – in whatever language it was. I didn't mind being looked at. I – I liked it. And then you speaking to me so quietly – as if you had expected me – made me hold on a little longer. It had been a confounded lonely time – I don't mean while swimming. I was glad to talk a little to somebody that didn't belong to the *Sephora*. As to asking for the captain, that was a mere impulse. It could have been no use, with all the ship knowing about me and the other people pretty certain to be round here in the morning. I don't know – I wanted to be seen, to talk with somebody, before I went on. I don't know what I would have said. . . . "Fine night, isn't it?" or something of the sort.'

'Do you think they will be round here presently?' I asked with some incredulity.

'Quite likely,' he said, faintly.

He looked extremely haggard all of a sudden. His head rolled on his shoulders.

'H'm. We shall see then. Meantime get into that bed,' I whispered. 'Want help? There.'

It was a rather high bed-place with a set of drawers underneath. This amazing swimmer really needed the lift I gave him by seizing his leg. He tumbled in, rolled over on his back, and flung one arm across his eyes. And then, with his face nearly hidden, he must have looked exactly as I used to look in that bed. I gazed upon my

other self for a while before drawing across carefully
the two green serge curtains which ran on a brass rod.
I thought for a moment of pinning them together for
greater safety, but I sat down on the couch, and once
there I felt unwilling to rise and hunt for a pin. I would
do it in a moment. I was extremely tired, in a peculiarly
intimate way, by the strain of stealthiness, by the effort
of whispering and the general secrecy of this excitement.
It was three o'clock by now and I had been on my feet
since nine, but I was not sleepy; I could not have gone
to sleep. I sat there, fagged out, looking at the curtains,
trying to clear my mind of the confused sensation of being
in two places at once, and greatly bothered by an exasperating knocking in my head. It was a relief to discover
suddenly that it was not in my head at all, but on the
outside of the door. Before I could collect myself the
words 'Come in' were out of my mouth, and the steward
entered with a tray, bringing in my morning coffee. I had
slept, after all, and I was so frightened that I shouted,
'This way! I am here, steward,' as though he had been
miles away. He put down the tray on the table next the
couch and only then said, very quietly, 'I can see you
are here, sir.' I felt him give me a keen look, but I dared
not meet his eyes just then. He must have wondered why
I had drawn the curtains of my bed before going to sleep
on the couch. He went out, hooking the door open as
usual.

I heard the crew washing decks above me. I knew I
would have been told at once if there had been any wind.
Calm, I thought, and I was doubly vexed. Indeed, I felt
dual more than ever. The steward reappeared suddenly
in the doorway. I jumped up from the couch so quickly
that he gave a start.

'What do you want here?'

'Close your port, sir – they are washing decks.'

'It is closed,' I said, reddening.

'Very well, sir.' But he did not move from the doorway and returned my stare in an extraordinary, equivocal

manner for a time. Then his eyes wavered, all his expression changed, and in a voice unusually gentle, almost coaxingly:

'May I come in to take the empty cup away, sir?'

'Of course!' I turned my back on him while he popped in and out. Then I unhooked and closed the door and even pushed the bolt. This sort of thing could not go on very long. The cabin was as hot as an oven, too. I took a peep at my double, and discovered that he had not moved, his arm was still over his eyes; but his chest heaved; his hair was wet; his chin glistened with perspiration. I reached over him and opened the port.

'I must show myself on deck,' I reflected.

Of course, theoretically, I could do what I liked, with no one to say nay to me within the whole circle of the horizon; but to lock my cabin door and take the key away I did not dare. Directly I put my head out of the companion I saw the group of my two officers, the second mate barefooted, the chief mate in long india-rubber boots, near the break of the poop, and the steward half-way down the poop-ladder talking to them eagerly. He happened to catch sight of me and dived, the second ran down on the main-deck shouting some order or other, and the chief mate came to meet me, touching his cap.

There was a sort of curiosity in his eye that I did not like. I don't know whether the steward had told them that I was 'queer' only, or downright drunk, but I know the man meant to have a good look at me. I watched him coming with a smile which, as he got into point-blank range, took effect and froze his very whiskers. I did not give him time to open his lips.

'Square the yards by lifts and braces before the hands go to breakfast.'

It was the first particular order I had given on board that ship; and I stayed on deck to see it executed, too. I had felt the need of asserting myself without loss of time. That sneering young cub got taken down a peg or two on that occasion, and I also seized the opportunity of having a good look at the face of every foremast man as they filed past me to go to the after braces. At breakfast time, eating nothing myself, I presided with such frigid dignity that the two mates were only too glad to escape from the cabin as soon as decency permitted; and all the time the dual working of my mind distracted me almost to the point of insanity. I was constantly watching myself, my secret self, as dependent on my actions as my own personality, sleeping in that bed, behind that door which faced me as I sat at the head of the table. It was very much like being mad, only it was worse because one was aware of it.

I had to shake him for a solid minute, but when at last he opened his eyes it was in the full possession of his senses, with an inquiring look.

'All's well so far,' I whispered. 'Now you must vanish into the bath-room.'

He did so, as noiseless as a ghost, and then I rang for the steward, and facing him boldly, directed him to tidy up my stateroom while I was having my bath – 'and be quick about it.' As my tone admitted of no excuses, he said, 'Yes, sir,' and ran off to fetch his dust-pan and brushes. I took a bath and did most of my dressing, splashing, and whistling softly for the steward's edification, while the secret sharer of my life stood drawn up bolt-upright in that little space, his face looking very sunken in daylight, his eyelids lowered under the stern, dark line of his eyebrows drawn together by a slight frown.

When I left him there to go back to my room the steward was finishing dusting. I sent for the mate and engaged him in some insignificant conversation. It was, as it were, trifling with the terrific character of his whiskers; but my object was to give him an opportunity for a good look at my cabin. And then I could at last shut, with a clear conscience, the door of my stateroom and get my double back into the recessed part. There was nothing else for it. He had to sit still on a small folding stool, half smothered by the heavy coats hanging there. We listened to the steward going into the bath-room out of the saloon, filling the water-bottles there, scrubbing the bath, setting things to rights, whisk, bang, clatter – out again into the saloon – turn the key – click. Such was my scheme for keeping my second self invisible. Nothing better could be contrived under the circumstances. And there we sat; I at my writing-desk ready to appear busy with some papers, he behind me out of sight of the door. It would not have been prudent to talk in day-time; and I could not have stood the excitement of that queer sense of whispering to myself. Now and then, glancing over my shoulder, I saw him far back there, sitting rigidly on the low stool, his bare feet close together, his arms folded, his head hanging on his breast – and perfectly still. Anybody would have taken him for me.

I was fascinated by it myself. Every moment I had to glance over my shoulder. I was looking at him when a voice outside the door said:

'Beg pardon, sir.'

'Well!' . . . I kept my eyes on him, and so when the voice outside the door announced, 'There's a ship's boat coming our way, sir,' I saw him give a start – the first movement he had made for hours. But he did not raise his bowed head.

'All right. Get the ladder over.'

I hesitated. Should I whisper something to him? But what? His immobility seemed to have been never disturbed. What could I tell him he did not know already? . . . Finally I went on deck.

2

The skipper of the *Sephora* had a thin red whisker all round his face, and the sort of complexion that goes with hair of that colour; also the particular, rather smeary shade of blue in the eyes. He was not exactly a showy figure; his shoulders were high, his stature but middling – one leg slightly more bandy than the other. He shook hands, looking vaguely around. A spiritless tenacity was his main characteristic, I judged. I behaved with a politeness which seemed to disconcert him. Perhaps he was shy. He mumbled to me as if he were ashamed of what he was saying; gave his name (it was something like Archbold – but at this distance of years I hardly am sure), his ship's name, and a few other particulars of that sort, in the manner of a criminal making a reluctant and doleful confession. He had had terrible weather on the passage out – terrible – terrible – wife aboard, too.

By this time we were seated in the cabin and the steward brought in a tray with a bottle and glasses. 'Thanks! No.' Never took liquor. Would have some water, though. He drank two tumblerfuls. Terrible thirsty work. Ever since daylight had been exploring the islands round his ship.

'What was that for – fun?' I asked, with an appearance of polite interest.

'No!' He sighed. 'Painful duty.'

As he persisted in his mumbling and I wanted my double to hear every word, I hit upon the notion of informing him that I regretted to say I was hard of hearing.

'Such a young man, too!' he nodded, keeping his smeary blue, unintelligent eyes fastened upon me. What was the cause of it – some disease? he inquired, without the least sympathy and as if he thought that, if so, I'd got no more than I deserved.

'Yes; disease,' I admitted in a cheerful tone which semed to shock him. But my point was gained, because he had to raise his voice to give me his tale. It is not worth while to record that version. It was just over two months since all this had happened, and he had thought so much about it that he seemed completely muddled as to its bearings, but still immensely impressed.

'What would you think of such a thing happening on board your own ship? I've had the *Sephora* for these fifteen years. I am a well-known shipmaster.'

He was densely distressed – and perhaps I should have sympathised with him if I had been able to detach my mental vision from the unsuspected sharer of my cabin as though he were my second self. There he was on the other side of the bulkhead, four or five feet from us, no more, as we sat in the saloon. I looked politely at Captain Archbold (if that was his name), but it was the other I saw, in a grey sleeping-suit, seated on a low stool, his bare feet close together, his arms folded, and every word said between us falling into the ears of his dark head bowed on his chest.

'I have been at sea now, man and boy, for seven-and-thirty years, and I've never heard of such a thing happening in an English ship. And that it should be my ship. Wife on board, too.'

I was hardly listening to him.

'Don't you think,' I said, 'that the heavy sea which, you told me, came aboard just then might have killed the man? I have seen the sheer weight of a sea kill a man very neatly, by simply breaking his neck.'

'Good God!' he uttered, impressively, fixing his smeary blue eyes on me. 'The sea! No man killed by the sea ever looked like that.' He seemed positively scandalised at my suggestion. And as I gazed at him, certainly not prepared for anything original on his part, he advanced his head close to mine and thrust his tongue out at me so suddenly that I couldn't help starting back.

After scoring over my calmness in this graphic way he nodded wisely. If I had seen the sight, he assured me, I would never forget it as long as I lived. The weather was too bad to give the corpse a proper sea burial. So next day at dawn they took it up on the poop, covering its face with a bit of bunting; he read a short prayer, and then, just as it was, in its oilskins and long boots, they launched it amongst those mountainous seas that seemed ready every moment to swallow up the ship herself and the terrified lives on board of her.

'That reefed foresail saved you,' I threw in.

'Under God – it did,' he exclaimed fervently. 'It was by a special mercy, I firmly believe, that it stood some of those hurricane squalls.'

'It was the setting of that sail which—' I began.

'God's own hand in it,' he interrupted me. 'Nothing less could have done it. I don't mind telling you that I hardly dared give the order. It seemed impossible that we could touch anything without losing it, and then our last hope would have been gone.'

The terror of that gale was on him yet. I let him go on for a bit, then said, casually – as if returning to a minor subject:

'You were very anxious to give up your mate to the shore people, I believe?'

He was. To the law. His obscure tenacity on that point had in it something incomprehensible and a little awful; something, as it were, mystical, quite apart from his anxiety that he should not be suspected of 'countenancing any doings of that sort'. Seven-and-thirty virtuous years at sea, of which over twenty of immaculate command, and the last fifteen in the *Sephora,* seemed to have laid him under some pitiless obligation.

'And you know,' he went on, groping shamefacedly amongst his feelings, 'I did not engage that young fellow. His people had some interest with my owners. I was in a way forced to take him on. He looked very smart, very gentlemanly, and all that. But do you know – I never liked him, somehow. I am a plain man. You see, he wasn't exactly the sort for the chief mate of a ship like the *Sephora.*'

I had become so connected in thoughts and impressions with the secret sharer of my cabin that I felt as if I, personally, were being given to understand that I, too, was not the sort that would have done for the chief mate of a ship like the *Sephora.* I had no doubt of it in my mind.

'Not at all the style of man. You understand,' he insisted, superfluously, looking hard at me.

I smiled urbanely. He seemed at a loss for a while.

'I suppose I must report a suicide.'

'Beg pardon?'

'Sui-cide! That's what I'll have to write to my owners directly I get in.'

'Unless you manage to recover him before to-morrow,' I assented, dispassionately.... 'I mean, alive.'

He mumbled something which I really did not catch, and I turned my ear to him in a puzzled manner. He fairly bawled:

'The land – I say, the mainland is at least seven miles off my anchorage.'

'About that.'

My lack of excitement, of curiosity, of surprise, of any sort of pronounced interest, began to arouse his distrust. But except for the felicitous pretence of deafness I had not tried to pretend anything. I had felt utterly incapable of playing the part of ignorance properly, and therefore was afraid to try. It is also certain that he had brought some ready-made suspicions with him, and that he viewed my politeness as a strange and unnatural phenomenon. And yet how else could I have received him? Not heartily! That was impossible for psychological reasons, which I need not state here. My only object was to keep off his inquiries. Surlily? Yes, but surliness might have provoked a point-blank question. From its novelty to him and from its nature, punctilious courtesy was the manner best calculated to restrain the man. But there was the danger of his breaking through my defence bluntly. I could not, I think, have met him by a direct lie, also for psychological (not moral) reasons. If he had only known how afraid I was of his putting my feeling of identity with the other to the test! But, strangely enough – (I thought of it only afterwards) – I believe that he was not a little disconcerted by the reverse side of that weird situation, by something in me that reminded him of the man he was seeking – suggested a mysterious similitude to the young fellow he had distrusted and disliked from the first.

However that might have been, the silence was not very prolonged. He took another oblique step.

'I reckon I had no more than a two-mile pull to your ship. Not a bit more.'

'And quite enough, too, in this awful heat,' I said.

Another pause full of mistrust followed. Necessity, they say, is mother of invention, but fear, too, is not barren of ingenious suggestions. And I was afraid he would ask me point-blank for news of my other self.

'Nice little saloon, isn't it?' I remarked, as if noticing for the first time the way his eyes roamed from one closed door to the other. 'And very well fitted out, too. Here for instance,' I continued, reaching over the back of my seat negligently and flinging the door open, 'is my bath-room.'

He made an eager movement, but hardly gave it a glance. I got up, shut the door of the bath-room, and invited him to have a look round, as if I were very proud of my accommodation. He had to rise and be shown round, but he went through the business without any raptures whatever.

'And now we'll have a look at my stateroom,' I declared, in a voice as loud as I dared to make it, crossing the cabin to the starboard side with purposely heavy steps.

He followed me in and gazed around. My intelligent double had vanished. I played my part.

'Very convenient – isn't it?'

'Very nice. Very comf . . .' He didn't finish and went out brusquely as if to escape from some unrighteous wiles of mine. But it was not to be. I had been too frightened not to feel vengeful; I felt I had him on the run, and I meant to keep him on the run. My polite insistence must have had something menacing in it, because he gave in suddenly. And I did not let him off a single item; mate's room, pantry, storerooms, the very sail-locker which was also under the poop – he had to look into them all. When at last I showed him out on the quarter-deck he drew a long, spiritless sigh, and mumbled dismally that he must really be going back to his ship now. I desired my mate, who had joined us, to see to the captain's boat.

The man of whiskers gave a blast on the whistle which he used to wear hanging round his neck, and yelled, '*Sephora*'s away!' My double down there in my cabin must have heard, and certainly could not feel more re-

lieved than I. Four fellows came running out from somewhere forward and went over the side, while my own
men, appearing on deck too, lined the rail. I escorted my
visitor to the gangway ceremoniously, and nearly overdid
it. He was a tenacious beast. On the very ladder he lingered, and in that unique, guiltily concientious manner of
sticking to the point:

'I say ... you ... you don't think that—'

I covered his voice loudly:

'Certainly not. . . . I am delighted. Good-bye.'

I had an idea of what he meant to say, and just saved
myself by the privilege of defective hearing. He was too
shaken generally to insist, but my mate, close witness of
that parting, looked mystified and his face took on a
thoughtful cast. As I did not want to appear as if I wished
to avoid all communication with my officers, he had the
opportunity to address me.

'Seems a very nice man. His boat's crew told our chaps
a very extraordinary story, if what I am told by the
steward is true. I suppose you had it from the captain,
sir?'

'Yes. I had a story from the captain.'

' A very horrible affair – isn't it, sir?'

'It is.'

'Beats all these tales we here about murders in Yankee
ships.'

'I don't think it beats them. I don't think it resembles
them in the least.'

'Bless my soul – you don't say so! But of course I've
no acquaintance whatever with American ships, not I, so
I couldn't go against your knowledge. It's horrible enough
for me. . . . But the queerest part is that those fellows
seemed to have some idea the man was hidden aboard
here. They had really. Did you ever hear of such a thing?'

'Preposterous – isn't it?'

We were walking to and fro athwart the quarter-deck.
No one of the crew forward could be seen (the day was
Sunday), and the mate pursued:

'There was some little dispute about it. Our chaps took offence. "As if we would harbour a thing like that," they said. "Wouldn't you like to look for him in our coal-hole?" Quite a tiff. But they made it up in the end. I suppose he did drown himself. Don't you, sir?'

'I don't suppose anything.'

'You have no doubt in the matter, sir?'

'None whatever.'

I left him suddenly. I felt I was producing a bad impression, but with my double down there it was most trying to be on deck. And it was almost as trying to be below. Altogether a nerve-trying situation. But on the whole I felt less torn in two when I was with him. There was no one in the whole ship whom I dared take into my confidence. Since the hands had got to know his story, it would have been impossible to pass him off for any one else, and an accidental discovery was to be dreaded now more than ever. . . .

The steward being engaged in laying the table for dinner, we could talk only with our eyes when I first went down. Later in the afternoon we had a cautious try at whispering. The Sunday quietness of the ship was against us; the stillness of air and water around her was against us; the elements, the men were against us – everything was against us in our secret partnership; time itself – for this could not go on forever. The very trust in Providence was, I suppose, denied to his guilt. Shall I confess that this thought cast me down very much? And as to the chapter of accidents which counts for so much in the book of success, I could only hope that it was closed. For what favourable accident could be expected?

'Did you hear everything?' were my first words as soon as we took up our position side by side, leaning over my bed-place.

He had. And the proof of it was his earnest whisper, 'The man told you he hardly dared to give the order.'

I understood the reference to be to that saving foresail.

'Yes. He was afraid of it being lost in the setting.'

'I assure you he never gave the order. He may think he did, but he never gave it. He stood there with me on the break of the poop after the maintopsail blew away, and whimpered about our last hope – positively whimpered about it and nothing else – and the night coming on! To hear one's skipper go on like that in such weather was enough to drive any fellow out of his mind. It worked me up into a sort of desperation. I just took it into my own hands and went away from him boiling, and— But what's the use telling you? *You* know! . . . Do you think that if I had not been pretty fierce with them I should have got the men to do anything? Not it! The bo's'n perhaps? Perhaps! It wasn't a heavy sea – it was a sea gone mad! I suppose the end of the world will be something like that; and a man may have the heart to see it coming once and be done with it – but to have to face it day after day— I don't blame anybody. I was precious little better than the rest. Only – I was an officer of that old coal-wagon, any-how—'

'I quite understand,' I conveyed that sincere assurance into his ear. He was out of breath with whispering; I could hear him pant slightly. It was all very simple. The same strung-up force which had given twenty-four men a chance, at least, for their lives, had, in a sort of recoil, crushed an unworthy mutinous existence.

But I had no leisure to weigh the merits of the matter – footsteps in the saloon, a heavy knock. 'There's enough wind to get under way with, sir.' Here was the call of a new claim upon my thoughts and even upon my feelings.

'Turn the hands up,' I cried through the door. 'I'll be on deck directly.'

I was going out to make the acquaintance of my ship. Before I left the cabin our eyes met – the eyes of the only two strangers on board. I pointed to the recessed part where the little camp-stool awaited him and laid my finger on my lips. He made a gesture – somewhat vague – a little mysterious, accompanied by a faint smile, as if of regret.

This is not the place to enlarge upon the sensations of

a man who feels for the first time a ship move under his feet to his own independent word. In my case they were unalloyed. I was not wholly alone with my command; for there was that stranger in my cabin. Or rather, I was not completely and wholly with her. Part of me was absent. That mental feeling of being in two places at once affected me physically as if the mood of secrecy had penetrated my very soul. Before an hour had elapsed since the ship had begun to move, having occasion to ask the mate (he stood by my side) to take a compass bearing of the Pagoda, I caught myself reaching up to his ear in whispers. I say I caught myself, but enough had escaped to startle the man. I can't describe it otherwise than by saying that he shied. A grave, preoccupied manner, as though he were in possession of some perplexing intelligence, did not leave henceforth. A little later I moved away from the rail to look at the compass with such a stealthy gait that the helmsman noticed it – and I could not help noticing the unusual roundness of his eyes. These are trifling instances, though it's to no commander's advantage to be suspected of ludicrous eccentricities. But I was also more seriously affected. There are to a seaman certain words, gestures, that should in given conditions come as naturally, as instinctively as the winking of a menaced eye. A certain order should spring on to his lips without thinking; a certain sign should get itself made, so to speak, without reflection. But all unconscious alertness had abandoned me. I had to make an effort of will to recall myself back (from the cabin) to the conditions of the moment. I felt that I was appearing an irresolute commander to those people who were watching me more or less critically.

And, besides, there were the scares. On the second day out, for instance, coming off the deck in the afternoon (I had straw slippers on my bare feet) I stopped at the open pantry door and spoke to the steward. He was doing something there with his back to me. At the sound of my voice he nearly jumped out of his skin, as the saying is, and incidentally broke a cup.

'What on earth's the matter with you?' I asked, astonished.

He was extremely confused. 'Beg your pardon, sir. I made sure you were in your cabin.'

'You see I wasn't.'

'No, sir. I could have sworn I had heard you moving in there not a moment ago. It's most extraordinary . . . very sorry, sir.'

I passed on with an inward shudder. I was so identified with my secret double that I did not even mention the fact in those scanty, fearful whispers we exchanged. I suppose he had made some slight noise of some kind or other. It would have been miraculous if he hadn't at one time or another. And yet, haggard as he appeared, he looked always perfectly self-controlled, more than calm – almost invulnerable. On my suggestion, he remained almost entirely in the bath-room, which, upon the whole, was the safest place. There could be really no shadow of an excuse for any one ever wanting to go in there, once the steward had done with it. It was a very tiny place. Sometimes he reclined on the floor, his legs bent, his head sustained on one elbow. At others I would find him on the camp-stool, sitting in his grey sleeping-suit and with his cropped dark hair like a patient, unmoved convict. At night I would smuggle him into my bed-place, and we would whisper together, with the regular foot-falls of the officer of the watch passing and repassing over our heads. It was an infinitely miserable time. It was lucky that some tins of fine preserves were stowed in a locker in my stateroom; hard bread I could always get hold of; and so he lived on stewed chicken, paté de foie gras, asparagus, cooked oysters, sardines – on all sorts of abominable sham delicacies out of tins. My early morning coffee he always drank; and it was all I dared do for him in that respect.

Every day there was the horrible manoeuvring to go through so that my room and then the bath-room should be done in the usual way. I came to hate the sight of the steward, to abhor the voice of that harmless man. I felt that it was he who would bring on the disaster of discovery. It hung like a sword over our heads.

The fourth day out, I think (we were then working down the east side of the Gulf of Siam, tack for tack, in light winds and smooth water) – the fourth day, I say, of this miserable juggling with the unavoidable, as we sat at our evening meal, that man, whose slightest movement I dreaded, after putting down the dishes ran up on deck busily. This could not be dangerous. Presently he came down again; and then it appeared that he had remembered a coat of mine which I had thrown over a rail to dry after having been wetted in a shower which had passed over the ship in the afternoon. Sitting stolidly at the head of the table I became terrified at the sight of the garment on his arm. Of course he made for my door. There was no time to lose.

'Steward,' I thundered. My nerves were so shaken that I could not govern my voice and conceal my agitation. This was the sort of thing that made my terrifically whiskered mate tap his forehead with his forefinger. I had detected him using that gesture while talking on deck with a confidential air to the carpenter. It was too far to hear a word, but I had no doubt that this pantomime could only refer to the strange new captain.

'Yes, sir,' the pale-faced steward turned resignedly to me. It was this maddening course of being shouted at, checked without rhyme or reason, arbitrarily chased out of my cabin, suddenly called into it, sent flying out of his pantry on incomprehensible errands, that accounted for the growing wretchedness of his expression.

'Where are you going with that coat?'

'To your room, sir.'

'Is there another shower coming?'

'I'm sure I don't know, sir. Shall I go up again and see, sir?'

'No! never mind.'

My object was attained, as of course my other self in

there would have heard everything that passed. During this interlude my two officers never raised their eyes off their respective plates; but the lip of that confounded cub, the second mate, quivered visibly.

I expected the steward to hook my coat on and come out at once. He was very slow about it; but I dominated my nervousness sufficiently not to shout after him. Suddenly I became aware (it could be heard plainly enough) that the fellow for some reason or other was opening the door of the bath-room. It was the end. The place was literally not big enough to swing a cat in. My voice died in my throat and I went stony all over. I expected to hear a yell of surprise and terror, and made a movement, but had not the strength to get on my legs. Everything remained still. Had my second self taken the poor wretch by the throat? I don't know what I could have done next moment if I had not seen the steward come out of my room, close the door, and then stand quietly by the sideboard.

'Saved,' I thought. 'But, no! Lost! Gone! He was gone!'

I laid my knife and fork down and leaned back in my chair. My head swam. After a while, when sufficiently recovered to speak in a steady voice, I instructed my mate to put the ship round at eight o'clock himself.

'I won't come on deck,' I went on. 'I think I'll turn in, and unless the wind shifts I don't want to be disturbed before midnight. I feel a bit seedy.'

'You did look middling bad a little while ago,' the chief mate remarked without showing any great concern.

They both went out, and I stared at the steward clearing the table. There was nothing to be read on that wretched man's face. But why did he avoid my eyes, I asked myself. Then I thought I should like to hear the sound of his voice.

'Steward!'

'Sir!' Startled as usual.

'Where did you hang up that coat?'

'In the bath-room, sir.' The usual anxious tone. 'It's not quite dry yet, sir.'

For some time longer I sat in the cuddy. Had my double vanished as he had come? But of his coming there was an explanation, whereas his disappearance would be inexplicable. . . . I went slowly into my dark room, shut the door, lighted the lamp, and for a time dared not turn round. When at last I did I saw him standing bolt-upright in the narrow recessed part. It would not be true to say I had a shock, but an irresistible doubt of his bodily existence flitted through my mind. Can it be, I asked myself, that he is not visible to other eyes than mine? It was like being haunted. Motionless, with a grave face, he raised his hands slightly at me in a gesture which meant clearly, 'Heavens! what a narrow escape!' Narrow indeed. I think I had come creeping quietly as near insanity as any man who has not actually gone over the border. That gesture restrained me, so to speak.

The mate with the terrific whiskers was now putting the ship on the other tack. In the moment of profound silence which follows upon the hands going to their stations I heard on the poop his raised vioce: 'Hard alee!' and the distant shout of the order repeated on the maindeck. The sails, in that light breeze, made but a faint fluttering noise. It ceased. The ship was coming round slowly; I held my breath in the renewed stillness of expectation; one wouldn't have thought that there was a single living soul on her decks. A sudden brisk shout, 'Mainsail haul!' broke the spell, and in the noisy cries and rush overhead of the men running away with the main-brace we two, down in my cabin, came together in our usual position by the bed-place.

He did not wait for my question. 'I heard him fumbling here and just managed to squat myself down in the bath,' he whispered to me. 'The fellow only opened the door and put his arm in to hang the coat up. All the same—'

'I never thought of that,' I whispered back, even more appalled than before at the closeness of the shave, and marvelling at that something unyielding in his character which was carrying him through so finely. There was no agitation in his whisper. Whoever was being driven distracted, it was not he. He was sane. And the proof of his sanity was continued when he took up the whispering again.

'It would never do for me to come to life again.'

It was something that a ghost might have said. But what he was alluding to was his old captain's reluctant admission of the theory of suicide. It would obviously serve his turn – if I had understood at all the view which seemed to govern the unalterable purpose of his action.

'You must maroon me as soon as ever you can get amongst these islands off the Cambodje shore,' he went on.

'Maroon you! We are not living in a boy's adventure tale,' I protested. His scornful whispering took me up.

'We aren't indeed! There's nothing of a boy's tale in this. But there's nothing else for it. I want no more. You don't suppose I am afraid of what can be done to me? You don't see me coming back to explain such things to an old fellow in a wig and twelve respectable tradesmen, do you? What can they know whether I am guilty or not – or of *what* I am guilty, either? That's my affair. What does the Bible say? "Driven off the face of the earth." Very well. I am off the face of the earth now. As I came at night so I shall go.'

'Impossible!' I murmured. 'You can't.'

'Can't? . . . Not naked like a soul on the Day of Judgment. I shall freeze on to this sleeping-suit. The Last Day is not yet – and . . . you have understood thoroughly. Didn't you?'

I felt suddenly ashamed of myself. I may say truly that I understood – and my hesitation in letting that man swim away from my ship's side had been a mere sham sentiment, a sort of cowardice.

'It can't be done now till next night,' I breathed out. 'The ship is on the off-shore tack and the wind may fail us.'

'As long as I know that you understand,' he whispered. 'But of course you do. It's a great satisfaction to have got somebody to understand. You seem to have been there on purpose.' And in the same whisper, as if we two whenever we talked had to say things to each other which were not fit for the world to hear, he added, 'It's very wonderful.'

We remained side by side talking in our secret way – but sometimes silent or just exchanging a whispered word or two at long intervals. And as usual he stared through the port. A breath of wind came now and again into our faces. The ship might have been moored in dock, so gently and on an even keel she slipped through the water, that did not murmur even at our passage, shadowy and silent like a phantom sea.

At midnight I went on deck, and to my mate's great surprise put the ship round on the other tack. His terrible whiskers flitted round me in silent criticism. I certainly should not have done it if it had been only a question of getting out of that sleepy gulf as quickly as possible. I believe he told the second mate, who relieved him, that it was a great want of judgment. The other only yawned. That intolerable cub shuffled about so sleepily and lolled against the rails in such a slack, improper fashion that I came down on him sharply.

'Aren't you properly awake yet?'

'Yes, sir! I am awake.'

'Well, then, be good enough to hold yourself as if you were. And keep a look-out. If there's any current we'll be closing with some islands before daylight.'

The east side of the gulf is fringed with islands, some solitary, others in groups. On the blue background of the high coast they seem to float on silvery patches of calm water, arid and grey, or dark green and rounded like clumps of evergreen bushes, with the larger ones, a mile or two long, showing the outlines of ridges, ribs of grey rock under the dank mantle of matted leafage. Unknown to trade, to travel, almost to geography, the manner of life they harbour is an unsolved secret. There must be villages – settlements of fishermen at least – on the largest of them, and some communication with the world is probably kept up by native craft. But all that forenoon, as we headed for them, fanned along by the faintest of breezes, I saw no sign of man or canoe in the field of the telescope I kept on pointing at the scattered group.

At noon I gave no orders for a change of course, and the mate's whiskers became much concerned and seemed to be offering themselves unduly to my notice. At last I said:

'I am going to stand right in. Quite in –as far as I can take her.'

The stare of extreme surprise imparted an air of ferocity also to his eyes, and he looked truly terrific for a moment.

'We're not doing well in the middle of the gulf,' I continued, casually. 'I am going to look for the land breezes to-night.'

'Bless my soul! Do you mean, sir, in the dark amongst the lot of all them islands and reefs and shoals?'

'Well – if there are any regular land breezes at all on this coast one must get close inshore to find them, musn't one?'

'Bless my soul!' he exclaimed again under his breath. All that afternoon he wore a dreamy, contemplative appearance which in him was a mark of perplexity. After dinner I went into my stateroom as if I meant to take some rest. There we two bent our dark heads over a half-unrolled chart lying on my bed.

'There,' I said. 'It's got to be Koh-ring. I've been looking at it ever since sunrise. It has got two hills and a low point. It must be inhabited. And on the coast opposite there is what looks like the mouth of a biggish river – with some town, no doubt, not far up. It's the best chance for you that I can see.'

'Anything. Koh-ring let it be.'

He looked thoughtfully at the chart as if surveying chances and distances from a lofty height – and following with his eyes his own figure wandering on the blank land of Cochin-China, and then passing off that piece of paper clean out of sight into uncharted regions. And it was as if the ship had two captains to plan her course for her. I had been so worried and restless running up and down that I had not had the patience to dress that day. I had remained in my sleeping-suit, with straw slippers and a soft floppy hat. The closeness of the heat in the gulf had been most oppressive, and the crew were used to see me wandering in that airy attire.

'She will clear the south point as she heads now,' I whispered into his ear. 'Goodness only knows when, though, but certainly after dark. I'll edge her in to half a mile, as far as I may be able to judge in the dark—'

'Be careful,' he murmured, warningly – and I realised suddenly that all my future, the only future for which I was fit, would perhaps go irretrievably to pieces in any mishap to my first command.

I could not stop a moment longer in the room. I motioned him to get out of sight and made my way on the poop. That unplayful cub had the watch. I walked up and down for a while thinking things out, then beckoned him over.

'Send a couple of hands to open the two quarter-deck ports,' I said, mildly.

He actually had the impudence, or else so forgot himself in his wonder at such an incomprehensible order, as to repeat:

'Open the quarter-deck ports! What for, sir?'

'The only reason you need concern yourself about is because I tell you to do so. Have them open wide and fastened properly.'

He reddened and went off, but I believe made some jeering remark to the carpenter as to the sensible practice of ventilating a ship's quarter-deck. I know he popped into the mate's cabin to impart the fact to him because the whiskers came on deck, as it were by chance, and stole glances at me from below – for signs of lunacy or drunkenness, I suppose.

A little before supper, feeling more restless than ever, I rejoined, for a moment, my second self. And to find him sitting so quietly was surprising, like something against nature, inhuman.

I developed my plan in a hurried whisper.

'I shall stand in as close as I dare and then put her round. I will presently find means to smuggle you out of here into the sail-locker, which communicates with the lobby. But there is an opening, a sort of square for hauling the sails out, which gives straight on the quarter-deck and which is never closed in fine weather, so as to give air to the sails. When the ship's way is deadened in stays and all the hands are aft at the main-braces you will have a clear road to slip out and get overboard through the open quarter-deck port. I've had them both fastened up. Use a rope's end to lower yourself into the water so as to avoid a splash – you know. It could be heard and cause some beastly complication.'

He kept silent for a while, then whispered, 'I understand.'

'I won't be there to see you go,' I began with an effort. 'The rest . . . I only hope I have understood, too.'

'You have. From first to last' – and for the first time there seemed to be a faltering, something strained in his whisper. He caught hold of my arm, but the ringing of the supper bell made me start. He didn't, though; he only released his grip.

After supper I didn't come below again till well past eight o'clock. The faint, steady breeze was loaded with dew; and the wet, darkened sails held all there was of propelling power in it. The night, clear and starry, sparkled darkly, and the opaque, lightless patches shifting slowly against the low stars were the drifting islets. On the port bow there was a big one more distant and shadowily imposing by the great space of sky it eclipsed.

On opening the door I had a back view of my very own self looking at a chart. He had come out of the recess and was standing near the table.

'Quite dark enough,' I whispered.

He stepped back and leaned against my bed with a level, quiet glance. I sat on the couch. We had nothing to say to each other. Over our heads the officer of the watch moved here and there. Then I heard him move quickly. I knew what that meant. He was making for the companion; and presently his voice was outside my door.

'We are drawing in pretty fast, sir. Land looks rather close.'

'Very well,' I answered. 'I am coming on deck directly.'

I waited till he was gone out of the cuddy, then rose. My double moved too. The time had come to exchange our last whispers, for neither of us was ever to hear each other's natural voice.

'Look here!' I opened a drawer and took out three sovereigns. 'Take this anyhow. I've got six and I'd give you the lot, only I must keep a little money to buy some fruit and vegetables for the crew from native boats as we go through Sunda Straits.'

He shook his head.

'Take it,' I urged him, whispering desperately. 'No one can tell what—'

He smiled and slapped meaningly the only pocket of the sleeping-jacket. It was not safe, certainly. But I produced a large old silk handkerchief of mine, and tying the three pieces of gold in a corner, pressed it on him. He was touched, I suppose, because he took it at last and tied it quickly round his waist under the jacket, on his bare skin.

Our eyes met; several seconds elapsed, till, our glances still mingled, I extended my hand and turned the lamp out. Then I passed through the cuddy, leaving the door of my room wide open. . . .

'Steward!'

He was lingering in the pantry in the greatness of his zeal, giving a rub-up to a plated cruet-stand the last thing before going to bed. Being careful not to wake up the mate, whose room was opposite, I spoke in an undertone.

He looked round anxiously. 'Sir!'

'Can you get me a little hot water from the galley?'

'I am afraid, sir, the galley fire's been out for some time now.'

'Go and see.'

He flew up the stairs.

'Now,' I whispered, loudly, into the saloon – too loudly, perhaps, but I was afraid I couldn't make a sound. He was by my side in an instant – the double captain slipped past the stairs – through a tiny dark passage . . . a sliding door. We were in the sail-locker, scrambling on our knees over the sails. A sudden thought struck me. I saw myself wandering barefooted, bareheaded, the sun beating on my dark poll. I snatched off my floppy hat and tried hurriedly in the dark to ram it on my other self. He dodged and fended off silently. I wonder what he thought had come to me before he understood and suddenly desisted. Our hands met gropingly, lingered united in a steady, motionless clasp for a second. . . . No word was breathed by either of us when they separated.

I was standing quietly by the pantry door when the steward returned.

'Sorry, sir. Kettle barely warm. Shall I light the spirit-lamp?'

'Never mind.'

I came out on deck slowly. It was now a matter of conscience to shave the land as close as possible – for now he must go overboard whenever the ship was put in stays. Must! There could be no going back for him. After a moment I walked over to leeward and my heart flew into my mouth at the nearness of the land on the bow. Under any other circumstances I would not have held on a minute longer. The second mate had followed me anxiously.

I looked on till I felt I could command my voice.

'She may weather,' I said then in a quiet tone.

'Are you going to try that, sir?' he stammered out incredulously.

I took no notice of him and raised my tone just enough to be heard by the helmsman.

'Keep her good full.'

'Good full, sir.'

The wind fanned my cheek, the sails slept, the world was silent. The strain of watching the dark loom of the land grow bigger and denser was too much for me. I had shut my eyes – because the ship must go closer. She must! The stillness was intolerable. Were we standing still?

When I opened my eyes the second view started my heart with a thump. The black southern hill of Koh-ring seemed to hang right over the ship like a towering fragment of the everlasting night. On that enormous mass of blackness there was not a gleam to be seen, not a sound to be heard. It was gliding irresistibly towards us and yet seemed already within reach of the hand. I saw the vague figures of the watch grouped in the waist, gazing in awed silence.

'Are you going on, sir?' inquired an unsteady voice at my elbow.

I ignored it. I had to go on.

'Keep her full. Don't check her way. That won't do now,' I said, warningly.

'I can't see the sails very well,' the helmsman answered me, in strange, quavering tones.

Was she close enough? Already she was, I won't say in the shadow of the land, but in the very blackness of it, already swallowed up as it were, gone too close to be recalled, gone from me altogether.

'Give the mate a call,' I said to the young man who stood at my elbow as still as death. 'And turn all hands up.'

My tone had a borrowed loudness reverberated from the height of the land. Several voices cried out together: 'We are all on deck, sir.'

Then stillness again, with the great shadow gliding closer, towering higher, without light, without a sound. Such a hush had fallen on the ship that she might have been a bark of the dead floating in slowly under the very gate of Erebus.

'My God! Where are we?'

It was the mate moaning at my elbow. He was thunder-struck, and as it were deprived of the moral support of his whiskers. He clapped his hands and absolutely cried out, 'Lost!'

'Be quiet,' I said, sternly.

He lowered his tone, but I saw the shadowy gesture of his despair. 'What are we doing here?'

'Looking for the land wind.'

He made as if to tear his hair, and addressed me recklessly.

'She will never get out. You have done it, sir. I knew it'd end in something like this. She will never weather, and you are too close now to stay. She'll drift ashore before she's round. O my God!'

I caught his arm as he was raising it to batter his poor devoted head, and shook it violently.

'She's ashore already,' he wailed, trying to tear himself away.

'Is she? ... Keep good full there!'

'Good full, sir,' cried the helmsman in a frightened, thin, child-like voice.

I hadn't let go the mate's arm and went on shaking it. 'Ready about, do you hear? You go forward' – shake – 'and see these head-sheets properly overhauled' – shake, shake, – shake.

And all the time I dared not look towards the land lest my heart should fail me. I released my grip at last and he ran forward as if fleeing for dear life.

I wondered what my double there in the sail-locker thought of this commotion. He was able to hear everything – and perhaps he was able to understand why, on my conscience, it had to be thus close – no less. My first order 'Hard alee!' re-echoed ominously under the towering shadow of Koh-ring as if I had shouted in a mountain gorge. And then I watched the land intently. In that smooth water and light wind it was impossible to feel the ship coming-to. No! I could not feel her. And my second self was making now ready to slip out and lower himself overboard. Perhaps he was gone already . . . ?

The great black mass brooding over our very mastheads began to pivot away from the ship's side silently. And now I forgot the secret stranger ready to depart, and remembered only that I was a total stranger to the ship. I did not know her. Would she do it? How was she to be handled?

I swung the mainyard and waited helplessly. She was perhaps stopped, and her very fate hung in the balance, with the black mass of Koh-ring like the gate of the everlasting night towering over her taffrail. What would she do now? Had she way on her yet? I stepped to the side swiftly, and on the shadowy water I could see nothing except a faint phosphorescent flash revealing the glassy smoothness of the sleeping surface. It was impossible to tell – and I had not learned yet the feel of my ship. Was she moving? What I needed was something easily seen, a piece of paper, which I could throw overboard and watch. I had nothing on me. To run down for it I didn't dare. There was no time. All at once my strained, yearning stare distinguished a white object floating within a yard of the ship's side. White on the black water. A phosphorescent flash passed under it. What was that thing? . . . I recognised my own floppy hat. It must have fallen off his head . . . and he didn't bother. Now I had what I wanted – the saving mark for my eyes. But I hardly thought of my other self, now gone from the ship, to be hidden for ever from all friendly faces, to be a fugitive and a vagabond on the earth, with no brand of the curse on his sane forehead to stay a slaying hand ... too proud to explain.

And I watched the hat – the expression of my sudden pity for his mere flesh. It had been meant to save his homeless head from the dangers of the sun. And now – behold – it was saving the ship, by serving me for a mark to help out the ignorance of my strangeness. Ha! It was drifting forward, warning me just in time that the ship had gathered sternway.

'Shift the helm,' I said in a low voice to the seaman standing still like a statue.

The man's eyes glistened wildly in the binnacle light as he jumped round to the other side and spun round the wheel.

I walked to the break of the poop. On the overshadowed deck all hands stood by the forebraces waiting for my order. The stars ahead seemed to be gliding from right to left. And all was so still in the world that I heard the quiet remark 'She's round,' passed in a tone of intense relief between two seamen.

'Let go and haul.'

The foreyards ran round with a great noise, amidst cheery cries. And now the frightful whiskers made themselves heard giving various orders. Already the ship was drawing ahead. And I was alone with her. Nothing! no one in the world should stand now between us, throwing a shadow on the way of silent knowledge and mute affection, the perfect communion of a seaman with his first command.

Walking to the taffrail, I was in time to make out, on the very edge of a darkness thrown by a towering black mass like the very gateway of Erebus – yes, I was in time to catch an evanescent glimpse of my white hat left behind to mark the spot where the secret sharer of my cabin and of my thoughts, as though he were my second self, had lowered himself into the water to take his punishment: a free man, a proud swimmer striking out for a new destiny.

GEORGE MOORE

Albert Nobbs

When we went up to Dublin in the 'sixties, Alec, we always put up at Morrison's Hotel, a big family hotel at the corner of Dawson Street, one that was well patronised by the gentry from all over Ireland, my father paying his bill every six months when he was able, which wasn't very often, for what with racing stables and elections following one after the other, Moore Hall wasn't what you'd call overflowing with money. Now that I come to think of it, I can see Morrison's as clearly almost as I do Moore Hall: the front door opening into a short passage, with some half-dozen steps leading up into the house, the glass doors of the coffee-room showing through the dimness, and in front of the visitor a big staircase running up to the second landing. I remember long passages on the second landing, and half-way down these passages was the well. I don't know if it's right to speak of the well of a staircase, but I used to think of it as a well. It was always being drummed into me that I mustn't climb on to the banisters, a thing I wished to do, but was afraid to get astride of them, lest I should lose my head and fall all the way down to the ground floor. There was nothing to stop me from reaching it, if I lost my balance, except a few gas lamps. I think that both the long passages led to minor stairs, but I never followed either lest I should miss my way. A very big building was Morrison's Hotel, with passages running hither and thither, and little flights of stairs in all kinds of odd corners by which the visitors climbed to their apartments, and it needed all my attention to remember the way to our rooms on the second floor. We were always on the second floor in a big sitting-room overlooking College Green, and I remember the pair of windows, their lace curtains and their rep curtains, better than the passages, and better than the windows I can remember myself looking through the pane interested in the coal carts going by, the bell hitched on to the horse's collar jangling all the way down the street, the coalman himself sitting with his legs hanging over the shafts, driving from the wrong side and looking up at the windows to see if he could spy out an order. Fine horses were in these coal carts, stepping out as well as those in our own carriage.

I'm telling you these things for the pleasure of looking back and nothing else. I can see the sitting-room and myself as plainly as I can see the mountains beyond, in some ways plainer, and the waiter that used to attend on us, I can see him, though not as plainly as I see you, Alec; but I'm more knowledgeable of him, if you understand me rightly, and to this day I can recall the frights he gave me when he came behind me, awaking me from my dream of a coalman's life — what he said is forgotten, but his squeaky voice remains in my ears. He seemed to be always laughing at me, showing long, yellow teeth, and I used to be afraid to open the sitting-room door, for I'd be sure to find him waiting on the landing, his napkin thrown over his right shoulder. I think I was afraid he'd pick me up and kiss me. As the whole of my story is about him, perhaps I'd better describe him more fully, and to do that I will tell you that he was a tall, scraggy fellow, with big hips sticking out, and a long, thin throat. It was his throat that frightened me as much as anything about him, unless it was his nose, which was a great high one, or his melancholy eyes, which were pale blue and very small, deep in the head. He was old, but how old I cannot say, for everybody except children seems old to children. He was the ugliest thing I'd seen out of a fairy-book, and I'd beg not to be left alone in the sitting-room; and I'm sure I often asked my father and mother to take another set of rooms, which they never did, for they liked Albert Nobbs. And the guests liked him, and the proprietress liked him, as well she might, for he was the most dependable servant in the hotel: no running round to public-houses and coming back with the smell of whisky and tobacco upon him; no rank pipe in his pocket; and of all, no playing the fool with the maid-servants. Nobody had ever been heard to say he had seen Albert out with one of them – a queer, hobgoblin sort of fellow that they mightn't have cared to be seen with, but all the same it seemed to them funny that he should never propose to walk out with one of them. I've heard the hall-porter say it was hard to understand a man living without taking pleasure in something outside of his work. Holidays he never asked for, and when Mrs Baker pressed him to go to the salt water for a week, he'd try to rake up an excuse for not going away, asking if it wasn't true that the Blakes, the Joyces, and the Ruttledges were coming up to town, saying that he didn't like to be away, so used were they to him and he to them. A strange life his was, and mysterious, though every hour of it was before them, saving the hours he was asleep, which weren't many, for he was no great sleeper. From the time he got up in the morning till he went to bed at night he was before their eyes, running up and down the staircase, his napkin over his arm, taking orders with cheerfulness, as if an order were as good as a half-crown tip to him, always good-humoured, and making amends for his lack of interest in other people by his willingness to oblige. No one had ever heard him object to doing anything he was asked to do, or even put forward an excuse for not being able to do it. In fact, his willingness to oblige was so notorious in the hotel that Mrs Baker (the proprietress of Morrison's Hotel at the time) could hardly believe she was listening to him when he began to stumble from one excuse to another for not sharing his bed with Hubert Page, and this after she had told him that his bed was Page's only chance of getting a stretch that night. All the other waiters were married men and went home to their wives. You see, Alec, it was Punchestown week, and beds are as scarce in Dublin that week as diamonds are on the slopes of Croagh Patrick.

But you haven't told me yet who Page was, Alec interjected, and I thought reprovingly. I'm just coming to him, I answered. Hubert Page was a house-painter, well known and well liked by Mrs Baker. He came over every season, and was always welcome at Morrison's Hotel, and so pleasant were his manners that one forgot the smell of his paint. It is hardly saying too much to say that when Hubert Page had finished his job everybody in the hotel, men and women alike, missed the pleasant sight of this young man going to and fro in his suit of hollands, the long coat buttoned loosely to his figure with large bone buttons, going to and fro about his work, up and down the passages, with a sort of lolling, idle gait that attracted and pleased the eye – a young man that would seem preferable to most men if a man had to choose a bed-fellow, yet seemingly the very one that Albert Nobbs couldn't abide lying down with, a dislike that Mrs Baker could understand so little that she stood staring at her confused and embarrassed waiter, who was still seeking excuses for his dislike to share his bed with Hubert Page. I suppose you fully understand, she said, that Page is leaving for Belfast by the morning train, and has come over here to ask us for a bed, there not being one at the hotel in which he is working? Albert answered that he understood well enough, but was thinking— He began again to fumble with words. Now, what are you trying to say? Mrs Baker asked, and rather sharply. My bed is full of lumps, Albert answered. Your mattress full of lumps! the proprietress rapped out; why, your mattress was repicked and buttoned six months ago, and came back as good as any mattress in the hotel. What kind of story are you telling me? So it was, ma'am, so it was, Albert mumbled, and it was some time before he got out his next excuse: he was a very light sleeper and had never slept with anybody before and was sure he wouldn't close his eyes; not that that would matter much, but his sleeplessness might keep Mr Page awake. Mr Page would get a better stretch on one of the sofas in the coffee-room than in my bed, I'm thinking, Mrs Baker. A better stretch on the sofa in the coffee-room? Mrs Baker repeated angrily. I don't understand you, not a little bit; and she stood staring at the two men, so dissimilar. But, ma'am, I wouldn't be putting Mr Nobbs to the inconvenience of my company, the house-painter began. The night is a fine one; I'll keep myself warm with a sharp walk, and the train starts early. You'll do nothing of the kind, Page, she answered; and seeing that Mrs Baker was now very angry Albert thought it time to give in, and without more ado he began to assure them both that he'd be glad of Mr Page's company in his bed. I should think so indeed! interjected Mrs Baker. But I'm a light sleeper, he added. We've heard that before, Albert! Of course, if Mr Page is pleased to share my bed, Albert continued, I shall be very glad. If Mr Nobbs doesn't like my company I should— Don't say another word, Albert whispered, you'll only set her against me. Come upstairs at once; it'll be all right. Come along.

Good-night, ma'am, and I hope— No inconvenience whatever, Page, Mrs Baker answered. This way, Mr Page, Albert cried; and as soon as they were in the room he said: I hope you aren't going to cut up rough at anything I've said; it isn't at all as Mrs Baker put it. I'm glad enough of your company, but you see, as I've never slept with anybody in my life, it may be that I shall be tossing about all night, keeping you awake. Well, if it's to be like that, Page answered, I might as well have a doze on the chair until it's time to go, and not trouble you at all. You won't be giving me any trouble; what I'm afraid of is – but enough has been said; we have to lie down together, whether we like it or whether we don't, for if Mrs Baker heard that we hadn't been in the same bed together all the fault would lie with me. I'd be sent out of the hotel in double-quick time. But how can she know? Page cried. It's been settled one way, so let us make no more fuss about it.

Albert began to undo his white neck-tie, saying he would try to lie quiet, and Page started pulling off his clothes, thinking he'd be well pleased to be out of the job of lying down with Albert. But he was so dog-tired that he couldn't think any more about whom he was to sleep with, only of the long days of twelve and thirteen hours he had been doing, with a walk to and from his work; only sleep mattered to him, and Albert saw him tumble into bed in the long shirt that he wore under his clothes, and lay himself down next to the wall. It would be better for him to lie on the outside, Albert said to himself, but he didn't like to say anything lest Page might get out of his bed in a fit of ill-humour; but Page, as I've said, was too tired to trouble himself which side of the bed he was to doss on. A moment after he was asleep, and Albert stood listening, his loosened tie dangling, till the heavy breathing from the bed told him that Page was sound asleep. To make full sure he approached the bed stealthily, and overlooking Page, said: Poor fellow, I'm glad he's in my bed, for he'll get a good sleep there and he wants it; and considering that things had fallen out better than he hoped for, he began to undress.

He must have fallen asleep at once, and soundly, for he awoke out of nothingness. Flea! he muttered, and a strong one, too. It must have come from the house-painter alongside of me; a flea will leave anyone to come to me. And turning round in bed he remembered the look of dismay that had appeared on the housemaids' faces yesterday on his telling them that no man would ever love their hides as much as a flea loved his, which was so true that he couldn't understand how it was that the same flea had taken so long to find him out. Fleas must be as partial to him, he said, as they are to me. There it is again, trying to make up for lost time! and out went Albert's leg. I'm afraid I've awakened him, he said, but Hubert only turned over in the bed to sleep more soundly. It's a mercy indeed that he is so tired, Albert said, for if he wasn't very tired that last jump I gave would have awakened him. A moment after Albert was nipped again by another flea, or by the same one, he couldn't tell; he thought it must be a second one, so vigorous was the bite, and he was hard put to it to keep his nails off the spots. I shall only make them worse if I scratch, he said, and he strove to lie quiet. But the torment was too great. I've got to get up, he muttered, and raising himself up quietly, he listened. The striking of a match won't awaken him out of that sleep! and remembering where he had put the match-box, his hand was on it at once. The match flared up; he lighted the candle, and stood a while overlooking his bed-fellow. I'm safe, he said, and set himself to the task of catching the flea. There he is on the tail of my shirt, hardly able to move with all the blood he's taken from me. Now for the soap; and as he was about to dab it upon the blood-filled insect the painter awoke with a great yawn, and turning round, he said: Lord amassy! what is the meaning of this? Why, you're a woman!

If Albert had had the presence of mind to drop her shirt over her shoulders and to answer: You're dreaming, my man, Page might have turned over and fallen asleep and in the morning forgotten all about it, or thought he had been dreaming. But Albert hadn't a word in her chops. At last she began to blub. You won't tell on me, and ruin a poor man, will you, Mr Page? That is all I ask of you, and on my knees I beg it. Get up from your knees, my good woman, said Hubert. My good woman! Albert repeated, for she had been about so long as a man that she only remembered occasionally that she was a woman. My good woman, Hubert repeated, get up from your knees and tell me how long you have been playing this part. Ever since I was a girl, Albert answered. You won't tell upon me, will you, Mr Page, and prevent a poor woman from getting her living? Not likely, I've no thought of telling on you, but I'd like to hear how it all came about. How I went out as a youth to get my living? Yes; tell me the story, Hubert answered, for though I was very sleepy just now, the sleep has left my eyes and I'd like to hear it. But before you begin, tell me what you were doing with your shirt off. A flea, Albert answered. I suffer terribly from fleas, and you must have brought some in with you, Mr Page. I shall be covered in blotches in the morning. I'm sorry for that, Hubert said; but tell me how long ago it was that you became a man. Before you came to Dublin, of course? Oh, yes, long before. It is very cold, she said, and shuddering, dropped her shirt over her shoulders and pulled on her trousers.

2

It was in London, soon after the death of my old nurse, she began. You know I'm not Irish, Mr Page. My parents may have been, for all I know. The only one who knew who they were was my old nurse, and she never told me. Never told you! interjected Hubert. No, she never told me, though I often asked her, saying no good could come of holding it back from me. She might have told me before she died, but she died suddenly. Died suddenly, Hubert repeated, without telling you who you were! You'd better begin at the beginning.

I don't know how I'm to do that, for the story seems to me to be without a beginning; anyway I don't know the beginning. I was a bastard, and no one but my old nurse, who brought me up, knew who I was; she said she'd tell me some day, and she hinted more than once that my people were grand folk, and I know she had a big allowance from them for my education. Whoever they were, a hundred a year was paid to her for my keep and education, and all went well with us so long as my parents lived, but when they died the allowance was no longer paid, and my nurse and myself had to go out to work. It was all very sudden: one day the Reverend Mother (I got my education at a convent school) told me that Mrs Nobbs, my old nurse, had sent for me, and the first news I had on coming home was that my parents were dead and that we'd have to get our own living henceforth. There was no time for picking and choosing. We hadn't what would keep us until the end of the month in the house, so out we had to go in search of work; and the first job that came our way was looking after chambers in the Temple. We had three gentlemen to look after, so there was eighteen shillings a week between my old nurse and myself; the omnibus fares had to come out of these wages, and to save sixpence a day we went to live in Temple Lane. My old nurse didn't mind the lane; she had been a working woman all her life; but with me it was different, and the change was so great from the convent that I often thought I would sooner die than continue to live amid rough people. There was nothing wrong with them; they were honest enough; but they were poor, and when you are very poor you live like the animals, indecently, and life without decency is hardly bearable, so I thought. I've been through a great deal since in different hotels, and have become used to hard work, but even now I can't think of Temple Lane without goose-flesh; and when Mrs Nobbs' brother lost his berth (he'd been a bandmaster, a bugler, or something to do with music in the country), my old nurse was obliged to give him sixpence a day, and the drop from eighteen shillings to fourteen and sixpence is a big one. My old nurse worried about the food, but it was the rough men I worried about; the bandsman wouldn't leave me alone, and many's the time I've waited until the staircase was clear, afraid that if I met him or another that I'd be caught hold of and held and pulled about. I was different then from what I am now, and might have been tempted if one of them had been less rough than the rest, and if I hadn't known I was a bastard; it was that, I think, that kept me straight more than anything else, for I had just begun to feel what a great misfortune it is for a poor girl to find herself in the family way; no greater misfortune can befall anyone in this world, but it would have been worse in my case, for I should have known that I was only bringing another bastard into the world.

I escaped being seduced in the lane, and in the chambers the barristers had their own mistresses; pleasant and considerate men they all were – pleasant to work for; and it wasn't until four o'clock came and our work was over for the day that my heart sank, for after four o'clock till we went to bed at night there was nothing for us to do but to listen to the screams of drunken women; I don't know which was the worser, the laughter or the curses.

One of the barristers we worked for was Mr Congreve; he had chambers in Temple Gardens overlooking the river, and it was a pleasure to us to keep his pretty things clean, never breaking one of them; it was a pleasure for my old nurse as well as myself, myself more than for her, for though I wasn't very sure of myself at the time, looking back now I can see that I must have loved Mr Congreve very dearly; and it couldn't be else, for I had come out of a convent of nuns where I had been given a good education, where all was good, quiet, refined and gentle, and Mr Congreve seemed in many ways to remind me of the convent, for he never missed Church; as rare for him to miss a service as for parson. There was plenty of books in his chambers and he'd lend them to me, and talk to me over his newspaper when I took in his breakfast, and ask about the convent and what the nuns were like, and I'd stand in front of him, my eyes fixed on him, not feeling the time going by. I can see him now as plainly as if he were before me – very thin and elegant, with long white hands, and beautifully dressed. Even in the old clothes that he wore of a morning there wasn't much fault to find; he wore old clothes more elegantly than any man in the Temple wore his new clothes. I used to know all his suits, as well I might, for it was my job to look after them, to brush them; and I used to spend a great deal more time than was needed taking out spots with benzine, arranging his neck-ties – he had fifty or sixty, all kinds – and seven or eight greatcoats. A real

toff – my word he was that, but not one of those haughty
ones too proud to give one a nod. He always smiled and
nodded if we met under the clock, he on his way to the
library and I returning to Temple Lane. I used to look
round after him saying: He's got on the striped trousers
and the embroidered waistcoat. Mr Congreve was a com-
pensation for Temple Lane; he had promised to take me
into his private service, and I was counting the days when
I should leave Temple Lane, when one day I said to myself: Why, here's a letter from a woman. You see, Mr
Congreve wasn't like the other young men in the Temple;
I never found a hairpin in his bed, and if I had I shouldn't
have thought as much of him as I did. Nice is in France,
I said, and thought no more about the matter until
another letter arrived from Nice. Now what can she be
writing to him about? I asked, and thought no more about
it until the third letter arrived. Yesterday is already more
than half forgotten, but the morning I took in that last
letter is always before me. And it was a few mornings
afterwards that a box of flowers came for him. A parcel for
you, sir, I said. He roused himself up in bed. For me? he
cried, putting out his hand, and the moment he saw the
writing, he said: Put the flowers in water. He knows all
about it, I said to myself, and so overcome was I as I
picked them up out of the box that a sudden faintness
came over me, and my old nurse said: What is the matter
with thee? She never guessed, and I couldn't have told
her if I had wished to, for at the time it was no more than
a feeling that so far as I was concerned all was over. Of
course I never thought that Mr Congreve would look at
me, and I don't know that I wanted him to, but I didn't
want another woman about the place, and I seemed to
know from that moment what was going to happen. She
isn't far away now, in the train maybe, I said, as I went
about my work, and these rooms will be mine no longer.
Of course they never were mine, but you know what I
mean.

A week later he said to me: There's a lady coming to

luncheon here, and I remember the piercing that the words caused me; I can feel them here still; and Albert put her hand to her heart. Well, I had to serve the luncheon, working round the table and they not minding me at all, but sitting looking at each other lost in a sense of delight; the luncheon was forgotten. They don't want me waiting about, I thought. I knew all this, and said to myself in the kitchen: It's disgraceful, it's wicked, to lead a man into sin – for all my anger went out against the woman, and not against Mr Congreve; in my eyes he seemed to be nothing more than a victim of a designing woman; that is how I looked at it at the time, being but a youngster only just come from a convent school.

I don't think that anyone suffered more than I did in those days. It all seems very silly now when I look back upon it, but it was very real then. It does seem silly to tell that I used to lie awake all night thinking to myself that Mr Congreve was an elegant gentleman and I but a poor serving girl that he'd never look twice at, thinking of her only as somebody to go to the cellar for coal or to the kitchen to fetch his breakfast. I don't think I ever hoped he'd fall in love with me. It wasn't as bad as that. It was the hopelessness of it that set the tears streaming down my cheeks over my pillow, and I used to stuff the sheet into my mouth to keep back the sobs lest my old nurse should hear me; it wouldn't do to keep her awake, for she was very ill at that time; and soon afterwards she died, and then I was left alone, without a friend in the world. The only people I knew were the charwomen that lived in Temple Lane, and the bugler, who began to bully me, saying that I must continue to give him the same money he had had from my old nurse. He caught me on the stairs once and twisted my arm until I thought he'd broken it. The month after my old nurse's death till I went to earn my living as a waiter was the hardest time of all, and Mr Congreve's kindness seemed to hurt me more than anything. If only he'd spared me his kind words, and not spoken about the extra money he was going to give me for

my attendance on this lady, I shouldn't have felt so much
that they had lain side by side in the bed that I was making. She brought a dressing-gown to the chambers and
some slippers, and then more luggage came along; and I
think she must have guessed I was in love with Mr
Congreve, for I heard them quarrelling – my name was
mentioned; and I said: I can't put up with it any longer;
whatever the next life may be like, it can't be worse than
this one for me at least; and as I went to and fro between
Temple Lane and the chambers in Temple Gardens I
began to think how I might make away with myself. I
don't know if you know London, Hubert? Yes, he said;
I'm a Londoner, but I come here to work every year. Then
if you know the Temple, you know that the windows of
Temple Gardens overlook the river. I used to stand at
those windows watching the big brown river flowing
through its bridges, thinking all the while of the sea into
which it went, and that I must plunge into the river and
be carried away down to the sea, or be picked up before I
got there. I could only think about making an end to my
trouble and of the Frenchwoman. Her suspicions that I
cared for him made her harder on me than she need have
been; she was always coming the missis over me. Her airs
and graces stiffened my back more than anything else, and
I'm sure if I hadn't met Bessie Lawrence I should have
done away with myself. She was the woman who used to
look after the chambers under Mr Congreve's. We stopped
talking outside the gateway by King's Bench Walk – if
you know the Temple, you know where I mean. Bessie
kept talking, but I wasn't listening, only catching a word
here and there, not waking up from the dream how to
make away with myself till I heard the words: If I had a
figure like yours. As no one had ever spoken about my
figure before, I said: Now what has my figure got to do
with it? You haven't been listening to me, she said, and
I answered that I had only missed the last few words.
Just missed the last few words, she said testily; you didn't
hear me telling you that there is a big dinner at the

Freemason's Tavern to-night, and they're short of waiters. But what has that go to do with my figure? I asked. That shows, she rapped out, that you haven't been listening to me. Didn't I say that if it wasn't for my hips and bosom I'd very soon be into a suit of evening clothes and getting ten shillings for the job. But what has that got to do with my figure? I repeated. Your figure is just the one for a waiter's. Oh, I'd never thought of that, says I, and we said no more. But the words: Your figure is just the one for a waiter's, kept on in my head till my eyes caught sight of a bundle of old clothes that Mr Congreve had given me to sell. A suit of evening clothes was in it. You see, Mr Congreve and myself were about the same height and build. The trousers will want a bit of shortening, I said to myself, and I set to work; and at six o'clock I was in them and down at the Freemason's Tavern answering questions, saying that I had been accustomed to waiting at table. All the waiting I had done was bringing in Mr Congreve's dinner from the kitchen to the sitting-room: a roast chicken or a chop, and in my fancy it seemed to me that the waiting at the Freemason's Tavern would be much the same. The head waiter looked me over a bit doubtfully and asked if I had had experience with public dinners. I thought he was going to turn me down, but they were short-handed, so I was taken on, and it was a mess that I made of it, getting in everybody's way; but my awkwardness was taken in good part and I received ten shillings, which was good money for the sort of work I did that night. But what stood to me was not so much the ten shillings that I earned as the bit I had learned. It was only a bit, not much bigger than a threepenny bit; but I had worked round a table at a big dinner, and feeling certain that I could learn what I didn't know, I asked for another job. I suppose the head waiter could see that there was the making of a waiter in me, for on coming out of the Freemason's Tavern he stopped me to ask if I was going back to private service as soon as I could get a place. The food I'd had and the excitement of the dinner, the guests, the lights, the talk, stood to me, and things seemed clearer than they had ever seemed before. My feet were of the same mind, for they wouldn't walk towards the Temple, and I answered the head waiter that I'd be glad of another job. Well, said he, you don't much know about the work, but you're an honest lad, I think, so I'll see what I can do for you; and at the moment a thought struck him. Just take this letter, said he, to the Holborn Restaurant. There's a dinner there and I've had word that they're short of a waiter or two. Be off as fast as you can. And away I went as fast as my legs could carry me, and they took me there in good time, in front, by a few seconds, of two other fellows who were after the job. I got it. Another job came along, and another and another. Each of them jobs was worth ten shillings to me, to say nothing of the learning of the trade; and having, as I've said, the making of a waiter in me, it didn't take more than about three months for me to be as quick and as smart and as watchful as the best of them, and without them qualities no one will succeed in waiting. I have worked round the tables in the biggest places in London and all over England in all the big towns, in Manchester, in Liverpool, and Birmingham; I am well known at the old Hen and Chickens, at the Queen's, and the Plough and Harrow in Birmingham. It was seven years ago that I came here, and here it would seem that I've come to be looked on as a fixture, for the Bakers are good people to work for and I didn't like to leave them when, three years ago, a good place was offered to me, so kind were they to me in my illness. I suppose one never remains always in the same place, but I may as well be here as elsewhere.

Seven years working in Morrison's Hotel, Page said, and on the second floor? Yes, the second floor is the best in the hotel; the money is better than in the coffee-room, and that is why the Bakers have put me here, Albert replied. I wouldn't care to leave them; they've often said they don't know what they'd do without me. Seven years, Hubert repeated, the same work up the stairs and down the stairs, banging into the kitchen and out again. There's more variety in the work than you think for, Hubert, Albert answered. Every family is different, and so you're always learning. Seven years, Page repeated, neither man nor woman, just a perhapser. He spoke these words more to himself than to Nobbs, but feeling he had expressed himself incautiously he raised his eyes and read on Albert's face that the words had gone home, and that this outcast from both sexes felt her loneliness perhaps more keenly than before. As Hubert was thinking what words he might use to conciliate Albert with her lot, Albert repeated the words: Neither man nor woman; yet nobody ever suspected, she muttered, and never would have suspected me till the day of my death if it hadn't been for that flea that you brought in with you. But what harm did the flea do? I'm bitten all over, said Albert, scratching her thighs. Never mind the bites, said Hubert; we wouldn't have had this talk if it hadn't been for the flea, and I shouldn't have heard your story.

Tears trembled on Albert's eyelids; she tried to keep them back, but they overflowed the lids and were soon running quickly down her cheeks. You've heard my story, she said. I thought nobody would ever hear it, and I thought I should never cry again; and Hubert watched the gaunt woman shaking with sobs under a coarse nightshirt. It's all much sadder than I thought it was, and if I'd known how sad it was I shouldn't have been able to live through it. But I've jostled along somehow, she added, always merry and bright, with never anyone to speak to, not really to speak to, only to ask for plates and dishes, for knives and forks and such like, tablecloths and napkins, cursing betimes the life you've been through; for the feeling cannot help coming over us, perhaps over the biggest as over the smallest, that all our trouble is for nothing and can end in nothing. It might have been better if I had taken the plunge. But why am I thinking these things? It's you that has set me thinking, Hubert. I'm sorry if— Oh, it's no use being sorry, and I'm a great silly to cry like this. I

thought that regrets had passed away with the petticoats.
But you've awakened the woman in me. You've brought it
all up again. But I mustn't let on like this; it's very foolish
of an old perhapser like me, neither man nor woman! But
I can't help it. She began to sob again, and in the midst
of her grief the word loneliness was uttered, and when the
paroxysm was over, Hubert said: Lonely, yes, I suppose it
is lonely; and he put his hand out towards Albert. You're
very good, Mr Page, and I'm sure you'll keep my secret,
though indeed I don't care very much whether you do or
not. Now, don't let on like that again, Hubert said. Let us
have a little chat and try to understand each other. I'm
sure it's lonely for you to live without man or without
woman, thinking like a man and feeling like a woman.
You seem to know all about it, Hubert. I hadn't thought
of it like that before myself, but when you speak the
words I feel you have spoken the truth. I suppose I was
wrong to put off my petticoats and step into those trousers.
I won't go so far as to say that, Hubert answered, and the
words were so unexpected that Albert forgot her grief for
a moment and said: Why do you say that, Hubert? Well,
because I was thinking, he replied, that you might marry.
But I was never a success as a girl. Men didn't look at me
then, so I'm sure they wouldn't now I'm a middle-aged
woman. Marriage! whom should I marry? No, there's no
marriage for me in the world; I must go on being a man.
But you won't tell on me? You've promised, Hubert. Of
course I won't tell, but I don't see why you shouldn't
marry. What do you mean, Hubert? You aren't putting a
joke upon me, are you? If you are it's very unkind. A joke
upon you? no, Hubert answered. I didn't mean that you
should marry a man, but you might marry a girl. Marry a
girl? Albert repeated, her eyes wide open and staring. A
girl? Well, anyway, that's what I've done, Hubert replied.
But you're a young man and a very handsome young man
too. Any girl would like to have you, and I dare say they
were all after you before you met the right girl. I'm not a
young man, I'm a woman, Hubert replied. Now I know

for certain, cried Albert, you're putting a joke upon me. A woman! Yes, a woman; you can feel for yourself if you won't believe me. Put your hand under my shirt; you'll find nothing there. Albert moved away instinctively, her modesty having been shocked. You see I offered myself like that feeling you couldn't take my word for it. It isn't a thing there can be any doubt about. Oh, I believe you, Albert replied. And now that that matter is settled, Hubert began, perhaps you'd like to hear my story; and without waiting for an answer she related the story of her unhappy marriage: her husband, a house-painter, had changed towards her altogether after the birth of her second child, leaving her without money for food and selling up the home twice. At last I decided to have another cut at it, Hubert went on, and catching sight of my husband's working clothes one day I said to myself: He's often made me put these on and go out and help him with his job; why shouldn't I put them on for myself and go away for good? I didn't like leaving the children, but I couldn't remain with him. But the marriage? Albert asked. It was lonely going home to an empty room; I was as lonely as you, and one day, meeting a girl as lonely as myself, I said: Come along, and we arranged to live together, each paying our share. She had her work and I had mine, and between us we made a fair living; and this I can say with truth, that we haven't known an unhappy hour since we married. People began to talk, so we had to. I'd like you to see our home. I always return to my home after a job is finished with a light heart and leave it with a heavy one. But I don't understand, Albert said. What don't you understand? Hubert asked. Whatever Albert's thoughts were, they faded from her, and her eyelids dropped over her eyes. You're falling asleep, Hubert said, and I'm doing the same. It must be three o'clock in the morning and I've to catch the five o'clock train. I can't think now of what I was going to ask you, Albert muttered, but you'll tell me in the morning; and turning over, she made a place for Hubert.

3

What has become of him? Albert said, rousing herself, and then, remembering that Hubert's intention was to catch the early train, she began to remember. His train, she said, started from Amiens Street at – I must have slept heavily for him – for her not to have awakened me, or she must have stolen away very quietly. But, lord amassy, what time is it? And seeing she had overslept herself a full hour, she began to dress herself, muttering all the while: Such a thing never happened to me before. And the hotel as full as it can hold. Why didn't they send for me? The missis had a thought of my bed-fellow, mayhap, and let me sleep it out. I told her I shouldn't close an eye till she left me. But I mustn't fall into the habit of sheing him. Lord, if the missis knew everything! But I've overslept myself a full hour, and if nobody has been up before somebody soon will be. The greater haste the less speed. All the same, despite the difficulty of finding her clothes, Albert was at work on her landing some twenty minutes after, running up and down the stairs, preparing for the different breakfasts in the half-dozen sitting-rooms given to her charge, driving everybody before her, saying: We're late to-day, and the house full of visitors. How is it that 54 isn't turned out? Has 35 rung his bell? Lord, Albert, said a housemaid, I wouldn't worry my fat because I was down late; once in a way don't hurt. And sitting up half the night talking to Mr Page, said another maid and then rounding on us. Half the night talking, Albert repeated. My bed-fellow! Where is Mr Page? I didn't hear him go away; he may have missed his train for aught I know. But do you be getting on with your work, and let me be getting on with mine. You're very cross this morning, Albert, the maid-servant muttered, and retired to chatter with two other maids who were looking over the banisters at the time.

Well, Mr Nobbs, the head porter began, when Albert came running downstairs to see some visitors off, and to receive her tips – well, Mr Nobbs, how did you find your bed-fellow? Oh, he was all right, but I'm not used to bed-fellows, and he brought a flea with him, and it kept me awake; and when I did fall asleep, I slept so heavily that I was an hour late. I hope he caught his train. But what is all this pother about bed-fellows? Albert asked herself, as she returned to her landing. Page hasn't said anything, no, she's said nothing, for we are both in the same boat, and to tell on me would be to tell on herself. I'd never have believed if – Albert's modesty prevented her from finishing the sentence. She's a woman right enough. But the cheek of it, to marry an innocent girl! Did she let the girl into the secret, or leave her to find it out when— The girl might have called in the police! This was a question one might ponder on, and by luncheon time Albert was inclined to believe that Hubert told his wife before— She couldn't have had the cheek to wed her, Albert said, without warning her that things might not turn out as she fancied. Mayhap, Albert continued, she didn't tell her before they wedded and mayhap she did, and being one of them like myself that isn't always hankering after a man she was glad to live with Hubert for companionship. Albert tried to remember the exact words that Hubert had used. It seemed to her that Hubert had said that she lived with a girl first and wedded her to put a stop to people's scandal. Of course they could hardly live together except as man and wife. She remembered Hubert saying that she always returned home with a light heart and never left it without a heavy one. So it would seem that this marriage was as successful as any and a great deal more than most.

At that moment 35 rang his bell. Albert hurried to answer it, and it was not till late in the evening, between nine and ten o'clock, when the guests were away at the theatres and concerts and nobody was about but two maids, that Albert, with her napkin over her shoulder, dozed and meditated on the advice that Hubert had given her. She should marry, Hubert had said; Hubert had married. Of course it wasn't a real marriage, it couldn't be that, but a very happy one it would seem. But the girl must have understood that she was not marrying a man. Did Hubert tell her before wedding her or after, and what were the words? She would have liked to know the words. For after all I've worked hard, she said, and her thoughts melted away into meditation of what her life had been for the last five-and-twenty years, a mere drifting, it seemed to her, from one hotel to another, without friends; meeting, it is true, sometimes men and women who seemed willing to be friendly. But her secret forced her to live apart from men as well as women; the clothes she wore smothered the woman in her; she no longer thought and felt as she used to when she wore petticoats, and she didn't think and feel like a man though she wore trousers. What was she? Nothing, neither man nor woman, so small wonder she was lonely. But Hubert had put off her sex, so she said. . . . Albert turned over in her mind the possibility that a joke had been put upon her, and fell to thinking what Hubert's home might be like, and was vexed with herself for not having asked if she had a clock and vases on the chimney-piece. One of the maids called from the end of the passage, and when Albert received 54's order and executed it, she returned to her seat in the passage, her napkin over her shoulder, and resumed her reverie. It seemed to her that Hubert once said that her wife was a milliner; Hubert may not have spoken the word milliner; but if she hadn't, it was strange that the word should keep on coming up in her mind. There was no reason why the wife shouldn't be a milliner, and if that were so it was as likely as not that they owned a house in some quiet, insignificant street, letting the dining-room, back room and kitchen to a widow or to a pair of widows. The drawing-room was the workroom and showroom; Page and his wife slept in the room above. On second thoughts it seemed to Albert that if the business were millinery it might be that Mrs Page would prefer the ground floor for her showroom. A third and fourth distribution of the 'premises' presented itself to Albert's imagination. On thinking the matter over again it seemed to her that Hubert did not

speak of a millinery business but of a seamstress, and if
that were so, a small dressmaker's business in a quiet
street would be in keeping with all Hubert had said about
the home. Albert was not sure, however, that if she found
a girl willing to share her life with her, it would be a
seamstress's business she would be on the look-out for.
She thought that a sweetmeat shop, newspapers and tobacco, would be her choice.

Why shouldn't she make a fresh start? Hubert had no
difficulties. She had said – Albert could recall the very
words – I didn't mean you should marry a man, but a
girl. Albert had saved, oh! how she had tried to save, for
she didn't wish to end her days in the workhouse. She had
saved upwards of five hundred pounds, which was enough
to purchase a little business, and her heart dilated as she
thought of her two successful investments in house
property. In six months' time she hoped to have six hundred pounds, and if it took her two years to find a partner
and a business, she would have at least seventy or eighty
pounds more, which would be a great help, for it would
be a mistake to put one's money into a falling business. If
she found a partner, she'd have to do like Hubert; for
marriage would put a stop to all tittle-tattle; she'd be able
to keep her place at Morrison's Hotel, or perhaps leave
Morrison's and rely on jobs; and with her connection it
would be a case of picking and choosing the best: ten and
sixpence a night, nothing under. She dreamed of a round.
Belfast, Liverpool, Manchester, Bradford, rose up in her
imagination, and after a month's absence, a couple of
months maybe, she would return home, her heart antici-
pating a welcome – a real welcome, for though she would
continue to be a man to the world, she would be a woman
to the dear one at home. With a real partner, one whose
heart was in the business, they might make as much as
two hundred pounds a year – four pounds a week! And
with four pounds a week their home would be as pretty
and happy as any in the city of Dublin. Two rooms and a
kitchen were what she foresaw. The furniture began to

creep into her imagination little by little. A large sofa by the fireplace covered with a chintz! But chintz dirtied quickly in the city; a dark velvet sofa might be more suitable. It would cost a great deal of money, five or six pounds; and at that rate fifty pounds wouldn't go very far, for they must have a fine double-bed mattress; and if they were going to do things in that style, the home would cost them eighty pounds. With luck these eighty pounds could be earned within the next two years at Morrison's Hotel.

Albert ran over in her mind the tips she had received. The people in 34 were leaving to-morrow; they were always good for half a sovereign, and she decided then and there that to-morrow's half-sovereign must be put aside as a beginning of a sum of money for the purchase of a clock to stand on a marble chimney-piece or a mahogany chiffonier. A few days after she got a sovereign from a departing guest, and it revealed a pair of pretty candlesticks and a round mirror. Her tips were no longer mere white and yellow metal stamped with the effigy of a dead king or a living queen, but symbols of the future that awaited her. An unexpected crown set her pondering on the colour of the curtains in their sitting-room, and Albert became suddenly conscious that a change had come into her life: the show was the same – carrying plates and dishes upstairs and downstairs, and taking orders for drinks and cigars; but behind the show a new life was springing up – a life strangely personal and associated with the life without only in this much, that the life without was now a vassal state paying tribute to the life within. She wasn't as good a servant as heretofore. She knew it. Certain absences of mind, that was all; and the servants as they went by with their dusters began to wonder whatever Albert could be dreaming of.

It was about this time that the furnishing of the parlour at the back of the shop was completed, likewise that of the bedroom above the shop, and Albert had just entered on another dream – a dream of a shop with two counters, one at which cigars, tobacco, pipes and matches were sold, and at the other all kinds of sweetmeats, a shop with a door leading to her wife's parlour. A changing figure the wife was in Albert's imagination, turning from fair to dark, from plump to slender, but capturing her imagination equally in all her changes; sometimes she was accompanied by a child of three or four, a boy, the son of a dead man, for in one of her dreams Albert married a widow. In another and more frequent dream she married a woman who had transgressed the moral code and been deserted before the birth of her child. In this case it would be supposed that Albert had done the right thing, for after leading the girl astray he had made an honest woman of her. Albert would be the father in everybody's eyes except the mother's, and she hoped that the child's mother would outgrow all the memory of the accidental seed sown, as the saying runs, in a foolish five minutes. A child would be a pleasure to them both, and a girl in the family way appealed to her more than a widow; a girl that some soldier, the boot-boy, or the hotel porter, had gotten into trouble; and Albert kept her eyes and ears open, hoping to rescue from her precarious situation one of those unhappy girls that were always cropping up in Morrison's Hotel. Several had had to leave the hotel last year, but not one this year. But some revivalist meetings were going to be held in Dublin. Many of our girls attend them, and an unlucky girl will be in luck's way if we should run across one another. Her thoughts passed into a dream of the babe that would come into the world some three or four months after their marriage, her little soft hands and expressive eyes claiming their protection, asking for it. What matter whether she calls me father or mother? They are but mere words that the lips speak, but love is in the heart and only love matters.

Now whatever can Albert be brooding? an idle housemaid asked herself as she went by. Brooding a love-story? Not likely. A marriage with some girl outside? He isn't over-partial to any of us. That Albert was brooding something, that there was something on his mind, became the talk of the hotel, and soon after it came to be noticed that Albert was eager to avail himself of every excuse to absent himself from duty in the hotel. He had been seen in the smaller streets looking up at the houses. He had saved a good deal of money, and some of his savings were invested in house property, so it was possible that his presence in these streets might be explained by the supposition that he was investing new sums of money in house property, or, and it was the second suggestion that stimulated the imagination, that Albert was going to be married and was looking out for a house for his wife. He had been seen talking with Annie Watts; but she was not in the family way after all, and despite her wistful eyes and gentle voice she was not chosen. Her heart is not in her work, Albert said; she thinks only of when she can get out, and that isn't the sort for a shop, whereas Dorothy Keyes is a glutton for work; but Albert couldn't abide the tall, angular woman, built like a boy, with a neck like a swan's. Besides her unattractive appearance, her manner was abrupt. But Alice's small, neat figure and quick intelligence marked her out for the job. Alas! Alice was hottempered. We should quarrel, Albert said, and picking up her napkin, which had slipped from her knee to the floor, she considered the maids on the floor above. A certain stateliness of figure and also of gait put the thought into her mind that Mary O'Brien would make an attractive shopwoman. But her second thoughts were that Mary O'Brien was a Papist, and the experience of Irish Protestants shows that Papists and Protestants don't mix.

She had just begun to consider the next housemaid, when a voice interrupted her musing. That lazy girl, Annie Watts, on the look-out for an excuse to chatter the time away instead of being about her work, were the words that crossed Albert's mind as she raised her eyes, and so unwelcoming were they that Annie in her nervousness began to hesitate and stammer, unable for the moment to find a subject, plunging at last, and rather awkwardly, into the news of the arrival of the new kitchen-maid, Helen Dawes, but never dreaming that the news could have any interest for Albert. To her surprise, Albert's eyes lighted up. Do you know her? Annie asked. Know her? Albert answered. No, I don't know her, but— At that moment a bell rang. Oh, bother, Annie said, and while she moved away idling along the banisters, Albert hurried down the passage to enquire what No. 47 wanted, and to learn that he needed writing-paper and envelopes. He couldn't write with the pens the hotel furnished; would Albert be so kind as to ask the page-boy to fetch some J's? With pleasure, Albert said; with pleasure. Would you like to have the writing-paper and envelopes before the boy returns with the pens, sir? The visitor answered that the writing-paper and envelopes would be of no use to him till he had gotten the pens. With pleasure, sir; with pleasure; and whilst waiting for the page to return she passed through the swing doors and searched for a new face among the different young women passing to and fro between the white-aproned and white-capped chefs, bringing the dishes to the great zinc counter that divided the kitchen-maids and the scullions from the waiters. She must be here, she said, and returned again to the kitchen in the hope of meeting the new-comer, Helen Dawes, who, when she was found, proved to be very unlike the Helen Dawes of Albert's imagination. A thick-set, almost swarthy girl of three-and-twenty, rather under than above the medium height, with white, even teeth, but unfortunately protruding, giving her the appearance of a rabbit. Her eyes seemed to be dark brown, but on looking into them Albert discovered them to be grey-green, round eyes that dilated and flashed wonderfully while she talked. Her face lighted up; and there was a vindictiveness in her voice that appeared and disappeared; Albert suspected her, and was at once frightened and attracted. Vindictiveness in her voice! How could such a thing have come into my mind? she said a few days after. A more kindly girl it would be difficult to find. How could I have been so stupid? She is one of those, Albert

continued, that will be a success in everything she under-
takes; and dreams began soon after that the sweetstuff and
tobacco shop could hardly fail to prosper under her direction. Nobody could befool Helen, and when I am away at
work I shall feel certain that everything will be all right at
home. It's a pity that she isn't in the family way, for it
would be pleasant to have a little one running about the
shop asking for lemon drops and to hear him calling us
father and mother. At that moment a strange thought
flitted across Albert's mind – after all, it wouldn't matter
much to her if Helen were to get into the family way later;
of course, there would be the expense of the lying-in. Her
second thoughts were that women live happily enough till
a man comes between them, and that it would be safer for
her to forgo a child and choose an older woman. All the
same, she could not keep herself from asking Helen to
walk out with her, and the next time they met the words
slipped out of her mouth: I shall be off duty at three to-
day, and if you are not engaged— I am off duty at three,
Helen answered. Are you engaged? Albert asked. Helen
hesitated, it being the truth that she had been and was still
walking out with one of the scullions, and was not sure
how he would look upon her going out with another, even
though that one was such a harmless fellow as Albert
Nobbs. Harmless in himself, she thought, and with a very
good smell of money rising out of his pockets, very
different from Joe, who seldom had a train fare upon him.
But she hankered after Joe, and wouldn't give Albert a
promise until she had asked him. Wants to walk out with
you? Why, he has never been known to walk out with
man, woman or child before. Well, that's a good one! I'd
like to know what he's after, but I'm not jealous; you can
go with him, there's no harm in Albert. I'm on duty: just
go for a turn with him. Poke him up and see what he's
after, and take him into a sweetshop and bring back a box
of chocolates. Do you like chocolates? Helen asked, and
her eyes flashing, she stood looking at Joe, who, thinking
that her temper was rising, and wishing to quell it, asked

hurriedly where she was going to meet him. At the corner, she answered. He is there already. Then be off, he said, and his tone grated. You wouldn't like me to keep him waiting? Helen said. Oh, dear no, not for Joe, not for Joseph, if he knows it, the scullion replied, lilting the song.

Helen turned away hoping that none of the maids would peach upon her, and Albert's heart rejoiced at seeing her on the other side of the street waiting for the tram to go by before she crossed it. Were you afraid I wasn't coming? she asked, and Albert, not being ready with words, answered shyly: Not very. A stupid answer this seemed to be to Helen, and it was in the hope of shuffing out of a tiresome silence that Albert asked her if she liked chocolates. Something under the tooth will help the time away, was the answer she got; and they went in search of a sweetmeat shop, Albert thinking that a shilling or one and sixpence would see her through it. But in a moment Helen's eyes were all over the shop, and spying out some large pictured boxes, she asked Albert if she might have one, and it being their first day out, Albert answered: Yes; but could not keep back the words: I'm afraid they'd cost a lot. For these words Albert got a contemptuous look, and Helen shook her shoulders so disdainfully that Albert pressed a second box on Helen – one to pass the time with, another to take home. To such a show of goodwill Helen felt she must respond, and her tongue rattled on pleasantly as she walked, crunching the chocolates, two between each lamp-post, Albert stinting herself to one, which she sucked slowly, hardly enjoying it at all, so worried was she by the loss of three and sixpence. As if Helen guessed the cause of Albert's disquiet, she called on her suitor to admire the damsel on the box, but Albert could not disengage her thoughts sufficiently from Helen's expensive tastes. If every walk were to cost three and sixpence there wouldn't be a lot left for the home in six months' time. And she fell to calculating how much it would cost her if they were to walk out once a week. Three fours are twelve and four sixpences are two shillings, four-

teen shillings a month, twice that is twenty-eight; twenty-
eight shillings a month, that is if Helen wanted two boxes
a week. At this rate she'd be spending sixteen pounds
sixteen shillings a year. Lord amassy! But perhaps Helen
wouldn't want two boxes of chocolates every time they
went out together— If she didn't, she'd want other things,
and catching sight of a jeweller's shop, Albert called
Helen's attention to a cyclist that had only just managed
to escape a tram car by a sudden wriggle. But Albert was
always unlucky. Helen had been wishing this long while
for a bicycle, and if she did not ask Albert to buy her one
it was because another jeweller's came into view. She
stopped to gaze, and for a moment Albert's heart seemed
to stand still, but Helen continued her chocolates, secure
in her belief that the time had not yet come for substantial
presents.

At Sackville Street bridge she would have liked to turn
back, having little taste for the meaner parts of the city,
but Albert wished to show her the north side, and she
began to wonder what he could find to interest him in
these streets, and why he should stand in admiration before all the small newspaper and tobacco shops, till she
remembered suddenly that he had invested his savings in
house property. Could these be his houses? All his own?
and, moved by this consideration, she gave a more attentive ear to Albert's account of the daily takings of these
shops, calculating that he was a richer man than anybody
believed him to be, but a mean one. The idea of his thinking twice about a box of chocolates! I'll show him! and
coming upon a big draper's shop in Sackville Street she
asked him for a pair of six-button gloves. She needed a
parasol and some shoes and stockings, and a silk kerchief
would not be amiss, and at the end of the third month
of their courtship it seemed to her that the time had come
for her to speak of bangles, saying that for three pounds
she could have a pretty one – one that would be a real
pleasure to wear; it would always remind her of him.
Albert coughed up with humility, and Helen felt that she

had 'got him', as she put it to herself, and afterwards to Joe Mackins. So he parted easily, Joe remarked, and pushing Helen aside he began to whip up the *rémoulade,* that had begun to show signs of turning, saying he'd have the chef after him. But I say, old girl, since he's coughing up so easily you might bring me something back; and a briarwood pipe and a pound or two of tobacco seemed the least she might obtain for him. And Helen answered that to get these she would have to ask Albert for money. And why shouldn't you? Joe returned. Ask him for a thin 'un, and mayhap he'll give you a thick 'un. It's the first quid that's hard to get; every time after it's like shelling peas. Do you think he's that far gone on me? Helen asked. Well, don't you? Why should he give you these things if he wasn't? Joe answered. Joe asked her of what she was thinking, and she replied that it was hard to say: she had walked out with many a man before but never with one like Albert Nobbs. In what way is he different? Joe asked. Helen was perplexed in her telling of Albert Nobbs' slackness. You mean that he doesn't pull you about, Joe rapped out; and she answered that there was something of that in it. All the same, she continued, that isn't the whole of it. I've been out before with men that didn't pull me about, but he seems to have something on his mind, and half the time he's thinking. Well, what does it matter, Joe asked, so long as there is coin in the pocket and so long as you have a hand to pull it out? Helen didn't like this description of Albert Nobbs' courtship, and the words rose to her lips to tell Joseph that she didn't want to go out any more with Albert, that she was tired of her job, but the words were quelled on her lips by a remark from Joe. Next time you go out with him work him up a bit and see what he is made of; just see if there's a sting in him or if he is no better than a capon. A capon! and what is a capon? she asked. A capon is a cut fowl. He may be like one. You think that, do you? she answered, and resolved to get the truth of the matter next time they went out together. It did seem odd that Albert should be willing to buy presents and not want to kiss her. In fact, it was more than odd. It might be as Joe had said. I might as well go out with my mother. Now what did it all mean? Was it a blind? Some other girl that he— Not being able to concoct a sufficiently reasonable story, Helen relinquished the attempt, without, however, regaining control of her temper, which had begun to rise, and which continued to boil up in her and overflow until her swarthy face was almost ugly. I'm beginning to feel ugly towards him, she said to herself. He is either in love with me or he's— And trying to discover his purpose, she descended the staircase, saying to herself: Now Albert must know that I'm partial to Joe Mackins. It can't be that he doesn't suspect. Well, I'm damned.

4

But Helen's perplexity on leaving the hotel was no greater than Albert's as she stood waiting by the kerb. She knew that Helen carried on with Joe Mackins, and she also knew that Joe Mackins had nothing to offer Helen but himself. She even suspected that some of the money she had given to Helen had gone to purchase pipes and tobacco for Joe: a certain shrewdness is not inconsistent with innocence, and it didn't trouble her much that Helen was perhaps having her fling with Joe Mackins. She didn't want Helen to fall into evil ways, but it was better for her to have her fling before than after marriage. On the other hand, a woman that had been bedded might be dissatisfied to settle down with another woman, though the home offered her was better than any she could get from a man. She might hanker for children, which was only natural, and Albert felt that she would like a child as well as another. A child might be arranged for if Helen wanted one, but it would never do to have the father hanging about the shop: he would have to be got rid of as soon as Helen was in the family way. But could he be got rid of? Not very easily if Joe Mackins was the father; she foresaw trouble and would prefer another father, almost any other. But why trouble herself about the father of Helen's child before she knew whether Helen would send Joe packing? which she'd have to do clearly if they were to wed – she and Helen. Their wedding was what she had to look to, whether she should confide her sex to Helen to-night or wait. Why not to-night as well as to-morrow night? she asked herself. But how would she tell it to Helen? Blurt it out –I've something to tell you, Helen. I'm not a man, but a woman like yourself. No, that wouldn't do. How did Hubert tell her wife she was a woman? If she had only asked she'd have been spared all this trouble. After hearing Hubert's story she should have said: I've something to ask you; but sleep was so heavy on their eyelids that they couldn't think any more and both of them were falling asleep, which wasn't to be wondered at, for they had been talking for hours. It was on her mind to ask how her wife found out. Did Hubert tell her or did the wife— Albert's modesty prevented her from pursuing the subject; and she turned on herself, saying that she could not leave Helen to find out she was a woman; of that she was certain, and of that only. She'd have to tell Helen that. But should the confession come before they were married, or should she reserve it for the wedding night in the bridal chamber on the edge of the bed afterwards? If it were not for Helen's violent temper— I in my night-shirt, she in her nightgown. On the other hand, she might quieten down after an outburst and begin to see that it might be very much to her advantage to accept the situation, especially if a hope were held out to her of a child by Joe Mackins in two years' time; she'd have to agree to wait till then, and in two years Joe would probably be after another girl. But if she were to cut up rough and do me an injury! Helen might call the neighbours in, or the policeman, who'd take them both to the station. She'd have to return to Liverpool or to Manchester. She didn't know what the penalty would be for marrying one of her own sex. And her thoughts wandered on to the morning boat.

One of the advantages of Dublin is that one can get out

of it as easily as any other city. Steamers were always leaving, morning and evening; she didn't know how many, but a great many. On the other hand, if she took the straight course and confided her sex to Helen before the marriage, Helen might promise not to tell; but she might break her promise; life in Morrison's Hotel would be unendurable, and she'd have to endure it. What a hue and cry! But one way was as bad as the other. If she had only asked Hubert Page! but she hadn't a thought at the time of going to do likewise. What's one man's meat is another man's poison, and she began to regret Hubert's confession to her. If it hadn't been for that flea she wouldn't be in this mess; and she was deep in it! Three months' company isn't a day, and everybody in Morrison's Hotel asking whether she or Joe Mackins would be the winner, urging her to make haste else Joe would come with a rush at the finish. A lot of racing talk that she didn't understand – or only half. If she could get out of this mess somehow— But it was too late. She must go through with it. But how? A different sort of girl altogether was needed, but she liked Helen. Her way of standing on a doorstep, her legs a little apart, jawing a tradesman, and she'd stand up to Mrs Baker and to the chef himself. She liked the way Helen's eyes lighted up when a thought came into her mind; her cheery laugh warmed Albert's heart as nothing else did. Before she met Helen she often feared her heart was growing cold. She might try the world over and not find one that would run the shop she had in mind as well as Helen. But the shop wouldn't wait; the owners of the shop would withdraw their offer if it was not accepted before next Monday. And to-day is Friday, Albert said to herself. This evening or never. To-morrow Helen'll be on duty all day; on Sunday she'll contrive some excuse to get out to meet Joe Mackins. After all, why not this evening? for what must be had better be faced bravely; and while the tram rattled down the long street, Rathmines Avenue, past the small houses atop of high steps, pretty boxes with ornamental trees in the garden, some with lawns, with here and there a more substantial house set in the middle of three or four fields at least, Albert meditated, plan after plan rising up in her mind; and when the car turned to the right and then to the left and proceeded at a steady pace up the long incline, Rathgar Avenue, Albert's courage was again at ebb. All the subterfuges she had woven – the long discussion in which she would maintain that marriage should not be considered as a sexual adventure, but a community of interests – seemed to have lost all significance; the points that had seemed so convincing in Rathmines Avenue were forgotten in Rathgar Avenue, and at Terenure she came to the conclusion that there was no use trying to think the story out beforehand; she would have to adapt her ideas to the chances that would arise as they talked under the trees in the dusk in a comfortable hollow, where they could lie at length out of hearing of the other lads and lasses whom they would find along the banks, resting after the labour of the day in dim contentment, vaguely conscious of each other, satisfied with a vague remark, a kick or a push.

It was the hope that the river's bank would tempt him into confidence that had suggested to Helen that they might spend the evening by the Dodder. Albert had welcomed the suggestion, feeling sure that if there was a place in the world that would make the telling of her secret easy it was the banks of the Dodder; and she was certain she would be able to speak it in the hollow under the ilex-trees. But speech died from her lips, and the silence round them seemed sinister and foreboding. She seemed to dread the river flowing over its muddy bottom, without ripple or eddy; and she started when Helen asked her of what she was thinking. Albert answered: Of you, dear; and how pleasant it is to be sitting with you. On these words the silence fell again, and Albert tried to speak, but her tongue was too thick in her mouth; she felt like choking, and the silence was not broken for some seconds, each seeming a minute. At last a lad's voice was

heard: I'll see if you have any lace on your drawers; and
the lass answered: You shan't. There's a pair that's enjoying themselves, Helen said, and she looked upon the
remark as fortunate, and hoped it would give Albert the
courage to pursue his courtship. Albert, too, looked upon
the remark as fortunate, and she tried to ask if there was
lace on all women's drawers; and meditated a reply that
would lead her into a confession of her sex. But the words:
It's so long since I've worn any, died on her lips; and
instead of speaking these words she spoke of the Dodder,
saying: What a pity it isn't nearer Morrison's. Where
would you have it? Helen replied – flowing down Sackville Street into the Liffey? We should be lying there as
thick as herrings, without room to move, or we should be
unable to speak to each other without being overheard.
I dare say you are right, Albert answered, and she was
so frightened that she added: But we have to be back
at eleven o'clock, and it takes an hour to get there. We
can go back now if you like, Helen rapped out. Albert
apologised, and hoping that something would happen to
help her out of her difficulty, she began to represent
Morrison's Hotel as being on the whole advantageous to
servants. But Helen did not respond. She seems to be
getting angrier and angrier, Albert said to herself, and she
asked, almost in despair, if the Dodder was pretty all the
way down to the sea. And remembering a walk with Joe,
Helen answered: There are woods as far as Dartry – the
Dartry Dye Works, don't you know them? But I don't
think there are any very pretty spots. You know Ring's
End, don't you? Albert said she had been there once; and
Helen spoke of a large three-masted vessel that she had
seen some Sundays ago by the quays. You were there
with Joe Mackins, weren't you? Well, what if I was?
Only this, Albert answered, that I don't think it is usual
for a girl to keep company with two chaps, and I thought—
Now, what did you think? Helen said. That you didn't
care for me well enough— For what? she asked. You
know we've been going out for three months, and it

doesn't seem natural to keep talking always, never wanting to put your arm round a girl's waist. I suppose Joe isn't like me, then? Albert asked; and Helen laughed, a scornful little laugh. But, Albert went on, isn't the time for kissing when one is wedded? This is the first time you've said anything about marriage, Helen rapped out. But I thought there had always been an understanding between us, said Albert, and it's only now I can tell you what I have to offer. The words were well chosen. Tell me about it, Helen said, her eyes and voice revealing her cupidity to Albert, who continued all the same to unfold her plans, losing herself in details that bored Helen, whose thoughts returned to the dilemma she was in — to refuse Albert's offer or to break with Joe; and that she should be obliged to do either one or the other was a disappointment to her. All you say about the shop is right enough, but it isn't a very great compliment to a girl. What, to ask her to marry? Albert interjected. Well, no, not if you haven't kissed her first. Don't speak so loud, Albert whispered; I'm sure that couple heard what you said, for they went away laughing. I don't care whether they laughed or cried, Helen answered. You don't want to kiss me, do you? and I don't want to marry a man who isn't in love with me. But I do want to kiss you, and Albert bent down and kissed Helen on both cheeks. Now you can't say I haven't kissed you, can you? You don't call that kissing, do you? Helen asked. But how do you wish me to kiss you, Helen? Well, you are an innocent! she said, and she kissed Albert vindictively. Helen, leave go of me; I'm not used to such kisses. Because you're not in love, Helen replied. In love? Albert repeated. I loved my old nurse very much, but I never wished to kiss her like that. At this Helen exploded with laughter. So you put me in the same class with your old nurse! Well, after that! Come, she said, taking pity upon Albert for a moment, are you or are you not in love with me? I love you deeply, Helen, Albert said. Love? She repeated: the men who have walked out with me were in love with me— In love, Albert repeated after her. I'm sure I love you. I like men to be in love with me, she answered. But that's like an animal, Helen. Whatever put all that muck in your head? I'm going home, she replied, and rose to her feet and started out on the path leading across the darkening fields. You're not angry with me, Helen? Angry? No, I'm not angry with you; you're a fool of a man, that's all. But if you think me a fool of a man, why did you come out this evening to sit under those trees? And why have we been keeping company for the last three months, Albert continued, going out together every week? You didn't always think me a fool of a man, did you? Yes, I did, she answered; and Albert asked Helen for a reason for choosing her company. Oh, you bother me asking reasons for everything, Helen said. But why did you make me love you? Albert asked. Well, if I did, what of it? and as for walking out with you, you won't have to complain of that any more. You don't mean, Helen, that we are never going to walk out again? Yes, I do, she said sullenly. You mean that for the future you'll be walking out with Joe Mackins, Albert lamented. That's my business, she answered. By this time they were by the stile at the end of the field, and in the next field there was a hedge to get through and a wood, and the little path they followed was full of such vivid remembrances that Albert could not believe that she was treading it with Helen for the last time, and besought Helen to take back the words that she would never walk out with her again.

The tram was nearly empty and they sat at the far end, close together, Albert beseeching Helen not to cast her off. If I've been stupid to-day, Albert pleaded, it's because I'm tired of the work in the hotel; I shall be different when we get to Lisdoonvarna: we both want a change of air; there's nothing like the salt water and the cliffs of Clare to put new spirits into a man. You will be different and I'll be different; everything will be different. Don't say no, Helen; don't say no. I've looked forward to this week in Lisdoonvarna, and Albert urged the expense of the lodgings she had already engaged. We shall have to pay for the lodgings; and there's the new suit of clothes that has just come back from the tailor's; I've looked forward to wearing it, walking with you in the strand, the waves crashing up into cliffs, with green fields among them, I've been told! We shall see the ships passing and wonder whither they are going. I've bought three neckties and some new shirts, and what good will these be to me if you'll not come to Lisdoonvarna with me? The lodgings will have to be paid for, a great deal of money, for I said in my letter we shall want two bedrooms. But there need only be one bedroom; but perhaps I shouldn't have spoken like that. Oh, don't talk to me about Lisdoonvarna, Helen answered. I'm not going to Lisdoonvarna with you. But what is to become of the hat I have ordered for you? Albert asked; the hat with the big feather in it; and I've bought stockings and shoes for you. Tell me, what shall I do with these, and with the gloves? Oh, the waste of money and the heart-breaking! What shall I do with the hat? Albert repeated. Helen didn't answer at once. Presently she said: You can leave the hat with me. And the stockings? Albert asked. Yes, you can leave the stockings. And the shoes? Yes, you can leave the shoes too. Yet you won't go to Lisdoonvarna with me? No, she said, I'll not go to Lisdoonvarna with you. But you'll take the presents? It was to please you I said I would take them, because I thought it would be some satisfaction to you to know that they wouldn't be wasted. Not wasted? Albert repeated. You'll wear them when you go out with Joe Mackins. Oh, well, keep your presents. And then the dispute took a different turn, and was continued until they stepped out of the tram at the top of Dawson Street. Albert continued to plead all the way down Dawson Street, and when they were within twenty yards of the hotel, and she saw Helen passing away from her for ever into the arms of Joe Mackins, she begged Helen not to leave her. We cannot part like this, she cried; let us walk up and down the street from Nassau

Street to Clare Street, so that we may talk things over
and do nothing foolish. You see, Albert began, I had set
my heart on driving on an outside car to the Broadstone
with you, and catching a train, and the train going into
lovely country, arriving at a place we had never seen,
with cliffs, and the sunset behind the cliffs. You've told
all that before, Helen said, and, she rapped out, I'm not
going to Lisdoonvarna with you. And if that is all you had
to say to me we might have gone into the hotel. But
there's much more, Helen. I haven't told you about the
shop yet. Yes, you have told me all there is to tell about
the shop; you've been talking about that shop for the last
three months. But, Helen, it was only yesterday that I
got a letter saying that they had had another offer for the
shop, and that they could give me only till Monday morning to close with them; if the lease isn't signed by then
we've lost the shop. But do you think, Helen asked, that
the shop will be a success? Many shops promise well in
the beginning and fade away till they don't get a customer
a day. Our shop won't be like that, I know it won't; and
Albert began an appraisement of the shop's situation and
the custom it commanded in the neighbourhood and the
possibility of developing that custom. We shall be able to
make a great success of that shop, and people will be
coming to see us, and they will be having tea with us in
the parlour, and they'll envy us, saying that never have
two people had such luck as we have had. And our wedding will be— Will be what? Helen asked. Will be a
great wonder. A great wonder indeed, she replied, but
I'm not going to wed you, Albert Nobbs, and now I see
it's beginning to rain. I can't remain out any longer.
You're thinking of your hat; I'll buy another. We may as
well say good-bye, she answered, and Albert saw her
going towards the doorway. She'll see Joe Mackins before
she goes to her bed, and lie dreaming of him; and I shall
lie awake in my bed, my thoughts flying to and fro the
livelong night, zigzagging up and down like bats. And
then remembering that if she went into the hotel she might

meet Helen and Joe Mackins, she rushed on with a hope
in her mind that after a long walk round Dublin she
might sleep.

At the corner of Clare Street she met two women strol-
ling after a fare – ten shillings or a sovereign, which? she
asked herself – and terrified by the shipwreck of all her
hopes, she wished she were one of them. For they at least
are women, whereas I am but a perhapser— In the midst
of her grief a wish to speak to them took hold of her.
But if I speak to them they'll expect me to— All the
same her steps quickened, and as she passed the two
street-walkers she looked round, and one woman, wishing
to attract her attention, said: It was almost a love dream.
Almost a love dream? Albert repeated. What are you
two women talking about? and the woman next to Albert
said: My friend here was telling me of a dream she had
last night. A dream, and what was her dream about? Albert asked. Kitty was telling me that she was better than
a love dream; now do you think she is, sir? I'll ask Kitty
herself, Albert replied, and Kitty answered him: A shade.
Only a shade, Albert returned, and as they crossed the
street a gallant attached himself to Kitty's companion.
Albert and Kitty were left together, and Albert asked
her companion to tell her name. My name is Kitty Mac-
Can, the girl replied. It's odd we've never met before,
Albert replied, hardly knowing what she was saying.
We're not often this way, was the answer. And where
do you walk usually – of an evening? Albert asked. In
Grafton Street or down by College Green; sometimes we
cross the river. To walk in Sackville Street, Albert interjected; and she tried to lead the woman into a story of
her life. But you're not one of them, she said, that think
that we should wash clothes in a nunnery for nothing?
I'm a waiter in Morrison's Hotel. As soon as the name of
Morrison's Hotel passed Albert's lips she began to regret
having spoken about herself. But what did it matter now?
and the woman didn't seem to have taken heed of the
name of the hotel. Is the money good in your hotel?

Kitty asked; I've heard that you get as much as half-a-crown for carrying up a cup of tea; and her story dribbled out in remarks, a simple story that Albert tried to listen to, but her attention wandered, and Kitty, who was not unintelligent, began to guess Albert to be in the middle of some great grief. It doesn't matter about me, Albert answered her, and Kitty being a kind girl said to herself: If I can get him to come home with me I'll help him out of his sorrow, if only for a little while. So she continued to try to interest him in herself till they came to Fitzwilliam Place; and it was not till then that Kitty remembered she had only three and sixpence left out of the last money she had received, and that her rent would be due on the morrow. She daren't return home without a gentleman; her landlady would be at her; and the best time of the night was going by talking to a man who seemed like one who would bid her a curt good-night at the door of his hotel. Where did he say his hotel was? she asked herself; and then, aloud, she said: You're a waiter, aren't you? I've forgotten which hotel you said. Albert didn't answer, and, troubled by her companion's silence, Kitty continued: I'm afraid I'm taking you out of your way. No, you aren't; all ways are the same to me. Well, they aren't to me, she replied. I must get some money to-night. I'll give you some money, Albert said. But won't you come home with me? the girl asked. Albert hesitated, tempted by her company. But if they were to go home together her sex would be discovered. But what did it matter if it were discovered? Albert asked herself, and the temptation came again to go home with this woman, to lie in her arms and tell the story that had been locked up so many years. They could both have a good cry together, and what matter would it be to the woman as long as she got the money she desired. She didn't want a man; it was money she was after, money that meant bread and board to her. She seems a kind, nice girl, Albert said, and she was about to risk the adventure when a man came by whom Kitty knew. Excuse me, he said, and Albert saw them walk away together. I'm sorry, said the woman, returning, but I've just met an old friend; another evening, perhaps. Albert would have liked to put her hand in her pocket and pay the woman with some silver for her company, but she was already half-way back to her friend, who stood waiting for her by the lamp-post. The street-walkers have friends, and when they meet them their troubles are over for the night; but my chances have gone by me; and, checking herself in the midst of the irrelevant question, whether it were better to be casual, as they were, or to have a husband that you could not get rid of, she plunged into her own grief, and walked sobbing through street after street, taking no heed of where she was going.

Why, lord, Mr Nobbs, whatever has kept you out until this hour? the hall-porter muttered. I'm sorry, she answered, and while stumbling up the stairs she remembered that even a guest was not received very amiably by the hall-porter after two; and for a servant to come in at that time! Her thoughts broke off and she lay too tired to think any more of the hall-porter, of herself, of anything. If she got an hour's sleep it was the most she got that night, and when the time came for her to go to her work she rose indifferently. But her work saved her from thinking, and it was not until the middle of the afternoon, when the luncheon-tables had been cleared, that the desire to see and to speak to Helen could not be put aside; but Helen's face wore an ugly, forbidding look, and Albert returned to the second floor without speaking to her. It was not long after that 34 rang his bell, and Albert hoped to get an order that would send her to the kitchen. Are you going to pass me by without speaking again, Helen? We talked enough last night, Helen retorted; there's nothing more to say, and Joe, in such disorder of dress as behooves a scullion, giggled as he went past, carrying a huge pile of plates. I loved my old nurse, but I never thought of kissing her like that, he said, turning on his heel and so suddenly that some of the plates fell with a great clatter. The ill luck that had befallen him seemed well deserved, and Albert returned upstairs and sat in the passages waiting for the sitting-rooms to ring their bells; and the housemaids, as they came about the head of the stairs with their dusters, wondered how it was that they could not get any intelligible conversation out of the love-stricken waiter. Albert's lovelorn appearance checked their mirth, pity entered their hearts, and they kept back the words: I loved my old nurse, etc. After all, he loves the girl, one said to the other, and a moment after they were joined by another housemaid, who, after listening for a while, went away, saying: There's no torment like the love torment; and the three housemaids, Mary, Alice, and Dorothy, offered Albert their sympathy, trying to lead her into little talks with a view to withdrawing her from the contemplation of her own grief, for women are always moved by a love story. Before long their temper turned against Helen, and they often went by asking themselves why she should have kept company with Albert all these months if she didn't mean to wed him. No wonder the poor man was disappointed. He is destroyed with his grief, said one; look at him, without any more colour in his face than is in my duster. Another said: He doesn't swallow a bit of food. And the third said: I poured out a glass of wine for him that was left over, but he put it away. Isn't love awful? But what can he see in her? another asked, a stumpy, swarthy woman, a little blackthorn bush and as full of prickles; and the three women fell to thinking that Albert would have done better to have chosen one of them. The shop entered into the discussion soon after, and everybody was of opinion that Helen would live to regret her cruelty. The word cruelty did not satisfy; treachery was mentioned, and somebody said that Helen's face was full of treachery. Albert will never recover himself as long as she's here, another remarked. He'll just waste away unless Miss Right comes along. He put all his eggs into one basket, a man said; you see he'd never been known to walk out with a girl before. And what age do you think he is? I put him down at forty-five, and when love takes a man at that age it takes him badly. This is no calf love, the man said, looking into the women's faces, and you'll never be able to mend matters, any of you; and they all declared they didn't wish to, and dispersed in different directions, flicking their dusters and asking themselves if Albert would ever look at another woman.

It was felt generally that he would not have the courage to try again, which was indeed the case, for when it was suggested to Albert that a faint heart never wins a fair lady she answered that her spirit was broken. I shall boil my pot and carry my can, but the spring is broken in me; and it was these words that were remembered and pondered, whereas the joke – I loved my old nurse, etc. – raised no laugh; and the sympathy that Albert felt to be gathering about her cheered her on her way. She was no longer friendless; almost any one of the women in the hotel would have married Albert out of pity for her. But there was no heart in Albert for another adventure; nor any thought in her for anything but her work. She rose every morning and went forth to her work, and was sorry when her work was done, for she had come to dread every interval, knowing that as soon as she sat down to rest the old torment would begin again. Once more she would begin to think that she had nothing more to look forward to; that her life would be but a round of work; a sort of treadmill. She would never see Lisdoonvarna, and the shop with two counters, one at which tobacco, cigarettes and matches were sold, and at the other counter all kinds of sweetstuffs. Like Lisdoonvarna, it had passed away, it had only existed in her mind – a thought, a dream. Yet it had possessed her completely; and the parlour behind the shop that she had furnished and refurnished, hanging a round mirror above the mantelpiece, papering the walls with a pretty colourful paper that she had seen in Wicklow Street and had asked the man to put aside for her. She had hung curtains about the windows in her imagination, and had set two armchairs on either side of the hearth, one in green and one in red velvet, for herself and Helen. The parlour too had passed away like Lisdoonvarna, like the shop, a thought, a dream, no more. There had never been anything in her life but a few dreams, and henceforth there would be not even dreams. It was strange that some people came into the world lucky, and others, for no reason, unlucky; she had been unlucky from her birth; she was a bastard; her parents were grand people whose name she did not know, who paid her nurse a hundred a year to keep her, and who died without making any provision for her. She and her old nurse had to go and live in Temple Lane, and to go out charing every morning; Mr Congreve had a French mistress, and if it hadn't been for Bessie Lawrence she might have thrown herself in the Thames; she was very near to it that night, and if she had drowned herself all this worry and torment would have been over. She was more resolute in those days than she was now, and would have faced the river, but she shrank from this Dublin river, perhaps because it was not her own river. If one wishes to drown oneself it had better be in one's own country. But why is it a mistake? For a perhapser like herself, all countries were the same; go or stay, it didn't matter. Yes, it did; she stayed in Dublin in the hope that Hubert Page would return to the hotel. Only to Hubert could she confide the misfortune that had befallen her, and she'd like to tell somebody. The three might set up together. A happy family they might make. Two women in men's clothes and one in petticoats. If Hubert were willing. Hubert's wife might not be willing. But she might be dead and Hubert on the look-out for another helpmate. He had never been away so long before; he might return any day. And from the moment that she foresaw herself as Hubert's future wife her life began to expand itself more eagerly than ever in watching for tips, collecting half-crowns, crowns and half-sovereigns. She must at least replace the money that she had spent giving presents to Helen, and as the months went by and the years, she remembered, with increasing bitterness, that she had wasted nearly twenty pounds on Helen, a cruel, heartless girl that had come into her life for three months and had left her for Joe Mackins. She took to counting her money in her room at night. The half-crowns were folded up in brown-paper packets, the half-sovereigns in blue, the rare sovereigns were in pink paper, and all these little packets were hidden away in different corners; some were put in the chimney, some under the carpet. She often thought that these hoards would be safer in the Post Office Bank, but she who has nothing else likes to have her money with her, and a sense of almost happiness awoke in her when she discovered herself to be again as rich as she was before she met Helen. Richer by twenty-five pounds twelve and sixpence, she said, and her eyes roved over the garret floor in search of a plank that might be lifted. One behind the bed was chosen, and henceforth Albert slept securely over her hoard, or lay awake thinking of Hubert, who might return, and to whom she might confide the story of her misadventure; but as Hubert did not return her wish to see him faded, and she began to think that it might be just as well if he stayed away, for, who knows? a wandering fellow like him might easily run out of his money and return to Morrison's Hotel to borrow from her, and she wasn't going to give her money to be spent for the benefit of another woman. The other woman was Hubert's wife. If Hubert came back he might threaten to publish her secret if she didn't give him money to keep it. An ugly thought, of which she was ashamed and which she tried to keep out of her mind. But as time went on a dread of Hubert took possession of her. After all, Hubert knew her secret, and somehow it didn't occur to her that in betraying her secret Hubert would be betraying his own. Albert didn't think as clearly as she used to; and one day she answered Mrs Baker in a manner that Mrs Baker did not like. Whilst speaking to Albert the thought crossed Mrs Baker's mind that it was a long while since they had

seen the painter. I cannot think, she said, what has become of Hubert Page; we've not had news of him for a
long time; have you heard from him, Albert? Why should
you think, ma'am, that I hear from him? I only asked,
Mrs Baker replied, and she heard Albert mumbling something about a wandering fellow, and the tone in which the
words were spoken was disrespectful, and Mrs Baker
began to consider Albert; and though a better servant now
than he had ever been in some respects, he had developed
a fault which she didn't like, a way of hanging round the
visitor as he was preparing to leave the hotel that almost
amounted to persecution. Worse than that, a rumour had
reached her that Albert's service was measured according
to the tip he expected to receive. She didn't believe it,
but if it were true she would not hesitate to have him out
of the hotel in spite of the many years he had spent with
them. Another thing: Albert was liked, but not by everybody. The little red-headed boy on the second floor told
me, Mrs Baker said (her thoughts returning to last Sunday,
when she had taken the child out to Bray), that he was
afraid of Albert, and he confided to me that Albert had
tried to pick him up and kiss him. Why can't he leave the
child alone? Can't he see the child doesn't like him?

But the Bakers were kind-hearted proprietors, and
could not keep sentiment out of their business, and Albert remained at Morrison's Hotel till she died.

An easy death I hope it was, your honour, for if any
poor creature deserved an easy one it was Albert herself.
You think so, Alec, meaning that the disappointed man
suffers less at parting with this world than the happy one?
Maybe you're right. That is as it may be, your honour,
he answered, and I told him that Albert awoke one morning hardly able to breathe, and returned to bed and lay
there almost speechless till the maid-servant came to
make the bed. She ran off again to fetch a cup of tea, and
after sipping it Albert said that she felt much better. But
she never roused completely, and the maid-servant who
came up in the evening with a bowl of soup did not press

her to try to eat it, for it was plain that Albert could not eat or drink, and it was almost plain that she was dying, but the maid-servant did not like to alarm the hotel and contented herself with saying: He'd better see the doctor to-morrow. She was up betimes in the morning, and on going to Albert's room she found the waiter asleep, breathing heavily. An hour later Albert was dead, and everybody was asking how a man who was in good health on Tuesday could be a corpse on Thursday morning, as if such a thing had never happened before. However often it had happened, it did not seem natural, and it was whispered that Albert might have made away with himself. Some spoke of apoplexy, but apoplexy in a long, thin man is not usual; and when the doctor came down his report that Albert was a woman put all thought of the cause of death out of everybody's mind. Never before or since was Morrison's Hotel agog as it was that morning, everybody asking the other why Albert had chosen to pass herself off as a man, and how she had succeeded in doing this year after year without any one of them suspecting her. She would be getting better wages as a man than as a woman, somebody said, but nobody cared to discuss the wages question; all knew that a man is better paid than a woman. But what Albert would have done with Helen if Helen hadn't gone off with Joe Mackins stirred everybody's imagination. What would have happened on the wedding night? Nothing, of course; but how would she have let on? The men giggled over their glasses, and the women pondered over their cups of tea; the men asked the women and the women asked the men, and the interest in the subject had not quite died down when Hubert Page returned to Morrison's Hotel, in the spring of the year, with her paint pots and brushes. How is Albert Nobbs? was one of her first enquiries, and it fired the train. Albert Nobbs! Don't you know? How should I know? Hubert Page replied. I've only just come back to Dublin. What is there to know? Don't you ever read the papers? Read the papers? Hubert repeated. Then you haven't heard that Albert Nobbs is dead? No, I haven't heard of it. I'm sorry for him, but after all, men die; there's something wonderful in that, is there? No; but if you had read the papers you'd have learnt that Albert Nobbs wasn't a man at all. Albert Nobbs was a woman. Albert Nobbs a woman! Hubert replied, putting as much surprise as she could into her voice. So you never heard? And the story began to fall out from different sides, everybody striving to communicate bits to her, until at last she said: If you all speak together, I shall never understand it. Albert Nobbs a woman! A woman as much as you're a man, was the answer, and the story of her courtship of Helen, and Helen's preference for Joe Mackins, and Albert's grief at Helen's treatment of her trickled into a long relation. The biggest deception in the whole world, a scullion cried from his saucepans. Whatever would she have done with Helen if they had married? But the question had been asked so often that it fell flat. So Helen went away with Joe Mackins? Hubert said. Yes; and they don't seem to get on over well together. Serve her right for her unkindness, cried a kitchen-maid. But after all, you wouldn't want her to marry a woman? a scullion answered. Of course not; of course not. The story was taken up by another voice, and the hundreds of pounds that Albert had left behind in many securities were multiplied; nearly a hundred in ready money rolled up in paper, half-crowns, half-sovereigns and sovereigns in his bedroom; his bedroom – her bedroom, I mean; but we are so used to thinking of her as a him that we find it difficult to say her; we're always catching each other up. But what I'm thinking of, said a waiter, is the waste of all that money. A great scoop it was for the Government, eight hundred pounds. The pair were to have bought a shop and lived together, Mr Page, Annie Watts rapped out, and when the discussion was carried from the kitchen upstairs to the second floor: True for you, said Dorothy, now you mention it, I remember; it's you that should be knowing better than anybody else, Mr

Page, what Albert's sex was like. Didn't you sleep with her? I fell asleep the moment my head was on the pillow, Page answered, for if you remember rightly I was that tired Mrs Baker hadn't the heart to turn me out of the hotel. I'd been working ten, twelve, fourteen hours a day, and when he took me up to his room I tore off my clothes and fell asleep and went away in the morning before he was awake. Isn't it wonderful? A woman, Hubert continued, and a minx in the bargain, and an artful minx if ever there was one in the world, and there have been a good many. And now, ladies, I must be about my work. I wonder what Annie Watts was thinking of when she stood looking into my eyes; does she suspect me? Hubert asked herself as she sat on her derrick. And what a piece of bad luck that I shouldn't have found Albert alive when I returned to Dublin

You see, Alec, this is how it was. Polly, that was Hubert's wife, died six months before Albert; and Hubert had been thinking ever since of going into partnership with Albert. In fact Hubert had been thinking about a shop, like Albert, saying to herself almost every day after the death of her wife: Albert and I might set up together. But it was not until she lay in bed that she fell to thinking the matter out, saying to herself: One of us would have had to give up our job to attend to it. The shop was Albert's idea more than mine, so perhaps she'd have given up waiting, which would not have suited me, for I'm tired of going up these ladders. My head isn't altogether as steady as it used to be; swinging about on a derrick isn't suited to women. So perhaps it's as well that things have fallen out as they have. Hubert turned herself over, but sleep was far from her, and she lay a long time thinking of everything and of nothing in particular, as we all do in our beds, with this thought often uppermost: I wonder what is going to be the end of my life. What new chance do the years hold for me?

And of what would Hubert be thinking, being a married woman? Of what else should she be thinking but

of her husband, who might now be a different man from
the one she left behind? Fifteen years, she said, makes
a great difference in all of us, and perhaps it was the
words, fifteen years, that put the children she had left
behind her back into her thought. I wouldn't be saying
that she hadn't been thinking of them, off and on, in the
years gone by, but the thought of them was never such
a piercing thought as it was that night. She'd have liked
to have jumped out of her bed and run away to them;
and perhaps she would have done if she only knew where
they were. But she didn't, so she had to keep to her bed;
and she lay for an hour or more thinking of them as little
children, and wondering what they were like now. Lily
was five when she left home. She's a young woman now.
Agnes was only two. She is now seventeen, still a girl,
Hubert said to herself; but Lily's looking round, thinking of young men, and the other won't be delaying much
longer, for young women are much more wide-awake
than they used to be in the old days. The rest of my
life belongs to them. Their father could have looked
after them till now; but now they are thinking of young
men he won't be able to cope with them, and maybe
he's wanting me too. Bill is forty, and at forty we begin
to think of them as we knew them long ago. He must
have often thought of me, perhaps oftener than I thought
of him; and she was surprised to find that she had forgotten all Bill's ill-usage, and remembered only the good
time she had had with him. The rest of my life belongs to
him, she said, and to the girls. But how am I to get back
to him? how, indeed? ... Bill may be dead; the children
too. But that isn't likely. I must get news of them somehow. The house is there; and lying in the darkness she
recalled the pictures on the wall, the chairs that she had
sat in, the coverlets on the beds, everything. Bill isn't
a wanderer, she said; I'll find him in the same house if
he isn't dead. And the children? Did they know anything
about her? Had Bill spoken ill of her to them? She didn't
think he would do that. But did they want to see her?

Well, she could never find that out except by going to
see. But how was she going to return home? Pack up
her things and go dressed as a man to the house and,
meeting Bill on the threshold, say: Don't you know me,
Bill? and are you glad to see your mother back, children?
No; that wouldn't do. She must return home as a woman,
and none of them must know the life she had been living.
But what story would she tell him? It would be difficult
to tell the story of fifteen years, for fifteen years is a long
time, and sooner or later they'd find out she was lying,
for they would keep asking her questions.

But sure, said Alec, 'tis an easy story to tell. Well,
Alec, what story should she tell them? In these parts,
Alec said, a woman who left her husband and returned
to him after fifteen years would say she was taken away
by the fairies whilst wandering in a wood. Do you think
she'd be believed? Why shouldn't she, your honour? A
woman that marries another woman, and lives happily
with her, isn't a natural woman; there must be something of the fairy in her. But I could see it all happening
as you told it, the maid-servants and the serving-men
going their own roads, and the only fault I've to find
with the story is that you left out some of the best parts.
I'd have liked to know what the husband said when she
went back to him, and they separated all the years. If he
liked her better than he did before, or less. And there
is a fine story in the way the mother would be vexed by
the two daughters and the husband, and they at her all
the time with questions, and she hard set to find answers
for them. But mayhap the best bit of all is when Albert
began to think that it wouldn't do to have Joe Mackins
hanging round, making their home his own, eating and
drinking of the best, and when there was a quarrel he'd
have a fine threat over them, as good as the Murrigan
herself when she makes off of a night to the fair, whirling herself over the people's heads, stirring them up agin
each other, making cakes of their skulls. I'm bet, fairly
bet, crowed down by the Ballinrobe cock. And now,

your honour, you heard the Angelus ringing, and my dinner is on the hob, and I'll be telling you what I think of the story when I come back; but I'm thinking already 'tis the finest that ever came out of Ballinrobe, I am so.

A. E. COPPARD

The Black Dog

I

Having pocketed his fare the freckled rustic took himself
and his antediluvian cab back to the village limbo from
which they had briefly emerged. Loughlin checked his
luggage into the care of the porter, an angular man with
one eye who was apparently the only other living being
in this remote minute station, and sat down in the platform shade. July noon had a stark eye-tiring brightness,
and a silence so very deep – when that porter ceased his
intolerable clatter – that Loughlin could hear footsteps
crunching on the road half a mile away. The train was late.
There were no other passengers. Nothing to look at except
his trunks, two shiny rails in the grim track, red holly-
hocks against white pailings on the opposite bank.

The holiday in this quiet neighbourhood had delighted
him, but its crowning experience had been too brief. On
the last day but one the loveliest woman he had ever
known had emerged almost as briefly as that cabman.
Some men are constantly meeting that woman. Not so the
Honourable Gerald Loughlin, but no man turns his back
tranquilly on destiny even if it is but two days old and
already some half-dozen miles away. The visit had come
to its end, Loughlin had come to his station, the cab had
gone back to its lair, but on reflection he could find no
other reasons for going away and denying himself the
delight of this proffered experience. Time was his own, as
much as he could buy of it, and he had an income that
enabled him to buy a good deal.

Moody and hesitant he began to fill his pipe when the one-eyed porter again approached him.

'Take a pipe of that?' said Loughlin, offering him the pouch.

'Thanky, sir, but I can't smoke a pipe; a cigarette I take now and again, thanky, sir, not often, just to keep me from cussing and damning. My wife buys me a packet sometimes, she says I don't swear so much then, but I don't know, I has to knock 'em off soon's they make me feel bad, and then, damn it all, I be worsen ever . . .'

'Look here,' said the other, interrupting him, 'I'm not going by this train after all. Something I have forgotten. Now look after my bags and I'll come along later, this afternoon.' He turned and left the station as hurriedly as if his business was really of the high importance the porter immediately conceived it to be.

The Honourable Gerald, though handsome and honest, was not a fool. A fool is one who becomes distracted between the claims of instinct and common sense; the larger foolishness is the peculiar doom of imaginative people, artists and their kind, while the smaller foolishness is the mark of all those who have nothing but their foolishness to endorse them. Loughlin responded to this impulse unhesitatingly but without distraction, calmly and directly as became a well-bred bachelor in the early thirties. He might have written to the young beauty with the queer name, Orianda Crabbe, but that course teemed with absurdities and difficulties, for he was modest, his romantic imagination weak, and he had only met her at old Lady Tillington's a couple of days before. Of this mere girl, just twenty-three or twenty-four, he knew nothing save that they had been immediately and vividly charming to each other. That was no excuse for presenting himself again to the old invalid of Tillington Park, it would be impossible for him to do so, but there had been one vague moment of their recalled intercourse, a glimmering intimation, which just seemed to offer a remote possibility of achievement, and so he walked on in the direction of the park.

Tillington was some miles off and the heat was oppressive. At the end of an hour's stroll he stepped into The Three Pigeons at Denbury and drank a deep drink. It was quiet and deliciously cool in the taproom there, yes, as silent as that little station had been. Empty the world seemed today, quite empty; he had not passed a human creature. Happily bemused he took another draught. Eighteen small panes of glass in that long window and perhaps as many flies buzzing in the room. He could hear and see a breeze saluting the bright walled ivy outside and the bushes by a stream. This drowsiness was heaven, it made so clear his recollection of Orianda. It was impossible to particularise but she was in her way, her rather uncultured way, just perfection. He had engaged her upon several themes, music, fishing (Loughlin loved fishing), golf, tennis, and books; none of these had particularly stirred her but she had brains, quite an original turn of mind. There had been neither time nor opportunity to discover anything about her, but there she was, staying there, that was the one thing certain, apparently indefinitely, for she described the park in a witty detailed way even to a certain favourite glade which she always visited in the afternoons. When she had told him that, he could swear she was not finessing; no, no, it was a most engaging simplicity, a frankness that was positively marmoreal.

He would certainly write to her; yes, and he began to think of fine phrases to put in a letter, but could there be anything finer, now, just at this moment, than to be sitting with her in this empty inn. It was not a fair place, though it was clean, but how she would brighten it, yes! there were two long settles and two short ones, two tiny tables and eight spittoons (he *had* to count them), and somehow he felt her image flitting adorably into this setting, defeating with its native glory all the scrupulous beer-smelling impoverishment. And then, after a while, he would take her, and they would lie in the grass under a deep-bosomed tree and speak of love. How beautiful she would be. But she was not there, and so he left the inn and crossed the road to a church, pleasant and tiny and tidy, white-walled and clean-ceilinged. A sparrow chirped in the porch, flies hummed in the nave, a puppy was barking in the vicarage garden. How trivial, how absurdly solemn, everything seemed. The thud of the great pendulum in the tower had the sound of a dead man beating on a bar of spiritless iron. He was tired of the vapid tidiness of these altars with their insignificant tapestries, candlesticks of gilded wood, the bunches of pale flowers oppressed by the rich glow from the windows. He longed for an altar that should be an inspiring symbol of belief, a place of green and solemn walls with a dark velvet shrine sweeping aloft to the peaked roof unhindered by tarnishing lustre and tedious linen. Holiness was always something richly dim. There was no more holiness here than in the tough hassocks and rush-bottomed chairs; not here, surely, the apple of Eden flourished. And yet, turning to the lectern, he noted the large prayer book open at the office of marriage. He idly read over the words of the ceremony, filling in at the gaps the names of Gerald Wilmot Loughlin and Orianda Crabbe.

What a fool! He closed the book with a slam and left the church. Absurd! You *couldn't* fall in love with a person as sharply as all that, could you? But why not? Unless fancy was charged with the lightning of gods it was nothing at all.

Tramping away still in the direction of Tillington Park he came in the afternoon to that glade under a screen of trees spoken of by the girl. It was green and shady, full of scattering birds. He flung himself down in the grass under a deep-bosomed tree. She had spoken delightfully of this delightful spot.

When she came, for come she did, the confrontation left him very unsteady as he sprang to his feet. (Confound that potation at The Three Pigeons! Enormously hungry, too!) But he was amazed, entranced, she was so happy to see him again. They sat down together, but he was still bewildered and his confusion left him all at sixes and sevens. Fortunately her own rivulet of casual chatter carried them on until he suddenly asked, 'Are you related to the Crabbes of Cotterton – I fancy I know them?'

'No, I think not, no, I am from the south country, near the sea, nobody at all, my father keeps an inn.'

'An inn! How extraordinary! How very . . . very . . .'

'Extraordinary?' Nodding her head in the direction of the hidden mansion she added, 'I am her companion.'

'Lady Tillington's?'

She assented coolly, was silent, while Loughlin ransacked his brains for some delicate reference that would clear him over this . . . this . . . cataract. But he felt stupid – that confounded potation at The Three Pigeons! Why, that was where he had thought of her so admirably, too. He asked if she cared for the position, was it pleasant, and so on. Heavens, what an astonishing creature for a domestic; quite positively lovely, a compendium of delightful qualities, this girl, so frank, so simple!

'Yes, I like it, but home is better. I should love to go back to my home, to father, but I can't, I'm still afraid – I ran away from home three years ago, to go with my mother. I'm like my mother, she ran away from home too.'

Orianda picked up the open parasol which she had dropped, closed it in a thoughtful manner, and laid its crimson folds beside her. There was no other note of colour in her white attire; she was without a hat. Her fair hair had a quenching tinge upon it that made it less bright than gold, but more rare. Her cheeks had the colour of homely flowers, the lily and the pink. Her teeth were as even as the peas in a newly opened pod, as clear as milk.

'Tell me about all that. May I hear it?'

'I have not seen him or heard from him since, but I love him very much now.'

'Your father?'

'Yes, but he is stern, a simple man, and he is so just. We live at a tiny old inn at the end of a village near the hills. The Black Dog. It is thatched and has tiny rooms.

It's painted all over with pink, pink whitewash.'

'Ah, I know.'

'There's a porch, under a sycamore tree, where people sit, and an old rusty chain hanging on a hook just outside the door.'

'What's that for?'

'I don't know what it is for, horses, perhaps, but it is always there, I always see that rusty chain. And on the opposite side of the road there are three lime trees and behind them is the yard where my father works. He makes hurdles and ladders. He is the best hurdle maker in three counties, he has won many prizes at the shows. It is splendid to see him working at the willow wood, soft and white. The yard is full of poles and palings, spars and faggots, and long shavings of the thin bark like seaweed. It smells so nice. In the spring the chaffinches and wrens are singing about him all day long; the wren is lovely, but in the summer of course it's the whitethroats come chippering, and yellow-hammers.'

'Ah, blackbirds, thrushes, nightingales!'

'Yes, but it's the little birds seem to love my father's yard.'

'Well then, but why did you, why did you run away?'

'My mother was much younger, and different from father; she was handsome and proud too, and in all sorts of ways superior to him. They got to hate each other; they were so quiet about it, but I could see. Their only common interest was me, they both loved me very much. Three years ago she ran away from him. Quite suddenly, you know; there was nothing at all leading up to such a thing. But I could not understand my father, not then, he took it all so calmly. He did not mention even her name to me for a long time, and I feared to intrude; you see, I did not understand, I was only twenty. When I did ask about her he told me not to bother him, forbade me to write to her. I didn't know where she was, but he knew, and at last I found out too.'

'And you defied him, I suppose?'

'No, I deceived him. He gave me money for some purpose – to pay a debt – and I stole it. I left him a letter and
ran away to my mother. I loved her.'

'O well, that was only to be expected,' said Loughlin.
'It was all right, quite right.'

'She was living with another man. I didn't know. I was
a fool.'

'Good lord! That was a shock for you,' Loughlin said.
'What did you do?'

'No, I was not shocked, she was so happy. I lived with
them for a year . . .'

'Extraordinary!'

'And then she died.'

'Your mother died!'

'Yes, so you see I could not stop with my . . . I could
not stay where I was, and I couldn't go back to my father.'

'I see, no, but you want to go back to your father now.'

'I'm afraid. I love him, but I'm afraid. I don't blame
my mother, I feel she was right, quite right – it was such
happiness. And yet I feel, too, that father was deeply
wronged. I can't understand that, it sounds foolish. I
should so love to go home again. This other kind of life
doesn't seem to eclipse me – things have been extraordinarily kind – I don't feel out of my setting, but still it
doesn't satisfy, it is polite and soft, like silk, perhaps it
isn't barbarous enough, and I want to live, somehow –
well, I have not found what I wanted to find.'

'What did you want to find?'

'I shan't know until I have found it. I do want to go
home now, but I am full of strange feelings about it. I
feel as if I was bearing the mark of something that can't
be hidden or disguised of what my mother did, as if I
were all a burning recollection for him that he couldn't
fail to see. He is good, a just man. He . . . he is the best
hurdle maker in three counties.'

While listening to this daughter of a man who made
ladders the Honourable Gerald had been swiftly thinking
of an intriguing phrase that leaped into his mind. Social

plesiomorphism, that was it! Caste was humbug, no
doubt, but even if it was conscious humbug it was there,
really there, like the patterned frost upon a window pane,
beautiful though a little incoherent, and conditioned only
by the size and number of your windows. (Eighteen windows in that pub!) But what did it amount to, after all?
It was stuck upon your clear polished outline for every
eye to see, but within was something surprising as the
sight of a badger in church – until you got used to the
indubitable relation of such badgers to such churches.
Fine turpitudes!

'My dear girl,' he burst out, 'your mother and you were
right, absolutely. I am sure life is enhanced not by amass-
ing conventions, but by destroying them. And your feeling for your father is right, too, rightest of all. Tell me
. . . let me . . . may I take you back to him?'

The girl's eyes dwelt upon his with some intensity.

'Your courage is kind,' she said, 'but he doesn't know
you, nor you him.' And to that she added, 'You don't even
know me.'

'I have known you for ten thousand years. Come home
to him with me, we will go back together. Yes, you can
explain. Tell him,' the Honourable Gerald had got the bit
between his teeth now, 'tell him I'm your sweetheart, will
you – will you?'

'Ten thousand . . . ! Yes, I know; but it's strange to
think you have only seen me just once before!'

'Does that matter? Everything grows from that one
small moment into a world of . . . well of . . . boundless
admiration.'

'I don't want,' said Orianda, reopening her crimson
parasol, 'to grow into a world of any kind.'

'No, of course you don't. But I mean the emotion is
irresistible, "the desire of the moth for the star", that sort
of thing, you know, and I immolate myself, the happy
victim of your attractions.'

'All that has been said before.' Orianda adjusted her
parasol as a screen for her raillery.

'I swear,' said he, 'I have not said it before, never to a living soul.'

Fountains of amusement beamed in her brilliant eyes. She was exquisite; he was no longer in doubt about the colour of her eyes – though he could not describe them. And the precise shade of her hair was – well, it was extraordinarily beautiful.

'I mean – it's been said to me!'

'O damnation! Of course it's been said to you. Ah, and isn't that my complete justification? But you agree, do you not? Tell me if it's possible. Say you agree, and let me take you back to your father.'

'I think I would like you to,' the jolly girl said, slowly.

2

On an August morning a few weeks later they travelled down together to see her father. In the interim Orianda had resigned her appointment, and several times Gerald had met her secretly in the purlieus of Tillington Park. The girl's cool casual nature fascinated him not less than her appearance. Admiration certainly outdistanced his happiness, although that also increased; but the bliss had its shadow, for the outcome of their friendship seemed mysteriously to depend on the outcome of the proposed return to her father's home, devotion to that project form- ing the first principle, as it were, of their intercourse. Orianda had not dangled before him the prospect of any serener relationship; she took his caresses as naturally and undemonstratively as a pet bird takes a piece of sugar. But he had begun to be aware of a certain force behind all her charming naïveté; the beauty that exhaled the fresh- ness, the apparent fragility, of a drop of dew had none the less a savour of tyranny which he vowed should never, least of all by him, be pressed to vulgar exercise.

When the train reached its destination Orianda con- fided calmly that she had preferred not to write to her father. Really she did not know for certain whether he was alive or even living on at the old home she so loved. And there was a journey of three miles or more which Orianda proposed to walk. So they walked.

The road lay across an expanse of marshy country and approached the wooded uplands of her home only by numerous eccentric divagations made necessary by culverts that drained the marsh. The day was bright; the sky, so vast an arch over this flat land, was a very oven for heat; there were cracks in the earth, the grass was like stubble. At the mid journey they crossed a river by its wooden bridge, upon which a boy sat fishing with stick and string. Near the water was a long white hut with a flag; a few tethered boats floated upon the stream. Gerald gave a shilling to a travelling woman who carried a burden on her back and shuffled slowly upon the harsh road sighing, looking neither to right nor left; she did not look into the sky, her gaze was fastened upon her dolorous feet, one two, one two, one two; her shift, if she had such a garment, must have clung to her old body like a shrimping net.

In an hour they had reached the uplands and soon, at the top of a sylvan slope where there was shade and cooling air, Gerald saw a sign hung upon a sycamore tree, THE BLACK DOG BY NATHANIEL CRABBE. The inn was small, pleasant with pink wash and brown paint, and faced across the road a large yard encircled by hedges, trees, and a gate. The travellers stood peeping into the enclosure which was stocked with new ladders, hurdles, and poles of various sizes. Amid them stood a tall burly man at a block, trimming with an axe the butt of a willow rod. He was about fifty, clad in rough country clothes, a white shirt, and a soft straw hat. He had mild simple features coloured, like his arms and neck, almost to the hue of a bay horse.

'Hullo!' called the girl. The man with the axe looked round at her unrecognizingly. Orianda hurried through the gateway. 'Father!' she cried.

'I did not know. I was not rightly sure of ye,' said the man, dropping the axe, 'such a lady you've grown.'

As he kissed his daughter his heavy discoloured hands

rested on her shoulders, her gloved ones lay against his
breast. Orianda took out her purse.

'Here is the money I stole, father.'

She dropped some coins one by one into his palm. He
counted them over, and saying simply 'Thank you, my
dear,' put them into his pocket.

'I'm dashed!'— thought Loughlin, who had followed
the girl— 'it's exactly how *she* would take it; no explanation, no apology. They do not know what reproach means.
Have they no code at all?

She went on chatting with her father, and seemed to
have forgotten her companion.

'You mean you want to come back!' exclaimed her
father eagerly, 'come back here? That would be grand,
that would. But look, tell me what I am to do. I've – you
see – this is how it is—'

He spat upon the ground, picked up his axe, rested one
foot upon the axe-block and one arm upon his knee.
Orianda sat down upon a pile of the logs.

'This is how it is . . . be you married?'

'Come and sit here, Gerald,' called the girl. As he came
forward Orianda rose and said: 'This is my very dear
friend, father, Gerald Loughlin. He has been so kind. It is
he who has given me the courage to come back. I wanted
to for so long. O, a long time, father, a long time. And
yet Gerald had to drag me here in the end.'

'What was you afraid of, my girl?' asked the big man.

'Myself.'

The two visitors sat upon the logs. 'Shall I tell you
about mother?' asked the girl.

Crabbe hesitated; looked at the ground.

'Ah, yes, you might,' he said.

'She died, did you know?'

The man looked up at the trees with their myriads of
unmoving leaves; each leaf seemed to be listening.

'She died?' he said softly. 'No, I did not know she died.'

'Two years ago,' continued the girl, warily, as if probing his mood.

'Two years!' He repeated it without emotion. 'No, I did not know she died. 'Tis a bad job.' He was quite still, his mind seemed to be turning over his own secret memories, but what he bent forward and suddenly said was, 'Don't say anything about it in there.' He nodded towards the inn.

'No?' Orianda opened her crimson parasol.

'You see,' he went on, again resting one foot on the axe-block and addressing himself more particularly to Gerald, 'I've . . . this is how it is. When I was left alone I could not get along here, not by myself. That's for certain. There's the house and the bar and the yard – I'd to get help, a young woman from Brighton. I met her at Brighton.' He rubbed the blade of the axe reflectively across his palm – 'And she manages house for me now, you see.'

He let the axe fall again and stood upright. 'Her name's Lizzie.'

'O, quite so, you could do no other,' Gerald exclaimed cheerfully, turning to the girl. But Orianda said softly, 'What a family we are! He means he is living with her. And so you don't want your undutiful daughter after all, father?' Her gaiety was a little tremulous.

'No, no!' he retorted quickly, 'you must come back, you must come back, if so be you can. There's nothing I'd like better, nothing on this mortal earth. My God, if something don't soon happen I don't know what *will* happen.' Once more he stooped for the axe. 'That's right, Orianda, yes, yes, but you've no call to mention to her'— he glared uneasily at the inn doorway— 'that . . . that about your mother.'

Orianda stared up at him though he would not meet her gaze.

'You mean she doesn't know?' she asked, 'you mean she would want you to marry her if she did know?'

'Yes, that's about how it is with us.'

Loughlin was amazed at the girl's divination. It seemed miraculous, what a subtle mind she had, extraordinary!

And how casually she took the old rascal's – well, what could you call it? – effrontery, shame, misdemeanour, helplessness. But was not her mother like it too? He had grasped nothing at all of the situation yet, save that Nathaniel Crabbe appeared to be netted in the toils of this housekeeper, this Lizzie from Brighton. Dear Orianda was 'dished' now, poor girl. She could not conceivably return to such a menage.

Orianda was saying: 'Then I may stay, father, mayn't I, for good with you?'

Her father's eyes left no doubt of his pleasure.

'Can we give Gerald a bedroom for a few days? Or do we ask Lizzie?'

'Ah, better ask her,' said the shameless man. 'You want to make a stay here, sir?'

'If it won't incommode you,' replied Loughlin.

'O, make no doubt about that, to be sure no, I make no doubt about that.'

'Have you still got my old bedroom?' asked Orianda, for the amount of dubiety in his air was in prodigious antagonism to his expressed confidence.

'Why yes, it may happen,' he replied slowly.

'Then Gerald can have the spare room. It's all wainscot and painted dark blue. It's a shrimp of a room, but there's a preserved albatross in a glass case as big as a van.'

'I make no doubt about that,' chimed in her father, straightening himself and scratching his chin uneasily, 'you must talk to Lizzie.'

'Splendid!' said Gerald to Orianda, 'I've never seen an albatross.'

'We'll ask Lizzie,' said she, 'at once.'

Loughlin was experiencing not a little inward distress at this turn in the affair, but it was he who had brought Orianda to her home, and he would have to go through with the horrid business.

'Is she difficult, father?'

'No, she's not difficult, not difficult, so to say, you must make allowance.'

The girl was implacable. Her directness almost froze the blood of the Honourable Loughlin.

'Are you fond of her? How long has she been here?'

'O, a goodish while, yes, let me see – no, she's not difficult, if that's what you mean – three years, perhaps.'

'Well, but that's long enough!'

(Long enough for what – wondered Loughlin?)

'Yes, it is longish.'

'If you really want to get rid of her you could tell her ...'

'Tell her what?'

'You know what to tell her!'

But her father looked bewildered and professed his ignorance.

'Take me in to her,' said Orianda, and they all walked across to The Black Dog. There was no one within; father and daughter went into the garden while Gerald stayed behind in a small parlour. Through the window that looked upon a grass plot he could see a woman sitting in a deck chair under a tree. Her face was turned away so that he saw only a curve of pink cheek and a thin mound of fair hair tossed and untidy. Lizzie's large red fingers were slipping a sprig of watercress into a mouth that was hidden round the corner of the curve. With her other hand she was caressing a large brown hen that sat on her lap. Her black skirt wrapped her limbs tightly, a round hip and a thigh being rigidly outlined, while the blouse of figured cotton also seemed strained upon her buxom breast, for it was torn and split in places. She had strong white arms and holes in her stockings. When she turned to confront the others it was easy to see that she was a foolish, untidy, but still a rather pleasant woman of about thirty.

'How do you do, Lizzie?' cried Orianda, offering a cordial hand. The hen fluttered away as, smiling a little wanly, the woman rose.

'Who is it, 'Thaniel?' she asked.

Loughlin heard no more, for some men came noisily into the bar and Crabbe hurried back to serve them.

3

In the afternoon Orianda drove Gerald in the gig back to the station to fetch the baggage.

'Well, what success, Orianda?' he asked as they jogged along.

'It would be perfect but for Lizzie – that *was* rather a blow. But I should have foreseen her – Lizzies are inevitable. And she *is* difficult – she weeps. But, O I am glad to be home again. Gerald, I feel I shall not leave it, ever.'

'Yes, Orianda,' he protested, 'leave it for me. I'll give your nostalgia a little time to fade. I think it was a man named Pater said, "All life is a wandering to find home." You don't want to omit the wandering?'

'Not if I have found my home again?'

'A home with Lizzie!'

'No, not with Lizzie.' She flicked the horse with the whip. 'I shall be too much for Lizzie; Lizzie will resume her wandering. She's as stupid as a wax widow in a show. Nathaniel is tired of Lizzie, and Lizzie of Nathaniel. The two wretches! But I wish she did not weep.'

Gerald had not observed any sign of tearfulness in Lizze at the midday dinner; on the contrary, she seemed rather a jolly creature, not that she had spoken much beyond 'Yes, 'Thaniel, no, 'Thaniel,' or Gerald, or Orianda, as the case had been. Her use of his Christian name, which had swept him at once into the bosom of the family, shocked him rather pleasantly. But he did not know what had taken place between the two women; perhaps Lizzie had already perceived and tacitly accepted her displacement.

He was wakened next morning by unusual sounds, chatter of magpies in the front trees, and the ching of hammers on a bulk of iron at the smithy. Below his window a brown terrier stood on its barrel barking at a goose. Such common simple things had power to please him, and for a few days everything at The Black Dog seemed planned on this scale of novel enjoyment. The old inn

itself, the log yard, harvesting, the chatter of the evening
topers, even the village Sunday delighted him with its
parade of Phyllis and Corydon, though it is true Phyllis
wore a pink frock, stockings of faint blue, and walked like
a man, while Corydon had a bowler hat and walked like a
bear. He helped 'Thaniel with axe, hammer, and plane,
but best of all was to serve mugs of beer nightly in the bar
and to drop the coins into the drawer of money. The rest
of the time he spent with Orianda whom he wooed happily enough, though without establishing any marked
progress. They roamed in fields and in copses, lounged in
lanes, looking at things and idling deliciously, at last returning home to be fed by Lizzie, whose case somehow
hung in the air, faintly deflecting the perfect stream of
felicity.

In their favourite glade a rivulet was joined by a number of springs bubbling from a pool of sand and rock.
Below it the enlarged stream was dammed into a small
lake once used for turning a mill, but now, since the mill
was dismantled, covered with arrow heads and lily leaves,
surrounded by inclining trees, bushes of rich green
growth, terraces of willow herb, whose fairy-like pink
steeples Orianda called 'codlins and cream', and catmint
with knobs of agreeable odour. A giant hornbeam tree had
fallen and lay buried in the lake. This, and the black
poplars whose vacillating leaves underscored the solemn
clamour of the outfall, gave to it the very serenity of
desolation.

Here they caught sight of the two woodpeckers bathing
in the springs, a cock and his hen, who had flown away
yaffling, leaving a pretty mottled feather tinged with green
floating there. It was endless pleasure to watch each spring
bubble upwards from a pouch of sand that spread smoke-
like in the water, turning each cone into a midget Vesu-
vius. A wasp crawled laboriously along a flat rock lying
in the pool. It moved weakly, as if, marooned like a
mariner upon some unknown isle, it could find no way of
escape; only, this isle was no bigger than a dish in an

ocean as small as a cartwheel. The wasp seemed to have forgotten that it had wings, it creepingly examined every inch of the rock until it came to a patch of dried dung. Proceeding still as wearily it paused upon a dead leaf until a breeze blew leaf and insect into the water. The wasp was overwhelmed by the rush from the bubbles, but at last it emerged, clutching the woodpecker's floating feather, and dragged itself into safety as a swimmer heaves himself into a boat. In a moment it preened its wings, flew back to the rock, and played at Crusoe again. Orianda picked the feather from the pool.

'What a fool that wasp is,' declared Gerald. 'I wonder what it is doing?'

Orianda, placing the feather in his hat, told him it was probably wandering to find home.

One day, brightest of all days, they went to picnic in the marshes, a strange place to choose, all rank with the musty smell of cattle, and populous with grasshoppers that burred below you and millions, quadrillions of flies that buzzed above. But Orianda loved it. The vast area of coarse pasture harboured not a single farmhouse, only a shed here and there marking a particular field, for a thousand shallow brooks flowed like veins from all directions to the arterial river moving through its silent leagues. Small frills of willow curving on the river brink, and elsewhere a temple of lofty elms, offered the only refuge from sun or storm. Store cattle roamed unchecked from field to field, and in the shade of gaunt rascally bushes sheep were nestling. Green reeds and willow herb followed the water-courses with endless efflorescence, beautiful indeed.

In the late afternoon they had come to a spot where they could see their village three or four miles away, but between them lay the inexorable barrier of the river without a bridge. There was a bridge miles away to the right, they had crossed it earlier in the day; and there was another bridge on the left, but that also was miles distant.

'Now what are we to do?' asked Orianda. She wore a white muslin frock, a country frock, and a large straw hat

with poppies, a country hat. They approached a column
of trees. In the soft smooth wind the foliage of the willows
was tossed into delicate greys. Orianda said they looked
like cock-shy heads on spindly necks. She would like to
shy at them, but she was tired. 'I know what we *could* do.'
Orianda glanced around the landscape, trees, and bushes;
the river was narrow, though deep, not more than forty
feet across, and had high banks.

'You can swim, Gerald?'

Yes, Gerald could swim rather well.

'Then let's swim it, Gerald, and carry our own clothes
over.'

'Can you swim, Orianda?'

Yes, Orianda could swim rather well.

'All right then,' he said. 'I'll go down here a little way.'

'O, don't go far, I don't want you to go far away,
Gerald,' and she added softly, 'my dear.'

'No, I won't go far,' he said, and sat down behind a bush
a hundred yards away. Here he undressed, flung his shoes
one after the other across the river, and swimming on his
back carried his clothes over in two journeys. As he sat
drying in the sunlight he heard a shout from Orianda. He
peeped out and saw her sporting in the stream quite close
below him. She swam with a graceful overarm stroke that
tossed a spray of drops behind her and launched her body
as easily as a fish's. Her hair was bound in a handkerchief.
She waved a hand to him. 'You've done it! Bravo! What
courage! Wait for me. Lovely.' She turned away like an
eel, and at every two or three strokes she spat into the air
a gay little fountain of water. How extraordinary she was.
Gerald wished he had not hurried. By and by he slipped
into the water again and swam upstream. He could not see
her.

'Have you finished?' he cried.

'I have finished, yes.' Her voice was close above his
head. She was lying in the grass, her face propped between
her palms, smiling down at him. He could see bare arms
and shoulders.

'Got your clothes across?'

'Of course.'

'All dry?'

She nodded.

'How many journeys? I made two.'

'Two,' said Orianda briefly.

'You're all right then.' He wafted a kiss, swam back, and dressed slowly. Then as she did not appear he wandered along to her humming a discreet and very audible hum as he went. When he came upon her she still lay upon the grass most scantily clothed.

'I beg your pardon,' he said hastily, and full of surprise and modesty walked away. The unembarrassed girl called after him, 'Drying my hair.'

'All right'— he did not turn round— 'no hurry.'

But what sensations assailed him. They aroused in his decent gentlemanly mind not exactly a tumult, but a flux of emotions, impressions, and qualms; doubtful emotions, incredible impressions, and torturing qualms. That alluring picture of Orianda, her errant father, the abandoned Lizzie! Had the water perhaps heated his mind though it had cooled his body? He felt he would have to urge her, drag her if need be, from this Black Dog. The setting was fair enough and she was fair, but lovely as she was not even she could escape the brush of its vulgarity, its plebeian pressure.

And if all this has, or seems to have, nothing or little enough to do with the drying of Orianda's hair, it is because the Honourable Gerald was accustomed to walk from grossness with an averted mind.

'Orianda,' said he, when she rejoined him, 'when are you going to give it up? You cannot stay here . . . with Lizzie . . . can you?'

'Why not?' she asked, sharply tossing back her hair. 'I stayed with my mother, you know.'

'That was different from this. I don't know how, but it must have been.'

She took his arm. 'Yes, it was. Lizzie I hate, and poor

stupid father loves her as much as he loves his axe or his handsaw. I hate her meekness, too. She has taken the heart out of everything. I must get her away.'

'I see your need, Orianda, but what can you do?'

'I shall lie to her, lie like a libertine. And I shall tell her that my mother is coming home at once. No Lizzie could face that.'

He was silent. Poor Lizzie did not know that there was now no Mrs Crabbe.

'You don't like my trick, do you?' Orianda shook his arm caressingly.

'It hasn't any particular grandeur about it, you know.'

'Pooh! You shouldn't waste grandeur on clearing up a mess. This is a very dirty Eden.'

'No, all's fair, I suppose.'

'But it isn't war, you dear, if that's what you mean. I'm only doing for them what they are naturally loth to do for themselves.' She pronounced the word 'loth' as if it rimed with moth.

'Lizzie,' he said, 'I'm sure about Lizzie. I'll swear there is still some fondness in her funny little heart.'

'It isn't love, though; she's just sentimental in her puffy kind of way. My dear Honourable, you don't know what love is.' He hated her to use his title, for there was then always a breath of scorn in her tone. Just at odd times she seemed to be – not vulgar, that was unthinkable – she seemed to display a contempt for good breeding. He asked with a stiff smile, 'What *is* love?'

'For me,' said Orianda, fumbling for a definition, 'for me it is a compound of anticipation and gratitude. When either of these two ingredients is absent love is dead.'

Gerald shook his head, laughing. 'It sounds like a malignant bolus that I shouldn't like to take. I feel that love is just self-sacrifice. Apart from the taste of the thing or the price of the thing, why and for what this anticipation, this gratitude?'

'For the moment of passion, of course. Honour thy moments of passion and keep them holy. But O, Gerald

Loughlin,' she added mockingly, 'this you cannot understand, for you are not a lover; you are not, no, you are not even a good swimmer.' Her mockery was adorable, but baffling.

'I do not understand you,' he said. Now why in the whole world of images should she refer to his swimming? He *was* a good swimmer. He was silent for a long time and then again he began to speak of marriage, urging her to give up her project and leave Lizzie in her simple peace.

Then, not for the first time, she burst into a strange perverse intensity that may have been love but might have been rage, that was toned like scorn and yet must have been a jest.

'Lovely Gerald, you must never marry, Gerald, you are too good for marriage. All the best women are already married, yes, they are – to all the worst men.' There was an infinite slow caress in her tone but she went on rapidly. 'So I shall never marry you, how should I marry a kind man, a good man? I am a barbarian, and want a barbarian lover, to crush and scarify me, but you are so tender and I am so crude. When your soft eyes look on me they look on a volcano.'

'I have never know anything half as lovely,' he broke in.

Her sudden emotion, though controlled, was unconcealed and she turned away from him.

'My love is a gentleman, but with him I should feel like a wild bee in a canary cage.'

'What are you saying!' cried Gerald, putting his arms around her. 'Orianda!'

'O yes, we do love in a mezzotinted kind of way. You could do anything with me short of making me marry you, anything, Gerald.' She repeated it tenderly. 'Anything. But short of marrying me I could make you do nothing.' She turned from him again for a moment or two. Then she took his arm and as they walked on she shook it and said chaffingly, 'And what a timid swimmer my Gerald is.'

But he was dead silent. That flux of sensations in his

mind had taken another twist, fiery and exquisite. Like rich clouds they shaped themselves in the sky of his mind, fancy's bright towers with shining pinnacles.

Lizzie welcomed them home. Had they enjoyed themselves – yes, the day had been fine – and so they had enjoyed themselves – well, well, that was right. But throughout the evening Orianda hid herself from him, so he wandered almost distracted about the village until in a garth he saw some men struggling with a cow. Ropes were twisted around its horns and legs. It was flung to the earth. No countryman ever speaks to an animal without blaspheming it, although if he be engaged in some solitary work and inspired to music, he invariably sings a hymn in a voice that seems to have some vague association with wood pulp. So they all blasphemed and shouted. One man, with sore eyes, dressed in a coat of blue fustian and brown cord trousers, hung to the end of a rope at an angle of forty-five degrees. His posture suggested that he was trying to pull the head off the cow. Two other men had taken turns of other rope around some stout posts, and one stood by with a handsaw.

'What are you going to do?' asked Gerald.

'Its harns be bent, yeu see,' said the man with the saw, 'they be going into its head. 'Twill blind or madden the beast.'

So they blasphemed the cow, and sawed off its crumpled horns.

When Gerald went back to the inn Orianda was still absent. He sat down but he could not rest. He could never rest now until he had won her promise. That lovely image in the river spat fountains of scornful fire at him. 'Do not leave me, Gerald,' she had said. He would never leave her, he would never leave her. But the men talking in the inn scattered his fiery thoughts. They discoursed with a vacuity whose very endlessness was transcendent. Good God! Was there ever a living person more magnificently inane than old Tottel, the registrar? He would have inspired a stork to protest. Of course, a man of his age should not have worn a cap, a small one especially; Tottel himself was small, and it made him look rumpled. He was bandy: his intellect was bandy too.

'Yes,' Mr Tottel was saying, 'it's very interesting to see interesting things, no matter if it's man, woman, or a object. The most interesting man as I ever met in my life I met on my honeymoon. Years ago. He made a lifelong study of railways, that man, knew 'em from Alpha to . . . to . . . what is it?'

'Abednego,' said someone.

'Yes, the trunk lines, the fares, the routes, the junctions of anywheres in England or Scotland or Ireland or Wales. London, too, the Underground. I tested him, every station in correct order from South Kensington to King's Cross. A strange thing! Nothing to do with railways in 'imself, it was just his 'obby. Was a Baptist minister, really, but still a most interesting man.'

Loughlin could stand it no longer, he hurried away into the garden. He could not find her. Into the kitchen – she was not there. He sat down excited and impatient, but he must wait for her, he wanted to know, to know at once. How divinely she could swim! What was it he wanted to know? He tried to read a book there, a ragged dusty volume about the polar regions. He learned that when a baby whale is born it weighs at least a ton. How horrible!

He rushed out into the fields full of extravagant melancholy and stupid distraction. That! All that was to be her life here! This was your rustic beauty, idiots and railways, boors who could choke an ox and chop off its horns – maddening doubts, maddening doubts – foul-smelling rooms, darkness, indecency. She held him at arm's length still, but she was dove-like, and he was grappled to her soul with hoops of steel, yes, indeed.

But soon this extravagance was allayed. Dim loneliness came imperceivably into the fields and he turned back. The birds piped oddly; some wind was caressing the higher foliage, turning it all one way, the way home. Telegraph poles ahead looked like half-used pencils; the small cross

on the steeple glittered with a sharp and shapely perman-
ence.

When he came to the inn Orianda was gone to bed.

4

The next morning an air of uneasy bustle crept into the
house after breakfast, much going in and out and up and
down in restrained perturbation.

Orianda asked him if he could drive the horse and trap
to the station. Yes, he thought he could drive it.

'Lizzie is departing,' she said, 'there are her boxes and
things. It is very good of you, Gerald, if you will be so
kind. It is a quiet horse.'

Lizzie, then, had been subdued. She was faintly affable
during the meal, but thereafter she had been silent;
Gerald could not look at her until the last dreadful
moment had come and her things were in the trap.

'Goodbye, 'Thaniel,' she said to the innkeeper, and
kissed him.

'Goodbye, Orianda,' and she kissed Orianda, and then
climbed into the trap beside Gerald, who said 'Click click,'
and away went the nag.

Lizzie did not speak during the drive – perhaps she was
in tears. Gerald would have liked to comfort her, but the
nag was unusually spirited and clacked so freshly along
that he did not dare turn to the sorrowing woman. They
trotted down from the uplands and into the windy road
over the marshes. The church spire in the town ahead
seemed to change its position with every turn of that
twisting route. It would have a background now of high
sour-hued down, now of dark woodland, anon of nothing
but sky and cloud; in a few miles farther there would be
the sea. Hereabout there were no trees, few houses, the
world was vast and bright, the sky vast and blue. What
was prettiest of all was a windmill turning its fans steadily
in the draught from the sea. When they crossed the river
its slaty slow-going flow was broken into blue waves.

At the station Lizzie dismounted without a word and

Gerald hitched the nag to a tree. A porter took the luggage and labelled it while Gerald and Lizzie walked about the platform. A calf with a sack over its loins, tied by the neck to a pillar, was bellowing deeply; Lizzie let it suck at her finger for a while, but at last she resumed her walk and talked with her companion.

'She's a fine young thing, clever, his daughter; I'd do anything for her, but for him I've nothing to say. What can I say? What could I do? I gave up a great deal for that man, Mr Loughlin – I'd better not call you Gerald any more now – a great deal. I knew he'd had trouble with his wicked wife, and now to take her back after so many years, eh! It's beyond me, I know how he hates her. I gave up everything for him, I gave him what he can't give back to me, and he hates her; you know?'

'No, I did not know. I don't know anything of this affair.'

'No, of course, you would not know anything of this affair,' said Lizzie with a sigh. 'I don't want to see him again. I'm a fool, but I got my pride, and that's something to the good, it's almost satisfactory, ain't it?'

As the train was signalled she left him and went into the booking office. He marched up and down, her sad case affecting him with sorrow. The poor wretch, she had given up so much and could yet smile at her trouble. He himself had never surrendered to anything in life – that was what life demanded of you – surrender. For reward it gave you love, this swarthy, skin-deep love that exacted remorseless penalties. What German philosopher was it who said 'Woman pays the debt of life not by what she does, but by what she suffers'? The train rushed in. Gerald busied himself with the luggage, saw that it was loaded, but did not see its owner. He walked rapidly along the carriages, but he could not find her. Well, she was sick of them all, probably hiding from him. Poor woman. The train moved off, and he turned away.

But the station yard outside was startlingly empty, horse and trap were gone. The tree was still there, but with a man leaning against it, a dirty man with a dirty pipe and a dirty smell. Had he seen a horse and trap?

'A brown mare?'

'Yes.'

'Trap with yaller wheels?'

'That's it.'

'O ah, a young ooman druv away in that . . .'

'A young woman!'

'Ah, two minutes ago.' And he described Lizzie. 'Out yon,' said the dirty man, pointing with his dirty pipe to the marshes.

Gerald ran until he saw a way off on the level winding road the trap bowling along at a great pace; Lizzie was lashing the cob.

'The damned cat!' He puffed large puffs of exasperation and felt almost sick with rage, but there was nothing now to be done except walk back to The Black Dog, which he began to do. Rage gave place to anxiety, fear of some unthinkable disaster, some tragic horror at the inn.

'What a clumsy fool! All my fault, my own stupidity!' He groaned when he crossed the bridge at the half distance. He halted there: 'It's dreadful, dreadful!' A tremor in his blood, the shame of his foolishness, the fear of catastrophe, all urged him to turn back to the station and hasten away from these miserable complications.

But he did not do so, for across the marshes at the foot of the uplands he saw the horse and trap coming back furiously towards him. Orianda was driving it.

'What has happened?' she cried, jumping from the trap. 'O, what fear I was in, what's happened?' She put her arms around him tenderly.

'And I was in great fear,' he said with a laugh of relief. 'What has happened?'

'The horse came home, just trotted up to the door and stood still. Covered with sweat and foam, you see. The trap was empty. We couldn't understand it, anything, unless you had been flung out and were bleeding on the road somewhere. I turned the thing back and came on at once.' She was without a hat; she had been anxious and touched him fondly. 'Tell me, what's the scare?'

He told her all.

'But Lizzie was not in the trap,' Orianda declared excitedly. 'She has not come back. What does it mean, what does she want to do? Let us find her. Jump up, Gerald.'

Away they drove again, but nobody had seen anything of Lizzie. She had gone, vanished, dissolved, and in that strong warm air her soul might indeed have been blown to Paradise. But they did not know how or why. Nobody knew. A vague search was carried on in the afternoon, guarded though fruitless inquiries were made, and at last it seemed clear, tolerably clear, that Lizzie had conquered her mad impulse or intention or whatever it was, and walked quietly away across the fields to a station in another direction.

5

For a day or two longer time resumed its sweet slow delightfulness, though its clarity was diminished and some of its enjoyment dimmed. A village woman came to assist in the mornings, but Orianda was now seldom able to leave the inn; she had come home to a burden, a happy, pleasing burden, that could not often be laid aside, and therefore a somewhat lonely Loughlin walked the high and the low of the country by day and only in the evenings sat in the parlour with Orianda. Hope too was slipping from his heart as even the joy was slipping from his days, for the spirit of vanished Lizzie, defrauded and indicting, hung in the air of the inn, an implacable obsession, a triumphant foreboding that was proved a prophecy when some boys fishing in the mill dam hooked dead Lizzie from the pool under the hornbeam tree.

Then it was that Loughlin's soul discovered to him a mass of feelings – fine sympathy, futile sentiment, a passion for righteousness, morbid regrets – from which a tragic bias was born. After the dread ordeal of the inquest, which gave a passive verdict of Found Drowned, it was not possible for him to stem this disloyal tendency of his mind. It laid that drowned figure accusatively at the feet of his beloved girl, and no argument or sophistry could disperse the venal savour that clung to the house of The Black Dog. 'To analyse or assess a person's failings or deficiencies,' he declared to himself, 'is useless, not because such blemishes are immovable, but because they affect the mass of beholders in divers ways. Different minds perceive utterly variant figures in the same being. To Brown Robinson is a hero, to Jones a snob, to Smith a fool. Who then is right? You are lucky if you can put your miserable self in relation at an angle where your own deficiencies are submerged or minimized, and wise if you can maintain your vision of that interesting angle.' But embedded in Loughlin's modest intellect there was a stratum of probity that was rock to these sprays of the casuist; and although Orianda grew more alluring than ever, he packed his bag, and on a morning she herself drove him in the gig to the station.

Upon that miserable departure it was fitting that rain should fall. The station platform was piled with bushel baskets and empty oil barrels. It rained with a quiet remorselessness. Neither spoke a word, no one spoke, no sound was uttered but the faint flicking of the raindrops. Her kiss to him was long and sweet, her goodbye almost voiceless.

'You will write?' she whispered.

'Yes, I will write.'

But he does not do so. In London he has not forgotten, but he cannot endure the thought of that countryside — to be far from the madding crowd is to be mad indeed. It is only after some trance of recollection, when his fond experience is all delicately and renewingly there, that he wavers; but time and time again he relinquishes or postpones his return. And sometimes he thinks he really will write a letter to his friend who lives in the country.

But he does not do so.

WALTER DE LA MARE

The Almond Tree

My old friend, 'the Count' as we used to call him, made very strange acquaintances at times. Let but a man have plausibility, a point of view, a crotchet, an enthusiasm, he would find in him an eager and exhilarating listener. And though he was often deceived and disappointed in his finds, the Count had a heart proof against lasting disillusionment. I confess, however, that these planetary cronies of his were rather disconcerting at times. And I own that meeting him one afternoon in the busy High Street, with a companion on his arm even more than usually voluble and odd – I own I crossed the road to avoid meeting the pair.

But the Count's eyes had been too sharp for me. He twitted me unmercifully with my snobbishness. 'I am afraid we must have appeared to avoid you to-day,' he said; and received my protestations with contemptuous indifference.

But the next afternoon we took a walk together over the heath; and perhaps the sunshine, something in the first freshness of the May weather, reminded him of bygone days.

'You remember that rather out-of-the-world friend of mine yesterday that so shocked your spruce proprieties, Richard? Well, I'll tell you a story.'

As closely as I can recall this story of the Count's childhood I have related it. I wish, though, I had my old friend's gift for such things; then, perhaps, his story might retain something of the charm in the reading which he gave to it in the telling. Perhaps that charm lies wholly in the memory of his voice, his companionship, his friendship. To revive these, what task would be a burden?...

'The house of my first remembrance, the house that to my last hour on earth will seem home to me, stood in a small green hollow on the verge of a wide heath. Its five upper windows faced far eastwards towards the weathercocked tower of a village which rambled down the steep inclination of a hill. And, walking in its green old garden – ah, Richard, the crocuses, the wallflowers, the violets! – you could see in the evening the standing fields of corn, and the dark furrows where the evening star was stationed; and a little to the south, upon a crest, a rambling wood of fir-trees and bracken.

'The house, the garden, the deep quiet orchard, all had been a wedding gift to my mother from a great-aunt, a very old lady in a kind of turban, whose shrewd eyes used to watch me out of her picture sitting in my high cane chair at meal-times – with not a little keenness; sometimes, I fancied, with a faint derision. Here passed by, to the singing of the lark, and the lamentation of autumn wind and rain, the first long nine of all these heaped-up inextricable years. Even now, my heart leaps up with longing to see again with those untutored eyes the lofty clouds of evening; to hear again as then I heard it the two small notes of the yellow-hammer piping from his green spray. I remember every room of the old house, the steep stairs, the cool apple-scented pantry; I remember the cobbles by the scullery, the well, my old dead raven, the bleak and whistling elms; but best of all I remember the unmeasured splendour of the heath, with its gorse, and its deep canopy of sunny air, the haven of every wild bird of the morning.

'Martha Rodd was a mere prim snippet of a maid then, pale and grave, with large contemplative, Puritan eyes. Mrs Ryder, in her stiff blue martial print and twisted gold brooch, was cook. And besides these, there was only old Thomas the gardener (as out-of-doors and as distantly seen a creature as a dryad); my mother; and that busy-minded little boy, agog in wits and stomach and spirit – myself. For my father seemed but a familiar guest in the house, a guest ever eagerly desired and welcome, but none too eager to remain. He was a dark man with grey eyes and a long chin; a face unusually impassive, unusually mobile. Just as his capricious mood suggested, our little household was dejected or wildly gay. I never shall forget the spirit of delight he could conjure up at a whim, when my mother would go singing up and down stairs, and in her tiny parlour; and Martha in perfect content would prattle endlessly on to the cook, basting the twirling sirloin, while I watched in the firelight. And the long summer evenings too, when my father would find a secret, a magic, a mystery in everything; and we would sit together in the orchard while he told me tales, with the small green apples overhead, and beyond contorted branches, the first golden twilight of the moon.

'It's an old picture now, Richard, but true to the time.

'My father's will, his word, his caprice, his frown, these were the tables of the law in that small household. To my mother he was the very meaning of her life. Only that little boy was in some wise independent, busy, inquisitive, docile, sedate; though urged to a bitterness of secret rebellion at times. In his childhood he experienced such hours of distress as the years do not in mercy bring again to a heart that may analyse as well as remember. Yet there also sank to rest the fountain of life's happiness. In among the gorse bushes were the green mansions of the fairies; along the furrows before his adventurous eyes stumbled crooked gnomes, hopped bewitched robins. Ariel trembled in the sunbeams and glanced from the dewdrops; and he heard the echo of distant and magic waters in the falling of the rain.

'But my father was never long at peace in the house. Nothing satisfied him; he must needs be at an extreme. And if he was compelled to conceal his discontent, there was something so bitter and imperious in his silence, so scornful a sarcasm in his speech, that we could scarcely bear it. And the knowledge of the influence he had over us served only at such times to sharpen his contempt.

'I remember one summer's evening we had been gathering strawberries. I carried a little wicker basket, and went rummaging under the aromatic leaves, calling ever and again my mother to see the "tremenjous" berry I had found. Martha was busy beside me, vexed that her two hands could not serve her master quick enough. And in a wild race with my mother my father helped us pick. At every ripest one he took her in his arms to force it between her lips; and of those pecked by the birds he made a rhymed offering to Pan. And when the sun had descended behind the hill, and the clamour of the rooks had begun to wane in the elm-tops, he took my mother on his arm, and we trooped all together up the long straggling path, and across the grass, carrying our spoil of fruit into the cool dusky corridor. As we passed into the gloaming I saw my mother stoop impulsively and kiss his arm. He brushed off her hand impatiently, and went into his study. I heard the door shut. A moment afterwards he called for candles. And, looking on those two other faces in the twilight, I knew with the intuition of childhood that he was suddenly sick to death of us all; and I knew that my mother shared my intuition. She sat down, and I beside her, in her little parlour, and took up her sewing. But her face had lost again all its girlishness as she bent her head over the white linen.

'I think she was happier when my father was away; for then, free from anxiety to be for ever pleasing his variable moods, she could entertain herself with hopes and preparations for his return. There was a little summer-house, or arbour, in the garden, where she would sit alone, while the swallows coursed in the evening air. Sometimes, too, she would take me for a long walk, listening distantly to my chatter, only, I think, that she might entertain the pleasure of supposing that my father might have returned home unforeseen, and be even now waiting to greet us. But these fancies would forsake her. She would speak harshly and coldly to me, and scold Martha for her owlishness, and find nothing but vanity and mockery in all that but a little while since had been her daydream.

'I think she rarely knew where my father stayed in his long absences from home. He would remain with us for a week, and neglect us for a month. She was too proud, and when he was himself, too happy and hopeful to question him, and he seemed to delight in keeping his affairs secret from her. Indeed, he sometimes appeared to pretend a mystery where none was, and to endeavour in all things to make his character and conduct appear quixotic and inexplicable.

'So time went on. Yet, it seemed, as each month passed by, the house was not so merry and happy as before; something was fading and vanishing that would not return; estrangement had pierced a little deeper. I think care at last put out of my mother's mind even the semblance of her former gaiety. She sealed up her heart lest love should break forth anew into the bleakness.

'On Guy Fawkes' Day Martha told me at bedtime that a new household had moved into the village on the other side of the heath. After that my father stayed away from us but seldom.

'At first my mother showed her pleasure in a thousand ways, with dainties of her own fancy and cooking, with ribbons in her dark hair, with new songs (though she had but a small thin voice). She read to please him; and tired my legs out in useless errands in his service. And a word of praise sufficed her for many hours of difficulty. But by and by, when evening after evening was spent by my father away from home, she began to be uneasy and depressed; and though she made no complaint, her anxious face, the incessant interrogation of her eyes vexed and irritated him beyond measure.

' "Where does my father go after dinner?" I asked Martha one night, when my mother was in my bedroom, folding my clothes.

' " How dare you ask such a question?" said my mother,

"and how dare you talk to the child about your master's comings and goings?"

' "But where does he?" I repeated to Martha, when my mother was gone out of the room.

' "Ssh now, Master Nicholas," she answered, "didn't you hear what your mamma said? She's vexed, poor lady, at master's never spending a whole day at home, but nothing but them cards, cards, cards, every night at Mr Grey's. Why, often it's twelve and one in the morning when I've heard his foot on the gravel beneath the window. But there, I'll be bound, she doesn't *mean* to speak unkindly. It's a terrible scourge is jealousy, Master Nicholas; and not generous or manly to give it cause. Mrs Ryder was kept a widow all along of jealousy, and but a week before her wedding with her second."

' "But why is Mother jealous of my father playing cards?"

'Martha slipped my nightgown over my head. "Ssh, Master Nicholas, little boys mustn't ask so many questions. And I hope when you are grown up to be a man, my dear, you will be a comfort to your mother. She needs it, poor soul, and sakes alive, just now of all times!" I looked inquisitively into Martha's face; but she screened my eyes with her hand; and instead of further questions, I said my prayers to her.

'A few days after this I was sitting with my mother in her parlour, holding her grey worsted for her to wind, when my father entered the room and bade me put on my hat and muffler. "He is going to pay a call with me," he explained curtly. As I went out of the room, I heard my mother's question, "To your friends at the Grange, I suppose?"

' "You may suppose whatever you please," he answered. I heard my mother rise to leave the room, but he called her back and the door was shut. . . .

'The room in which the card-players sat was very low-ceiled. A piano stood near the window, a rosewood table with a fine dark crimson work-basket upon it by the fireside, and some little distance away, a green card-table with candles burning. Mr Grey was a slim, elegant man, with a high, narrow forehead and long fingers. Major Aubrey was a short, red-faced, rather taciturn man. There was also a younger man with fair hair. They seemed to be on the best of terms together; and I helped to pack the cards and to pile the silver coins, sipping a glass of sherry with Mr Grey. My father said little, paying me no attention, but playing gravely with a very slight frown.

'After some little while the door opened, and a lady appeared. This was Mr Grey's sister, Jane, I learned. She seated herself at her work-table, and drew me to her side.

'"Well, so this is Nicholas!" she said. "Or is it Nick?"

'"Nicholas," I said.

'"Of course," she said, smiling, "and I like that too, much the best. How very kind of you to come to see me! It was to keep *me* company, you know, because I am very stupid at games, but I love talking. Do you?"

'I looked into her eyes, and knew we were friends. She smiled again, with open lips, and touched my mouth with her thimble. "Now, let me see, business first, and – me afterwards. You see I have three different kinds of cake, because, I thought, I cannot in the least tell which kind he'll like best. Could I now? Come, you shall choose."

'She rose and opened the long door of a narrow cupboard, looking towards the card-players as she stooped. I remember the cakes to this day; little oval shortbreads stamped with a beehive, custards and mince-pies; and a great glass jar of goodies which I carried in both arms round the little square table. I took a mince-pie, and sat down on a footstool near by Miss Grey, and she talked to me while she worked with slender hands at her lace embroidery. I told her how old I was; about my great-aunt and her three cats. I told her my dreams, and that I was very fond of Yorkshire pudding, "from under the meat, you know". And I told her I thought my father the handsomest man I had ever seen.

' "What, handsomer than Mr Spencer?' she said laughing, looking along her needle.

'I answered that I did not very much like clergymen.

' "And why?" she said gravely.

' "Because they do not talk like real," I said.

'She laughed very gaily. "Do men ever?" she said.

'And her voice was so quiet and so musical, her neck so graceful, I thought her a very beautiful lady, admiring especially her dark eyes when she smiled brightly and yet half sadly at me; I promised, moreover, that if she would meet me on the heath, I would show her the rabbit warren and the "Miller's Pool".

' "Well, Jane, and what do you think of my son?" said my father when we were about to leave.

'She bent over me and squeezed a lucky fourpenny-piece into my hand. "I love fourpence, pretty little fourpence, I love fourpence better than my life," she whispered into my ear. "But that's a secret," she added, glancing up over her shoulder. She kissed lightly the top of my head. I was looking at my father while she was caressing me, and I fancied a faint sneer passed over his face. But when we had come out of the village on to the heath, in the bare keen night, as we walked along the path together between the gorse-bushes, now on turf, and now on stony ground, never before had he seemed so wonderful a companion. He told me little stories; he began a hundred, and finished none; yet with the stars above us, they seemed a string of beads all of bright colours. We stood still in the vast darkness, while he whistled that strangest of all old songs – "the Song the Sirens sang". He pilfered my wits and talked like my double. But when – how much too quickly, I thought with sinking heart – we were come to the house-gates, he suddenly fell silent, turned an instant, and stared far away over the windy heath.

' "How weary, flat, stale—" he began, and broke off between uneasy laughter and a sigh. "Listen to me, Nicholas," he said, lifting my face to the starlight, "you must grow up a man – a Man, you understand; no vapourings, no posings, no caprices; and above all, no sham. No sham. It's your one and only chance in this unfaltering Scheme." He scanned my face long and closely. "You have your mother's eyes," he said musingly. "And that," he added under his breath, "*that's* no joke." He pushed open the squealing gate and we went in.

'My mother was sitting in a low chair before a dying and cheerless fire.

' "Well, Nick," she said very suavely, "and how have you enjoyed your evening?"

'I stared at her without answer. "Did you play cards with the gentlemen; or did you turn over the music?"

' "I talked to Miss Grey," I said.

' "Really,' said my mother, raising her eyebrows, "and who then is Miss Grey?" My father was smiling at us with sparkling eyes.

' "Mr Grey's sister," I answered in a low voice.

' "Not his wife, then?" said my mother, glancing furtively at the fire. I looked towards my father in doubt but could lift my eyes no higher than his knees.

' "You little fool!" he said to my mother with a laugh, "what a sharpshooter! Never mind, Sir Nick; there, run off to bed, my man."

'My mother caught me roughly by the sleeve as I was passing her chair. "Aren't you going to kiss me good night, then," she said furiously, her narrow under-lip quivering, "you too!" I kissed her cheek. "That's right, my dear," she said scornfully, "that's how little fishes kiss." She rose and drew back her skirts. "I refuse to stay in the room," she said haughtily, and with a sob she hurried out.

'My father continued to smile, but only a smile it seemed gravity had forgotten to smooth away. He stood very still, so still that I grew afraid he must certainly hear me thinking. Then with a kind of sigh he sat down at my mother's writing table, and scribbled a few words with his pencil on a slip of paper.

' "There, Nicholas, just tap at your mother's door with that. Good night, old fellow." He took my hand and smiled down into my eyes with a kind of generous dark appeal that called me straight to his side. I hastened conceitedly upstairs, and delivered my message. My mother was crying when she opened the door.

' "Well?" she said in a low, trembling voice.

'But presently afterwards, while I was still lingering in the dark corridor, I heard her run down quickly, and in a while my father and mother came upstairs together, arm in arm, and by her light talk and laughter you might suppose she had no knowledge of care or trouble at all.

'Never afterwards did I see so much gaiety and youthfulness in my mother's face as when she sat next morning with us at breakfast. The honeycomb, the small bronze chrysanthemums, her yellow gown seemed dainty as a miniature. With every word her eyes would glance covertly at my father; her smile, as it were, hesitating between her lashes. She was so light and girlish and so versatile I should scarcely have recognized the weary and sallow face of the night before. My father seemed to find as much pleasure, or relief, in her good spirits as I did; and to delight in exercising his ingenuity to quicken her humour.

'It was but a transient morning of sunshine, however, and as the brief and sombre day waned, its gloom pervaded the house. In the evening my father left us to our solitude as usual. And that night was very misty over the heath, with a small, warm rain falling.

'So it happened that I began to be left more and more to my own devices, and grew so inured at last to my own narrow company and small thoughts and cares, that I began to look on my mother's unhappiness almost with indifference, and learned to criticize almost before I had learned to pity. And so I do not think I enjoyed Christmas very much the less, although my father was away from home and all our little festivities were dispirited. I had plenty of good things to eat, and presents, and a picture-book from Martha. I had a new rocking-horse – how changeless and impassive its mottled battered face looks out at me across the years! It was brisk, clear weather, and on St Stephen's Day I went to see if there was any ice yet on the Miller's Pool.

'I was stooping down at the extreme edge of the pool, snapping the brittle splinters of the ice with my finger, when I heard a voice calling me in the still air. It was Jane Grey, walking on the heath with my father, who had called me having seen me from a distance stooping beside the water.

' "So you see I have kept my promise," she said, taking my hand.

' "But you promised to come by yourself," I said.

' "Well, so I will then," she answered, nodding her head. "Good-bye," she added, turning to my father. "It's three's none, you see. Nicholas shall take me home to tea, and you can call for him in the evening, if you will; that is, if you are coming."

' "Are you asking me to come?" he said moodily, "do you care whether I come or not?"

'She lifted her face and spoke gravely. "You are my friend," she said, "of course I care whether you are with me or not." He scrutinized her through half-closed lids. His face was haggard, gloomy with *ennui*. "How you harp on the word, you punctilious Jane. Do you suppose I am still in my teens? Twenty years ago, now— It amuses me to hear you women talk. It's little you ever really feel."

' "I don't think I am quite without feeling," she replied, "you are a little difficult, you know."

' "Difficult," he echoed in derision. He checked himself and shrugged his shoulders. "You see, Jane, it's all on the surface; I boast of my indifference. It's the one rag of philosophy age denies no one. It is so easy to be mock-heroic – debonair, iron-grey, rhetorical, dramatic – you know it only too well, perhaps? But after all, life's comedy, when one stops smiling, is only the tepidest farce. Or the gilt wears off and the pinchbeck tragedy shows through. And so, as I say, we talk on, being past feeling. One by one our hopes come home to roost, our delusions find themselves out, and the mystery proves to be nothing but sleight-of-hand. It's age, my dear Jane – age; it turns one to stone. With you young people life's a dream; ask Nicholas here!" He shrugged his shoulders, adding under his breath, "But one wakes on a devilish hard pallet."

' "Of course," said Jane slowly, "you are only talking cleverly, and then it does not matter whether it's true or not, I suppose. I can't say. I don't think you mean it, and so it comes to nothing. I can't and won't believe you feel so little – I can't." She continued to smile, yet, I fancied, with the brightness of tears in her eyes. "It's all mockery and make-believe; we are not the miserable slaves of time you try to fancy. There must be some way to win through." She turned away, then added slowly, "You ask me to be fearless, sincere, to speak my heart; I wonder, do you?"

'My father did not look at her, appeared not to have seen the hand she had half held out to him, and as swiftly withdrawn. "The truth is, Jane," he said slowly, "I am past sincerity now. And as for *heart* it is a quite discredited organ at forty. Life, thought, selfishness, egotism, call it what you will; they have all done their worst with me; and I really haven't the sentiment to pretend that they haven't. And when bright youth and sentiment are gone; why, go too, dear lady! Existence proves nothing but brazen inanity afterwards. But there's always that turning left to the dullest and dustiest road – oblivion." He remained silent a moment. Silence deep and strange lay all around us. The air was still, the winter sky unutterably calm. And again that low dispassionate voice continued: "It's only when right seems too easy a thing, too trivial, and not worth the doing; and wrong a foolish thing – too dull. . . . There, take care of her, Nicholas; take care of her, 'snips and snails', you know. *Au revoir*, 'pon my word, I almost wish it was good-bye."

'Jane Grey regarded him attentively. "So then do I," she replied in a low voice, "for I shall never understand you; perhaps I should hate to understand you."

'My father turned with an affected laugh, and left us.

194

'Miss Grey and I walked slowly along beside the frosty bulrushes until we came to the wood. The bracken and heather were faded. The earth was dark and rich with autumnal rains. Fir-cones lay on the moss beneath the dark green branches. It was all now utterly silent in the wintry afternoon. Far away rose tardily, and alighted, the hoarse rooks upon the ploughed earth; high in the pale sky passed a few on ragged wing.

' "What does my father mean by wishing it was good-bye?" I said.

'But my companion did not answer me in words. She clasped my hand; she seemed very slim and gracious walking by my side on the hardened ground. My mother was small now and awkward beside her in my imagination. I questioned her about the ice, about the red sky, and if there was any mistletoe in the woods. Sometimes she, in turn, asked me questions too, and when I answered them we would look at each other and smile, and it seemed it was with her as it was with me – of the pure gladness I found in her company. In the middle of our walk to the Thorns she bent down in the cold twilight, and putting her hands on my shoulders, "My dear, dear Nicholas," she said, "you must be a good son to your mother – brave and kind; will you?"

' "He hardly ever speaks to Mother now," I answered instinctively.

'She pressed her lips to my cheek, and her cheek was cold against mine, and she clasped her arms about me. "Kiss me," she said. "We must do our best, mustn't we?" she pleaded, still holding me. I looked mournfully into the gathering darkness. "That's easy when you're grown up," I said. She laughed and kissed me again, and then we took hands and ran till we were out of breath, towards the distant lights of the Thorns. . . .

'I had been some time in bed, lying awake in the warmth, when my mother came softly through the darkness into my room. She sat down at the bedside, breathing hurriedly. "Where have you been all the evening?" she said.

' "Miss Grey asked me to stay to tea," I answered.

' "Did I give you permission to go to tea with Miss Grey?"

'I made no answer.

' "If you go to that house again, I shall beat you. You hear me, Nicholas? Alone, or with your father, if you go there again, without my permission, I shall beat you. You have not been whipped for a long time, have you?" I could not see her face, but her head was bent towards me in the dark, as she sat – almost crouched – on my bed-side.

'I made no answer. But when my mother had gone, without kissing me, I cried noiselessly on into my pillow. Something had suddenly flown out of memory, never to sing again. Life had become a little colder and stranger. I had always been my own chief company; now another sentimental barrier had arisen between the world and me, past its heedlessness, past my understanding to break down.

'Hardly a week passed now without some bitter quarrel. I seemed to be perpetually stealing out of sound of angry voices; fearful of being made the butt of my father's serene taunts, of my mother's passions and desperate remorse. He disdained to defend himself against her, never reasoned with her; he merely shrugged his shoulders, denied her charges, ignored her anger; coldly endeavouring only to show his indifference, to conceal by every means in his power his own inward weariness and vexation. I saw this, of course, only vaguely, yet with all a child's certainty of insight, though I rarely knew the cause of my misery; and I continued to love them both in my selfish fashion, not a whit the less.

'At last, on St Valentine's Day, things came to a worse pass than ever. It had always been my father's custom to hang my mother a valentine on the handle of her little parlour door, a string of pearls, a fan, a book of poetry, whatever it might be. She came down early this morning, and sat in the window-seat, looking out at the falling snow. She said nothing at breakfast, only feigned to eat, lifting her eyes at intervals to glance at my father with a strange intensity, as if of hatred, tapping her foot on the floor. He took no notice of her, sat quiet and moody with his own thoughts. I think he had not really forgotten the day, for I found long afterwards in his old bureau a bracelet purchased but a week before with her name written on a scrap of paper, inside the case. Yet it seemed to be the absence of this little gift that had driven my mother beyond reason.

'Towards evening, tired of the house, tired of being alone, I went out and played for a while listlessly in the snow. At nightfall I went in; and in the dark heard angry voices. My father came out of the dining-room and looked at me in silence, standing in the gloom of the wintry dusk. My mother followed him. I can see her now, leaning in the doorway, white with rage, her eyes ringed and darkened with continuous trouble, her hand trembling.

' "It shall learn to hate you," she cried in a low, dull voice. "I will teach it every moment to hate and despise you as I— Oh, *I* hate and despise you."

'My father looked at her calmly and profoundly before replying. He took up a cloth hat and brushed it with his hand. "Very well then, you have chosen," he said coldly. "It has always lain with you. You have exaggerated, you have raved, and now you have said what can never be recalled or forgotten. Here's Nicholas. Pray do not imagine, however, that I am defending myself. I have nothing to defend. I think of no one but myself – no one. Endeavour to understand me, no one. Perhaps, indeed, you yourself – no more than— But words again – the dull old round!" He made a peculiar gesture with his hand. "Well, life is . . . ach! I have done. So be it." He stood looking out of the door. "You see, it's snowing," he said, as if to himself.

'All the long night before and all day long, snow had been falling continuously. The air was wintry and cold. I could discern nothing beyond the porch but a gloomy accumulation of cloud in the twilight air, now darkened with the labyrinthine motion of the snow. My father glanced back for an instant into the house, and, as I fancy, regarded me with a kind of strange, close earnestness. But he went out and his footsteps were instantly silenced.

'My mother peered at me in a dreadful perplexity, her eyes wide with terror and remorse. "What? What?" she said. I stared at her stupidly. Three snowflakes swiftly and airily floated together into the dim hall from the gloom without. She clasped her hand over her mouth. Overburdened her fingers seemed to be, so slender were they, with her many rings.

' "Nicholas, Nicholas, tell me; what was I saying? What was I saying?" She stumbled hastily to the door. "Arthur, Arthur," she cried from the porch, "it's St Valentine's Day. That was all I meant; come back, come back!" But perhaps my father was already out of hearing; I do not think he made any reply.

'My mother came in doubtfully, resting her hand on the wall. And she walked very slowly and laboriously upstairs. While I was standing at the foot of the staircase, looking out across the hall into the evening, Martha climbed primly up from the kitchen with her lighted taper, shut-to the door and lit the hall lamp. Already the good smell of the feast cooking floated up from the kitchen, and gladdened my spirits. "Will he come back?" Martha said, looking very scared in the light of her taper. "It's such a fall of snow, already it's a hand's breadth on the windowsill. Oh, Master Nicholas, it's a hard world for us women." She followed my mother upstairs, carrying light to all the gloomy upper rooms.

'I sat down in the window-seat of the dining-room, and read in my picture-book as well as I could by the flamelight. By and by, Martha returned to lay the table.

'As far back as brief memory carried me, it had been our custom to make a Valentine's feast on the Saint's day. This was my father's mother's birthday also. When she was alive I well remember her. visiting us with her companion, Miss Schreiner, who talked in such good-humoured

English to me. This same anniversary had last year brought about a tender reconciliation between my father and mother, after a quarrel that meant how little then. And I remember on this day to have seen the first fast-sealed buds upon the almond tree. We would have a great spangled cake in the middle of the table, with marzipan and comfits, just as at Christmas-time. And when Mrs Merry lived in the village, her little fair daughters used to come in a big carriage to spend the evening with us and to share my Valentine's feast.

'But all this was changed now. My wits were sharper, but I was none the less only the duller for that; my hopes and dreams had a little fallen and faded. I looked idly at my picture-book, vaguely conscious that its colours pleased me less than once upon a time; that I was rather tired of seeing them, and they just as tired of seeing me. And yet I had nothing else to do, so I must go on with a hard face, turning listlessly the pictured pages.

'About seven o'clock my mother sent for me. I found her sitting in her bedroom. Candles were burning before the looking-glass. She was already dressed in her handsome black silk gown, and wearing her pearl necklace. She began to brush my hair, curling its longer ends with her fingers, which she moistened in the pink bowl that was one of the first things I had set eyes on in this world. She put me on a clean blouse and my buckle shoes, talking to me the while, almost as if she were telling me a story. Then she looked at herself long and earnestly in the glass; throwing up her chin with a smile, as was a habit of hers in talk. I wandered about the room, fingering the little toilet-boxes and nick-nacks on the table. By mischance I upset one of these, a scent-bottle that held rose-water. The water ran out and filled the warm air with its fragrance. "You foolish, clumsy boy!" said my mother, and slapped my hand. More out of vexation and tiredness than because of the pain, I began to cry. And then, with infinite tenderness, she leaned her head on my shoulder. "Mother can't think very well just now," she said; and cried so bitterly in silence that I was only too ready to extricate myself and run away when her hold on me relaxed.

'I climbed slowly upstairs to Martha's bedroom, and kneeling on a cane chair looked out of the window. The flakes had ceased to fall now, although the snowy heath was encompassed in mist. Above the snow the clouds had parted, drifting from beneath the stars, and these in their constellations were trembling very brightly, and here and there burned one of them in solitude, larger and wilder in its radiance than the rest. But though I did not tire of looking out of the window, my knees began to ache; and the little room was very cold and still so near the roof. So I went down to the dining-room, with all its seven candlesticks kindled, seeming to my unaccustomed eyes a very splendid blaze out of the dark. My mother was kneeling on the rug by the fireside. She looked very small, even dwarfish, I thought. She was gazing into the flames; one shoe curved beneath the hem of her gown, her chin resting on her hand.

'I surveyed the table with its jellies and sweetmeats and glasses and fruit, and began to be very hungry, so savoury was the smell of the turkey roasting downstairs. Martha knocked at the door when the clock had struck eight.

' "Dinner is ready, ma'am."

'My mother glanced fleetingly at the clock. "Just a little, only a very little while longer, tell Mrs Ryder; your master will be home in a minute." She rose and placed the claret in the hearth at some distance from the fire.

' "Is it nicer warm, Mother?" I said. She looked at me with startled eyes and nodded. "Did you hear anything, Nicholas? Run to the door and listen; was that a sound of footsteps?"

'I opened the outer door and peered into the darkness; but it seemed the world ended here with the warmth and the light: beyond could extend only winter and silence, a region that, familiar though it was to me, seemed now to terrify me like an enormous sea.

' "It's stopped snowing," I said, "but there isn't anybody there; nobody at all, Mother."

'The hours passed heavily from quarter on to quarter. The turkey, I grieved to hear, was to be taken out of the oven, and put away to cool in the pantry. I was bidden help myself to what I pleased of the trembling jellies, and delicious pink blanc-mange. Already midnight would be the next hour to be chimed. I felt sick, yet was still hungry and very tired. The candles began to burn low. "Leave me a little light here, then," my mother said at last to Martha, "and go to bed. Perhaps your master has missed his way home in the snow." But Mrs Ryder had followed Martha into the room.

' "You must pardon my interference, ma'am, but it isn't right, it isn't really right of you to sit up longer. Master will not come back, maybe, before morning. And I shouldn't be doing my bounden duty, ma'am, except I spoke my mind. Just now too, of all times."

' "Thank you very much, Mrs Ryder," my mother answered simply, "but I would prefer not to go to bed yet. It's very lonely on the heath at night. But I shall not want anything else, thank you."

' "Well, ma'am, I've had my say, and done my conscience's bidding. And I have brought you up this tumbler of mulled wine; else you'll be sinking away or something with the fatigue."

'My mother took the wine, sipped of it with a wan smile at Mrs Ryder over the brim; and Mrs Ryder retired with Martha. I don't think they had noticed me sitting close in the shadow on my stool beside the table. But all through that long night, I fancy, these good souls took it in turn to creep down stealthily and look in on us; and in the small hours of the morning, when the fire had fallen low, they must have wrapped us both warm in shawls. They left me then, I think, to be my mother's company. Indeed, I remember we spoke in the darkness, and she took my hand.

'My mother and I shared the steaming wine together

when they were gone; our shadows looming faintly huge upon the ceiling. We said very little, but I looked softly into her grey childish eyes, and we kissed one another kneeling there together before the fire. And afterwards, I jigged softly round the table, pilfering whatever sweet or savoury mouthful took my fancy. But by and by in the silent house – a silence broken only by the fluttering of the flames, and the odd far-away stir of the frost, drowsiness vanquished me; I sat down by the fireside, leaning my head on a chair. And sitting thus, vaguely eyeing firelight and wavering shadow, I began to nod, and very soon dream stalked in, mingling with reality.

'It was early morning when I awoke, dazed and cold and miserable in my uncomfortable resting-place. The rare odour of frost was on the air. The ashes of the fire lay iron-grey upon the cold hearth. An intensely clear white ray of light leaned up through a cranny of the shutters to the cornice of the ceiling. I got up with difficulty. My mother was still asleep, breathing heavily, and as I stooped, regarding her curiously, I could almost watch her transient dreams fleeting over her face; and now she smiled faintly; and now she raised her eyebrows as if in some playful and happy talk with my father; then again utterly still darkness would descend on brow and lid and lip.

'I touched her sleeve, suddenly conscious of my loneliness in the large house. Her face clouded instantly, she sighed profoundly. "What?" she said, "nothing – nothing?" She stretched out her hand towards me; the lids drew back from eyes still blind from sleep. But gradually time regained its influence over her. She moistened her lips and turned to me, and suddenly, in a gush of agony, remembrance of the night returned to her. She hid her face in her hands, rocking her body gently to and fro; then rose and smoothed back her hair at the looking-glass. I was surprised to see no trace of tears on her cheeks. Her lips moved, as if unconsciously a heart worn out with grief addressed that pale reflection of her sorrow in the glass. I took hold of the hand that hung down listlessly on her silk skirt, and fondled it, kissing punctiliously each loose ring in turn.

'But I do not think she heeded my kisses. So I returned to the table on which was still set out the mockery of our Valentine feast, strangely disenchanted in the chill dusk of daybreak. I put a handful of wine biscuits and a broken piece of cake in my pocket; for a determination had taken me to go out on to the heath. My heart beat thick and fast in imagination of the solitary snow and of myself wandering in loneliness across its untrampled surface. A project also was forming in my mind of walking over to the Thorns; for somehow I knew my mother would not scold or punish me that day. Perhaps, I thought, my father would be there. And I would tell Miss Grey all about my adventure of the night spent down in the dining-room. So moving very stealthily, and betraying no eagerness, lest I should be forbidden to go, I stole at length unnoticed from the room, and leaving the great hall door ajar, ran out joyously into the wintry morning.

'Already dawn was clear and high in the sky, already the first breezes were moving in the mists; and breathed chill, as if it were the lingering darkness itself on my cheeks. The air was cold, yet with a fresh faint sweetness. The snow lay crisp across its perfect surface, mounded softly over the gorse-bushes, though here and there a spray of parched blossom yet protruded from its cowl. Flaky particles of ice floated invisible in the air. I called out with pleasure to see the little ponds where the snow had been blown away from the black ice. I saw on the bushes too the webs of spiders stretched from thorn to thorn, and festooned with crystals of hoar-frost. I turned and counted as far as I could my footsteps leading back to the house, which lay roofed in gloomy pallor, dim and obscured in the darkened west.

'A waning moon that had risen late in the night shone, it seemed, very near to the earth. But every moment light swept invincibly in, pouring its crystal like a river; and darkness sullenly withdrew into the north. And when at last the sun appeared, glittering along the rosy snow, I turned in an ecstasy and with my finger pointed him out, as if the house I had left behind me might view him with my own delight. Indeed, I saw its windows transmuted, and heard afar a thrush pealing in the bare branches of a pear-tree; and a robin startled me, so suddenly shrill and sweet he broke into song from a snowy tuft of gorse.

'I was now come to the beginning of a gradual incline, from the summit of which I should presently descry in the distance the avenue of lindens that led towards the village from the margin of the heath. As I went on my way, munching my biscuits, looking gaily about me, I brooded deliciously on the breakfast which Miss Grey would doubtless sit me down to; and almost forgot the occasion of my errand, and the troubled house I had left behind me. At length I climbed to the top of the smooth ridge and looked down. At a little distance from me grew a crimson hawthorn-tree that often in past Aprils I had used for a green tent from the showers; but now it was closely hooded, darkening with its faint shadow the long expanse of unshadowed whiteness. Not very far from this bush I perceived a figure lying stretched along the snow and knew instinctively that this was my father lying here.

'The sight did not then surprise or dismay me. It seemed only the lucid sequel to that long heavy night-watch, to all the troubles and perplexities of the past. I felt no sorrow, but stood beside the body, regarding it only with deep wonder and a kind of earnest curiosity, yet perhaps with a remote pity too, that he could not see me in the beautiful morning. His grey hand lay arched in the snow, his darkened face, on which showed a smear of dried blood, was turned away a little as if out of the oblique sunshine. I understood that he was dead, and had already begun speculating on what changes it would make; how I should spend my time; what would happen in the house now that he was gone, his influence, his authority, his discord. I remembered too that I was alone, was master of this immense secret, that I must go home sedately, as if it were a Sunday, and in a low voice tell my mother, concealing any exultation I might feel in the office. I imagined the questions that would be asked me, and was considering the proper answers to make to them, when my morbid dreams were suddenly broken in on by Martha Rodd. She stood in my footsteps, looking down on me from the ridge from which I had but just now descended. She hastened towards me, stooping a little as if she were carrying a heavy bundle, her mouth ajar, her forehead wrinkled beneath its wispy light brown hair.

' "Look, Martha, look," I cried, "I found him in the snow; he's dead." And suddenly a bond seemed to snap in my heart. The beauty and solitude of the morning, the perfect whiteness of the snow – it was all an uncouth mockery against me – a subtle and quiet treachery. The tears gushed into my eyes and in my fear and affliction I clung to the poor girl, sobbing bitterly, protesting my grief, hiding my eyes in terror from that still, inscrutable shape. She smoothed my hair with her hand again and again, her eyes fixed; and then at last, venturing cautiously nearer, she stooped over my father. "O Master Nicholas," she said, "his poor dark hair! What will we do now? What will your poor mamma do now, and him gone?" She hid her face in her hands, and our tears gushed out anew.

'But my grief was speedily forgotten. The novelty of being left entirely alone, my own master; to go where I would; to do as I pleased; the experience of being pitied most when I least needed it, and then – when misery and solitariness came over me like a cloud – of being utterly ignored, turned my thoughts gradually away. My father's body was brought home and laid in my mother's little parlour that looked out on to the garden and the snowy orchard. The house was darkened. I took a secret pleasure in peeping in on the sunless rooms, and stealing from door to door through corridors screened from the daylight. My mother was ill; and for some inexplicable reason I connected her illness with the bevy of gentlemen dressed in black who came one morning to the house and walked away together over the heath. Finally Mrs Marshall drove up one afternoon from Islington, and by the bundles she had brought with her and her grained box with the iron handles I knew that she was come, as once before in my experience, to stay.

'I was playing on the morrow in the hall with my leaden soldiers when there came into my mind vaguely the voices of Mrs Ryder and of Mrs Marshall gossiping together on their tedious way upstairs from the kitchen.

' "No, Mrs Marshall, nothing," I heard Mrs Ryder saying, "not one word, not one word. And now the poor dear lady left quite alone, and only the doctor to gainsay that fatherless mite from facing the idle inquisitive questions of all them strangers. It's neither for me nor you, Mrs Marshall, to speak out just what comes into our heads here and now. The ways of the Almighty are past understanding – but a kinder at *heart* never trod this earth."

' "Ah," said Mrs Marshall.

' "I knew to my sorrow," continued Mrs Ryder, "there was words in the house; but there, wheresoever you be there's that. Human beings ain't angels, married or single, and in every—"

' "Wasn't there talk of some—?" insinuated Mrs Marshall discreetly.

' "Talk, Mrs Marshall," said Mrs Ryder, coming to a standstill, "I scorn the word! A pinch of truth in a hogshead of falsehood. I don't gainsay it even. I just shut my ears – there – with the dead." Mrs Marshall had opened her mouth to reply when I was discovered, crouched as small as possible at the foot of the stairs.

' "Well, here's pitchers!" said Mrs Marshall pleasantly. "And this is the poor fatherless manikin, I suppose. It's hard on the innocent, Mrs Ryder, and him grown such a sturdy child too, as I said from the first. Well, now, and don't you remember me, little man, don't you remember Mrs Marshall? He ought to, now!"

' "He's a very good boy in general," said Mrs Ryder, "and I'm sure I hope and pray he'll grow up to be a comfort to his poor widowed mother, if so be—" They glanced earnestly at one another, and Mrs Marshall stooped with a sigh of effort and drew a big leather purse from a big loose pocket under her skirt, and selected a bright ha'penny-piece from among its silver and copper.

' "I make no doubt he will, poor mite," she said cheerfully; I took the ha'penny in silence and the two women passed slowly upstairs.

'In the afternoon, in order to be beyond call of Martha, I went out on to the heath with a shovel, intent on building a great tomb in the snow. Yet more snow had fallen during the night; it now lay so deep as to cover my socks above my shoes. I laboured very busily, shovelling, beating, moulding, stamping. So intent was I that I did not see Miss Grey until she was close beside me. I looked up from the snow and was surprised to find the sun already set and the low mists of evening approaching. Miss Grey was veiled and dressed in furs to the throat. She drew her ungloved hand from her muff.

' "Nicholas," she said in a low voice.

'I stood for some reason confused and ashamed without answering her. She sat down on my shapeless mound of snow, and took me by the hand. Then she drew up her veil, and I saw her face pale and darkened, and her clear dark eyes gravely gazing into mine.

' "My poor, poor Nicholas," she said, and continued to gaze at me with her warm hand clasping mine. "What can I say? What can I do? Isn't it very, very lonely out here in the snow?"

' "I didn't feel lonely much," I answered, "I was making a – I was playing at building."

' "And I am sitting on your beautiful snow-house, then?" she said, smiling sadly, her hand trembling upon mine.

' "It isn't a house," I answered, turning away.

'She pressed my hand on the furs at her throat.

' "Poor cold, blue hands," she said. "Do you like playing alone?"

' "I like you being here," I answered. "I wish you would come always, or at least sometimes."

'She drew me close to her, smiling, and bent and kissed my head.

' "There," she said, "I am here now."

' "Mother's ill," I said.

'She drew back and looked out over the heath towards the house.

' "They have put my father in the little parlour, in his coffin, of course; you know he's dead, and Mrs Marshall's come; she gave me a ha'penny this morning. Dr Graham gave me a whole crown, though." I took it out of my breeches pocket and showed it her.

' "That's very, very nice," she said. "What lots of nice things you can buy with it! And, look, I am going to give you a little keepsake too, between just you and me."

'It was a small silver box that she drew out of her muff, and embossed in the silver of the lid was a crucifix. "I thought, perhaps, I should see you to-day, you know," she continued softly. "Now, who's given you this?" she said, putting the box into my hand.

' "You," I answered softly.

' "And who am I?"

' "Miss Grey," I said.

' "Your friend, Jane Grey," she repeated, as if she were fascinated by the sound of her own name. "Say it now— Always my friend, Jane Grey."

'I repeated it after her.

' "And now," she continued, "tell me which room is – is the little parlour. Is it that small window at the corner under the ivy?"

'I shook my head.

' "Which?" she said in a whisper, after a long pause.

'I twisted my shovel in the snow. "Would you like to see my father?" I asked her. "I am sure, you know, Martha would not mind; and Mother's in bed." She started, her dark eyes dwelling strangely on mine. "But Nicholas, you poor lamb; where?" she said, without stirring.

' "It's at the back, a little window that comes out — if you were to come this evening, I would be playing in the hall; I always play in the hall, after tea, if I can; and now, always. Nobody would see you at all, you know."

'She sighed. "O what are you saying?" she said, and stood up, drawing down her veil.

' "But would you like to?" I repeated. She stooped suddenly, pressing her veiled face to mine. "I'll come, I'll come," she said, her face utterly changed so close to my eyes. "We can both still — still be loyal to him, can't we, Nicholas?"

'She walked away quickly, towards the pool and the little darkened wood. I looked after her and knew that she would be waiting there alone till evening. I looked at my silver box with great satisfaction, and after opening it, put it into my pocket with my crown piece and my ha'penny, and continued my building for awhile.

'But now zest for it was gone; and I began to feel cold, the frost closing in keenly as darkness gathered. So I went home.

'My silence and suspicious avoidance of scrutiny and question passed unnoticed. Indeed, I ate my tea in solitude, except that now and again one or other of the women would come bustling in on some brief errand. A peculiar suppressed stir was in the house. I wondered what could be the cause of it; and began suddenly to be afraid of my project being discovered.

'None the less I was playing in the evening, as I had promised, close to the door, alert to catch the faintest sign of the coming of my visitor.

' "Run down to the kitchen, dearie," said Martha. Her cheeks were flushed. She was carrying a big can of steaming water. "You must keep very, *very* quiet this evening and go to bed like a good boy, and perhaps to-morrow morning I'll tell you a great, great secret." She kissed me with hasty rapture. I was not especially inquisitive of her secret just then, and eagerly promised to be quite quiet if I might continue to play where I was.

' "Well, very, *very* quiet then, and you mustn't let Mrs Marshall," she began, but hurried hastily away in answer to a peremptory summons from upstairs.

'Almost as soon as she was gone I heard a light tap on the door. It seemed that Jane Grey had brought in with her the cold and freshness of the woods. I led the way on tiptoe down the narrow corridor and into the small, silent room. The candles burned pure and steadfastly in their brightness. The air was still and languid with the perfume of flowers. Overhead passed light, heedful footsteps; but they seemed not a disturbing sound, only a rumour beyond the bounds of silence.

' "I am very sorry," I said, "but they have nailed it down. Martha says the men came this afternoon."

'Miss Grey took a little bunch of snowdrops from her bosom, and hid them in among the clustered wreaths of flowers; and she knelt down on the floor, with a little silver cross which she sometimes wore pressed tight to her lips. I felt ill at ease to see her praying, and wished I could go back to my soldiers. But while I watched her, seeing in marvellous brilliancy everything in the little room, and re-membering dimly the snow lying beneath the stars in the darkness of the garden, I listened also to the quiet foot-steps passing to and fro in the room above. Suddenly, the silence was broken by a small, continuous, angry crying.

'Miss Grey looked up. Her eyes were very clear and wonderful in the candlelight.

' "What was that?" she said faintly, listening.

'I stared at her. The cry welled up anew, piteously; as if of a small, remote and helpless indignation.

' "Why, it sounds just like a – little baby," I said.

'She crossed herself hastily and arose. "Nicholas!" she said in a strange, quiet, bewildered voice – yet her face was most curiously bright. She looked at me lovingly and yet so strangely I wished I had not let her come in.

'She went out as she had entered. I did not so much as peep into the darkness after her, but busy with a hundred thoughts returned to my play.

'Long past my usual bedtime, as I sat sipping a mug of hot milk before the glowing cinders of the kitchen fire, Martha told me her secret. . . .'

'So my impossible companion in the High Street yesterday was own and only brother to your crazy old friend, Richard,' said the Count. 'His only brother,' he added, in a muse.

JAMES JOYCE

The Dead

Lily, the caretaker's daughter, was literally run off her feet. Hardly had she brought one gentleman into the little pantry behind the office on the ground floor and helped him off with his overcoat, than the wheezy hall-door bell clanged again and she had to scamper along the bare hallway to let in another guest. It was well for her she had not to attend to the ladies also. But Miss Kate and Miss Julia had thought of that and had converted the bathroom upstairs into a ladies' dressing-room. Miss Kate and Miss Julia were there, gossiping and laughing and fussing, walking after each other to the head of the stairs, peering down over the banisters and calling down to Lily to ask her who had come.

It was always a great affair, the Misses Morkan's annual dance. Everybody who knew them came to it, members of the family, old friends of the family, the members of Julia's choir, any of Kate's pupils that were grown up enough, and even some of Mary Jane's pupils too. Never once had it fallen flat. For years and years it had gone off in splendid style, as long as anyone could remember; ever since Kate and Julia, after the death of their brother Pat, had left the house in Stoney Batter and taken Mary Jane, their only niece, to live with them in the dark, gaunt house on Usher's Island, the upper part of which they had rented from Mr Fulham, the corn-factor on the ground floor. That was a good thirty years ago if it was a day. Mary Jane, who was then a little girl in short clothes, was now the main prop of the household, for she had the organ in Haddington Road. She had been through the Academy and gave a pupils' concert every year in the upper room of the Antient Concert Rooms. Many of her pupils belonged to the better-class families on the Kingstown and Dalkey line. Old as they were, her aunts also did their share. Julia, though she was quite grey, was still the leading soprano in Adam and Eve's, and Kate, being too feeble to go about much, gave music lessons to beginners on the old square piano in the back room. Lily, the caretaker's daughter, did housemaid's work for them. Though their life was modest, they believed in eating well; the best of everything: diamond-bone sirloins, three-shilling tea and the best bottled stout. But Lily seldom made a mistake in the orders, so that she got on well with her three mistresses. They were fussy, that was all. But the only thing they would not stand was back answers.

Of course, they had good reason to be fussy on such a night. And then it was long after ten o'clock and yet there was no sign of Gabriel and wife. Besides they were dreadfully afraid that Freddy Malins might turn up screwed. They would not wish for worlds that any of Mary Jane's pupils should see him under the influence; and when he was like that it was sometimes very hard to manage him. Freddy Malins always came late, but they wondered what could be keeping Gabriel: and that was what brought them every two minutes to the banisters to ask Lily had Gabriel or Freddy come.

'O, Mr Conroy,' said Lily to Gabriel when she opened the door for him, 'Miss Kate and Miss Julia thought you were never coming. Good night, Mrs Conroy.'

'I'll engage they did,' said Gabriel, 'but they forgot that my wife here takes three mortal hours to dress herself.'

He stood on the mat, scraping the snow from his goloshes, while Lily led his wife to the foot of the stairs and called out:

'Miss Kate, here's Mrs Conroy.'

Kate and Julia came toddling down the stairs at once.

Both of them kissed Gabriel's wife, said she must be perished alive, and asked was Gabriel with her.

'Here I am as right as the mail, Aunt Kate! Go on up. I'll follow,' called out Gabriel from the dark.

He continued scraping his feet vigorously while the three women went upstairs, laughing, to the ladies' dressing-room. A light fringe of snow lay like a cape on the shoulders of his overcoat and like toecaps on the toes of his goloshes; and, as the buttons of his overcoat slipped with a squeaking noise through the snow-stiffened frieze, a cold, fragrant air from out-of-doors escaped from crevices and folds.

'Is it snowing again, Mr Conroy?' asked Lily.

She had preceded him into the pantry to help him off with his overcoat. Gabriel smiled at the three syllables she had given his surname and glanced at her. She was a slim, growing girl, pale in complexion and with hay-coloured hair. The gas in the pantry made her look still paler. Gabriel had known her when she was a child and used to sit on the lowest step nursing a rag doll.

'Yes, Lily,' he answered, 'and I think we're in for a night of it.'

He looked up at the pantry ceiling, which was shaking with the stamping and shuffling of feet on the floor above, listened for a moment to the piano and then glanced at the girl, who was folding his overcoat carefully at the end of a shelf.

'Tell me, Lily,' he said in a friendly tone, 'do you still go to school?'

'O no, sir,' she answered. 'I'm done schooling this year and more.'

'O, then,' said Gabriel gaily, 'I suppose we'll be going to your wedding one of these fine days with your young man, eh?'

The girl glanced back at him over her shoulder and said with great bitterness:

'The men that is now is only all palaver and what they can get out of you.'

Gabriel coloured, as if he felt he had made a mistake and, without looking at her, kicked off his goloshes and flicked actively with his muffler at his patent-leather shoes.

He was a stout, tallish young man. The high colour of his cheeks pushed upwards even to his forehead, where it scattered itself in a few formless patches of pale red; and on his hairless face there scintillated restlessly the polished lenses and the bright gilt rims of the glasses which screened his delicate and restless eyes. His glossy black hair was parted in the middle and brushed in a long curve behind his ears where it curled slightly beneath the groove left by his hat.

When he had flicked lustre into his shoes he stood up and pulled his waistcoat down more tightly on his plump body. Then he took a coin rapidly from his pocket.

'O Lily,' he said, thrusting it into her hands, 'it's Christmas-time, isn't it? Just . . . here's a little . . .'

He walked rapidly towards the door.

'O no, sir' cried the girl, following him. 'Really, sir, I wouldn't take it.'

'Christmas-time! Christmas-time!' said Gabriel, almost trotting to the stairs and waving his hand to her in deprecation.

The girl, seeing that he had gained the stairs, called out after him:

'Well, thank you, sir.'

He waited outside the drawing-room door until the waltz should finish, listening to the skirts that swept against it and to the shuffling of feet. He was still discomposed by the girl's bitter and sudden retort. It had cast a gloom over him which he tried to dispel by arranging his cuffs and the bows of his tie. He then took from his waistcoat pocket a little paper and glanced at the headings he had made for his speech. He was undecided about the lines from Robert Browning, for he feared they would be above the heads of his hearers. Some quotation that they would recognise from Shakespeare or from the Melodies would be better. The indelicate clack-

ing of the men's heels and the shuffling of their soles reminded him that their grade of culture differed from his.
He would only make himself ridiculous by quoting poetry
to them which they could not understand. They would
think that he was airing his superior education. He would
fail with them just as he had failed with the girl in the
pantry. He had taken up a wrong tone. His whole speech
was a mistake from first to last, an utter failure.

Just then his aunts and his wife came out of the ladies'
dressing-room. His aunts were two small, plainly dressed
old women. Aunt Julia was an inch or so the taller. Her
hair, drawn low over the tops of her ears, was grey; and
grey also, with darker shadows, was her large flaccid face.
Though she was stout in build and stood erect, her slow
eyes and parted lips gave her the appearance of a woman
who did not know where she was or where she was going.
Aunt Kate was more vivacious. Her face, healthier than
her sister's, was all puckers and creases, like a shrivelled
red apple, and her hair, braided in the same old-fashioned
way, had not lost its ripe nut colour.

They both kissed Gabriel frankly. He was their favourite nephew, the son of their dead elder sister, Ellen, who
had married T. J. Conroy of the Port and Docks.

'Gretta tells me you're not going to take a cab back to
Monkstown tonight, Gabriel,' said Aunt Kate.

'No,' said Gabriel, turning to his wife, 'we had quite
enough of that last year, hadn't we? Don't you remember,
Aunt Kate, what a cold Gretta got out of it? Cab windows rattling all the way, and the east wind blowing in
after we passed Merrion. Very jolly it was. Gretta caught
a dreadful cold.'

Aunt Kate frowned severely and nodded her head at
every word.

'Quite right, Gabriel, quite right,' she said. 'You can't
be too careful.'

'But as for Gretta there,' said Gabriel, 'she'd walk
home in the snow if she were let.'

Mrs Conroy laughed.

'Don't mind him, Aunt Kate,' she said. 'He's really an awful bother, what with green shades for Tom's eyes at night and making him do the dumb-bells, and forcing Eva to eat the stirabout. The poor child! And she simply hates the sight of it! . . . O, but you'll never guess what he makes me wear now!'

She broke out into a peal of laughter and glanced at her husband, whose admiring and happy eyes had been wandering from her dress to her face and hair. The two aunts laughed heartily, too, for Gabriel's solicitude was a standing joke with them.

'Goloshes!' said Mrs Conroy. 'That's the latest. Whenever it's wet underfoot I must put on my goloshes. To-night even, he wanted me to put them on, but I wouldn't. The next thing he'll buy me will be a diving-suit.'

Gabriel laughed nervously and patted his tie reassuringly, while Aunt Kate nearly doubled herself, so heartily did she enjoy the joke. The smile soon faded from Aunt Julia's face and her mirthless eyes were directed towards her nephew's face. After a pause she asked:

'And what are goloshes, Gabriel?'

'Goloshes, Julia!' exclaimed her sister. 'Goodness me, don't you know what goloshes are? You wear them over your . . . over your boots, Gretta, isn't it?'

'Yes,' said Mrs Conroy. 'Gutta-percha things. We both have a pair now. Gabriel says everyone wears them on the Continent.'

'O, on the Continent,' murmured Aunt Julia, nodding her head slowly.

Gabriel knitted his brows and said, as if he were slightly angered:

'It's nothing very wonderful, but Gretta thinks it very funny because she says the word reminds her of Christy Minstrels.'

'But tell me, Gabriel,' said Aunt Kate, with brisk tact. 'Of course, you've seen about the room. Gretta was saying . . .'

'O, the room is all right,' replied Gabriel. 'I've taken one in the Gresham.'

'To be sure,' said Aunt Kate, 'by far the best thing to do. And the children, Gretta, you're not anxious about them?'

'O, for one night,' said Mrs Conroy. 'Besides, Bessie will look after them.'

'To be sure,' said Aunt Kate again. 'What a comfort it is to have a girl like that, one you can depend on! There's that Lily, I'm sure I don't know what has come over her lately. She's not the girl she was at all.'

Gabriel was about to ask his aunt some questions on this point, but she broke off suddenly to gaze after her sister, who had wandered down the stairs and was craning her neck over the banisters.

'Now, I ask you,' she said almost testily, 'where is Julia going? Julia! Julia! Where are you going?'

Julia, who had gone half-way down one flight, came back and announced blandly: 'Here's Freddy.'

At the same moment a clapping of hands and a final flourish of the pianist told that the waltz had ended. The drawing-room door was opened from within and some couples came out. Aunt Kate drew Gabriel aside hurriedly and whispered into his ear:

'Slip down, Gabriel, like a good fellow and see if he's all right, and don't let him up if he's screwed. I'm sure he's screwed. I'm sure he is.'

Gabriel went to the stairs and listened over the banisters. He could hear two persons talking in the pantry. Then he recognised Freddy Malins's laugh. He went down the stairs noisily.

'It's such a relief,' said Aunt Kate to Mrs Conroy, 'that Gabriel is here. I always feel easier in my mind when he's here . . . Julia, there's Miss Daly and Miss Power will take some refreshment. Thanks for your beautiful waltz, Miss Daly. It made lovely time.'

A tall wizen-faced man, with a stiff grizzled moustache and swarthy skin, who was passing out with his partner, said:

'And may we have some refreshment, too, Miss Morkan?'

'Julia,' said Aunt Kate summarily, 'and here's Mr Browne and Miss Furlong. Take them in, Julia, with Miss Daly and Miss Power.'

'I'm the man for the ladies,' said Mr Browne, pursing his lips until his moustache bristled and smiling in all his wrinkles. 'You know, Miss Morkan, the reason they are so fond of me is . . .'

He did not finish his sentence, but, seeing that Aunt Kate was out of earshot, at once led the three young ladies into the back room. The middle of the room was occupied by two square tables placed end to end, and on these Aunt Julia and the caretaker were straightening and smoothing a large cloth. On the sideboard were arrayed dishes and plates, and glasses and bundles of knives and forks and spoons. The top of the closed square piano served also as a sideboard for viands and sweets. At a smaller sideboard in one corner two young men were standing, drinking hop-bitters.

Mr Browne led his charges thither and invited them all, in jest, to some ladies' punch, hot, strong and sweet. As they said they never took anything strong, he opened three bottles of lemonade for them. Then he asked one of the young men to move aside, and, taking hold of the decanter, filled out for himself a goodly measure of whisky. The young men eyed him respectfully while he took a trial sip.

'God help me,' he said, smiling. 'It's the doctor's orders.'

His wizened face broke into a broader smile, and the three young ladies laughed in musical echo to his pleasantry, swaying their bodies to and fro, with nervous jerks of their shoulders. The boldest said:

'O, now, Mr Browne, I'm sure the doctor never ordered anything of the kind.'

Mr Browne took another sip of his whisky and said, with sidling mimicry:

'Well, you see, I'm like the famous Mrs Cassidy, who

is reported to have said: "Now, Mary Grimes, if I don't take it, make me take it, for I feel I want it." '

His hot face had leaned forward a little too confidentially and he had assumed a very low Dublin accent so that the young ladies, with one instinct, received his speech in silence. Miss Furlong, who was one of Mary Jane's pupils, asked Miss Daly what was the name of the pretty waltz she had played; and Mr Browne, seeing that he was ignored, turned promptly to the two young men who were more appreciative.

A red-faced young woman, dressed in pansy, came into the room, excitedly clapping her hands and crying:

'Quadrilles! Quadrilles!'

Close on her heels came Aunt Kate, crying:

'Two gentlemen and three ladies, Mary Jane!'

'O, here's Mr Bergin and Mr Kerrigan,' said Mary Jane. 'Mr Kerrigan, will you take Miss Power? Miss Furlong, may I get you a partner, Mr Bergin. O, that'll just do now.'

'Three ladies, Mary Jane,' said Aunt Kate.

The two young gentlemen asked the ladies if they might have the pleasure, and Mary Jane turned to Miss Daly.

'O, Miss Daly, you're really awfully good, after playing for the last two dances, but really we're so short of ladies tonight.'

'I don't mind in the least, Miss Morkan.'

'But I've a nice partner for you, Mr Bartell D'Arcy, the tenor. I'll get him to sing later on. All Dublin is raving about him.'

'Lovely voice, lovely voice!' said Aunt Kate.

As the piano had twice begun the prelude to the first figure Mary Jane led her recruits quickly from the room. They had hardly gone when Aunt Julia wandered slowly into the room, looking behind her at something.

'What is the matter, Julia?' asked Aunt Kate anxiously. 'Who is it?'

Julia, who was carrying in a column of table-napkins,

turned to her sister and said, simply, as if the question had surprised her:

'It's only Freddy, Kate, and Gabriel with him.'

In fact right behind her Gabriel could be seen piloting Freddy Malins across the landing. The latter, a young man of about forty, was of Gabriel's size and build, with very round shoulders. His face was fleshy and pallid, touched with colour only at the thick hanging lobes of his ears and at the wide wings of his nose. He had coarse features, a blunt nose, a convex and receding brow, tumid and protruded lips. His heavy-lidded eyes and the disorder of his scanty hair made him look sleepy. He was laughing heartily in a high key at a story which he had been telling Gabriel on the stairs and at the same time rubbing the knuckles of his left fist backwards and forwards into his left eye.

'Good evening, Freddy,' said Aunt Julia.

Freddy Malins bade the Misses Morkan good evening in what seemed an offhand fashion by reason of the habitual catch in his voice and then, seeing that Mr Browne was grinning at him from the sideboard, crossed the room on rather shaky legs and began to repeat in an undertone the story he had just told to Gabriel.

'He's not so bad, is he?' said Aunt Kate to Gabriel.

Gabriel's brows were dark, but he raised them quickly and answered:

'O, no, hardly noticeable.'

'Now, isn't he a terrible fellow!' she said. 'And his poor mother made him take the pledge on New Year's Eve. But come on, Gabriel, into the drawing-room.'

Before leaving the room with Gabriel she signalled to Mr Browne by frowning and shaking her forefinger in warning to and fro. Mr Browne nodded in answer and, when she had gone, said to Freddy Malins:

'Now, then, Teddy, I'm going to fill you out a good glass of lemonade just to buck you up.'

Freddy Malins, who was nearing the climax of his story, waved the offer aside impatiently, but Mr Browne, having first called Freddy Malins's attention to a disarray in his dress, filled out and handed him a full glass of lemonade. Freddy Malins's left hand accepted the glass mechanically, his right hand being engaged in the mechanical readjustment of his dress. Mr Browne, whose face was once more wrinkling with mirth, poured out for himself a glass of whisky while Freddy Malins exploded, before he had well reached the climax of his story, in a kink of high-pitched bronchitic laughter and, setting down his untasted and overflowing glass, began to rub the knuckles of his left fist backwards and forwards into his left eye, repeating words of his last phrase as well as his fit of laughter would allow him.

Gabriel could not listen while Mary Jane was playing her Academy piece, full of runs and difficult passages, to the hushed drawing-room. He liked music, but the piece she was playing had no melody for him and he doubted whether it had any melody for the other listeners, though they had begged Mary Jane to play something. Four young men, who had come from the refreshment-room to stand in the doorway at the sound of the piano, had gone away quietly in couples after a few minutes. The only persons who seemed to follow the music were Mary Jane herself, her hands racing along the keyboard or lifted from it at the pauses like those of a priestess in momentary imprecation, and Aunt Kate standing at her elbow to turn the page.

Gabriel's eyes, irritated by the floor, which glittered with beeswax under the heavy chandelier, wandered to the wall above the piano. A picture of the balcony scene in *Romeo and Juliet* hung there and beside it was a picture of the two murdered princes in the Tower which Aunt Julia had worked in red, blue and brown wools when she was a girl. Probably in the school they had gone to as girls that kind of work had been taught for one year. His mother had worked for him as a birthday present a waistcoat of purple tabinet, with little foxes' heads upon it, lined with brown satin and having round mulberry buttons. It was strange that his mother had had no musical talent, though Aunt Kate used to call her the brains carrier of the Morkan family. Both she and Julia had always seemed a little proud of their serious and matronly sister. Her photograph stood before the pierglass. She held an open book on her knees and was pointing out something in it to Constantine who, dressed in a man-o'-war suit, lay at her feet. It was she who had chosen the names of her sons, for she was very sensible of the dignity of family life. Thanks to her, Constantine was now senior curate in Balbriggan and, thanks to her, Gabriel himself had taken his degree in the Royal University. A shadow passed over his face as he remembered her sullen opposition to his marriage. Some slighting phrases she had used still rankled in his memory; she had once spoken of Gretta as being country cute and that was not true of Gretta at all. It was Gretta who had nursed her during all her last long illness in their house at Monkstown.

He knew that Mary Jane must be near the end of her piece, for she was playing again the opening melody with runs of scales after every bar, and while he waited for the end the resentment died down in his heart. The piece ended with a trill of octaves in the treble and a final deep octave in the bass. Great applause greeted Mary Jane as, blushing and rolling up her music nervously, she escaped from the room. The most vigorous clapping came from the four young men in the doorway who had gone away to the refreshment-room at the beginning of the piece but had come back when the piano had stopped.

Lancers were arranged. Gabriel found himself partnered with Miss Ivors. She was a frank-mannered talkative young lady, with a freckled face and prominent brown eyes. She did not wear a low-cut bodice, and the large brooch which was fixed in the front of her collar bore on it an Irish device and motto.

When they had taken their places she said abruptly:

'I have a crow to pluck with you.'

'With me?' said Gabriel.

She nodded her head gravely.

'What is it?' asked Gabriel, smiling at her solemn manner.

'Who is G. C.?' answered Miss Ivors, turning her eyes upon him.

Gabriel coloured and was about to knit his brows, as if he did not understand, when she said bluntly:

'O, innocent Amy! I have found out that you write for the *Daily Express.* Now, aren't you ashamed of yourself?'

'Why should I be ashamed of myself?' asked Gabriel, blinking his eyes and trying to smile.

'Well, I'm ashamed of you,' said Miss Ivors frankly. 'To say you'd write for a paper like that. I didn't think you were a West Briton.'

A look of perplexity appeared on Gabriel's face. It was true that he wrote a literary column every Wednesday in the *Daily Express,* for which he was paid fifteen shillings. But that did not make him a West Briton surely. The books he received for review were almost more welcome than the paltry cheque. He loved to feel the covers and turn over the pages of newly printed books. Nearly every day when his teaching in the college was ended he used to wander down the quays to the second-hand booksellers, to Hickey's on Bachelor's Walk, to Webb's or Massey's on Aston's Quay, or to O'Clohissey's in the by-street. He did not know how to meet her charge. He wanted to say that literature was above politics. But they were friends of many years' standing and their careers had been parallel, first at the University and then as teachers; he could not risk a grandiose phrase with her. He continued blinking his eyes and trying to smile and murmured lamely that he saw nothing political in writing reviews of books.

When their turn to cross had come he was still perplexed and inattentive. Miss Ivors promptly took his hand in a warm grasp and said in a soft friendly tone:

'Of course, I was only joking. Come, we cross now.'

When they were together again she spoke of the University question and Gabriel felt more at ease. A friend of hers had shown her his review of Browning's poems. That was how she had found out the secret: but she liked the review immensely. Then she said suddenly:

'O, Mr Conroy, will you come for an excursion to the Aran Isles this summer? We're going to stay there a whole month. It will be splendid out in the Atlantic. You ought to come. Mr Clancy is coming, and Mr Kilkelly and Kathleen Kearney. It would be splendid for Gretta too if she'd come. She's from Connacht, isn't she?'

'Her people are,' said Gabriel shortly.

'But you will come, won't you?' said Miss Ivors, laying her warm hand eagerly on his arm.

'The fact is,' said Gabriel, 'I have just arranged to go . . .'

'Go where?' asked Miss Ivors.

'Well, you know, every year I go for a cycling tour with some fellows and so . . .'

'But where?' asked Miss Ivors.

'Well, we usually go to France or Belgium or perhaps Germany,' said Gabriel awkwardly.

'And why do you go to France and Belgium,' said Miss Ivors, 'instead of visiting your own land?'

'Well,' said Gabriel, 'it's partly to keep in touch with the languages and partly for a change.'

'And haven't you your own language to keep in touch with – Irish?' asked Miss Ivors.

'Well,' said Gabriel, 'if it comes to that, you know, Irish is not my language.'

Their neighbours had turned to listen to the cross-examination. Gabriel glanced right and left nervously and tried to keep his good humour under the ordeal, which was making a blush invade his forehead.

'And haven't you your own land to visit,' continued Miss Ivors, 'that you know nothing of, your own people, and your own country?'

'O, to tell you the truth,' retorted Gabriel suddenly, 'I'm sick of my own country, sick of it!'

'Why?' asked Miss Ivors.

Gabriel did not answer for his retort had heated him.

'Why?' repeated Miss Ivors.

They had to go visiting together and, as he had not answered her, Miss Ivors said warmly:

'Of course, you've no answer.'

Gabriel tried to cover his agitation by taking part in the dance with great energy. He avoided her eyes for he had seen a sour expression on her face. But when they met in the long chain he was surprised to feel his hand firmly pressed. She looked at him from under her brows for a moment quizzically until he smiled. Then, just as the chain was about to start again, she stood on tiptoe and whispered into his ear:

'West Briton!'

When the lancers were over Gabriel went away to a remote corner of the room where Freddy Malins's mother was sitting. She was a stout, feeble old woman with white hair. Her voice had a catch in it like her son's and she stuttered slightly. She had been told that Freddy had come and that he was nearly all right. Gabriel asked her whether she had had a good crossing. She lived with her married daughter in Glasgow and came to Dublin on a visit once a year. She answered placidly that she had had a beautiful crossing and that the captain had been most attentive to her. She spoke also of the beautiful house her daughter kept in Glasgow, and of all the friends they had there. While her tongue rambled on Gabriel tried to banish from his mind all memory of the unpleasant incident with Miss Ivors. Of course the girl, or woman, or whatever she was, was an enthusiast, but there was a time for all things. Perhaps he ought not to have answered her like that. But she had no right to call him a West Briton before people, even in joke. She had tried to make him ridiculous before people, heckling him and staring at him with her rabbit's eyes.

He saw his wife making her way towards him through the waltzing couples. When she reached him she said into his ear:

'Gabriel, Aunt Kate wants to know won't you carve the goose as usual. Miss Daly will carve the ham and I'll do the pudding.'

'All right,' said Gabriel.

'She's sending in the younger ones first as soon as this waltz is over so that we'll have the table to ourselves.'

'Were you dancing?' asked Gabriel.

'Of course I was. Didn't you see me? What row had you with Molly Ivors?'

'No row. Why? Did she say so?'

'Something like that. I'm trying to get that Mr D'Arcy to sing. He's full of conceit, I think.'

'There was no row,' said Gabriel moodily, 'only she wanted me to go for a trip to the west of Ireland and I said I wouldn't.'

'O, do go, Gabriel,' she cried. 'I'd love to see Galway again.'

'You can go if you like,' said Gabriel coldly.

She looked at him for a moment, then turned to Mrs Malins and said:

'There's a nice husband for you, Mrs Malins.'

While she was threading her way back across the room Mrs Malins, without adverting to the interruption, went on to tell Gabriel what beautiful places there were in Scotland and beautiful scenery. Her son-in-law brought them every year to the lakes and they used to go fishing. Her son-in-law was a splendid fisher. One day he caught a beautiful big fish and the man in the hotel cooked it for dinner.

Gabriel hardly heard what she said. Now that supper was coming near he began to think again about his speech and about the quotation. When he saw Freddy Malins coming across the room to visit his mother Gabriel left the chair free for him and retired into the embrasure of the window. The room had already cleared and from the back of the room came the clatter of plates and knives. Those who still remained in the drawing-room seemed tired of dancing and were conversing quietly in little groups. Gabriel's warm trembling fingers tapped the cold pane of the window. How cool it must be outside! How pleasant it would be to walk out alone, first along by the river and then through the park! The snow would be lying on the branches of the trees and forming a bright cap on the top of the Wellington Monument. How much more pleasant it would be there than at the supper-table!

He ran over the headings of his speech: Irish hospitality, sad memories, the Three Graces, Paris, the quotation from Browning. He repeated to himself a phrase he had written in his review: 'One feels that one is listening to a thought-tormented music.' Miss Ivors had praised the review. Was she sincere? Had she really any life of her own behind all her propagandism? There had never been any ill-feeling between them until that night. It unnerved him to think that she would be at the supper-table, looking up at him while he spoke with her critical quizzing eyes. Perhaps she would not be sorry to see him fail in his speech. An idea came into his mind and gave him courage. He would say, alluding to Aunt Kate and Aunt Julia: 'Ladies and Gentlemen, the generation which is now on the wane among us may have had its faults, but for my part I think it had certain qualities of hospitality, of humour, of humanity, which the new and very serious and hypereducated generation that is growing up around us seems to me to lack.' Very good: that was one for Miss Ivors. What did he care that his aunts were only two ignorant old women?

A murmur in the room attracted his attention. Mr Browne was advancing from the door, gallantly escorting Aunt Julia, who leaned upon his arm, smiling and hanging her head. An irregular musketry of applause escorted her also as far as the piano and then, as Mary Jane seated herself on the stool, and Aunt Julia, no longer smiling, half turned so as to pitch her voice fairly into the room,

gradually ceased. Gabriel recognised the prelude. It was
that of an old song of Aunt Julia's – *Arrayed for the
Bridal*. Her voice, strong and clear in tone, attacked with
great spirit the runs which embellish the air and though
she sang very rapidly she did not miss even the smallest
of the grace notes. To follow the voice, without looking
at the singer's face, was to feel and share the excitement
of swift and secure flight. Gabriel applauded loudly with
all the others at the close of the song and loud applause
was bórne in from the invisible supper-table. It sounded
so genuine that a little colour struggled into Aunt Julia's
face as she bent to replace in the music-stand the old
leather-bound songbook that had her initials on the cover.
Freddy Malins, who had listened with his head perched
sideways to hear her better, was still applauding when
everyone else had ceased and talking animatedly to his
mother, who nodded her head gravely and slowly in
acquiescence. At last, when he could clap no more, he
stood up suddenly and hurried across the room to Aunt
Julia whose hand he seized and held in both his hands,
shaking it when words failed him or the catch in his
voice proved too much for him.

'I was just telling my mother,' he said, 'I never heard
you sing so well, never. No, I never heard your voice so
good as it is tonight. Now! Would you believe that now?
That's the truth. Upon my word and honour that's the
truth. I never heard your voice sound so fresh and so ...
so clear and fresh, never.'

Aunt Julia smiled broadly and murmured something
about compliments as she released her hand from his
grasp. Mr Browne extended his open hand towards her
and said to those who were near him in the manner of a
showman introducing a prodigy to an audience:

'Miss Julia Morkan, my latest discovery!'

He was laughing very heartily at this himself when
Freddy Malins turned to him and said:

'Well, Browne, if you're serious you might make a
worse discovery. All I can say is I never heard her sing

half so well as long as I am coming here. And that's the honest truth.'

'Neither did I,' said Mr Browne. 'I think her voice has greatly improved.'

Aunt Julia shrugged her shoulders and said with meek pride:

'Thirty years ago I hadn't a bad voice as voices go.'

'I often told Julia,' said Aunt Kate emphatically, 'that she was simply thrown away in that choir. But she never would be said by me.'

She turned as if to appeal to the good sense of the others against a refractory child while Aunt Julia gazed in front of her, a vague smile of reminiscence playing on her face.

'No,' continued Aunt Kate, 'she wouldn't be said or led by anyone, slaving there in that choir night and day, night and day. Six o'clock on Christmas morning! And all for what?'

'Well, isn't it for the honour of God, Aunt Kate?' asked Mary Jane, twisting round on the piano-stool and smiling.

Aunt Kate turned fiercely on her niece and said:

'I know all about the honour of God, Mary Jane, but I think it's not at all honourable for the Pope to turn out the women of the choirs that have slaved there all their lives and put little whipper-snappers of boys over their heads. I suppose it is for the good of the Church if the Pope does it. But it's not just, Mary Jane, and it's not right.'

She had worked herself into a passion and would have continued in defence of her sister, for it was a sore subject with her, but Mary Jane, seeing that all the dancers had come back, intervened pacifically:

'Now, Aunt Kate, you're giving scandal to Mr Browne who is of the other persuasion.'

Aunt Kate turned to Mr Browne, who was grinning at this allusion to his religion, and said hastily:

'O, I don't question the Pope's being right. I'm only a stupid old woman and I wouldn't presume to do such a thing. But there's such a thing as common everyday politeness and gratitude. And if I were in Julia's place I'd tell that Father Healey straight up to his face. . . .'

'And besides, Aunt Kate,' said Mary Jane, 'we really are all hungry and when we are hungry we are all very quarrelsome.'

'And when we are thirsty we are also quarrelsome,' added Mr Browne.

'So that we had better go to supper,' said Mary Jane, 'and finish the discussion afterwards.'

On the landing outside the drawing-room Gabriel found his wife and Mary Jane trying to persuade Miss Ivors to stay for supper. But Miss Ivors, who had put on her hat and was buttoning her cloak, would not stay. She did not feel in the least hungry and she had already overstayed her time.

'But only for ten minutes, Molly,' said Mrs Conroy. 'That won't delay you.'

'To take a pick itself,' said Mary Jane, 'after all your dancing.'

'I really couldn't,' said Miss Ivors.

'I am afraid you didn't enjoy yourself at all,' said Mary Jane hopelessly.

'Ever so much, I assure you,' said Miss Ivors, 'but you really must let me run off now.'

'But how can you get home?' asked Mrs Conroy.

'O, it's only two steps up the quay.'

Gabriel hesitated a moment and said:

'If you will allow me, Miss Ivors, I'll see you home if you are really obliged to go.'

But Miss Ivors broke away from them.

'I won't hear of it,' she cried. 'For goodness' sake go in to your suppers and don't mind me. I'm quite well able to take care of myself.'

'Well, you're the comical girl, Molly,' said Mrs Conroy frankly.

'*Beannacht libh*,' cried Miss Ivors, with a laugh, as she ran down the staircase.

Mary Jane gazed after her, a moody puzzled expression on her face, while Mrs Conroy leaned over the banisters to listen for the hall door. Gabriel asked himself was he the cause of her abrupt departure. But she did not seem to be in an ill humour: she had gone away laughing. He stared blankly down the staircase.

At the moment Aunt Kate came toddling out of the supper-room, almost wringing her hands in despair.

'Where is Gabriel?' she cried 'Where on earth is Gabriel? There's everyone waiting in there, stage to let, and nobody to carve the goose!'

'Here I am, Aunt Kate!' cried Gabriel, with sudden animation, 'ready to carve a flock of geese, if necessary.'

A fat brown goose lay at one end of the table and at the other end, on a bed of creased paper strewn with sprigs of parsley, lay a great ham, stripped of its outer skin and peppered over with crust crumbs, a neat paper frill round its shin, and beside this was a round of spiced beef. Between these rival ends ran parallel lines of side-dishes: two little minsters of jelly, red and yellow; a shallow dish full of blocks of blancmange and red jam a large green leaf-shaped dish with a stalk-shaped handle, on which lay bunches of purple raisins and peeled almonds, a companion dish on which lay a solid rectangle of Smyrna figs, a dish of custard topped with grated nutmeg, a bowl full of chocolates and sweets wrapped in gold and silver papers and a glass vase in which stood some tall celery stalks. In the centre of the table there stood, as sentries to a fruit-stand which upheld a pyramid of oranges and American apples, two squat old-fashioned decanters of cut glass, one containing port and the other dark sherry. On the closed square piano a pudding in a huge yellow dish lay in waiting and behind it were three squads of bottles of stout and ale and minerals, drawn up according to the colours of their uniforms, the first two black, with brown and red labels, the third and smallest squad white, with transverse green sashes.

Gabriel took his seat boldly at the head of the table

and, having looked to the edge of the carver, plunged his fork firmly into the goose. He felt quite at ease now for he was an expert carver and liked nothing better than to find himself at the head of a well-laden table.

'Miss Furlong, what shall I send you?' he asked. 'A wing or a slice of the breast?'

'Just a small slice of the breast.'

'Miss Higgins, what for you?'

'O, anything at all, Mr Conroy.'

While Gabriel and Miss Daly exchanged plates of goose and plates of ham and spiced beef, Lily went from guest to guest with a dish of hot floury potatoes wrapped in a white napkin. This was Mary Jane's idea and she had also suggested apple sauce for the goose, but Aunt Kate had said that plain roast goose without any apple sauce had always been good enough for her and she hoped she might never eat worse. Mary Jane waited on her pupils and saw that they got the best slices, and Aunt Kate and Aunt Julia opened and carried across from the piano bottles of stout and ale for the gentlemen and bottles of minerals for the ladies. There was a great deal of confusion and laughter and noise, the noise of orders and counter-orders, of knives and forks, of corks and glass-stoppers. Gabriel began to carve second helpings as soon as he had finished the first round without serving himself. Everyone protested loudly so that he compromised by taking a long draught of stout, for he had found the carving hot work. Mary Jane settled down quietly to her supper, but Aunt Kate and Aunt Julia were still toddling round the table, walking on each other's heels, getting in each other's way and giving each other unheeded orders. Mr Browne begged of them to sit down and eat their suppers and so did Gabriel, but they said there was time enough, so that, at last, Freddy Malins stood up and, capturing Aunt Kate, plumped her down on her chair amid general laughter.

When everyone had been well served Gabriel said, smiling:

'Now, if anyone wants a little more of what vulgar people call stuffing let him or her speak.'

A chorus of voices invited him to begin his own supper, and Lily came forward with three potatoes which she had reserved for him.

'Very well,' said Gabriel amiably, as he took another preparatory draught, 'kindly forget my existence, ladies and gentlemen, for a few minutes.'

He set to his supper and took no part in the conversation with which the table covered Lily's removal of the plates. The subject of talk was the opera company which was then at the Theatre Royal. Mr Bartell D'Arcy, the tenor, a dark-complexioned young man with a smart moustache, praised very highly the leading contralto of the company, but Miss Furlong thought she had a rather vulgar style of production. Freddy Malins said there was a Negro chieftain singing in the second part of the Gaiety pantomime who had one of the finest tenor voices he had ever heard.

'Have you heard him?' he asked Mr Bartell D'Arcy across the table.

'No,' answered Mr Bartell D'Arcy carelessly.

'Because,' Freddy Malins explained, 'now I'd be curious to hear your opinion of him. I think he has a grand voice.'

'It takes Teddy to find out the really good things,' said Mr Browne familiarly to the table.

'And why couldn't he have a voice too?' asked Freddy Malins sharply. 'Is it because he's only a black?'

Nobody answered this question and Mary Jane led the table back to the legitimate opera. One of her pupils had given her a pass for *Mignon*. Of course it was very fine, she said, but it made her think of poor Georgina Burns. Mr Browne could go back further still, to the old Italian companies that used to come to Dublin – Tietjens, Ilma de Murzka, Campinini, the great Trebelli, Giuglini, Ravelli, Aramburo. Those were the days, he said, when there was something like singing to be heard in Dublin. He told too of how the top gallery of the old Royal used to be packed night after night, of how one night an Italian tenor had sung five encores to *Let me like a Soldier Fall*, introducing a high C every time, and of how the gallery boys would sometimes in their enthusiasm unyoke the horses from the carriage of some great *prima donna* and pull her themselves through the streets to her hotel. Why did they never play the grand old operas now, he asked, *Dinorah, Lucrezia Borgia*? Because they could not get the voices to sing them: that was why.

'O, well,' said Mr Bartell D'Arcy, 'I presume there are as good singers today as there were then.'

'Where are they?' asked Mr Browne defiantly.

'In London, Paris, Milan,' said Mr Bartell D'Arcy warmly. 'I suppose Caruso, for example, is quite as good, if not better than any of the men you have mentioned.'

'Maybe so,' said Mr Browne. 'But I may tell you I doubt it strongly.'

'O, I'd give anything to hear Caruso sing,' said Mary Jane.

'For me,' said Aunt Kate, who had been picking a bone, 'there was only one tenor. To please me, I mean. But I suppose none of you ever heard of him.'

'Who was he, Miss Morkan?' asked Mr Bartell D'Arcy politely.

'His name,' said Aunt Kate, 'was Parkinson. I heard him when he was in his prime and I think he had then the purest tenor voice that was ever put into a man's throat.'

'Strange,' said Mr Bartell D'Arcy. 'I never even heard of him.'

'Yes, yes, Miss Morkan is right,' said Mr Browne. 'I remember hearing old Parkinson, but he's too far back for me.'

'A beautiful, pure, sweet mellow English tenor,' said Aunt Kate with enthusiasm.

Gabriel having finished, the huge pudding was transferred to the table. The clatter of forks and spoons began again. Gabriel's wife served out spoonfuls of the pudding and passed the plates down the table. Midway down they were held up by Mary Jane, who replenished them with raspberry or orange jelly or with blancmange and jam. The pudding was of Aunt Julia's making, and she received praises for it from all quarters. She herself said that it was not quite brown enough.

'Well, I hope, Miss Morkan,' said Mr Browne, 'that I'm brown enough for you because, you know, I'm all brown.'

All the gentlemen, except Gabriel, ate some of the pudding out of compliment to Aunt Julia. As Gabriel never ate sweets the celery had been left for him. Freddy Malins also took a stalk of celery and ate it with his pudding. He had been told that celery was a capital thing for the blood and he was just then under doctor's care. Mrs Malins, who had been silent all through the supper, said that her son was going down to Mount Melleray in a week or so. The table then spoke of Mount Melleray, how bracing the air was down there, how hospitable the monks were and how they never asked for a penny-piece from their guests.

'And do you mean to say,' asked Mr Browne incredulously, 'that a chap can go down there and put up there as if it were a hotel and live on the fat of the land and then come away without paying anything?'

'O, most people give some donation to the monastery when they leave,' said Mary Jane.

'I wish we had an institution like that in our Church,' said Mr Browne candidly.

He was astonished to hear that the monks never spoke, got up at two in the morning and slept in their coffins. He asked what they did it for.

'That's the rule of the order,' said Aunt Kate firmly.

'Yes, but why?' asked Mr Browne.

Aunt Kate repeated that it was the rule, that was all. Mr Browne still seemed not to understand. Freddy Malins explained to him, as best he could, that the monks were trying to make up for the sins committed by all the sinners in the outside world. The explanation was not very clear for Mr Browne grinned and said:

'I like that idea very much, but wouldn't a comfortable spring bed do them as well as a coffin?'

'The coffin,' said Mary Jane, 'is to remind them of their last end.'

As the subject had become lugubrious it was buried in a silence of the table, during which Mrs Malins could be heard saying to her neighbour in an indistinct undertone:

'They are very good men, the monks, very pious men.'

The raisins and almonds and figs and apples and oranges and chocolates and sweets were now passed about the table and Aunt Julia invited all the guests to have either port or sherry. At first Mr Bartell D'Arcy refused to take either, but one of his neighbours nudged him and whispered something to him, upon which he allowed his glass to be filled. Gradually as the last glasses were being filled the conversation ceased. A pause followed, broken only by the noise of the wine and by unsettlings of chairs. The Misses Morkan, all three, looked down at the table-cloth. Someone coughed once or twice and then a few gentlemen patted the table gently as a signal for silence. The silence came and Gabriel pushed back his chair and stood up.

The patting at once grew louder in encouragement and then ceased altogether. Gabriel leaned his ten trembling fingers on the tablecloth and smiled nervously at the company. Meeting a row of upturned faces he raised his eyes to the chandelier. The piano was playing a waltz tune and he could hear the skirts sweeping against the drawing-room door. People, perhaps, were standing in the snow on the quay outside, gazing up at the lighted windows and listening to the waltz music. The air was pure there. In the distance lay the park where the trees were weighted with snow. The Wellington Monument wore a gleaming cap of snow that flashed westwards over the white field of Fifteen Acres.

He began:

'Ladies and Gentlemen,

'It has fallen to my lot this evening, as in years past, to

perform a very pleasing task, but a task for which I am afraid my poor powers as a speaker are all too inadequate.'

'No, no!' said Mr Browne.

'But, however that may be, I can only ask you tonight to take the will for the deed, and to lend me your attention for a few moments while I endeavour to express to you in words what my feelings are on this occasion.

'Ladies and Gentlemen, it is not the first time that we have gathered together under this hospitable roof, around this hospitable board. It is not the first time that we have been the recipients – or perhaps, I had better say, the victims – of the hospitality of certain good ladies.'

He made a circle in the air with his arm and paused. Everyone laughed or smiled at Aunt Kate and Aunt Julia and Mary Jane who all turned crimson with pleasure. Gabriel went on more boldly:

'I feel more strongly with every recurring year that our country has no tradition which does it so much honour and which it should guard so jealously as that of its hospitality. It is a tradition that is unique as far as my experience goes (and I have visited not a few places abroad) among the modern nations. Some would say, perhaps, that with us it is rather a failing than anything to be boasted of. But granted even that, it is, to my mind, a princely failing, and one that I trust will long be cultivated among us. Of one thing, at least, I am sure. As long as this one roof shelters the good ladies aforesaid – and I wish from my heart it may do so, for many and many a long year to come – the tradition of genuine warm-hearted courteous Irish hospitality, which our forefathers have handed down to us and which we in turn must hand down to our descendants, is still alive among us.'

A hearty murmur of assent ran round the table. It shot through Gabriel's mind that Miss Ivors was not there and that she had gone away discourteously: and he said with confidence in himself:

'Ladies and Gentlemen,

'A new generation is growing up in our midst, a generation actuated by new ideas and new principles. It is serious and enthusiastic for these new ideas and its enthusiasm, even when it is misdirected, is, I believe, in the main sincere. But we are living in a sceptical and, if I may use the phrase, a thought-tormented age: and sometimes I fear that this new generation, educated or hypereducated as it is, will lack those qualities of humanity, of hospitality, of kindly humour which belonged to an older day. Listening tonight to the names of all those great singers of the past it seemed to me, I must confess, that we were living in a less spacious age. Those days might, without exaggeration, be called spacious days: and if they are gone beyond recall let us hope, at least, that in gatherings such as this we shall still speak of them with pride and affection, still cherish in our hearts the memory of those dead and gone great ones whose fame the world will not willingly let die.'

'Hear, hear!' said Mr Browne loudly.

'But yet,' continued Gabriel, his voice falling into a softer inflection, 'there are always in gatherings such as this sadder thoughts that will recur to our minds: thoughts of the past, of youth, of changes, of absent faces that we miss here tonight. Our path through life is strewn with many such sad memories: and were we to brood upon them always we could not find the heart to go on bravely with our work among the living. We have all of us living duties and living affections which claim, and rightly claim, our strenuous endeavours.

'Therefore, I will not linger on the past. I will not let any gloomy moralising intrude upon us here tonight. Here we are gathered together for a brief moment from the bustle and rush of our everyday routine. We are met here as friends, in the spirit of good-fellowship, as colleagues also to a certain extent, in the true spirit of *camaraderie*, and as the guests of – what shall I call them? – the Three Graces of the Dublin musical world.'

The table burst into applause and laughter at this

allusion. Aunt Julia vainly asked each of her neighbours in turn to tell her what Gabriel had said.

'He says we are the Three Graces, Aunt Julia,' said Mary Jane.

Aunt Julia did not understand, but she looked up, smiling, at Gabriel, who continued in the same vein:

'Ladies and Gentlemen,

'I will not attempt to play tonight the part that Paris played on another occasion. I will not attempt to choose between them. The task would be an invidious one and one beyond my poor powers. For when I view them in turn, whether it be our chief hostess herself, whose good heart, whose too good heart, has become a byword with all who know her; or her sister, who seems to be gifted with perennial youth and whose singing must have been a surprise and a revelation to us all tonight; or, last but not least, when I consider our youngest hostess, talented, cheerful, hard-working and the best of nieces, I confess, Ladies and Gentlemen, that I do not know to which of them I should award the prize.'

Gabriel glanced down at his aunts and, seeing the large smile on Aunt Julia's face and the tears which had risen to Aunt Kate's eyes, hastened to his close. He raised his glass of port gallantly, while every member of the company fingered a glass expectantly, and said loudly:

'Let us toast them all three together. Let us drink to their health, wealth, long life, happiness and prosperity, and may they long continue to hold the proud and self-won position which they hold in their profession and the position of honour and affection which they hold in our hearts.'

All the guests stood up, glass in hand, and turning towards the three seated ladies, sang in unison, with Mr Browne as leader:

> For they are jolly gay fellows,
> For they are jolly gay fellows,
> For they are jolly gay fellows,
> Which nobody can deny.

Aunt Kate was making frank use of her handkerchief and even Aunt Julia seemed moved. Freddy Malins beat time with his pudding-fork and the singers turned towards one another, as if in melodious conference, while they sang with emphasis:

> Unless he tells a lie,
> Unless he tells a lie,

Then, turning once more towards their hostesses, they sang:

> For they are jolly gay fellows,
> For they are jolly gay fellows,
> For they are jolly gay fellows,
> Which nobody can deny.

The acclamation which followed was taken up beyond the door of the supper-room by many of the other guests and renewed time after time, Freddy Malins acting as officer with his fork on high.

The piercing morning air came into the hall where they were standing so that Aunt Kate said:

'Close the door, somebody. Mrs Malins will get her death of cold.'

'Browne is out there, Aunt Kate,' said Mary Jane.

'Browne is everywhere,' said Aunt Kate, lowering her voice.

Mary Jane laughed at her tone.

'Really,' she said archly, 'he is very attentive.'

'He has been laid on here like the gas,' said Aunt Kate in the same tone, 'all during the Christmas.'

She laughed herself this time good-humouredly and then added quickly:

'But tell him to come in, Mary Jane, and close the door. I hope to goodness he didn't hear me.'

At that moment the hall door was opened and Mr Browne came in from the doorstep, laughing as if his heart would break. He was dressed in a long green overcoat with mock astrakhan cuffs and collar and wore on his head an oval fur cap. He pointed down the snow-covered quay from where the sound of shrill prolonged whistling was borne in.

'Teddy will have all the cabs in Dublin out,' he said.

Gabriel advanced from the little pantry behind the office, struggling into his overcoat and, looking round the hall, said:

'Gretta not down yet?'

'She's getting on her things, Gabriel,' said Aunt Kate.

'Who's playing up there?' asked Gabriel.

'Nobody. They're all gone.'

'O no, Aunt Kate,' said Mary Jane. 'Bartell D'Arcy and Miss O'Callaghan aren't gone yet.'

'Someone is fooling at the piano anyhow,' said Gabriel.

Mary Jane glanced at Gabriel and Mr Browne and said with a shiver:

'It makes me feel cold to look at you two gentlemen muffled up like that. I wouldn't like to face your journey home at this hour.'

'I'd like nothing better this minute,' said Mr. Browne stoutly, 'than a rattling fine walk in the country or a fast drive with a good spanking goer between the shafts.'

'We used to have a very good horse and trap at home,' said Aunt Julia sadly.

'The never-to-be-forgotten Johnny,' said Mary Jane, laughing.

Aunt Kate and Gabriel laughed too.

'Why, what was wonderful about Johnny?' asked Mr Browne.

'The late lamented Patrick Morkan, our grandfather, that is,' explained Gabriel, 'commonly known in his later years as the old gentleman, was a glue-boiler.'

'O, now, Gabriel,' said Aunt Kate, laughing, 'he had a starch mill.'

'Well, glue or starch,' said Gabriel, 'the old gentleman had a horse by the name of Johnny. And Johnny used to work in the old gentleman's mill, walking round and round in order to drive the mill. That was all very well;

but now comes the tragic part about Johnny. One fine day the old gentleman thought he'd like to drive out with the quality to a military review in the park.'

'The Lord have mercy on his soul,' said Aunt Kate compassionately.

'Amen,' said Gabriel. 'So the old gentleman, as I said, harnessed Johnny and put on his very best tall hat and his very best stock collar and drove out in grand style from his ancestral mansion somewhere near Back Lane, I think.'

Everyone laughed, even Mrs Malins, at Gabriel's manner and Aunt Kate said:

'O, now, Gabriel, he didn't live in Back Lane, really. Only the mill was there.'

'Out from the mansion of his forefathers,' continued Gabriel, 'he drove with Johnny. And everything went on beautifully until Johnny came in sight of King Billy's statue: and whether he fell in love with the horse King Billy sits on or whether he thought he was back again in the mill, anyhow he began to walk round the statue.'

Gabriel paced in a circle round the hall in his goloshes amid the laughter of the others.

'Round and round he went,' said Gabriel, 'and the old gentleman, who was a very pompous old gentleman, was highly indignant. "Go on, sir! What do you mean, sir? Johnny! Johnny! Most extraordinary conduct! Can't understand the horse!"'

The peals of laughter which followed Gabriel's imitation of the incident was interrupted by a resounding knock at the hall door. Mary Jane ran to open it and let in Freddy Malins. Freddy Malins, with his hat well back on his head and his shoulders humped with cold, was puffing and steaming after his exertions.

'I could only get one cab,' he said.

'O, we'll find another along the quay,' said Gabriel.

'Yes,' said Aunt Kate. 'Better not keep Mrs Malins standing in the draught.'

Mrs Malins was helped down the front steps by her son and Mr Browne, and, after many manœuvres, hoisted into the cab. Freddy Malins clambered in after her and spent a long time settling her on the seat, Mr Browne helping him with advice. At last she was settled comfortably and Freddy Malins invited Mr Browne into the cab. There was a good deal of confused talk, and then Mr Browne got into the cab. The cabman settled his rug over his knees, and bent down for the address. The confusion grew greater and the cabman was directed differently by Freddy Malins and Mr Browne, each of whom had his head out through a window of the cab. The difficulty was to know where to drop Mr Browne along the route, and Aunt Kate, Aunt Julia and Mary Jane helped the discussion from the doorstep with cross-directions and contradictions and abundance of laughter. As for Freddy Malins he was speechless with laughter. He popped his head in and out of the window every moment to the great danger of his hat, and told his mother how the discussion was progressing, till at last Mr Browne shouted to the bewildered cabman above the din of everybody's laughter:

'Do you know Trinity College?'

'Yes, sir,' said the cabman.

'Well, drive bang up against Trinity College gates,' said Mr Browne, 'and then we'll tell you where to go. You understand now?'

'Yes, sir,' said the cabman.

'Make like a bird for Trinity College.'

'Right, sir,' said the cabman.

The horse was whipped up and the cab rattled off along the quay amid a chorus of laughter and adieus.

Gabriel had not gone to the door with the others. He was in a dark part of the hall gazing up the staircase. A woman was standing near the top of the first flight, in the shadow also. He could not see her face but he could see the terra-cotta and salmon-pink panels of her skirt which the shadow made appear black and white. It was his wife. She was leaning on the banisters, listening to something. Gabriel was surprised at her stillness and strained his ear to listen also. But he could hear little save the noise of laughter and dispute on the front steps, a few chords struck on the piano and a few notes of a man's voice singing.

He stood still in the gloom of the hall, trying to catch the air that the voice was singing and gazing up at his wife. There was grace and mystery in her attitude as if she were a symbol of something. He asked himself what is a woman standing on the stairs in the shadow, listening to distant music, a symbol of. If he were a painter he would paint her in that attitude. Her blue felt hat would show off the bronze of her hair against the darkness and the dark panels of her skirt would show off the light ones. *Distant Music* he would call the picture if he were a painter.

The hall door was closed; and Aunt Kate, Aunt Julia and Mary Jane came down the hall, still laughing.

'Well, isn't Freddy terrible?' said Mary Jane. 'He's really terrible.'

Gabriel said nothing, but pointed up the stairs towards where his wife was standing. Now that the hall door was closed the voice and the piano could be heard more clearly. Gabriel held up his hand for them to be silent. The song seemed to be in the old Irish tonality and the singer seemed uncertain both of his words and of his voice. The voice, made plaintive by distance and by the singer's hoarseness, faintly illuminated the cadence of the air with words expressing grief:

> O, the rain falls on my heavy locks
> And the dew wets my skin,
> My babe lies cold . . .

'O,' exclaimed Mary Jane. 'It's Bartell D'Arcy singing and he wouldn't sing all the night. O, I'll get him to sing a song before he goes.'

'O do, Mary Jane,' said Aunt Kate.

Mary Jane brushed past the others and ran to the staircase, but before she reached it the singing stopped and the piano was closed abruptly.

'O, what a pity!' she cried. 'Is he coming down, Gretta?'

Gabriel heard his wife answer yes and saw her come down towards them. A few steps behind her were Mr Bartell D'Arcy and Miss O'Callaghan.

'O, Mr D'Arcy,' cried Mary Jane, 'it's downright mean of you to break off like that when we were all in raptures listening to you.'

'I have been at him all the evening,' said Miss O'Callaghan, 'and Mrs Conroy, too, and he told us he had a dreadful cold and couldn't sing.'

'O, Mr D'Arcy,' said Aunt Kate, 'now that was a great fib to tell.'

'Can't you see that I'm as hoarse as a crow?' said Mr D'Arcy roughly.

He went into the pantry and hastily put on his over-coat. The others, taken aback by his rude speech, could find nothing to say. Aunt Kate wrinkled her brows and made signs to the others to drop the subject. Mr D'Arcy stood swathing his neck carefully and frowning.

'It's the weather,' said Aunt Julia, after a pause.

'Yes, everybody has colds,' said Aunt Kate readily, 'everybody.'

'They say,' said Mary Jane, 'we haven't had snow like it for thirty years; and I read this morning in the news-papers that the snow is general all over Ireland.'

'I love the look of snow,' said Aunt Julia sadly.

'So do I,' said Miss O'Callaghan. 'I think Christmas is never really Christmas unless we have the snow on the ground.'

'But poor Mr D'Arcy doesn't like the snow,' said Aunt Kate, smiling.

Mr D'Arcy came from the pantry, fully swathed and buttoned, and in a repentant tone told them the history of his cold. Every one gave him advice and said it was a great pity and urged him to be very careful of his throat in the night air. Gabriel watched his wife, who did not join in the conversation. She was standing right under the dusty fanlight and the flame of the gas lit up the rich bronze of her hair, which he had seen her drying at the fire a few days before. She was in the same attitude and seemed unaware of the talk about her. At last she turned towards them and Gabriel saw that there was colour in her cheeks and that her eyes were shining. A sudden tide of joy went leaping out of his heart.

'Mr D'Arcy,' she said, 'what is the name of that song you were singing?'

'It's called *The Lass of Aughrim*,' said Mr D'Arcy, 'but I couldn't remember it properly. Why? Do you know it?'

'*The Lass of Aughrim*,' she repeated. 'I couldn't think of the name.'

'It's a very nice air,' said Mary Jane. 'I'm sorry you were not in voice tonight.'

'Now, Mary Jane,' said Aunt Kate, 'don't annoy Mr D'Arcy. I won't have him annoyed.'

Seeing that all were ready to start she shepherded them to the door, where good night was said:

'Well, good night, Aunt Kate, and thanks for the pleasant evening.'

'Good night, Gabriel. Good night, Gretta!'

'Good night, Aunt Kate, and thanks ever so much. Good night, Aunt Julia.'

'O, good night, Gretta, I didn't see you.'

'Good night, Mr D'Arcy. Good night, Miss O'Callaghan.'

'Good night, Miss Morkan.'

'Good night, again.'

'Good night, all. Safe home.'

'Good night. Good night.'

The morning was still dark. A dull, yellow light brooded over the houses and the river; and the sky seemed to be descending. It was slushy underfoot; and only streaks and patches of snow lay on the roofs, on the parapets of the quay and on the area railings. The lamps were still burning redly in the murky air and, across the river, the palace

of the Four Courts stood out menacingly against the heavy
sky.

She was walking on before him with Mr Bartell D'Arcy,
her shoes in a brown parcel tucked under one arm and her
hands holding her skirt up from the slush. She had no
longer any grace of attitude, but Gabriel's eyes were still
bright with happiness. The blood went bounding along
his veins; and the thoughts went rioting through his brain,
proud, joyful, tender, valorous.

She was walking on before him so lightly and so erect
that he longed to run after her noiselessly, catch her by
the shoulders and say something foolish, and affectionate
into her ear. She seemed to him so frail that he longed to
defend her against something and then to be alone with
her. Moments of their secret life together burst like stars
upon his memory. A heliotrope envelope was lying beside
his breakfast-cup and he was caressing it with his hand.
Birds were twittering in the ivy and the sunny web of the
curtain was shimmering along the floor: he could not eat
for happiness. They were standing on the crowded platform and he was placing a ticket inside the warm palm of
her glove. He was standing with her in the cold, looking
in through a grated window at a man making bottles in
a roaring furnace. It was very cold. Her face, fragrant in
the cold air, was quite close to his; and suddenly he called
out to the man at the furnace:

'Is the fire hot, sir?'

But the man could not hear with the noise of the furnace. It was just as well. He might have answered rudely.

A wave of yet more tender joy escaped from his heart
and went coursing in warm flood along his arteries. Like
the tender fire of stars moments of their life together, that
no one knew of or would ever know of, broke upon and
illumined his memory. He longed to recall to her those
moments, to make her forget the years of their dull existence together and remember only their moments of
ecstasy. For the years, he felt, had not quenched his soul
or hers. Their children, his writing, her household cares

had not quenched all their souls' tender fire. In one letter that he had written to her then he had said: 'Why is it that words like these seem to me so dull and cold? Is it because there is no word tender enough to be your name?'

Like distant music these words that he had written years before were borne towards him from the past. He longed to be alone with her. When the others had gone away, when he and she were in the room in the hotel, then they would be alone together. He would call her softly:

'Gretta!'

Perhaps she would not hear at once: she would be undressing. Then something in his voice would strike her. She would turn and look at him. . . .

At the corner of Winetavern Street they met a cab. He was glad of its rattling noise as it saved him from conversation. She was looking out of the window and seemed tired. The others spoke only a few words, pointing out some building or street. The horse galloped along wearily under the murky morning sky, dragging his old rattling box after his heels, and Gabriel was again in a cab with her, galloping to catch the boat, galloping to their honeymoon.

As the cab drove across O'Connell Bridge Miss Callaghan said:

'They say you never cross O'Connell Bridge without seeing a white horse.'

'I see a white man this time,' said Gabriel.

'Where?' asked Mr Bartell D'Arcy.

Gabriel pointed to the statue, on which lay patches of snow. Then he nodded familiarly to it and waved his hand.

'Good night, Dan,' he said gaily.

When the cab drew up before the hotel, Gabriel jumped out and, in spite of Mr Bartell D'Arcy's protest, paid the driver. He gave the man a shilling over his fare. The man saluted and said:

'A prosperous New Year to you, sir.'

'The same to you,' said Gabriel cordially.

She leaned for a moment on his arm in getting out of the cab and while standing at the kerbstone, bidding the others good night. She leaned lightly on his arm, as lightly as when she had danced with him a few hours before. He had felt proud and happy then, happy that she was his, proud of her grace and wifely carriage. But now, after the kindling again of so many memories, the first touch of her body, musical and strange and perfumed, sent through him a keen pang of lust. Under cover of her silence he pressed her arm closely to his side; and, as they stood at the hotel door, he felt that they had escaped from their lives and duties, escaped from home and friends and run away together with wild and radiant hearts to a new adventure.

An old man was dozing in a great hooded chair in the hall. He lit a candle in the office and went before them to the stairs. They followed him in silence, their feet falling in soft thuds on the thickly carpeted stairs. She mounted the stairs behind the porter, her head bowed in the ascent, her frail shoulders curved as with a burden, her skirt girt tightly about her. He could have flung his arms about her hips and held her still, for his arms were trembling with desire to seize her and only the stress of his nails against the palms of his hands held the wild impulse of his body in check. The porter halted on the stairs to settle his guttering candle. They halted, too, on the steps below him. In the silence Gabriel could hear the falling of the molten wax into the tray and the thumping of his own heart against his ribs.

The porter led them along a corridor and opened a door. Then he set his unstable candle down on a toilet-table and asked at what hour they were to be called in the morning.

'Eight,' said Gabriel.

The porter pointed to the tap of the electric-light and began a muttered apology, but Gabriel cut him short.

'We don't want any light. We have light enough from the street. And I say,' he added, pointing to the candle, 'you might remove that handsome article, like a good man.'

The porter took up his candle again, but slowly, for he was surprised by such a novel idea. Then he mumbled good night and went out. Gabriel shot the lock to.

A ghastly light from the street lamp lay in a long shaft from one window to the door. Gabriel threw his overcoat and hat on a couch and crossed the room towards the window. He looked down into the street in order that his emotion might calm a little. Then he turned and leaned against a chest of drawers with his back to the light. She had taken off her hat and cloak and was standing before a large swinging mirror, unhooking her waist. Gabriel paused for a few moments, watching her, and then said:

'Gretta!'

She turned away from the mirror slowly and walked along the shaft of light towards him. Her face looked so serious and weary that the words would not pass Gabriel's lips. No, it was not the moment yet.

'You look tired,' he said.

'I am a little,' she answered.

'You don't feel ill or weak?'

'No, tired: that's all.'

She went on to the window and stood there, looking out. Gabriel waited again and then, fearing that diffidence was about to conquer him, he said abruptly:

'By the way, Gretta!'

'What is it?'

'You know that poor fellow Malins?' he said quickly.

'Yes. What about him?'

'Well, poor fellow, he's a decent sort of chap after all,' continued Gabriel in a false voice. 'He gave me back that sovereign I lent him, and I didn't expect it, really. It's a pity he wouldn't keep away from that Browne, because he's not a bad fellow, really.'

He was trembling now with annoyance. Why did she seem so abstracted? He did not know how he could begin. Was she annoyed, too, about something? If she would only turn to him or come to him of her own accord! To take her as she was would be brutal. No, he must see some ardour in her eyes first. He longed to be master of her strange mood.

'When did you lend him the pound?' she asked, after a pause.

Gabriel strove to restrain himself from breaking out into brutal language about the sottish Malins and his pound. He longed to cry to her from his soul, to crush her body against his, to overmaster her. But he said:

'O, at Christmas, when he opened that little Christmas-card shop in Henry Street.'

He was in such a fever of rage and desire that he did not hear her come from the window. She stood before him for an instant, looking at him strangely. Then, suddenly raising herself on tiptoe and resting her hands lightly on his shoulders, she kissed him.

'You are a very generous person, Gabriel,' she said.

Gabriel, trembling with delight at her sudden kiss and at the quaintness of her phrase, put his hands on her hair and began smoothing it back, scarcely touching it with his fingers. The washing had made it fine and brilliant. His heart was brimming with happiness. Just when he was wishing for it she had come to him of her own accord. Perhaps her thoughts had been running with his. Perhaps she had felt the impetuous desire that was in him, and then the yielding mood had come upon her. Now that she had fallen to him so easily, he wondered why he had been so diffident.

He stood, holding her head between his hands. Then, slipping one arm swiftly about her body and drawing her towards him, he said softly:

'Gretta, dear, what are you thinking about?'

She did not answer nor yield wholly to his arm. He said again, softly:

'Tell me what it is, Gretta. I think I know what is the matter. Do I know?'

She did not answer at once. Then she said in an outburst of tears:

'O, I am thinking about that song, *The Lass of Aughrim.*'

She broke loose from him and ran to the bed and, throwing her arms across the bed-rail, hid her face. Gabriel stood stock-still for a moment in astonishment and then followed her. As he passed in the way of the cheval-glass he caught sight of himself in full length, his broad, well-filled shirt-front, the face whose expression always puzzled him when he saw it in a mirror, and his glimmering gilt-rimmed eyeglasses. He halted a few paces from her and said:

'What about the song? Why does that make you cry?'

She raised her head from her arms and dried her eyes with the back of her hand like a child. A kinder note than he had intended went into his voice.

'Why, Gretta?' he asked.

'I am thinking about a person long ago who used to sing that song.'

'And who was the person long ago?' asked Gabriel, smiling.

'It was a person I used to know in Galway when I was living with my grandmother,' she said.

The smile passed away from Gabriel's face. A dull anger began to gather again at the back of his mind and the dull fires of his lust began to glow angrily in his veins.

'Someone you were in love with?' he asked ironically.

'It was a young boy I used to know,' she answered, 'named Michael Furey. He used to sing that song, *The Lass of Aughrim.* He was very delicate.'

Gabriel was silent. He did not wish her to think that he was interested in this delicate boy.

'I can see him so plainly,' she said, after a moment. 'Such eyes as he had: big, dark eyes! And such an expression in them – an expression!'

'O, then, you are in love with him?' said Gabriel.

'I used to go out walking with him,' she said, 'when I was in Galway.'

A thought flew across Gabriel's mind.

'Perhaps that was why you wanted to go to Galway with that Ivors girl?' he said coldly.

She looked at him and asked in surprise:

'What for?'

Her eyes made Gabriel feel awkward. He shrugged his shoulders and said:

'How do I know? To see him, perhaps.'

She looked away from him along the shaft of light towards the window in silence.

'He is dead,' she said at length. 'He died when he was only seventeen. Isn't it a terrible thing to die so young as that?'

'What was he?' asked Gabriel, still ironically.

'He was in the gasworks,' she said.

Gabriel felt humiliated by the failure of his irony and by the evocation of this figure from the dead, a boy in the gasworks. While he had been full of memories of their secret life together, full of tenderness and joy and desire, she had been comparing him in her mind with another. A shameful consciousness of his own person assailed him. He saw himself as a ludicrous figure, acting as a pennyboy for his aunts, a nervous, well-meaning sentimentalist, orating to vulgarians and idealising his own clownish lusts, the pitiable fatuous fellow he had caught a glimpse of in the mirror. Instinctively he turned his back more to the light lest she might see the shame that burned upon his forehead.

He tried to keep up his tone of cold interrogation, but his voice when he spoke was humble and indifferent.

'I suppose you were in love with this Michael Furey, Gretta,' he said.

'I was great with him at that time,' she said.

Her voice was veiled and sad. Gabriel, feeling now how vain it would be to try to lead her whither he had purposed, caressed one of her hands and said, also sadly:

'And what did he die of so young, Gretta? Consumption, was it?'

'I think he died for me,' she answered.

A vague terror seized Gabriel at this answer, as if, at that hour when he had hoped to triumph, some impalpable and vindictive being was coming against him, gathering forces against him in its vague world. But he shook himself free of it with an effort of reason and continued to caress her hand. He did not question her again, for he felt that she would tell him of herself. Her hand was warm and moist: it did not respond to his touch, but he continued to caress it just as he had caressed her first letter to him that spring morning.

'It was in the winter,' she said, 'about the beginning of the winter when I was going to leave my grandmother's and come up here to the convent. And he was ill at the time in his lodgings in Galway and wouldn't be let out, and his people in Oughterard were written to. He was in decline, they said, or something like that. I never knew rightly.'

She paused for a moment and sighed.

'Poor fellow,' she said. 'He was very fond of me and he was such a gentle boy. We used to go out together, walking, you know, Gabriel, like they do in the country. He was going to study singing only for his health. He had a very good voice, poor Michael Furey.'

'Well; and then?' asked Gabriel.

'And then when it came to the time for me to leave Galway and come up to the convent he was much worse and I wouldn't be let see him so I wrote him a letter saying I was going up to Dublin and would be back in the summer, and hoping he would be better then.'

She paused for a moment to get her voice under control, and then went on:

"Then the night before I left, I was in my grandmother's house in Nuns' Island, packing up, and I heard gravel thrown up against the window. The window was so wet I couldn't see, so I ran downstairs as I was and slipped out the back into the garden and there was the poor fellow at the end of the garden, shivering.'

'And did you not tell him to go back?' asked Gabriel.

'I implored of him to go home at once and told him he would get his death in the rain. But he said he did not want to live. I can see his eyes as well as well! He was standing at the end of the wall where there was a tree.'

'And did he go home?' asked Gabriel.

'Yes, he went home. And when I was only a week in the convent he died and he was buried in Oughterard, where his people came from. O, the day I heard that, that he was dead!'

She stopped, choking with sobs, and, overcome by emotion, flung herself face downwards on the bed, sobbing in the quilt. Gabriel held her hand for a moment longer, irresolutely, and then, shy of intruding on her grief, let it fall gently and walked quietly to the window.

She was fast asleep.

Gabriel, leaning on his elbow, looked for a few moments unresentfully on her tangled hair and half-open mouth, listening to her deep-drawn breath. So she had had that romance in her life, a man had died for her sake. It hardly pained him now to think how poor a part he, her husband, had played in her life. He watched her while she slept, as though he and she had never lived together as man and wife. His curious eyes rested long upon her face and on her hair: and, as he thought of what she must have been then, in that time of her first girlish beauty, a strange, friendly pity for her entered his soul. He did not like to say even to himself that her face was no longer beautiful, but he knew that it was no longer the face for which Michael Furey had braved death.

Perhaps she had not told him all the story. His eyes moved to the chair over which she had thrown some of her clothes. A petticoat string dangled to the floor. One boot stood upright, its limp upper fallen down: the fellow of it lay upon its side. He wondered at his riot of emotions of an hour before. From what had it proceeded? From his aunt's supper, from his own foolish speech, from the wine and dancing, the merry-making when saying good night in the hall, the pleasure of the walk along the river in the snow. Poor Aunt Julia! She, too, would soon be a shade with the shade of Patrick Morkan and his horse. He had caught that haggard look upon her face for a moment when she was singing *Arrayed for the Bridal*. Soon, perhaps, he would be sitting in that same drawing-room, dressed in black, his silk hat on his knees. The blinds would be drawn down and Aunt Kate would be sitting beside him, crying and blowing her nose and telling him how Julia had died. He would cast about in his mind for some words that might console her, and would find only lame and useless ones. Yes, yes: that would happen very soon.

The air of the room chilled his shoulders. He stretched himself cautiously along under the sheets and lay down beside his wife. One by one, they were all becoming shades. Better pass boldly into that other world, in the full glory of some passion, than fade and wither dismally with age. He thought of how she who lay beside him had locked in her heart for so many years that image of her lover's eyes when he had told her that he did not wish to live.

Generous tears filled Gabriel's eyes. He had never felt that himself towards any woman, but he knew that such a feeling must be love. The tears gathered more thickly in his eyes and in the partial darkness he imagined he saw the form of a young man standing dripping under a tree. Other forms were near. His soul had approached that region where dwell the vast hosts of the dead. He was conscious of, but could not apprehend, their wayward and flickering existence. His own identity was fading out into a grey impalpable world: the solid world itself, which these dead had one time reared and lived in, was dissolving and dwindling.

A few light taps upon the pane made him turn to the

window. It had begun to snow again. He watched sleepily the flakes, silver and dark, falling obliquely against the lamplight. The time had come for him to set out on his journey westwards. Yes, the newspapers were right: snow was general all over Ireland. It was falling on every part of the dark central plain, on the treeless hills, falling softly upon the Bog of Allen and, further westwards, softly falling into the dark mutinous Shannon waves. It was falling, too, upon every part of the lonely churchyard on the hill where Michael Furey lay buried. It lay thickly drifted on the crooked crosses and headstones, on the spears of the little gate, on the barren thorns. His soul swooned slowly as he heard the snow falling faintly through the universe and faintly falling, like the descent of their last end, upon all the living and the dead.

ALDOUS HUXLEY

Little Mexican

The shopkeeper called it, affectionately, a little Mexican; and little, for a Mexican, it may have been. But in this Europe of ours, where space is limited and the scale smaller, the little Mexican was portentous, a giant among hats. It hung there, in the centre of the hatter's window, a huge black aureole, fit for a king among devils. But no devil walked that morning through the streets of Ravenna; only the mildest of literary tourists. Those were the days when very large hats seemed in my eyes very desirable, and it was on my head, all unworthy, that the aureole of darkness was destined to descend. On my head; for at the first sight of the hat, I had run into the shop, tried it on, found the size correct, and bought it, without bargaining, at a foreigner's price. I left the shop with the little Mexican on my head, and my shadow on the pavements of Ravenna was like the shadow of an umbrella pine.

The little Mexican is very old now, and moth-eaten and green. But I still preserve it. Occasionally, for old associations' sake, I even wear it. Dear Mexican! it represents for me a whole epoch of my life. It stands for emancipation and the first year at the university. It symbolises the discovery of how many new things, new ideas, new sensations! – of French literature, of alcohol, of modern painting, of Nietzsche, of love, of metaphysics, of Mallarmé, of syndicalism, and of goodness knows what else. But, above all, I prize it because it reminds me of my first discovery of Italy. It re-evokes for me, my little Mexican, all the thrills and astonishments and virgin raptures of that first

Italian tour in the early autumn of 1912. Urbino, Rimini, Ravenna, Ferrara, Modena, Mantua, Verona, Vicenza, Padua, Venice – my first impressions of all these fabulous names lie, like a hatful of jewels, in the crown of the little Mexican. Shall I ever have the heart to throw it away?

And then, of course, there is Tirabassi. Without the little Mexican I should never have made Tirabassi's acquaintance. He would never have taken me, in my small unemphatic English hat, for a painter. And I should never, in consequence, have seen the frescoes, never have talked with the old Count, never heard of the Colombella. Never. ... When I think of that, the little Mexican seems to me more than ever precious.

It was, of course, very typical of Tirabassi to suppose, from the size of my hat, that I must be a painter. He had a neat military mind that refused to accept the vague disorder of the world. He was for ever labelling and pigeonholing and limiting his universe; and when the classified objects broke out of their pigeon-holes and tore the labels from off their necks, Tirabassi was puzzled and annoyed. In any case, it was obvious to him from the first moment he saw me in the restaurant at Padua, that I must be a painter. All painters wear large black hats. I was wearing the little Mexican. Ergo, I was a painter. It was syllogistic, unescapable.

He sent the waiter to ask me whether I would do him the honour of taking coffee with him at his table. For the first moment, I must confess, I was a little alarmed. This dashing young lieutenant of cavalry – what on earth could he want with me? The most absurd fancies filled my mind: I had committed, all unconsciously, some frightful solecism; I had trodden on the toes of the lieutenant's honour, and he was about to challenge me to a duel. The choice of weapons, I rapidly reflected, would be mine. But what – oh, what on earth should I choose? Swords? I had never learnt to fence. Pistols? I had once fired six shots at a bottle, and missed it with every shot. Would there be time to write one or two letters, make some sort of a testament about my personal belongings? From this anguish of mind the waiter, returning a moment later with my fried octopus, delivered me. The Lieutenant Count, he explained in a whisper of confidence, had a villa on the Brenta, not far from Strà. A villa – he spread out his hands in a generous gesture – full of paintings. Full, full, full. And he was anxious that I should see them, because he felt sure that I was interested in paintings. Oh, of course – I smiled rather foolishly, for the waiter seemed to expect some sort of confirmatory interpolation from me – I *was* interested in paintings; very much. In that case, said the waiter, the Count would be delighted to take me to see them. He left me, still puzzled, but vastly relieved. At any rate, I was not being called upon to make the very embarrassing choice between swords and pistols.

Surreptitiously, whenever he was not looking in my direction, I examined the Lieutenant Count. His appearance was not typically Italian (but then what is a typical Italian?). He was not, that is to say, blue-jowled, beady-eyed, swarthy, and aquiline. On the contrary, he had pale ginger hair, grey eyes, a snub nose, and a freckled complexion. I knew plenty of young Englishmen who might have been Count Tirabassi's less vivacious brothers.

He received me, when the time came, with the most exquisite courtesy, apologising for the most unceremonious way in which he had made my acquaintance. 'But as I felt sure,' he said, 'that you were interested in art, I thought you would forgive me for the sake of what I have to show you.' I couldn't help wondering why the Count felt so certain about my interest in art. It was only later, when we left the restaurant together, that I understood; for, as I put on my hat to go, he pointed with a smile at the little Mexican. 'One can see,' he said, 'that you are a real artist.' I was left at a loss, not knowing what to answer.

After we had exchanged the preliminary courtesies, the Lieutenant plunged at once, entirely for my benefit I could see, into a conversation about art. 'Nowadays,' he said, 'we Italians don't take enough interest in art. In a modern country, you see...' He shrugged his shoulders, leaving the sentence unfinished. 'But I don't think that's right. I adore art. Simply adore it. When I see foreigners going round with their guide-books, standing for half an hour in front of one picture, looking first at the book, then at the picture' – and here he gave the most brilliantly finished imitation of an Anglican clergyman conscientiously 'doing' the Mantegna chapel: first a glance at the imaginary guide-book held open in his two hands, then, with the movement of a chicken that drinks, a lifting of the face towards an imaginary fresco, a long stare between puckered eyelids, a falling open of the mouth, and finally a turning back of the eyes towards the inspired pages of Baedeker – 'when I see them, I feel ashamed for us Italians.' The Count spoke very earnestly, feeling, no doubt, that his talent for mimicry had carried him a little too far. 'And if they stand for half an hour looking at the thing, I go and stand there for an hour. That's the way to understand great art. The only way.' He leaned back in his chair and sipped his coffee. 'Unfortunately,' he added, after a moment, 'one hasn't got much time.'

I agreed with him. 'When one can only get to Italy for a month at a stretch, like myself...'

'Ah, but if only I could travel about the world like you!' The Count sighed. 'But here I am, cooped up in this wretched town. And when I think of the enormous capital that's hanging there on the walls of my house...' He checked himself, shaking his head. Then, changing his tone, he began to tell me about his house on the Brenta. It sounded altogether too good to be true. Carpioni, yes – I could believe in frescoes by Carpioni; almost any one might have those. But a hall by Veronese, but rooms by Tiepolo, all in the same house – that sounded incredible. I could not help believing that the Count's enthusiasm for art had carried him away. But, in any case, to-morrow I should be able to judge for myself; the Count had invited me to lunch with him.

We left the restaurant. Still embarrassed by the Count's

references to my little Mexican, I walked by his side in silence up the arcaded street.

'I am going to introduce you to my father,' said the Count. 'He, too, adores the arts.'

More than ever I felt myself a swindler. I had wriggled into the Count's confidence on false pretences; my hat was a lie. I felt that I ought to do something to clear up the misunderstanding. But the Count was so busy complaining to me about his father that I had no opportunity to put in my little explanation. I didn't listen very attentively, I confess, to what he was saying. In the course of a year at Oxford, I had heard so many young men complain of their fathers. Not enough money, too much interference – the story was a stale one. And at that time, moreover, I was taking a very high philosophical line about this sort of thing. I was pretending that people didn't interest me – only books, only ideas. What a fool one can make of oneself at that age!

'*Eccoci*,' said the Count. We halted in front of the Café Pedrochi. 'He always comes here for his coffee.'

And where else, indeed, should he come for his coffee? Who, in Padua, would go anywhere else?

We found him sitting on the terrace at the farther end of the building. I had never, I thought, seen a jollier-looking old gentleman. The old Count had a red weather-beaten face, with white moustaches bristling gallantly upwards and a white imperial in the grand Risorgimento manner of Victor Emmanuel the Second. Under the white tufty eyebrows, and set in the midst of a webwork of fine wrinkles, the eyes were brown and bright like a robin's. His long nose looked, somehow, more practically useful than the ordinary human nose, as though made for fine judicial sniffing, for delicate burrowing and probing. Thick set and strong, he sat there solidly in his chair, his knees apart, his hands clasped over the knob of his cane, carrying his paunch with dignity, nobly I had almost said, before him. He was dressed all in white linen – for the weather was still very hot – and his wide grey hat was tilted rakishly forward over his left eye. It gave one a real satisfaction to look at him; he was so complete, so perfect in his kind.

The young Count introduced me. 'This is an English gentleman. Signor . . .' He turned to me for the name.

'Oosselay,' I said, having learnt by experience that that was as near as any Italian could be expected to get to it.

'Signor Oosselay,' the young Count continued, 'is an artist.'

'Well, not exactly an artist,' I was beginning; but he would not let me make an end.

'He is also very much interested in ancient art,' he continued. 'To-morrow I am taking him to Dolo to see the frescoes. I know he will like them.'

We sat down at the old Count's table; critically he looked at me and nodded. '*Benissimo*,' he said, and then added, 'Let's hope you'll be able to do something to help sell the things.'

This was startling. I looked in some perplexity towards the young Count. He was frowning angrily at his father. The old gentleman had evidently said the wrong thing; he had spoken, I guessed, too soon. At any rate, he took his son's hint and glided off serenely on another tack.

'The fervid phantasy of Tiepolo,' he began rotundly, 'the cool, unimpassioned splendour of Veronese – at Dolo you will see them contrasted.' I listened attentively, while the old gentleman thundered on in what was evidently a set speech. When it was over, the young Count got up; he had to be back at the barracks by half-past two. I too made as though to go; but the old man laid his hand on my arm. 'Stay with me,' he said. 'I enjoy your conversation infinitely.' And as he himself had hardly ceased speaking for one moment since I first set eyes on him, I could well believe it. With the gesture of a lady lifting her skirts out of the mud (and those were the days when skirts still had to be lifted) the young Count swaggered off, very military, very brilliant and glittering, like a soldier on the stage, into the sunlight, out of sight.

The old man's bird-bright eyes followed him as he went. 'A good boy, Fabio,' he said, turning back to me at last, 'a good son.' He spoke affectionately; but there was a hint, I thought, in his smile, in the tone of his voice, a hint of amusement, of irony. It was as though he were adding, by implication, 'But good boys, after all, are fools to be so good.' I found myself, in spite of my affectation of detachment, extremely curious about this old gentleman. And he, for his part, was not the man to allow any one in his company to remain for long in splendid isolation. He insisted on my taking an interest in his affairs. He told me all about them – or at any rate all about some of them – pouring out his confidences with an astonishing absence of reserve. Next to the intimate and trusted friend, the perfect stranger is the best of all possible confidants. There is no commercial traveller, of moderately sympathetic appearance, who has not, in the course of his days in the train, his evenings in the parlours of commercial hotels, been made the repository of a thousand intimate secrets – even in England. And in Italy – goodness knows what commercial travellers get told in Italy. Even I, a foreigner, speaking the language badly, and not very skilful anyhow in conducting a conversation with strangers, have heard queer things in the second-class carriages of Italian trains. . . . Here, too, on Pedrochi's terrace I was to hear queer things. A door was to be left ajar, and through the crack I was to have a peep at unfamiliar lives.

'What I should do without him,' the old gentleman continued, 'I really don't know. The way he manages the estate is simply wonderful.' And he went rambling off into long digressions about the stupidity of peasants, the incompetence and dishonesty of bailiffs, the badness of the weather, the spread of phylloxera, the high price of manure. The upshot of it all was that, since Fabio had taken over the estate, everything had gone well; even the weather had improved. 'It's such a relief,' the Count concluded, 'to feel that I have some one in charge on whom

I can rely, some one I can trust, absolutely. It leaves me free to devote my mind to more important things.'

I could not help wondering what the important things were; but it would have been impertinent, I felt, to ask. Instead, I put a more practical question. 'But what will happen,' I asked, 'when your son's military duties take him away from Padua?'

The old Count gave me a wink and laid his forefinger, very deliberately, to the side of his long nose. The gesture was rich with significance. 'They never will,' he said. 'It's all arranged. A little *combinazione*, you know. I have a friend in the Ministry. His military duties will always keep him in Padua.' He winked and smiled again.

I could not help laughing, and the old Count joined in with a joyous ha-ha that was the expression of a profound satisfaction, that was, as it were, a burst of self-applause. He was evidently proud of his little *combinazione*. But he was prouder still of the other combination, about which he now confidentially leaned across the table to tell me. It was decidedly the subtler of the two.

'And it's not merely his military duties,' he said, wagging at me the thick, yellow-nailed forefinger which he had laid against his nose, 'it's not merely his military duties that'll keep the boy in Padua. It's his domestic duties. He's married. I married him.' He leaned back in his chair, and surveyed me, smiling. The little wrinkles round his eyes seemed to be alive. 'That boy, I said to myself, must settle down. He must have a nest, or else he'll fly away. He must have roots, or else he'll run. And his poor old father will be left in the lurch. He's young, I thought, but he must marry. He *must* marry. At once.' And the old gentleman made great play with his forefinger. It was a long story. His old friend, the Avvocato Monaldeschi, had twelve children—three boys and nine girls. (And here there were digressions about the Avvocato and the size of good Catholic families.) The eldest girl was just the right age for Fabio. No money, of course; but a good girl and pretty, and very well brought up and religious. Religious – that was very important, for it was essential that Fabio should have a large family – to keep him more effectually rooted, the old Count explained – and with these modern young women brought up outside the Church one could never be certain of children. Yes, her religion was most important; he had looked into that very carefully before selecting her. Well, the next thing, of course, was that Fabio should be induced to select her. It had been a matter of bringing the horse to water *and* making him drink. Oh, a most difficult and delicate business! For Fabio prided himself on his independence; and he was obstinate, like a mule. Nobody should interfere with his affairs, nobody should make him do what he didn't want to. And he was so touchy, he was so pig-headed that often he wouldn't do what he really wanted, merely because somebody else had suggested that he ought to do it. So I could imagine – the old Count spread out his hands before me – just how difficult and delicate a business it had been. Only a consummate diplomat could have succeeded. He did it by throwing them together a great deal and talking, meanwhile, about the rashness of early marriages, the uselessness of poor wives, the undesirability of wives not of noble birth. It worked like a charm; within four months, Fabio was engaged; two months later he was married, and ten months after that he had a son and heir. And now he was fixed, rooted. The old gentleman chuckled, and I could fancy that I was listening to the chuckling of some old white-haired tyrant of the quattrocento, congratulating himself on the success of some peculiarly ingenious stroke of policy – a rich city induced to surrender itself by fraud, a dangerous rival lured by fair words into a cage and trapped. Poor Fabio, I thought; and also, what a waste of talent!

Yes, the old Count went on, now he would never go. He was not like his younger brother, Lucio. Lucio was a rogue, *furbo*, sly; he had no conscience. But Fabio had ideas about duty, and lived up to them. Once he had engaged himself, he would stick to his engagements, obstinately, with all the mulishness of his character. Well, now he lived on the estate, in the big painted house at Dolo. Three days a week he came into Padua for his military duties, and the rest of his time he devoted to the estate. It brought in, now, more than it had ever done before. But goodness knew, the old man complained, that was little enough. Bread and oil, and wine and milk, and chickens and beef – there was plenty of those and to spare. Fabio could have a family of fifty and they would never starve. But ready money – there wasn't much of that. 'In England,' the Count concluded, 'you are rich. But we Italians ...' He shook his head.

I spent the next quarter of an hour trying to persuade him that we were not all millionaires. But in vain. My statistics, based on somewhat imperfect memories of Mr and Mrs Sidney Webb, carried no conviction. In the end I gave it up.

The next morning Fabio appeared at the door of my hotel in a large, very old and very noisy Fiat. It was the family machine-of-all-work, bruised, scratched, and dirtied by years of service. Fabio drove it with a brilliant and easy recklessness. We rushed through the town, swerving from one side of the narrow street to the other, with a disregard for the rules of the road which, in a pedantic country like England, would have meant at the least a five-pound fine and an endorsed licence. But here the Carabiniers, walking gravely in couples under the arcades, let us pass without comment. Right or left – after all, what did it matter?

'Why do you keep the silencer out?' I shouted through the frightful clamour of the engine.

Fabio slightly shrugged his shoulders. '*È piu allegro così,*' he answered.

I said no more. From a member of this hardy race which enjoys discomfort, a nerve-ridden Englishman could hardly hope to get much sympathy.

We were soon out of the town. Trailing behind us a seething white wake of dust and with the engine rattling off its explosions like a battery of machine-guns, we raced along the Fusina road. On either hand extended the cultivated plain. The road was bordered by ditches, and on the banks beyond, instead of hedges, stood rows of little pollards, with grape-laden vines festooned from tree to tree. White with the dust, tendrils, fruit, and leaves hung there like so much goldsmith's work sculptured in frosted metal, hung like the swags of fruit and foliage looped round the flanks of a great silver bowl. We hurried on. Soon, on our right hand, we had the Brenta, sunk deep between the banks of its canal. And now we were at Strà. Through gateways rich with fantastic stucco, down tunnels of undeciduous shade, we looked in a series of momentary glimpses into the heart of the park. And now for an instant the statues on the roof of the villa beckoned against the sky and were passed. On we went. To right and left, on either bank of the river, I got every now and then a glimpse of some enchanting mansion, gay and brilliant even in decay. Little baroque garden houses peeped at me over walls; and through great gates, at the end of powdery cypress avenues, half humorously, it seemed, the magniloquent and frivolous façades soared up in defiance of all the rules. I should have liked to do the journey slowly, to stop here and there, to look, to savour at leisure; but Fabio disdained to travel at anything less than fifty kilometres to the hour, and I had to be content with momentary and precarious glimpses. It was in these villas, I reflected, as we bumped along at the head of our desolation of white dust, that Casanova used to come and spend the summer; seducing the chamber-maids, taking advantage of terrified marchionesses in *calèches* during thunderstorms, bamboozling soft-witted old senators of Venice with his fortune-telling and black magic. Gorgeous and happy scoundrel! In spite of my professed detachment, I envied him. And, indeed, what was that famous detachment but a disguised expression of the envy which the successes and audacities of a Casanova must necessarily arouse in every timid and diffident mind? If I lived in splendid isolation, it was because

I lacked the audacity to make war – even to make entangling alliances. I was absorbed in these pleasing self-condemnatory thoughts, when the car slowed down and came to a standstill in front of a huge imposing gate. Fabio hooted impatiently on his horn; there was a scurry of footsteps, the sound of bolts being drawn, and the gate swung open. At the end of a short drive, very large and grave, very chaste and austere, stood the house. It was considerably older than most of the other villas I had seen in glimpses on our way. There was no frivolousness in its façade, no irregular grandiloquence. A great block of stuccoed brick; a central portico approached by steps and topped with a massive pediment; a row of rigid statues on the balustrade above the cornice. It was correctly, coldly even, Palladian. Fabio brought the car to a halt in front of the porch. We got out. At the top of the steps stood a young woman with a red-headed child in her arms. It was the Countess with the son and heir.

The Countess impressed me very agreeably. She was slim and tall – two or three inches taller than her husband; with dark hair, drawn back from the forehead and twisted into a knot on the nape of her neck; dark eyes, vague, lustrous, and melancholy, like the eyes of a gentle animal; a skin brown and transparent like darkened amber. Her manner was gentle and unemphatic. She rarely gesticulated; I never heard her raise her voice. She spoke, indeed, very little. The old Count had told me that his daughter-in-law was religious, and from her appearance I could easily believe it. She looked at you with the calm, remote regard of one whose life mostly goes on behind the eyes.

Fabio kissed his wife and then, bending his face towards the child, he made a frightful grimace and roared like a lion. It was all done in affection; but the poor little creature shrank away, terrified. Fabio laughed and pinched its ear.

'Don't tease him,' said the Countess gently. 'You'll make him cry.'

Fabio turned to me. 'That's what comes of leaving a boy

to be looked after by women. He cries at everything. Let's come in,' he added. 'At present we only use two or three rooms on the ground floor, and the kitchen in the basement. All the rest is deserted. I don't know how these old fellows managed to keep up their palaces. I can't.' He shrugged his shoulders. Through a door on the right of the portico we passed into the house. 'This is our drawing-room and dining-room combined.'

It was a fine big room, nobly proportioned – a double cube, I guessed – with doorways of sculptured marble and a magnificent fireplace flanked by a pair of nymphs on whose bowed shoulders rested a sloping overmantel carved with coats of arms and festoons of foliage. Round the walls ran a frieze, painted in grisaille; in a graceful litter of cornucopias and panoplies, goddesses sumptuously reclined, cherubs wriggled and flew. The furniture was strangely mixed. Round a sixteenth-century dining-table that was a piece of Palladian architecture in wood, were ranged eight chairs in the Viennese secession style of 1905. A large chalet-shaped cuckoo clock from Bern hung on the wall between two cabinets of walnut, pilastered and pedimented to look like little temples, and with heroic statuettes in yellow boxwood, standing in niches between the pillars. And then the pictures on the walls, the cretonnes with which the arm-chairs were covered! Tactfully, however, I admired everything, new as well as old.

'And now,' said the Count, 'for the frescoes.'

I followed him through one of the marble-framed doorways and found myself at once in the great central hall of the villa. The Count turned round to me. 'There!' he said, smiling triumphantly with the air of one who has really succeeded in producing a rabbit out of an empty hat. And, indeed, the spectacle was sufficiently astonishing.

The walls of the enormous room were completely covered with frescoes which it did not need much critical judgment or knowledge to perceive were genuine Veroneses. The authorship was obvious, palpable. Who else could have painted those harmoniously undulating groups

273

of figures set in their splendid architectural frame? Who
else but Veronese could have combined such splendour
with such coolness, so much extravagant opulence with
exquisite suavity?

'*È grandioso!*' I said to the Count.

And indeed it was. Grandiose; there was no other word.
A rich triumphant arcade ran all round the room, four or
five arches appearing on each wall. Through the arches
one looked into a garden; and there, against a background
of cypresses and statues and far-away blue mountains,
companies of Venetian ladies and gentlemen gravely dis-
ported themselves. Under one arch they were making
music; through another, one saw them sitting round a
table, drinking one another's health in glasses of red wine,
while a little blackamoor in a livery of green and yellow
carried round the silver jug. In the next panel they were
watching a fight between a monkey and a cat. On the
opposite wall a poet was reading his verses to the assembled company, and next to him Veronese himself –
the self-portrait was recognisable – stood at his easel,
painting the picture of an opulent blonde in rose-coloured
satin. At the feet of the artist lay his dog; two parrots and
a monkey were sitting on the marble balustrade in the
middle distance.

I gazed with delight. 'What a marvellous thing to possess!' I exclaimed, fairly carried away by my enthusiasm.
'I envy you.'

The Count made a little grimace and laughed. 'Shall we
come and look at the Tiepolos?' he asked.

We passed through a couple of cheerful rooms by Carpioni – satyrs chasing nymphs through a romantic forest
and, on the fringes of a seascape, a very eccentric rape of
mermaids by centaurs – to step across a threshold into
that brilliant universe, at once delicate and violently extravagant, wild and subtly orderly, which Tiepolo, in the
last days of Italian painting, so masterfully and magically
created. It was the story of Eros and Psyche, and the tale
ran through three large rooms, spreading itself even on

to the ceilings, where, in a pale sky dappled with white and golden clouds, the appropriate deities balanced themselves, diving or ascending through the empyrean with that air of being perfectly at home in their element which seems to belong, in nature, only to fishes and perhaps a few winged insects and birds.

Fabio had boasted to me that, in front of a picture, he could outstare any foreigner. But I was such a mortally long time admiring these dazzling phantasies that in the end he quite lost patience.

'I wanted to show you the farm before lunch,' he said, looking at his watch. 'There's only just time.' I followed him reluctantly.

We looked at the cows, the horses, the prize bull, the turkeys. We looked at the tall, thin haystacks, shaped like giant cigars set on end. We looked at the sacks of wheat in the barn. For lack of any better comment I told the Count that they reminded me of the sacks of wheat in English barns; he seemed delighted.

The farm buildings were set round an immense courtyard. We had explored three sides of this piazza; now we came to the fourth, which was occupied by a long, low building pierced with round archways and, I was surprised to see, completely empty.

'What's this?' I asked, as we entered.

'It *is* nothing,' the Count replied. 'But it might, some day, become ... *chi sa*?' He stood there for a moment, frowning pensively, with the expression of Napoleon on St Helena – dreaming of the future, regretting past opportunities for ever lost. His freckled face, ordinarily a lamp for brightness, became incongruously sombre. Then all at once he burst out – damning life, cursing fate, wishing to God he could get away and do something instead of wasting himself here. I listened, making every now and then a vague noise of sympathy. What could I do about it? And then, to my dismay, I found that I could do something about it, that I was expected to do something. I was being asked to help the Count to sell his frescoes. As an artist, it was obvious, I must be acquainted with patrons, museums, millionaires. I had seen the frescoes; I could honestly recommend them. And now there was this perfected process for transferring frescoes on to canvas. The walls could easily be peeled of their painting, the canvases rolled up and taken to Venice. And from there it would be the easiest thing in the world to smuggle them on board a ship and get away with them. As for prices – if he could get a million and a half of lire, so much the better; but he'd take a million, he'd even take three-quarters. And he'd give me ten per cent commission. . . .

And afterwards, when he'd sold his frescoes, what would he do? To begin with – the Count smiled at me triumphantly – he'd turn this empty building in which we were now standing into an up-to-date cheese-factory. He could start the business handsomely on half a million, and then, using cheap female labour from the country round, he could be almost sure of making big profits at once. In a couple of years, he calculated, he'd be netting eighty or a hundred thousand a year from his cheeses. And then, ah then, he'd be independent, he'd be able to get away, he'd see the world. He'd go to Brazil and the Argentine. An enterprising man with capital could always do well out there. He'd go to New York, to London, to Berlin, to Paris. There was nothing he could not do.

But meanwhile the frescoes were still on the walls—beautiful, no doubt (for, the Count reminded me, he adored art), but futile; a huge capital frozen into the plaster, eating its head off, utterly useless. Whereas, with his cheese-factory. . . .

Slowly we walked back towards the house.

I was in Venice again in the September of the following year, 1913. There were, I imagine, that autumn, more German honeymoon-couples, more parties of rucksacked Wander-Birds than there had ever been in Venice before. There were too many, in any case, for me; I packed my bag and took the train for Padua.

I had not originally intended to see young Tirabassi

again. I didn't know, indeed, how pleased he would be to see me. For the frescoes, so far as I knew, at any rate, were still safely on the walls, the cheese-factory still remote in the future, in the imagination. I had written to him more than once, telling him that I was doing my best, but that at the moment, etcetera, etcetera. Not that I had ever held out much hope. I had made it clear from the first that my acquaintance among millionaires was limited, that I knew no directors of American museums, that I had nothing to do with any of the international picture dealers. But the Count's faith in me had remained, none the less, unshaken. It was the little Mexican, I believe, that inspired so much confidence. But now, after my letters, after all this lapse of time and nothing done, he might feel that I had let him down, deceived him somehow. That was why I took no steps to seek him out. But chance overruled my decision. On the third day of my stay in Padua, I ran into him in the street. Or rather he ran into me.

It was nearly six o'clock, and I had strolled down to the Piazzo del Santo. At that hour, when the slanting light is full of colour and the shadows are long and profound, the great church, with its cupolas and turrets and campaniles, takes on an aspect more than ever fantastic and oriental. I had walked round the church, and now I was standing at the foot of Donatello's statue, looking up at the grim bronze man, the ponderously stepping beast, when I suddenly became aware that some one was standing very close behind me. I took a step to one side and turned round. It was Fabio. Wearing his famous expression of the sight-seeing parson, he was gazing up at the statue, his mouth open in a vacant and fish-like gape. I burst out laughing.

'Did I look like that?' I asked.

'Precisely.' He laughed too. 'I've been watching you for the last ten minutes, mooning round the church. You English! Really . . .' He shook his head.

Together we strolled up the Via del Santo, talking as we went.

'I'm sorry I wasn't able to do anything about the frescoes,' I said. 'But really...' I entered into explanations.

'Some day, perhaps.' Fabio was still optimistic.

'And how's the Countess?'

'Oh, she's very well,' said Fabio, 'considering. You know she had another son three or four months after you came to see us.'

'No?'

'She's expecting another now.' Fabio spoke rather gloomily, I thought. More than ever I admired the old Count's sagacity. But I was sorry, for his son's sake, that he had not a wider field in which to exercise his talents.

'And your father?' I asked. 'Shall we find him sitting at Pedrochi's, as usual?'

Fabio laughed. 'We shall not,' he said significantly. 'He's flown.'

'Flown?'

'Gone, vanished, disappeared.'

'But where?'

'Who knows?' said Fabio. 'My father is like the swallows; he comes and he goes. Every year.... But the migration isn't regular. Sometimes he goes away in the spring; sometimes it's the autumn, sometimes it's the summer.... One fine morning his man goes into his room to call him as usual, and he isn't there. Vanished. He might be dead. Oh, but he isn't.' Fabio laughed. 'Two or three months later, in he walks again, as though he were just coming back from a stroll in the Botanical Gardens. "Good evening. Good evening." ' Fabio imitated the old Count's voice and manner, snuffing the air like a warhorse, twisting the ends of an imaginary white moustache. ' "How's your mother? How are the girls? How have the grapes done this year?" Snuff, snuff. "How's Lucio? And who the devil has left all this rubbish lying about in my study?" ' Fabio burst into an indignant roar that made the loiterers in the Via Roma turn, astonished, in our direction.

'And where does he go?' I asked.

'Nobody knows. My mother used to ask, once. But she soon gave it up. It was no good. "Where have you been, Ascanio?" "My dear, I'm afraid the olive crop is going to be very poor this year." Snuff, snuff. And when she pressed him, he would fly into a temper and slam the doors. . . . What do you say to an aperitif?' Pedrochi's open doors invited. We entered, chose a retired table, and sat down.

'But what do you suppose the old gentleman does when he's away?'

'Ah!' And making the richly significant gesture I had so much admired in his father, the young Count laid his finger against his nose and slowly, solemnly winked his left eye.

'You mean . . . ?'

Fabio nodded. 'There's a little widow here in Padua.' With his extended finger the young Count described in the air an undulating line. 'Nice and plump. Black eyes. I've noticed that she generally seems to be out of town just at the time the old man does his migrations. But it may, of course, be a mere coincidence.' The waiter brought us our vermouth. Pensively the young Count sipped. The gaiety went out of his open, lamp-like face. 'And meanwhile,' he went on slowly and in an altered voice, 'I stay here, looking after the estate, so that the old man can go running round the world with his little pigeon – *la sua colombella*.' (The expression struck me as particularly choice.) 'Oh, it's funny, no doubt,' the young Count went on. 'But it isn't right. If I wasn't married, I'd go clean away and try my luck somewhere else. I'd leave him to look after everything himself. But with a wife and two children – three children soon – how can I take the risk? At any rate, there's plenty to eat as long as I stay here. My only hope,' he added, after a little pause, 'is in the frescoes.'

Which implied, I reflected, that his only hope was in me; I felt sorry for him.

In the spring of 1914 I sent two rich Americans to look

at Fabio's villa. Neither of them made any offer to buy
the frescoes; it would have astonished me if they had.
But Fabio was greatly encouraged by their arrival. 'I feel,'
he wrote to me, 'that a beginning has now been made.
These Americans will go back to their country and tell
their friends. Soon there will be a procession of millionaires coming to see the frescoes. Meanwhile, life is the
same as ever. Rather worse, if anything. Our little daughter, whom we have christened Emilia, was born last
month. My wife had a very bad time and is still far from
well, which is very troublesome.' (It seemed a curious
adjective to use, in the circumstances. But coming from
Fabio, I understood it; he was one of those exceedingly
healthy people to whom any sort of illness is mysterious,
unaccountable, and above all extraordinarily tiresome and
irritating.) 'The day before yesterday my father disappeared again. I have not yet had time to find out if the
Colombella has also vanished. My brother, Lucio, has succeeded in getting a motor-bicycle out of him, which is
more than I ever managed to do. But then I was never
one for creeping diplomatically round and round a thing,
as he can do. . . . I have been going very carefully into the
cheese-factory business lately, and I am not sure that it
might not be more profitable to set up a silk-weaving
establishment instead. When you next come, I will go into
details with you.'

But it was a very long time before I saw Padua and
the Count again. . . . The war put an end to my yearly
visits to Italy, and for various reasons, even when it was
over, I could not go south again as soon as I should have
liked. Not until the autumn of 1921 did I embark again
on the Venice express.

It was in an Italy not altogether familiar that I now
found myself – an Italy full of violence and bloodshed.
The Fascists and the Communists were still busily fighting. Roaring at the head of their dust-storms, the motor-
lorries, loaded with cargoes of singing boys, careered
across the country in search of adventure and lurking Bol-

shevism. One stood respectfully in the gutter while they passed; and through the flying dust, through the noise of the engine, a snatch of that singing would be blown back: *'Giovinezza, giovinezza, primavera di bellezza...'* (Youth, youth, springtime of beauty). Where but in Italy would they have put such words to a political song? And then the proclamation, the manifestos, the denunciations, the appeals! Every hoarding and blank wall was plastered with them. Between the station and Pedrochi's I walked through a whole library of these things. 'Citizens!' they would begin. 'A heroic wind is to-day reviving the almost asphyxiated soul of our unhappy Italy, overcome by the poisonous fumes of Bolshevism and wallowing in ignoble abasement at the feet of the Nations.' And they finished, for the most part, with references to Dante. I read them all with infinite pleasure.

I reached Pedrochi's at last. On the terrace, sitting in the very corner where I had seen him first, years before, was the old Count. He stared at me blankly when I saluted him, not recognising me at all. I began to explain who I was; after a moment he cut me short, almost impatiently, protesting that he remembered now, perfectly well. I doubted very much whether he really did; but he was too proud to confess that he had forgotten. Meanwhile, he invited me to sit at his table.

At a first glance, from a distance, I fancied that the old Count had not aged a day since last I saw him. But I was wrong. From the street, I had only seen the rakish tilt of his hat, the bristling of his white moustache and imperial, the parted knees, the noble protrusion of the paunch. But, now that I could look at him closely and at leisure, I saw that he was in fact a very different man. Under the tilted hat his face was unhealthily purple; the flesh sagged into pouches. In the whites of his eyes, discoloured and as though tarnished with age, the little broken veins showed red. And, lustreless, the eyes themselves seemed to look without interest at what they saw. His shoulders were bent as though under a weight, and when he lifted his cup to his lips his hand trembled so much that a drop of coffee splashed on to the table. He was an old man now, old and tired.

'How's Fabio?' I asked; since 1916 I had had no news of him.

'Oh, Fabio's well,' the old Count answered, 'Fabio's very well. He has six children now, you know.' And the old gentleman nodded and smiled at me without a trace of malice. He seemed to have forgotten the reasons for which he had been at so much pains to select a good Catholic for a daughter-in-law. 'Six,' he repeated. 'And then, you know, he did very well in the war. We Tirabassi have always been warriors.' Full of pride, he went on to tell me of Fabio's exploits and sufferings. Twice wounded, special promotion on the field of battle, splendid decorations. He was a major now.

'And do his military duties still keep him in Padua?'

The old gentleman nodded, and suddenly there appeared on his face something like the old smile. 'A little *combinazione* of mine,' he said, and chuckled.

'And the estate?' I asked.

Oh, that was doing all right, everything considered. It had got rather out of hand during the war, while Fabio was at the front. And then, afterwards, there had been a lot of trouble with the peasants; but Fabio and his Fascists were putting all that to rights. 'With Fabio on the spot,' said the old gentleman, 'I have no anxieties.' And then he began to tell me, all over again, about Fabio's exploits in the war.

The next day I took the tram to Strà, and after an hour agreeably spent in the villa and the park, I walked on at my leisure towards Dolo. It took me a long time to get there, for on this occasion I was able to stop and look for as long as I liked at all the charming things on the way. Casanova seemed, now, a good deal less enviable, I noticed, looking inwards on myself, than he had when last I passed this way. I was nine years older.

The gates were open; I walked in. There stood the

house, as grave and ponderous as ever, but shabbier than when I saw it last. The shutters needed painting, and here and there the stucco was peeling off in scabs. I approached. From within the house came a cheerful noise of children's laughter and shouting. The family, I supposed, was playing hide-and-seek, or trains, or perhaps some topical game of Fascists and Communists. As I climbed the steps of the porch, I could hear the sound of small feet racing over the tiled floors; in the empty rooms footsteps and shouting strangely echoed. And then, suddenly, from the sitting-room on the right, came the sound of Fabio's voice, furiously shouting. 'Oh, for God's sake,' it yelled, 'keep those wretched children quiet.' And then, petulantly, it complained, 'How do you expect me to do accounts with this sort of thing going on?' There was at once a profound and as it were unnatural silence; then the sound of small feet tiptoeing away, some whispering, a little nervous laugh. I rang the bell.

It was the Countess who opened the door. She stood for a moment hesitatingly, wondering who I was; then remembered, smiled, held out her hand. She had grown, I noticed, very thin, and with the wasting of her face, her eyes seemed to have become larger. Their expression was as gentle and serene as ever; she seemed to be looking at me from a distance.

'Fabio will be delighted to see you,' she said, and she took me through the door on the right of the porch straight into the sitting-room. Fabio was sitting at the Palladian table in front of a heap of papers, biting the end of his pencil.

Even in his grey-green service uniform the young Count looked wonderfully brilliant, like a soldier on the stage. His face was still boyishly freckled, but the skin was deeply lined; he looked very much older than when I had seen him last – older than he really was. The open cheerfulness, the shining, lamp-like brightness were gone. On his snubby-featured face he wore a ludicrously incongruous expression of chronic melancholy. He brightened, it is true, for a moment when I appeared; I think he was genuinely glad to see me.

'*Caspita!*' he kept repeating. '*Caspita!*' (It was his favourite expression of astonishment, an odd, old-fashioned word.) 'Who would have thought it? After all this time!'

'And all the eternity of the war as well,' I said.

But when the first ebullition of surprise and pleasure subsided, the look of melancholy came back.

'It gives me the spleen,' he said, 'to see you again; still travelling about; free to go where you like. If you knew what life was like here . . .'

'Well, in any case,' I said, feeling that I ought, for the Countess's sake, to make some sort of protest, 'in any case the war's over and you have escaped a real revolution. That's something.'

'Oh, you're as bad as Laura,' said the Count impatiently. He looked towards his wife, as though hoping that she would say something. But the Countess went on with her sewing without even looking up. The Count took my arm. 'Come along,' he said, and his tone was almost one of anger. 'Let's take a turn outside.' His wife's religious resignation, her patience, her serenity angered him, I could see, like a reprimand – tacit, indeed, and unintentionally given, but none the less galling.

Along the weed-grown paths of what had once, in the ancient days of splendour, been the garden, slowly we walked towards the farm. A few ragged box-trees grew along the fringes of the paths; once there had been neat hedges. Poised over a dry basin a Triton blew his waterless conch. At the end of the vista a pair of rapes – Pluto and Proserpine, Apollo and Daphne – writhed desperately against the sky.

'I saw your father yesterday,' I said. 'He looks aged.'

'And so he ought,' said Fabio murderously. 'He's sixty-nine.'

I felt uncomfortably that the subject had become too serious for light conversation. I had wanted to ask after the Colombella; in the circumstances, I decided that it would be wiser to say nothing about her. I repressed my curiosity. We were walking now under the lea of the farm buildings.

'The cows look very healthy,' I said politely, looking through an open doorway. In the twilight within, six grey rumps plastered with dry dung presented themselves in file; six long leather tails swished impatiently from side to side. Fabio made no comment; he only grunted.

'In any case,' he went on slowly, after another silence, 'he can't live much longer. I shall sell my share and clear off to South America, family or no family.' It was a threat against his own destiny, a threat of which he must have known the vanity. He was deceiving himself to keep up his spirits.

'But I say,' I exclaimed, taking another and better opportunity to change the conversation, 'I see you have started a factory here after all.' We had walked round to the farther side of the square. Through the windows of the long low building which, at my last visit, had stood untenanted, I saw the complicated shapes of machines, rows of them in a double line down the whole length of the building. 'Looms? Then you decided against cheese? And the frescoes?' I turned questioningly towards the Count. I had a horrible fear that, when we got back to the house, I should find the great hall peeled of its Veroneses and a blank of plaster where once had been the history of Eros and Psyche.

'Oh, the frescoes are still there, what's left of them.' And in spite of Fabio's long face, I was delighted at the news. 'I persuaded my father to sell some of his house property in Padua, and we started this weaving business here two years ago. Just in time,' Fabio added, 'for the Communist revolution.'

Poor Fabio, he had no luck. The peasants had seized his factory and had tried to possess themselves of his land. For three weeks he had lived at the villa in a state of siege, defending the place, with twenty Fascists to help him, against all the peasants of the countryside. The danger was over now; but the machines were broken, and in any case it was out of the question to start them again; feeling was still too high. And what, for Fabio, made it worse was the fact that his brother Lucio, who had also got a little capital out of the old man, had gone off to Bulgaria and invested it in a bootlace factory. It was the only bootlace factory in the country, and Lucio was making money hand over fist. Free as air he was, well off, a lovely Turkish girl for a mistress. For Fabio, the Turkish girl was evidently the last straw. '*Una Turca, una vera Turca*,' he repeated, shaking his head. The female infidel symbolised in his eyes all that was exotic, irregular, undomestic; all that was not the family; all that was remote from Padua and the estate.

'And they were such beautiful machines,' said Fabio, pausing for a moment to look in at the last of the long line of windows. 'Whether to sell them, whether to wait till all this has blown over and have them put right and try to start again – I don't know.' He shrugged his shoulders hopelessly. 'Or just let things slide till the old man dies.' We turned the corner of the square and began to walk back towards the house. 'Sometimes,' he added, after a silence, 'I don't believe he ever will die.'

The children were playing in the great hall of the Veroneses. The majestic double doors which gave on to the portico were ajar; through the opening we watched them for a moment without being seen. The family was formed up in order of battle. A red-headed boy of ten or eleven led the van, a brown boy followed. Then came three little girls, diminishing regularly in size like graded pearls; and finally a little toddling creature in blue linen crawlers. All six of them carried shouldered bamboos, and they were singing in ragged unison to a kind of trumpet call of three notes: '*All' armi i Fascisti; a morte i Comunisti; a basso i Socialisti*' – over and over again. And as they sang they marched, round and round, earnestly, indefatigably. The huge empty room echoed like a swimming-bath. Remote under their triumphal arches, in their serene world of fantastic beauty, the silken ladies and gentlemen played their music, drank their wine; the poet declaimed, the painter poised his brush before the canvas; the monkeys clambered among the Roman ruins, the parrots dozed on the balustrades. *'All' armi i Fascisti; a morte i Comunisti ...'* I should have liked to stand there in silence, merely to see how long the children would continue their patriotic march. But Fabio had none of my scientific curiosity; or if he ever had, it had certainly been exhausted long before the last of his children was born. After indulging me for a moment with the spectacle, he pushed open the door and walked in. The children looked round and were immediately silent. What with his bad temper and his theory of education by teasing, they seemed to be thoroughly frightened of their father.

'Go on,' he said, 'go on.' But they wouldn't; they obviously couldn't, in his terrifying presence. Unobtrusively they slipped away.

Fabio led me round the painted room. 'Look here,' he said, 'and look here.' In one of the walls of the great hall there were half a dozen bullet holes. A chip had been taken off one of the painted cornices; one lady was horribly wounded in the face; there were two or three holes in the landscape, and a monkey's tail was severed. 'That's our friends, the peasants,' Fabio explained.

In the Carpioni rooms all was still well; the satyrs still pursued their nymphs, and in the room of the centaurs and the mermaids, the men who were half horses galloped as tumultuously as ever into the sea, to ravish the women who were half fish. But the tale of Eros and Psyche had suffered dreadfully. The exquisite panel in which Tiepolo had painted Psyche holding up the lamp to look at her mysterious lover was no more than a faint, mildewy smudge. And where once the indignant young god had flown upwards to rejoin his Olympian relatives (who still, fortunately, swam about intact among the clouds on the ceiling) there was nothing but the palest ghost of an ascending Cupid, while Psyche weeping on the earth below was now quite invisible.

'That's our friends the French,' said Fabio. 'They were quartered here in 1918, and they didn't trouble to shut the windows when it rained.'

Poor Fabio! Everything was against him. I had no consolation to offer. That autumn I sent him an art critic and three more Americans. But nothing came of their visits. The fact was that he had too much to offer. A picture – that might easily have been disposed of. But what could one do with a whole houseful of paintings like this?

The months passed. About Easter time of the next year I had another letter from Fabio. The olive crop had been poor. The Countess was expecting another baby and was far from well. The two eldest children were down with measles, and the last but one had what the Italians call an 'asinine cough'. He expected all the children to catch both diseases in due course. He was very doubtful now if it would ever be worth while to restart his looms; the position of the silk trade was not so sound as it had been at the end of 1919. If only he had stuck to cheese, as he first intended! Lucio had just made fifty thousand lire by a lucky stroke of speculation. But the female infidel had run off with a Rumanian. The old Count was ageing rapidly; when Fabio saw him last, he had told the same anecdote three times in the space of ten minutes. With these two pieces of good news – they were for him, I imagine, the only bright spots in the surrounding gloom – Fabio closed his letter. I was left wondering why he troubled to write to me at all. It may be that he got a certain lacerating satisfaction by thus enumerating his troubles.

That August there was a musical festival in Salzburg. I had never been in Austria; the occasion seemed to me a good one. I went, and I enjoyed myself prodigiously. Salzburg at the moment is all in the movement. There are baroque churches in abundance; there are Italianate fountains; there are gardens and palaces that mimic in their extravagantly ponderous Teutonic way the gardens and palaces of Rome. And, choicest treasure of all, there is a tunnel, forty feet high, bored through a precipitous crag – a tunnel such as only a Prince Bishop of the seventeenth century could have dreamed of, having at either end an arch of triumph, with pilasters, broken pediments, statues, scutcheons, all carved out of the living rock—a masterpiece among tunnels, and in a town where everything, without being really good, is exquisitely 'amusing', the most amusing feature of all. Ah, decidedly, Salzburg is in the movement.

One afternoon I took the funicular up to the castle. There is a beer-terrace under the walls of the fortress from which you get a view that is starred in Baedeker. Below you on one side lies the town, spread out in the curving valley, with a river running through it, like a small and German version of Florence. From the other side of the terrace you look out over a panorama that makes no pretence to Italianism; it is as sweetly and romantically German as an air out of Weber's *Freischütz*. There are mountains on the horizon, spiky and blue like mountains in a picture book; and in the foreground, extending to the very foot of the extremely improbable crag on which the castle and the beer-garden are perched, stretches a flat green plain – miles upon miles of juicy meadows dotted with minusculous cows, with here and there a neat toy farm, or, more rarely, a cluster of dolls' houses, with a spire going up glittering from the midst of them.

I was sitting with my blond beer in front of this delicious and slightly comical landscape, thinking comfortably of nothing in particular, when I heard behind me a rapturous voice exclaiming, *'Bello, bello!'* I looked round curiously – for it seemed to me somehow rather surprising to hear Italian spoken here – and saw one of those fine sumptuous women they admire so much in the South. She was a *bella grassa*, plump to the verge of overripeness and perilously near middle age; but still in her way exceedingly handsome. Her face had the proportions of an ice-berg – one-fifth above water, four-fifths below. Ample and florid from the eyes downwards, it was almost headless; the hair began immediately above the brows. The eyes themselves were dark, large, and, for my taste, at least, somewhat excessively tender in expression. I took her in in a moment and was about to look away again when her companion, who had been looking at the view on the other side, turned round. It was the old Count.

I was far more embarrassed, I believe, than he. I felt myself blushing, as our eyes met, as though it were I who had been travelling about the world with a Colombella and he who had caught me in the act. I did not know what to do – whether to smile and speak to him, or to turn away as though I had not recognised him, or to nod from a distance and then, discreetly, to disappear. But the old Count put an end to my irresolution by call-ing out my name in astonishment, by running up to me and seizing my hand. What a delight to see an old friend! Here of all places! In this God-forsaken country – though it was cheap enough, didn't I find? He would introduce me to a charming compatriot of his own, an Italian lady he had met yesterday in the train from Vienna.

I was made known to the Colombella, and we all sat down at my table. Speaking resolutely in Italian, the Count ordered two more beers. We talked. Or rather the Count talked; for the conversation was a monologue. He told us anecdotes of the Italy of fifty years ago; he gave us imitations of the queer characters he had known; he even, at one moment, imitated the braying of an ass – I forget in what context; but the braying remains vividly in my memory. Snuffing the air between every sentence, he gave us his views on women. The Colombella screamed indignant protests, dissolved herself in laughter. The old Count twisted his moustaches, twinkling at her through the network of his wrinkles. Every now and then he turned in my direction and gave me a little wink.

I listened in astonishment. Was this the man who had told the same anecdote three times in ten minutes? I looked at the old Count. He was leaning towards the Colombella whispering something in her ear which made her laugh so much that she had to wipe the tears from her eyes. Turning away from her, he caught my eye; smiling, he shrugged his shoulders as though to say, 'These women! What imbeciles, but how delicious, how indispensable!' Was this the tired old man I had seen a year ago sitting on Pedrochi's terrace? It seemed incredible.

'Well, good-bye, *a rivederci.*' They had to get down into the town again. The funicular was waiting.

'I'm delighted to have seen you,' said the old Count, shaking me affectionately by the hand.

'And so am I,' I protested. 'Particularly delighted to see you so well.'

'Yes, I'm wonderfully well now,' he said, blowing out his chest.

'And young,' I went on. 'Younger than I am! How have you done it?'

'Aha!' The old Count cocked his head on one side mysteriously.

More in joke than in earnest, 'I believe you've been seeing Steinach in Vienna,' I said. 'Having a rejuvenating operation.'

For all reply, the old Count raised the forefinger of his right hand, laying it first to his lips, then along the side of his nose, and as he did so he winked. Then clenching his fist, and with his thumb sticking rigidly up, he made a complicated gesture which would, I am sure, for an Italian, have been full of a profound and vital significance. To me, however, unfamiliar with the language of signs, the exact meaning was not entirely clear. But the Count offered no verbal explanation. Still without uttering a word, he raised his hat; then laying his finger once more to his lips, he turned and ran with an astonishing agility down the steep path towards the little carriage of the funicular, in which the Colombella had already taken her seat.

SOMERSET MAUGHAM

The Hairless Mexican

'Do you like macaroni?' said R.

'What do you mean by macaroni?' answered Ashenden. 'It is like asking me if I like poetry. I like Keats and Wordsworth and Verlaine and Goethe. When you say macaroni, do you mean *spaghetti, tagliatelli, vermicelli, fettucini, tufali, farfalli,* or just macaroni?'

'Macaroni,' replied R., a man of few words.

'I like all simple things, boiled eggs, oysters and caviare, *truite au bleu,* grilled salmon, roast lamb (the saddle by preference), cold grouse, treacle tart and rice pudding. But of all simple things the only one I can eat day in and day out, not only without disgust but with the eagerness of an appetite unimpaired by excess, is macaroni.'

'I am glad of that because I want you to go down to Italy.'

Ashenden had come from Geneva to meet R. at Lyons and having got there before him had spent the afternoon wandering about the dull, busy and prosaic streets of that thriving city. They were sitting now in a restaurant on the *place* to which Ashenden had taken R. on his arrival because it was reputed to give you the best food in that part of France. But since in so crowded a resort (for the Lyonese like a good dinner) you never knew what inquisitive ears were pricked up to catch any useful piece of information that might fall from your lips, they had contented themselves with talking of indifferent things. They had reached the end of an admirable repast.

'Have another glass of brandy?' said R.

'No, thank you,' answered Ashenden, who was of an abstemious turn.

'One should do what one can to mitigate the rigours of war,' remarked R. as he took the bottle and poured out a glass for himself and another for Ashenden.

Ashenden, thinking it would be affectation to protest, let the gesture pass, but felt bound to remonstrate with his chief on the unseemly manner in which he held the bottle.

'In my youth I was always taught that you should take a woman by the waist and a bottle by the neck,' he murmured.

'I am glad you told me. I shall continue to hold a bottle by the waist and give women a wide berth.'

Ashenden did not know what to reply to this and so remained silent. He sipped his brandy and R. called for his bill. It was true that he was an important person, with power to make or mar quite a large number of his fellows, and his opinions were listened to by those who held in their hands the fate of empires; but he could never face the business of tipping a waiter without an embarrassment that was obvious in his demeanour. He was tortured by the fear of making a fool of himself by giving too much or of exciting the waiter's icy scorn by giving too little. When the bill came he passed some hundred-franc notes over to Ashenden and said:

'Pay him, will you? I can never understand French figures.'

The groom brought them their hats and coats.

'Would you like to go back to the hotel?' asked Ashenden.

'We might as well.'

It was early in the year, but the weather had suddenly turned warm, and they walked with their coats over their arms. Ashenden knowing that R. liked a sitting-room had engaged one for him and to this, when they reached the hotel, they went. The hotel was old-fashioned and the sitting-room was vast. It was furnished with a heavy mahogany suite upholstered in green velvet and the chairs were set primly round a large table. On the walls, covered with a dingy paper, were large steel engravings of the battles of Napoleon, and from the ceiling hung an enormous chandelier once used for gas, but now fitted with electric bulbs. It flooded the cheerless room with a cold, hard light.

'This is very nice,' said R., as they went in.

'Not exactly cosy,' suggested Ashenden.

'No, but it looks as though it were the best room in the place. It all looks very *good* to me.'

He drew one of the green velvet chairs away from the table and, sitting down, lit a cigar. He loosened his belt and unbuttoned his tunic.

'I always thought I liked a cheroot better than anything,' he said, 'but since the war I've taken quite a fancy to Havanas. Oh well, I suppose it can't last for ever.' The corners of his mouth flickered with the beginning of a smile. 'It's an ill wind that blows nobody any good.'

Ashenden took two chairs, one to sit on and one for his feet, and when R. saw him he said: 'That's not a bad idea,' and swinging another chair out from under the table with a sigh of relief put his boots on it.

'What room is that next door?' he asked.

'That's your bedroom.'

'And on the other side?'

'A banqueting hall.'

R. got up and strolled slowly about the room and when he passed the windows, as though in idle curiosity, peeped through the heavy rep curtains that covered them, and then returning to his chair once more comfortably put his feet up.

'It's just as well not to take any more risk than one need,' he said.

He looked at Ashenden reflectively. There was a slight smile on his thin lips, but the pale eyes, too closely set together, remained cold and steely. R.'s stare would have been embarrassing if Ashenden had not been used to it. He knew that R. was considering how he would broach the subject that he had in mind. The silence must have lasted for two or three minutes.

'I'm expecting a fellow to come and see me to-night,' he said at last. 'His train gets in about ten.' He gave his wrist-watch a glance. 'He's known as the Hairless Mexican.'

'Why?'

'Because he's hairless and because he's a Mexican.'

'The explanation seems perfectly satisfactory,' said Ashenden.

'He'll tell you all about himself. He talks nineteen to the dozen. He was on his uppers when I came across him. It appears that he was mixed up in some revolution in Mexico and had to get out with nothing but the clothes he stood up in. They were rather the worse for wear when I found him. If you want to please him you call him General. He claims to have been a general in Huerta's army, at least I think it was Huerta; anyhow he says that if things had gone right he would be Minister of War now and no end of a big bug. I've found him very useful. Not a bad chap. The only thing I really have against him is that he will use scent.'

'And where do I come in?' asked Ashenden.

'He's going down to Italy. I've got rather a ticklish job for him to do and I want you to stand by. I'm not keen on trusting him with a lot of money. He's a gambler and he's a bit too fond of the girls. I suppose you came from Geneva on your Ashenden passport?'

'Yes.'

'I've got another for you, a diplomatic one, by the way, in the name of Somerville with visas for France and Italy. I think you and he had better travel together. He's an amusing cove when he gets going, and I think you ought to know one another.'

'What is the job?'

'I haven't yet quite made up my mind how much it's desirable for you to know about it.'

Ashenden did not reply. They eyed one another in a detached manner, as though they were strangers who sat together in a railway carriage and each wondered who and what the other was.

'In your place I'd leave the General to do most of the talking. I wouldn't tell him more about yourself than you find absolutely necessary. He won't ask you any questions, I can promise you that, I think he's by way of being a gentleman after his own fashion.'

'By the way, what is his real name?'

'I always call him Manuel, I don't know that he likes it very much, his name is Manuel Carmona.'

'I gather by what you have not said that he's an unmitigated scoundrel.'

R. smiled with his pale blue eyes.

'I don't know that I'd go quite so far as that. He hasn't had the advantages of a public-school education. His ideas of playing the game are not quite the same as yours or mine. I don't know that I'd leave a gold cigarette-case about when he was in the neighbourhood, but if he lost money to you at poker and had pinched your cigarette-case he would immediately pawn it to pay you. If he had half a chance he'd seduce your wife, but if you were up against it he'd share his last crust with you. The tears will run down his face when he hears Gounod's "Ave Maria" on the gramophone, but if you insult his dignity he'll shoot you like a dog. It appears that in Mexico it's an insult to get between a man and his drink and he told me himself that once when a Dutchman who didn't know passed between him and the bar he whipped out his revolver and shot him dead.'

'Did nothing happen to him?'

'No, it appears that he belongs to one of the best families. The matter was hushed up and it was announced in the papers that the Dutchman had committed suicide.

He did practically. I don't believe the Hairless Mexican has a great respect for human life.'

Ashenden, who had been looking intently at R., started a little and he watched more carefully than ever his chief's tired, lined and yellow face. He knew that he did not make this remark for nothing.

'Of course a lot of nonsense is talked about the value of human life. You might just as well say that the counters you use at poker have an intrinsic value, their value is what you like to make it; for a general giving battle, men are merely counters and he's a fool if he allows himself for sentimental reasons to look upon them as human beings.'

'But, you see, they're counters that feel and think and if they believe they're being squandered they are quite capable of refusing to be used any more.'

'Anyhow, that's neither here nor there. We've had information that a man called Constantine Andreadi is on his way from Constantinople with certain documents that we want to get hold of. He's a Greek. He's an agent of Enver Pasha and Enver has great confidence in him. He's given him verbal messages that are too secret and too important to be put on paper. He's sailing from the Piræus, on a boat called the *Ithaca*, and will land at Brindisi on his way to Rome. He's to deliver his despatches at the German Embassy and impart what he has to say personally to the ambassador.'

'I see.'

At this time Italy was still neutral; the Central Powers were straining every nerve to keep her so; the Allies were doing what they could to induce her to declare war on their side.

'We don't want to get into any trouble with the Italian authorities, it might be fatal, but we've got to prevent Andreadi from getting to Rome.'

'At any cost?' asked Ashenden.

'Money's no object,' answered R., his lips twisting into a sardonic smile.

'What do you propose to do?'

'I don't think you need bother your head about that.'

'I have a fertile imagination,' said Ashenden.

'I want you to go down to Naples with the Hairless Mexican. He's very keen on getting back to Cuba. It appears that his friends are organising a show and he wants to be as near at hand as possible so that he can hop over to Mexico when things are ripe. He needs cash. I've brought money down with me, in American dollars, and I shall give it to you to-night. You'd better carry it on your person.'

'Is it much?'

'It's a good deal, but I thought it would be easier for you if it wasn't bulky, so I've got it in thousand-dollar notes. You will give the Hairless Mexican the notes in return for the documents that Andreadi is bringing.'

A question sprang to Ashenden's lips, but he did not ask it. He asked another instead.

'Does this fellow understand what he has to do?'

'Perfectly.'

There was a knock at the door. It opened and the Hairless Mexican stood before them.

'I have arrived. Good evening, Colonel. I am enchanted to see you.'

R. got up.

'Had a nice journey, Manuel? This is Mr Somerville, who's going to Naples with you, General Carmona.'

'Pleased to meet you, sir.'

He shook Ashenden's hand with such force that he winced.

'Your hands are like iron, General,' he murmured.

The Mexican gave them a glance.

'I had them manicured this morning. I do not think they were very well done. I like my nails much more highly polished.'

They were cut to a point, stained bright red, and to Ashenden's mind shone like mirrors. Though it was not cold the General wore a fur coat with an astrakhan collar and with his every movement a wave of perfume was wafted to your nose.

'Take off your coat, General, and have a cigar,' said R.

The Hairless Mexican was a tall man, and though thinnish gave you the impression of being very powerful; he was smartly dressed in a blue serge suit, with a silk handkerchief neatly tucked in the breast pocket of his coat, and he wore a gold bracelet on his wrist. His features were good, but a little larger than life-size, and his eyes were brown and lustrous. He was quite hairless. His yellow skin had the smoothness of a woman's and he had no eyebrows nor eyelashes; he wore a pale brown wig, rather long, and the locks were arranged in artistic disorder. This and the unwrinkled sallow face, combined with his dandified dress, gave him an appearance that was at first glance a trifle horrifying. He was repulsive and ridiculous, but you could not take your eyes from him. There was a sinister fascination in his strangeness.

He sat down and hitched up his trousers so that they should not bag at the knee.

'Well, Manuel, have you been breaking any hearts to-day?' said R. with his sardonic joviality.

The General turned to Ashenden.

'Our good friend, the Colonel, envies me my successes with the fair sex. I tell him he can have just as many as I if he will only listen to me. Confidence, that is all you need. If you never fear a rebuff you will never have one.'

'Nonsense, Manuel, one has to have your way with the girls. There's something about you that they can't resist.'

The Hairless Mexican laughed with a self-satisfaction that he did not try to disguise. He spoke English very well, with a Spanish accent, but with an American intonation.

'But since you ask me, Colonel, I don't mind telling you that I got into conversation on the train with a little woman who was coming to Lyons to see her mother-in-law. She was not very young and she was thinner than I like a woman to be, but she was possible, and she helped me to pass an agreeable hour.'

'Well, let's get to business,' said R.

'I am at your service, Colonel.' He gave Ashenden a glance. 'Is Mr Somerville a military man?'

'No,' said R., 'he's an author.'

'It takes all sorts to make a world, as you say. I am happy to make your acquaintance, Mr Somerville. I can tell you many stories that will interest you; I am sure that we shall get on well together. You have a sympathetic air. I am very sensitive to that. To tell you the truth I am nothing but a bundle of nerves and if I am with a person who is antipathetic to me I go all to pieces.'

'I hope we shall have a pleasant journey,' said Ashenden.

'When does our friend arrive at Brindisi?' asked the Mexican, turning to R.

'He sails from the Piræus in the *Ithaca* on the fourteenth. It's probably some old tub, but you'd better get down to Brindisi in good time.'

'I agree with you.'

R. got up and with his hands in his pockets sat on the edge of the table. In his rather shabby uniform, his tunic unbuttoned, he looked a slovenly creature beside the neat and well-dressed Mexican.

'Mr Somerville knows practically nothing of the errand on which you are going and I do not desire you to tell him anything. I think you had much better keep your own counsel. He is instructed to give you the funds you need for your work, but your actions are your own affair. If you need his advice of course you can ask for it.'

'I seldom ask other people's advice and never take it.'

'And should you make a mess of things I trust you to keep Mr Somerville out of it. He must on no account be compromised.'

'I am a man of honour, Colonel,' answered the Hairless Mexican with dignity, 'and I would sooner let myself be cut in a thousand pieces than betray my friends.'

'That is what I have already told Mr Somerville. On the other hand, if everything pans out O.K. Mr Somerville is instructed to give you the sum we agreed on in return for the papers I spoke to you about. In what manner you get them is no business of his.'

'That goes without saying. There is only one thing I wish to make quite plain; Mr Somerville understands of course that I have not accepted the mission with which you have entrusted me on account of the money?'

'Quite,' replied R. gravely, looking him straight in the eyes.

'I am with the Allies body and soul, I cannot forgive the Germans for outraging the neutrality of Belgium, and if I accept the money that you have offered me it is because I am first and foremost a patriot. I can trust Mr Somerville implicitly, I suppose?'

R. nodded. The Mexican turned to Ashenden.

'An expedition is being arranged to free my unhappy country from the tyrants that exploit and ruin it and every penny that I receive will go on guns and cartridges. For myself I have no need of money; I am a soldier and I can live on a crust and a few olives. There are only three occupations that befit a gentleman, war, cards and women; it costs nothing to sling a rifle over your shoulder and take to the mountains – and that is real warfare, not this manœuvring of battalions and firing of great guns – women love me for myself, and I generally win at cards.'

Ashenden found the flamboyance of this strange creature, with his scented handkerchief and his gold bracelet, very much to his taste. This was far from being just the man in the street (whose tyranny we rail at but in the end submit to) and to the amateur of the baroque in human nature he was a rarity to be considered with delight. He was a purple patch on two legs. Notwithstanding his wig and his hairless big face, he had undoubtedly an air; he was absurd, but he did not give you the impression that he was a man to be trifled with. His self-complacency was magnificent.

'Where is your kit, Manuel?' asked R.

It was possible that a frown for an instant darkened the Mexican's brow at the abrupt question that seemed a little contemptuously to brush to one side his eloquent statement, but he gave no other sign of displeasure. Ashenden suspected that he thought the Colonel a barbarian insensitive to the finer emotions.

'I left it at the station.'

'Mr Somerville has a diplomatic passport so that he can get it through with his own things at the frontier without examination if you like.'

'I have very little, a few suits and some linen, but perhaps it would be as well if Mr Somerville would take charge of it. I bought half a dozen suits of silk pyjamas before I left Paris.'

'And what about you?' asked R., turning to Ashenden.

'I've only got one bag. It's in my room.'

'You'd better have it taken to the station while there's someone about. Your train goes at one ten.'

'Oh?'

This was the first Ashenden had heard that they were to start that night.

'I think you'd better get down to Naples as soon as possible.'

'Very well.'

R. got up.

'I'm going to bed. I don't know what you fellows want to do.'

'I shall take a walk about Lyons,' said the Hairless Mexican. 'I am interested in life. Lend me a hundred francs, Colonel, will you? I have no change on me.'

R. took out his pocket-book and gave the General the note he asked for. Then to Ashenden:

'What are you going to do? Wait here?'

'No,' said Ashenden, 'I shall go to the station and read.'

'You'd both of you better have a whisky and soda before you go, hadn't you? What about it, Manuel?'

303

'It is very kind of you, but I never drink anything but champagne and brandy.'

'Mixed?' asked R. dryly.

'Not necessarily,' returned the other with gravity.

R. ordered brandy and soda and when it came, whereas he and Ashenden helped themselves to both, the Hairless Mexican poured himself out three parts of a tumbler of neat brandy and swallowed it in two noisy gulps. He rose to his feet and put on his coat with the astrakhan collar, seized in one hand his bold black hat and, with the gesture of a romantic actor giving up the girl he loves to one more worthy of her, held out the other to R.

'Well, Colonel, I will bid you good-night and pleasant dreams. I do not expect that we shall meet again so soon.'

'Don't make a hash of things, Manuel, and if you do, keep your mouth shut.'

'They tell me that in one of your colleges where the sons of gentlemen are trained to become naval officers it is written in letters of gold: There is no such word as impossible in the British Navy. I do not know the meaning of the word failure.'

'It has a good many synonyms,' retorted R.

'I will meet you at the station, Mr Somerville,' said the Hairless Mexican, and with a flourish left them.

R. looked at Ashenden with that little smile of his that always made his face look so dangerously shrewd.

'Well, what d'you think of him?'

'You've got me beat,' said Ashenden. 'Is he a mountebank? He seems as vain as a peacock. And with that frightful appearance can he really be the lady's man he pretends? What makes you think you can trust him?'

R. gave a low chuckle and he washed his thin, old hands with imaginary soap.

'I thought you'd like him. He's quite a character, isn't he? I think we can trust him.' R.'s eyes suddenly grew opaque. 'I don't believe it would pay him to double-cross us.' He paused for a moment. 'Anyhow, we've got to risk it. I'll give you the tickets and the money and then you can take yourself off; I'm all in and I want to go to bed.'

Ten minutes later Ashenden set out for the station with his bag on a porter's shoulder.

Having nearly two hours to wait he made himself comfortable in the waiting-room. The light was good and he read a novel. When the time drew near for the arrival of the train from Paris that was to take them direct to Rome and the Hairless Mexican did not appear, Ashenden, beginning to grow a trifle anxious, went out on the platform to look for him. Ashenden suffered from that distressing malady known as train fever: an hour before his train was due he began to have apprehensions lest he should miss it; he was impatient with the porters who would never bring his luggage down from his room in time and he could not understand why the hotel bus cut it so fine; a block in the street would drive him to frenzy and the languid movements of the station porters infuriate him. The whole world seemed in a horrid plot to delay him; people got in his way as he passed through the barriers; others, a long string of them, were at the ticket-office getting tickets for other trains than his and they counted their change with exasperating care; his luggage took an interminable time to register; and then if he was travelling with friends they would go to buy newspapers, or would take a walk along the platform, and he was certain they would be left behind, they would stop to talk to a casual stranger or suddenly be seized with a desire to telephone and disappear at a run. In fact the universe conspired to make him miss every train he wanted to take and he was not happy unless he was settled in his corner, his things on the rack above him, with a good half-hour to spare. Sometimes by arriving at the station too soon he had caught an earlier train than the one he had meant to, but that was nerve-racking and caused him all the anguish of very nearly missing it.

The Rome express was signalled and there was no sign

of the Hairless Mexican; it came in and he was not to be seen. Ashenden became more and more harassed. He walked quickly up and down the platform, looked in all the waiting-rooms, went to the *consigne* where the luggage was left; he could not find him. There were no sleeping-cars, but a number of people got out and he took two seats in a first-class carriage. He stood by the door, looking up and down the platform and up at the clock; it was useless to go if his travelling companion did not turn up, and Ashenden made up his mind to take his things out of the carriage as the porter cried *en voiture*; but, by George! he would give the brute hell when he found him. There were three minutes more, then two minutes, then one; at that late hour there were few persons about and all who were travelling had taken their seats. Then he saw the Hairless Mexican, followed by two porters with his luggage and accompanied by a man in a bowler-hat, walk leisurely on to the platform. He caught sight of Ashenden and waved to him.

'Ah, my dear fellow, there you are, I wondered what had become of you.'

'Good God, man, hurry up or we shall miss the train.'

'I never miss a train. Have you got good seats? The *chef de gare* has gone for the night; this is his assistant.'

The man in the bowler-hat took it off when Ashenden nodded to him.

'But this is an ordinary carriage. I am afraid I could not travel in that.' He turned to the stationmaster's assistant with an affable smile. 'You must do better for me than that, *mon cher*.'

'*Certainement, mon général*, I will put you into a *salon-lit*. Of course.'

The assistant stationmaster led them along the train and opened the door of an empty compartment where there were two beds. The Mexican eyed it with satisfaction and watched the porters arrange the luggage.

'That will do very well. I am much obliged to you.' He held out his hand to the man in the bowler-hat. 'I shall not forget you and next time I see the Minister I will tell him with what civility you have treated me.'

'You are too good, General. I shall be very grateful.'

A whistle was blown and the train started.

'This is better than an ordinary first-class carriage, I think, Mr Somerville,' said the Mexican. 'A good traveller should learn how to make the best of things.'

But Ashenden was still extremely cross.

'I don't know why the devil you wanted to cut it so fine. We should have looked a pair of damned fools if we'd missed the train.'

'My dear fellow, there was never the smallest chance of that. When I arrived I told the stationmaster that I was General Carmona, Commander-in-Chief of the Mexican Army, and that I had to stop off in Lyons for a few hours to hold a conference with the British Field-Marshal. I asked him to hold the train for me if I was delayed and suggested that my government might see its way to conferring an order on him. I have been to Lyons before, I like the girls here; they have not the *chic* of the Parisians, but they have something, there is no denying that they have something. Will you have a mouthful of brandy before you go to sleep?'

'No, thank you,' said Ashenden morosely.

'I always drink a glass before going to bed, it settles the nerves.'

He looked in his suit-case and without difficulty found a bottle. He put it to his lips and had a long drink, wiped his mouth with the back of his hand and lit a cigarette. Then he took off his boots and lay down. Ashenden dimmed the light.

'I have never yet made up my mind,' said the Hairless Mexican reflectively, 'whether it is pleasanter to go to sleep with the kisses of a beautiful woman on your mouth or with a cigarette between your lips. Have you ever been to Mexico? I will tell you about Mexico tomorrow. Good-night.'

Soon Ashenden heard from his steady breathing that

he was asleep and in a little while himself dozed off. Presently he woke. The Mexican, deep in slumber, lay motionless; he had taken off his fur coat and was using it as a blanket; he still wore his wig. Suddenly there was a jolt and the train with a noisy grinding of brakes stopped; in the twinkling of an eye, before Ashenden could realize that anything had happened, the Mexican was on his feet with his hand to his hip.

'What is it?' he cried.

'Nothing. Probably only a signal against us.'

The Mexican sat down heavily on his bed. Ashenden turned on the light.

'You wake quickly for such a sound sleeper,' he said.

'You have to in my profession.'

Ashenden would have liked to ask him whether this was murder, conspiracy or commanding armies, but was not sure that it would be discreet. The General opened his bag and took out the bottle.

'Will you have a nip?' he asked. 'There is nothing like it when you wake suddenly in the night.'

When Ashenden refused he put the bottle once more to his lips and poured a considerable quantity of liquor down his throat. He sighed and lit a cigarette. Although Ashenden had seen him now drink nearly a bottle of brandy, and it was probable that he had had a good deal more when he was going about the town, he was certainly quite sober. Neither in his manner nor in his speech was there any indication that he had drunk during the evening anything but lemonade.

The train started and Ashenden again fell asleep. When he awoke it was morning and turning round lazily he saw that the Mexican was awake too. He was smoking a cigarette. The floor by his side was strewn with burnt-out butts and the air was thick and grey. He had begged Ashenden not to insist on opening a window, for he said the night air was dangerous.

'I did not get up, because I was afraid of waking you. Will you do your toilet first or shall I?'

'I'm in no hurry,' said Ashenden.

'I am an old campaigner, it will not take me long. Do you wash your teeth every day?'

'Yes,' said Ashenden.

'So do I. It is a habit I learned in New York. I always think that a fine set of teeth are an adornment to a man.'

There was a wash-basin in the compartment and the General scrubbed his teeth, with gurglings and garglings, energetically. Then he got a bottle of eau-de-Cologne from his bag, poured some of it on a towel and rubbed it over his face and hands. He took a comb and carefully arranged his wig; either it had not moved in the night or else he had set it straight before Ashenden awoke. He got another bottle out of his bag, with a spray attached to it, and squeezing a bulb covered his shirt and coat with a fine cloud of scent, did the same to his handkerchief, and then with a beaming face, like a man who has done his duty by the world and is well pleased, turned to Ashenden and said:

'Now I am ready to brave the day. I will leave my things for you, you need not be afraid of the eau-de-Cologne, it is the best you can get in Paris.'

'Thank you very much,' said Ashenden. 'All I want is soap and water.'

'Water? I never use water except when I have a bath. Nothing can be worse for the skin.'

When they approached the frontier, Ashenden, remembering the General's instructive gesture when he was suddenly awakened in the night, said to him:

'If you've got a revolver on you I think you'd better give it to me. With my diplomatic passport they're not likely to search me, but they might take it into their heads to go through you and we don't want to have any bothers.'

'It is hardly a weapon, it is only a toy,' returned the Mexican, taking out of his hip-pocket a fully loaded revolver of formidable dimensions. 'I do not like parting with it even for an hour, it gives me the feeling that I am not fully dressed. But you are quite right, we do not want to take any risks; I will give you my knife as well. I would always rather use a knife than a revolver; I think it is a more elegant weapon.'

'I dare say it is only a matter of habit,' answered Ashenden. 'Perhaps you are more at home with a knife.'

'Anyone can pull a trigger, but it needs a man to use a knife.'

To Ashenden it looked as though it were in a single movement that he tore open his waistcoat and from his belt snatched and opened a long knife of murderous aspect. He handed it to Ashenden with a pleased smile on his large, ugly and naked face.

'There's a pretty piece of work for you, Mr Somerville. I've never seen a better bit of steel in my life, it takes an edge like a razor and it's strong; you can cut a cigarette-paper with it and you can hew down an oak. There is nothing to get out of order and when it is closed it might be the knife a schoolboy uses to cut notches in his desk.'

He shut it with a click and Ashenden put it along with the revolver in his pocket.

'Have you anything else?'

'My hands,' replied the Mexican with arrogance, 'but those I dare say the Custom officials will not make trouble about.'

Ashenden remembered the iron grip he had given him when they shook hands and slightly shuddered. They were large and long and smooth; there was not a hair on them or on the wrists, and with the pointed, rosy, manicured nails there was really something sinister about them.

Ashenden and General Carmona went through the formalities at the frontier independently and when they returned to their carriage Ashenden handed back to his companion the revolver and the knife. He sighed.

'Now I feel more comfortable. What do you say to a game of cards?'

'I should like it,' said Ashenden.

The Hairless Mexican opened his bag again and from a corner extracted a greasy pack of French cards. He asked Ashenden whether he played *écarté* and when Ashenden told him that he did not suggested piquet. This was a game that Ashenden was not unfamiliar with, so they settled the stakes and began. Since both were in favour of quick action, they played the game of four hands, doubling the first and last. Ashenden had good enough cards, but the General seemed notwithstanding always to have better. Ashenden kept his eyes open and he was not careless of the possibility that his antagonist might correct the inequalities of chance, but he saw nothing to suggest that everything was not above board. He lost game after game. He was capoted and rubiconed. The score against him mounted up and up till he had lost something like a thousand francs, which at that time was a tidy sum. The General smoked innumerable cigarettes. He made them himself with a twist of the finger, a lick of his tongue and incredible celerity. At last he flung himself against the back of his seat.

'By the way, my friend, does the British Government pay your card losses when you are on a mission?' he asked.

'It certainly doesn't.'

'Well, I think you have lost enough. If it went down on your expense account I would have proposed playing till we reached Rome, but you are sympathetic to me. If it is your own money I do not want to win any more of it.'

He picked up the cards and put them aside. Ashenden somewhat ruefully took out a number of notes and handed them to the Mexican. He counted them and with his usual neatness put them carefully folded into his pocket-book. Then, leaning forward, he patted Ashenden almost affectionately on the knee.

'I like you, you are modest and unassuming, you have not the arrogance of your countrymen, and I am sure that you will take my advice in the spirit in which it is meant. Do not play piquet with people you don't know.'

Ashenden was somewhat mortified and perhaps his face showed it, for the Mexican seized his hand.

'My dear fellow, I have not hurt your feelings? I would not do that for the world. You do not play piquet worse than most piquet players. It is not that. If we were going to be together longer I would teach you how to win at cards. One plays cards to win money and there is no sense in losing.'

'I thought it was only in love and war that all things were fair,' said Ashenden, with a chuckle.

'Ah, I am glad to see you smile. That is the way to take a loss. I see that you have good humour and good sense. You will go far in life. When I get back to Mexico and am in possession of my estates again you must come and stay with me. I will treat you like a king. You shall ride my best horses, we will go to bull-fights together, and if there are girls you fancy you have only to say the word and you shall have them.'

He began telling Ashenden of the vast territories, the *haciendas* and the mines in Mexico, of which he had been dispossessed. He told him of the feudal state in which he lived. It did not matter whether what he said was true or not, for those sonorous phrases of his were fruity with the rich-distilled perfumes of romance. He described a spacious life that seemed to belong to another age and his eloquent gestures brought before the mind's eye tawny distances and vast green plantations, great herds of cattle and in the moonlit night the song of the blind singers that melted in the air and the twanging of guitars.

'Everything I lost, everything. In Paris I was driven to earn a pittance by giving Spanish lessons or showing Americans – *Americanos del Norte*, I mean – the night life of the city. I who have flung away a thousand *duros* on a dinner have been forced to beg my bread like a blind Indian. I who have taken pleasure in clasping a diamond bracelet round the wrist of a beautiful woman have been forced to accept a suit of clothes from a hag old enough to be my mother. Patience. Man is born to trouble as the sparks fly upward, but misfortune cannot last for ever. The time is ripe and soon we shall strike our blow.'

He took up the greasy pack of cards and set them out in a number of little piles.

'Let us see what the cards say. They never lie. Ah, if I had only had greater faith in them I should have avoided the only action of my life that has weighed heavily on me. My conscience is at ease. I did what any man would do under the circumstances, but I regret that necessity forced upon me an action that I would willingly have avoided.'

He looked through the cards, set some of them on one side on a system Ashenden did not understand, shuffled the remainder and once more put them in little piles.

'The cards warned me, I will never deny that, their warning was clear and definite. Love and a dark woman, danger, betrayal and death. It was as plain as the nose on your face. Any fool would have known what it meant and I have been using the cards all my life. There is hardly an action that I make without consulting them. There are no excuses. I was besotted. Ah, you of the Northern races do not know what love means, you do not know how it can prevent you from sleeping, how it can take your appetite for food away so that you dwindle as if from a fever, you do not understand what a frenzy it is so that you are like a madman and you will stick at nothing to satisfy your desire. A man like me is capable of every folly and every crime when he is in love, *si*, *Señor*, and of heroism. He can scale mountains higher than Everest and swim seas broader than the Atlantic. He is god, he is devil. Women have been my ruin.'

Once more the Hairless Mexican glanced at the cards,

took some out of the little piles and left others in. He shuffled them again.

'I have been loved by multitudes of women. I do not say it in vanity. I offer no explanation. It is mere matter of fact. Go to Mexico City and ask them what they know of Manuel Carmona and of his triumphs. Ask them how many women have resisted Manuel Carmona.'

Ashenden, frowning a little, watched him reflectively. He wondered whether R., that shrewd fellow who chose his instruments with such a sure instinct, had not this time made a mistake, and he was uneasy. Did the Hairless Mexican really believe that he was irresistible or was he merely a blatant liar? In the course of his manipulations he had thrown out all the cards in the pack but four, and these now lay in front of him face downwards and side by side. He touched them one by one but did not turn them up.

'There is fate,' he said, 'and no power on earth can change it. I hesitate. This is a moment that ever fills me with apprehension and I have to steel myself to turn over the cards that may tell me that disaster awaits me. I am a brave man, but sometimes I have reached this stage and not had the courage to look at the four vital cards.'

Indeed now he eyed the backs of them with an anxiety he did not try to hide.

'What was I saying to you?'

'You were telling me that women found your fascinations irresistible,' replied Ashenden dryly.

'Once all the same I found a woman who resisted me. I saw her first in a house, a *casa de mujeres* in Mexico City, she was going down the stairs as I went up; she was not very beautiful, I had had a hundred more beautiful, but she had something that took my fancy and I told the old woman who kept the house to send her to me. You will know her when you go to Mexico City; they call her La Marqueza. She said that the girl was not an inmate, but came there only from time to time and

314

had left. I told her to have her there next evening and
not to let her go till I came. But I was delayed and when
I arrived La Marqueza told me that the girl had said she
was not used to being kept waiting and had gone. I am
a good-natured fellow and I do not mind if women are
capricious and teasing, that is part of their charm, so
with a laugh I sent her a note of a hundred *duros* and
promised that on the following day I would be punctual.
But when I went, on the minute, La Marqueza handed
me back my hundred *duros* and told me the girl did not
fancy me. I laughed at her impertinence. I took off the
diamond ring I was wearing and told the old woman to
give her that and see whether it would induce her to
change her mind. In the morning La Marqueza brought
me in return for my ring – a red carnation. I did not
know whether to be amused or angry. I am not used to
being thwarted in my passions, I never hesitate to spend
money (what is it for but to squander on pretty women?),
and I told La Marqueza to go to the girl and say that I
would give her a thousand *duros* to dine with me that
night. Presently she came back with the answer that the
girl would come on the condition that I allowed her to
go home immediately after dinner. I accepted with a
shrug of the shoulders. I did not think she was serious.
I thought that she was saying that only to make herself
more desired. She came to dinner at my house. Did I
say she was not beautiful? She was the most beautiful,
the most exquisite creature I had ever met. I was intoxicated. She had charm and she had wit. She had all
the *gracia* of the Andalusian. In one word she was adorable. I asked her why she had treated me so casually and
she laughed in my face. I laid myself out to be agreeable.
I exercised all my skill. I surpassed myself. But when we
finished dinner she rose from her seat and bade me
good-night. I asked her where she was going. She said I
had promised to let her go and she trusted me as a man
of honour to keep my word. I expostulated, I reasoned,
I raved, I stormed. She held me to my word. All I could

induce her to do was to consent to dine with me the
following night on the same terms.

'You will think I was a fool, I was the happiest man
alive; for seven days I paid her a thousand silver *duros*
to dine with me. Every evening I waited for her with my
heart in my mouth, as nervous as a *novillero* at his first
bull-fight, and every evening she played with me, laughed
at me, coquetted with me and drove me frantic. I was
madly in love with her. I have never loved anyone so
much before or since. I could think of nothing else. I
was distracted. I neglected everything. I am a patriot
and I love my country. A small band of us had got together and made up our minds that we could no longer
put up with the misrule from which we were suffering.
All the lucrative posts were given to other people, we
were being made to pay taxes as though we were tradesmen, and we were exposed to abominable affronts. We
had money and men. Our plans were made and we were
ready to strike. I had an infinity of things to do, meetings to go to, ammunition to get, orders to give, I was
so besotted over this woman that I could attend to
nothing.

'You would have thought that I should be angry with
her for making such a fool of me, me who had never
known what it was not to gratify my smallest whim; I
did not believe that she refused me to inflame my desires,
I believed that she told the plain truth when she said
that she would not give herself to me until she loved
me. She said it was for me to make her love me. I
thought her an angel. I was ready to wait. My passion
was so consuming that sooner or later, I felt, it must
communicate itself to her; it was like a fire on the prairie
that devours everything around it; and at last — at last
she said she loved me. My emotion was so terrific that I
thought I should fall down and die. Oh, what rapture!
Oh, what madness! I would have given her everything I
possessed in the world, I would have torn down the stars
from heaven to deck her hair; I wanted to do something

to prove to her the extravagance of my love, I wanted to do the impossible, the incredible, I wanted to give her myself, my soul, my honour, all, all I had and all I was; and that night when she lay in my arms I told her of our plot and who we were that were concerned in it. I felt her body stiffen with attention, I was conscious of a flicker of her eyelids, there was something, I hardly knew what, the hand that stroked my face was dry and cold; a sudden suspicion seized me and all at once I remembered what the cards had told me: love and a dark woman, danger, betrayal and death. Three times they'd said it and I wouldn't heed. I made no sign that I had noticed anything. She nestled up against my heart and told me that she was frightened to hear such things and asked me if So-and-so was concerned. I answered her. I wanted to make sure. One after the other, with infinite cunning, between her kisses she cajoled me into giving every detail of the plot, and now I was certain, as certain as I am that you sit before me, that she was a spy. She was a spy of the President's and she had been set to allure me with her devilish charm and now she had wormed out of me all our secrets. The lives of all of us were in her hands and I knew that if she left that room in twenty-four hours we should be dead men. And I loved her, I loved her; oh, words cannot tell you the agony of desire that burned my heart; love like that is no pleasure; it is pain, pain, but the exquisite pain that transcends all pleasure. It is that heavenly anguish that the saints speak of when they are seized with a divine ecstasy. I knew that she must not leave the room alive and I feared that if I delayed my courage would fail me.

' "I think I shall sleep," she said.

' "Sleep, my dove," I answered.

' "*Alma de mi corazon*," she called me. "Soul of my heart." They were the last words she spoke. Those heavy lids of hers, dark like a grape and faintly humid, those heavy lids of hers closed over her eyes and in a little while I knew by the regular movement of her breast against mine that she slept. You see, I loved her, I could not bear that she should suffer; she was a spy, yes, but my heart bade me spare her the terror of knowing what must happen. It is strange, I felt no anger because she had betrayed me, I should have hated her because of her vileness; I could not, I only felt that my soul was enveloped in night. Poor thing, poor thing. I could have cried in pity for her. I drew my arm very gently from around her, my left arm that was, my right was free, and raised myself on my hand. But she was so beautiful, I turned my face away when I drew the knife with all my strength across her lovely throat. Without awaking she passed from sleep to death.'

He stopped and stared frowning at the four cards that still lay, their backs upward, waiting to be turned up.

'It was in the cards. Why did I not take their warning? I will not look at them. Damn them. Take them away.'

With a violent gesture he swept the whole pack on to the floor.

'Though I am a free-thinker I had masses said for her soul.' He leaned back and rolled himself a cigarette. He inhaled a long breathful of smoke. He shrugged his shoulders. 'The Colonel said you were a writer. What do you write?'

'Stories,' replied Ashenden.

'Detective stories?'

'No.'

'Why not? They are the only ones I read. If I were a writer I should write detective stories.'

'They are very difficult. You need an incredible amount of invention. I devised a murder story once, but the murder was so ingenious that I could never find a way of bringing it home to the murderer, and, after all, one of the conventions of the detective story is that the mystery should in the end be solved and the criminal brought to justice.'

'If your murder is as ingenious as you think the only means you have of proving the murderer's guilt is by the discovery of his motives. When once you have found a motive the chances are that you will hit upon evidence that till then had escaped you. If there is no motive the most damning evidence will be inconclusive. Imagine for instance that you went up to a man in a lonely street on a moonless night and stabbed him to the heart. Who would ever think of you? But if he was your wife's lover, or your brother, or had cheated or insulted you, then a scrap of paper, a bit of string or a chance remark would be enough to hang you. What were your movements at the time he was killed? Are there not a dozen people who saw you before and after? But if he was a total stranger you would never for a moment be suspected. It was inevitable that Jack the Ripper should escape unless he was caught in the act.'

Ashenden had more than one reason to change the conversation. They were parting at Rome and he thought it necessary to come to an understanding with his companion about their respective movements. The Mexican was going to Brindisi and Ashenden to Naples. He meant to lodge at the Hotel de Belfast, which was a large second-rate hotel near the harbour frequented by commercial travellers and the thriftier kind of tripper. It would be as well to let the General have the number of his room so that he could come up if necessary without enquiring of the porter, and at the next stopping-place Ashenden got an envelope from the station-buffet and made him address it in his own writing to himself at the post-office in Brindisi. All Ashenden had to do then was to scribble a number on a sheet of paper and post it.

The Hairless Mexican shrugged his shoulders.

'To my mind all these precautions are rather childish. There is absolutely no risk. But whatever happens you may be quite sure that I will not compromise you.'

'This is not the sort of job which I'm very familiar with,' said Ashenden. 'I'm content to follow the Colonel's instructions and know no more about it than it's essential I should.'

'Quite so. Should the exigencies of the situation force me to take a drastic step and I get into trouble I shall of course be treated as a political prisoner. Sooner or later Italy is bound to come into the war on the side of the Allies and I shall be released. I have considered everything. But I beg you very seriously to have no more anxiety about the outcome of our mission than if you were going for a picnic on the Thames.'

But when at last they separated and Ashenden found himself alone in a carriage on the way to Naples he heaved a great sigh of relief. He was glad to be rid of that chattering, hideous and fantastic creature. He was gone to meet Constantine Andreadi at Brindisi and if half of what he had told Ashenden was true, Ashenden could not but congratulate himself that he did not stand in the Greek spy's shoes. He wondered what sort of a man he was. There was a grimness in the notion of his coming across the blue Ionian, with his confidential papers and his dangerous secrets, all unconscious of the noose into which he was putting his head. Well, that was war, and only fools thought it could be waged with kid gloves on.

Ashenden arrived in Naples and, having taken a room at the hotel, wrote its number on a sheet of paper in block letters and posted it to the Hairless Mexican. He went to the British Consulate, where R. had arranged to send any instructions he might have for him, and found that they knew about him and everything was in order. Then he put aside these matters and made up his mind to amuse himself. Here in the South the spring was well advanced and in the busy streets the sun was hot. Ashenden knew Naples pretty well. The Piazza di San Ferdinando, with its bustle, the Piazza del Plebiscito, with its handsome church, stirred in his heart pleasant recollections. The Strada di Chiara was as noisy as ever. He stood at corners and looked up the narrow alleys that climbed the hill precipitously, those alleys of high houses with the washing set out to dry on lines across the street like pennants flying to mark a feast-day: and he sauntered along the shore, looking at the burnished sea with Capri faintly outlined against the bay, till he came to Posilippo, where there was an old, rambling and bedraggled *palazzo* in which in his youth he had spent many a romantic hour. He observed the curious little pain with which the memories of the past wrung his heart-strings. Then he took a fly drawn by a small and scraggy pony and rattled back over the stones to the *Galleria*, where he sat in the cool and drank an *americano* and looked at the people who loitered there, talking, for ever talking with vivacious gestures, and, exercising his fancy, sought from their appearance to divine their reality.

For three days Ashenden led the idle life that fitted so well the fantastical, untidy and genial city. He did nothing from morning till night but wander at random, looking, not with the eye of the tourist who seeks for what ought to be seen, nor with the eye of the writer who looks for his own (seeing in a sunset a melodious phrase or in a face the inkling of a character), but with that of the tramp to whom whatever happens is absolute. He went to the museum to look at the statue of Agrippina the Younger, which he had particular reasons for remembering with affection, and took the opportunity to see once more the Titian and the Brueghel in the picture gallery. But he always came back to the church of Santa Chiara. Its grace, its gaiety, the airy persiflage with which it seemed to treat religion and at the back of this its sensual emotion; its extravagance, its elegance of line; to Ashenden it seemed to express, as it were in one absurd and grandiloquent metaphor, the sunny, dusty, lovely city and its bustling inhabitants. It said that life was charming and sad; it's a pity one hadn't any money, but money wasn't everything, and anyway why bother when we are here to-day and gone to-morrow, and it was all very exciting and amusing, and after all we must make the best of things: *facciamo una piccola combinazione.*

But on the fourth morning, when Ashenden, having just stepped out of his bath, was trying to dry himself on a towel that absorbed no moisture, his door was quickly opened and a man slipped into his room.

'What d'you want?' cried Ashenden.

'It's all right. Don't you know me?'

'Good Lord, it's the Mexican. What have you done to yourself?'

He had changed his wig and wore now a black one, close-cropped, that fitted on his head like a cap. It entirely altered the look of him and though this was still odd enough, it was quite different from that which he had borne before. He wore a shabby grey suit.

'I can only stop a minute. He's getting shaved.'

Ashenden felt his cheeks suddenly redden.

'You found him then?'

'That wasn't difficult. He was the only Greek passenger on the ship. I went on board when she got in and asked for a friend who had sailed from the Piræus. I said I had come to meet a Mr George Diogenidis. I pretended to be much puzzled at his not coming, and I got into conversation with Andreadi. He's travelling under a false name. He calls himself Lombardos. I followed him when he landed and do you know the first thing he did? He went into a barber's and had his beard shaved. What do you think of that?'

'Nothing. Anyone might have his beard shaved.'

'That is not what I think. He wanted to change his appearance. Oh, he's cunning. I admire the Germans, they leave nothing to chance, he's got his whole story pat, but I'll tell you that in a minute.'

'By the way, you've changed your appearance too.'

'Ah, yes, this is a wig I'm wearing; it makes a difference, doesn't it?'

'I should never have known you.'

'One has to take precautions. We are bosom friends. We had to spend the day in Brindisi and he cannot speak Italian. He was glad to have me help him and we travelled up together. I have brought him to this hotel. He says he is going to Rome to-morrow, but I shall not let him out of my sight; I do not want him to give me the slip. He says that he wants to see Naples and I have offered to show him everything there is to see.'

'Why isn't he going to Rome to-day?'

'That is part of the story. He pretends he is a Greek business man who has made money during the war. He says he was the owner of two coasting steamers and has just sold them. Now he means to go to Paris and have his fling. He says he has wanted to go to Paris all his life and at last has the chance. He is close. I tried to get him to talk. I told him I was a Spaniard and had been to Brindisi to arrange communications with Turkey about war material. He listened to me and I saw he was interested, but he told me nothing and of course I did not think it wise to press him. He has the papers on his person.'

'How do you know?'

'He is not anxious about his grip, but he feels every now and then round his middle, they're either in a belt or in the lining of his vest.'

'Why the devil did you bring him to this hotel?'

'I thought it would be more convenient. We may want to search his luggage.'

'Are you staying here too?'

'No, I am not such a fool as that. I told him I was going to Rome by the night train and would not take a room. But I must go, I promised to meet him outside the barber's in fifteen minutes.'

'All right.'

'Where shall I find you to-night if I want you?'

Ashenden for an instant eyed the Hairless Mexican, then with a slight frown looked away.

'I shall spend the evening in my room.'

'Very well. Will you just see that there's nobody in the passage?'

Ashenden opened the door and looked out. He saw no one. The hotel in point of fact at that season was nearly empty. There were few foreigners in Naples and trade was bad.

'It's all right,' said Ashenden.

The Hairless Mexican walked boldly out. Ashenden closed the door behind him. He shaved and slowly dressed. The sun was shining as brightly as usual on the square and the people who passed, the shabby little carriages with their scrawny horses, had the same air as before, but they did not any longer fill Ashenden with gaiety. He was not comfortable. He went out and called as was his habit at the Consulate to ask if there was a telegram for him. Nothing. Then he went to Cook's and looked out the trains to Rome: there was one soon after midnight and another at five in the morning. He wished he could catch the first. He did not know what were the Mexican's plans; if he really wanted to get to Cuba he would do well to make his way to Spain, and, glancing at the notices in the office, Ashenden saw that next day there was a ship sailing from Naples to Barcelona.

Ashenden was bored with Naples. The glare in the streets tired his eyes, the dust was intolerable, the noise was deafening. He went to the *Galleria* and had a drink. In the afternoon he went to a cinema. Then, going back to his hotel, he told the clerk that since he was starting so early in the morning he preferred to pay his bill at once, and he took his luggage to the station, leaving in his room only a despatch-case in which were the printed part of his code and a book or two. He dined. Then returning to the hotel he sat down to wait for the Hairless Mexican. He could not conceal from himself the fact that he was exceedingly nervous. He began to read, but the book was tiresome, and he tried another; his attention wandered and he glanced at his watch. It was desperately early; he took up his book again, making up his mind that he would not look at his watch till he had read thirty pages, but though he ran his eyes conscientiously down one page after another he could not tell more than vaguely what it was he read. He looked at the time again. Good God, it was only half-past ten. He wondered where the Hairless Mexican was, and what he was doing; he was afraid he would make a mess of things. It was a horrible business. Then it struck him that he had better shut the window and draw the curtains. He smoked innumerable cigarettes. He looked at his watch and it was a quarter past eleven. A thought struck him and his heart began to beat against his chest; out of curiosity he counted his pulse and was surprised to find that it was normal. Though it was a warm night and the room was stuffy his hands and feet were icy. What a nuisance it was, he reflected irritably, to have an imagination that conjured up pictures of things that you didn't in the least want to see! From his standpoint as a writer he had often considered murder and his mind went to that fearful description of one in *Crime and Punishment*. He did not want to think of this topic, but it forced itself upon him; his book dropped to his knees and staring at the wall in front of him (it had a brown wall-paper with a pattern of dingy roses) he asked himself how, if one had to, one would commit a murder in Naples. Of course there was the Villa, the great leafy garden facing the bay in which stood the aquarium; that was deserted at night and very dark; things happened there that did not bear the light of day and prudent persons after dusk avoided its sinister paths. Beyond Posilippo the road was very solitary and there were byways that led up the hill in which by night you would never meet a soul, but how would you induce a man who had any nerves to go there? You might suggest a row in the bay, but the boatman who hired the boat would see you; it was doubtful indeed if he would let you go on the water alone; there were disreputable hotels down by the harbour where no questions were asked of persons who arrived late at night without luggage; but here again the waiter who showed you your room had the chance of a good look at you and you had on entering to sign an elaborate questionnaire.

Ashenden looked once more at the time. He was very

tired. He sat now not even trying to read, his mind a
blank.

Then the door opened softly and he sprang to his feet.
His flesh crept. The Hairless Mexican stood before him.

'Did I startle you?' he asked smiling. 'I thought you
would prefer me not to knock.'

'Did anyone see you come in?'

'I was let in by the night-watchman; he was asleep when
I rang and didn't even look at me. I'm sorry I'm so late,
but I had to change.'

The Hairless Mexican wore now the clothes he had
travelled down in and his fair wig. It was extraordinary
how different he looked. He was bigger and more flam-
boyant; the very shape of his face was altered. His eyes
were shining and he seemed in excellent spirits. He gave
Ashenden a glance.

'How white you are, my friend! Surely you're not
nervous?'

'Have you got the documents?'

'No. He hadn't got them on him. This is all he had.'

He put down on the table a bulky pocket-book and a
passport.

'I don't want them,' said Ashenden quickly. 'Take
them.'

With a shrug of the shoulders the Hairless Mexican put
the things back in his pocket.

'What was in his belt? You said he kept feeling round
his middle.'

'Only money. I've looked through the pocket-book. It
contains nothing but private letters and photographs of
women. He must have locked the documents in his grip
before coming out with me this evening.'

'Damn,' said Ashenden.

'I've got the key of his room. We'd better go and look
through his luggage.'

Ashenden felt a sensation of sickness in the pit of his
stomach. He hesitated. The Mexican smiled not unkindly.

'There's no risk, *amigo*,' he said, as though he were reassuring a small boy, 'but if you don't feel happy, I'll go alone.'

'No, I'll come with you,' said Ashenden.

'There's no one awake in the hotel and Mr Andreadi won't disturb us. Take off your shoes if you like.'

Ashenden did not answer. He frowned because he noticed that his hands were slightly trembling. He unlaced his shoes and slipped them off. The Mexican did the same.

'You'd better go first,' he said. 'Turn to the left and go straight along the corridor. It's number thirty-eight.'

Ashenden opened the door and stepped out. The passage was dimly lit. It exasperated him to feel so nervous when he could not but be aware that his companion was perfectly at ease. When they reached the door the Hairless Mexican inserted the key, turned the lock and went in. He switched on the light. Ashenden followed him and closed the door. He noticed that the shutters were shut.

'Now we're all right. We can take our time.'

He took a bunch of keys out of his pocket, tried one or two and at last hit upon the right one. The suitcase was filled with clothes.

'Cheap clothes,' said the Mexican contemptuously as he took them out. 'My own principle is that it's always cheaper in the end to buy the best. After all one is a gentleman or one isn't a gentleman.'

'Are you obliged to talk?' asked Ashenden.

'A spice of danger affects people in different ways. It only excites me, but it puts you in a bad temper, *amigo*.'

'You see, I'm scared and you're not,' replied Ashenden with candour.

'It's merely a matter of nerves.'

Meanwhile he felt the clothes, rapidly but with care, as he took them out. There were no papers of any sort in the suitcase. Then he took out his knife and slit the lining. It was a cheap piece and the lining was gummed to the material of which the suitcase was made. There was no possibility of anything being concealed in it.

327

'They're not here. They must be hidden in the room.'

'Are you sure he didn't deposit them in some office? At one of the consulates, for example?'

'He was never out of my sight for a moment except when he was getting shaved.'

The Hairless Mexican opened the drawers and the cupboard. There was no carpet on the floor. He looked under the bed, in it, and under the mattress. His dark eyes shot up and down the room, looking for a hiding-place, and Ashenden felt that nothing escaped him.

'Perhaps he left them in charge of the clerk downstairs?'

'I should have known it. And he wouldn't dare. They're not here. I can't understand it.'

He looked about the room irresolutely. He frowned in the attempt to guess at a solution of the mystery.

'Let's get out of here,' said Ashenden.

'In a minute.'

The Mexican went down on his knees, quickly and neatly folded the clothes, and packed them up again. He locked the bag and stood up. Then, putting out the light, he slowly opened the door and looked out. He beckoned to Ashenden and slipped into the passage. When Ashenden had followed him he stopped and locked the door, put the key in his pocket and walked with Ashenden to his room. When they were inside it and the bolt drawn Ashenden wiped his clammy hands and his forehead.

'Thank God, we're out of that!'

'There wasn't really the smallest danger. But what are we to do now? The Colonel will be angry that the papers haven't been found.'

'I'm taking the five o'clock train to Rome. I shall wire for instructions there.'

'Very well, I will come with you.'

'I should have thought it would suit you better to get out of the country more quickly. There's a boat to-morrow that goes to Barcelona. Why don't you take that and if necessary I can come to see you there?'

The Hairless Mexican gave a little smile.

'I see that you are anxious to be rid of me. Well, I won't thwart a wish that your inexperience in these matters excuses. I will go to Barcelona. I have a visa for Spain.'

Ashenden looked at his watch. It was a little after two. He had nearly three hours to wait. His companion comfortably rolled himself a cigarette.

'What do you say to a little supper?' he asked. 'I'm as hungry as a wolf.'

The thought of food sickened Ashenden, but he was terribly thirsty. He did not want to go out with the Hairless Mexican, but neither did he want to stay in that hotel by himself.

'Where could one go at this hour?'

'Come along with me. I'll find you a place.'

Ashenden put on his hat and took his despatch-case in his hand. They went downstairs. In the hall the porter was sleeping soundly on a mattress on the floor. As they passed the desk, walking softly in order not to wake him, Ashenden noticed in the pigeon-hole belonging to his room a letter. He took it out and saw that it was addressed to him. They tiptoed out of the hotel and shut the door behind them. Then they walked quickly away. Stopping after a hundred yards or so under a lamp-post Ashenden took the letter out of his pocket and read it; it came from the Consulate and said: *The enclosed telegram arrived to-night and in case it is urgent I am sending it round to your hotel by messenger.* It had apparently been left some time before midnight while Ashenden was sitting in his room. He opened the telegram and saw that it was in code.

'Well, it'll have to wait,' he said, putting it back in his pocket.

The Hairless Mexican walked as though he knew his way through the deserted streets and Ashenden walked by his side. At last they came to a tavern in a blind alley, noisome and evil, and this the Mexican entered.

'It's not the Ritz,' he said, 'but at this hour of the night it's only in a place like this that we stand a chance of getting something to eat.'

Ashenden found himself in a long sordid room at one end of which a wizened young man sat at a piano; there were tables standing out from the wall on each side and against them benches. A number of persons, men and women, were sitting about. They were drinking beer and wine. The women were old, painted, and hideous; and their harsh gaiety was at once noisy and lifeless. When Ashenden and the Hairless Mexican came in they all stared and when they sat down at one of the tables Ashenden looked away in order not to meet the leering eyes, just ready to break into a smile, that sought his insinuatingly. The wizened pianist strummed a tune and several couples got up and began to dance. Since there were not enough men to go round some of the women danced together. The General ordered two plates of spaghetti and a bottle of Capri wine. When the wine was brought he drank a glassful greedily and then waiting for the *pasta* eyed the women who were sitting at the other tables.

'Do you dance?' he asked Ashenden. 'I'm going to ask one of these girls to have a turn with me.'

He got up and Ashenden watched him go up to one who had at least flashing eyes and white teeth to recommend her; she rose and he put his arm round her. He danced well. Ashenden saw him begin talking; the woman laughed and presently the look of indifference with which she had accepted his offer changed to one of interest. Soon they were chatting gaily. The dance came to an end and putting her back at her table he returned to Ashenden and drank another glass of wine.

'What do you think of my girl?' he asked. 'Not bad, is she? It does one good to dance. Why don't you ask one of them? This is a nice place, is it not? You can always trust me to find anything like this. I have an instinct.'

The pianist started again. The woman looked at the Hairless Mexican and when with his thumb he pointed to the floor she jumped up with alacrity. He buttoned up his coat, arched his back and standing up by the side of the table waited for her to come to him. He swung her off, talking, smiling, and already he was on familiar terms with everyone in the room. In fluent Italian, with his Spanish accent, he exchanged badinage with one and the other. They laughed at his sallies. Then the waiter brought two heaped platefuls of macaroni and when the Mexican saw them he stopped dancing without ceremony and, allowing his partner to get back to her table as she chose, hurried to his meal.

'I'm ravenous,' he said. 'And yet I ate a good dinner. Where did you dine? You're going to eat some macaroni, aren't you?'

'I have no appetite,' said Ashenden.

But he began to eat and to his surprise found that he was hungry. The Hairless Mexican ate with huge mouthfuls, enjoying himself vastly; his eyes shone and he was loquacious. The woman he had danced with had in that short time told him all about herself and he repeated now to Ashenden what she had said. He stuffed huge pieces of bread into his mouth. He ordered another bottle of wine.

'Wine?' he cried scornfully. 'Wine is not a drink, only champagne; it does not even quench your thirst. Well, *amigo*, are you feeling better?'

'I'm bound to say I am,' smiled Ashenden.

'Practice, that is all you want, practice.'

He stretched out his hand to pat Ashenden on the arm.

'What's that?' cried Ashenden with a start. 'What's that stain on your cuff?'

The Hairless Mexican gave his sleeve a glance.

'That? Nothing. It's only blood. I had a little accident and cut myself.'

Ashenden was silent. His eyes sought the clock that hung over the door.

'Are you anxious about your train? Let me have one more dance and then I'll accompany you to the station.'

The Mexican got up and with his sublime self-assurance seized in his arms the woman who sat nearest to him and danced away with her. Ashenden watched him moodily. He was a monstrous, terrible figure with that blond wig and his hairless face, but he moved with a matchless grace; his feet were small and seemed to hold the ground like the pads of a cat or a tiger; his rhythm was wonderful and you could not but see that the bedizened creature he danced with was intoxicated by his gestures. There was music in his toes and in the long arms that held her so firmly, and there was music in those long legs that seemed to move strangely from the hips. Sinister and grotesque though he was, there was in him now a feline elegance, even something of beauty, and you felt a secret, shameful fascination. To Ashenden he suggested one of those sculptures of the pre-Aztec hewers of stone, in which there is barbarism and vitality, something terrible and cruel, and yet withal a brooding and significant loveliness. All the same he would gladly have left him to finish the night by himself in that sordid dance-hall, but he knew that he must have a business conversation with him. He did not look forward to it without misgiving. He had been instructed to give Manuel Carmona certain sums in return for certain documents. Well, the documents were not forthcoming, and as for the rest – Ashenden knew nothing about that; it was no business of his. The Hairless Mexican waved gaily as he passed him.

'I will come the moment the music stops. Pay the bill and then I shall be ready.'

Ashenden wished he could have seen into his mind. He could not even make a guess at its workings. Then the Mexican, with his scented handkerchief wiping the sweat from his brow, came back.

'Have you had a good time, General?' Ashenden asked him.

'I always have a good time. Poor white trash, but what do I care? I like to feel the body of a woman in my arms and see her eyes grow languid and her lips part as her desire for me melts the marrow in her bones like butter in the sun. Poor white trash, but women.'

They sallied forth. The Mexican proposed that they should walk and in that quarter, at that hour, there would

332

have been little chance of finding a cab; but the sky was starry. It was a summer night and the air was still. The silence walked beside them like the ghost of a dead man. When they neared the station the houses seemed on a sudden to take on a greyer, more rigid line, and you felt that the dawn was at hand. A little shiver trembled through the night. It was a moment of apprehension and the soul for an instant was anxious; it was as though, inherited down the years in their countless millions, it felt a witless fear that perhaps another day would not break. But they entered the station and the night once more enwrapped them. One or two porters lolled about like stage-hands after the curtain has rung down and the scene is struck. Two soldiers in dim uniforms stood motionless.

The waiting-room was empty, but Ashenden and the Hairless Mexican went to sit in the most retired part of it.

'I still have an hour before my train goes. I'll just see what this cable's about.'

He took it out of his pocket and from the despatch-case got his code. He was not then, using a very elaborate one. It was in two parts, one contained in a slim book and the other, given him on a sheet of paper and destroyed by him before he left allied territory, committed to memory. Ashenden put on his spectacles and set to work. The Hairless Mexican sat in a corner of the seat, rolling himself cigarettes and smoking; he sat there placidly, taking no notice of what Ashenden did, and enjoyed his well-earned repose. Ashenden deciphered the groups of numbers one by one and as he got it out jotted down each word on a piece of paper. His method was to abstract his mind from the sense till he had finished, since he had discovered that if you took notice of the words as they came along you often jumped to a conclusion and sometimes were led into error. So he translated quite mechanically, without paying attention to the words as he wrote them one after the other. When at last he had done he read the complete message. It ran as follows:

Constantine Andreadi has been detained by illness at

Piræus. He will be unable to sail. Return Geneva and await instructions.

At first Ashenden could not understand. He read it again. He shook from head to foot. Then, for once robbed of his self-possession, he blurted out, in a hoarse, agitated and furious whisper:

'You bloody fool, you've killed the wrong man.'

D. H. LAWRENCE

The Man Who Loved Islands

I

There was a man who loved islands. He was born on one,
but it didn't suit him, as there were too many other people
on it, besides himself. He wanted an island all of his own:
not necessarily to be alone on it, but to make it a world
of his own.

An island, if it is big enough, is no better than a continent. It has to be really quite small, before it *feels* like an
island; and this story will show how tiny it has to be,
before you can presume to fill it with your own personality.

Now circumstances so worked out that this lover of
islands, by the time he was thirty-five, actually acquired
an island of his own. He didn't own it as freehold property, but he had a ninety-nine years' lease of it, which, as
far as a man and an island are concerned, is as good as
everlasting. Since, if you are like Abraham, and want
your offspring to be numberless as the sands of the sea-
shore, you don't choose an island to start breeding on.
Too soon there would be over-population, overcrowding,
and slum conditions. Which is a horrid thought, for one
who loves an island for its insulation. No, an island is a
nest which holds one egg, and one only. This egg is the
islander himself.

The island acquired by our potential islander was not
in the remote oceans. It was quite near home, no palm
trees nor boom of surf on the reef, nor any of that kind of
thing; but a good solid dwelling-house, rather gloomy,

above the landing-place, and beyond, a small farmhouse with sheds, and a few outlying fields. Down in the little landing-bay were three cottages in a row, like coastguards' cottages, all neat and whitewashed.

What could be more cosy and home-like? It was four miles if you walked all round your island, through the gorse and the blackthorn bushes, above the steep rocks of the sea and down in the little glades where the primroses grew. If you walked straight over the two humps of hills, the length of it, through the rocky fields where the cows lay chewing, and through the rather sparse oats, on into the gorse again, and so to the low cliffs' edge, it took you only twenty minutes. And when you came to the edge, you could see another, bigger island lying beyond. But the sea was between you and it. And as you returned over the turf where the short, downland cowslips nodded, you saw to the east still another island, a tiny one this time, like the calf of the cow. This tiny island also belonged to the islander.

Thus it seems that even islands like to keep each other company.

Our islander loved his island very much. In early spring, the little ways and glades were a snow of blackthorn, a vivid white among the Celtic stillness of close green and grey rock, blackbirds calling out in the whiteness their first long, triumphant calls. After the blackthorn and the nestling primroses came the blue apparition of hyacinths, like elfin lakes and slipping sheets of blue, among the bushes and under the glade of trees. And many birds with nests you could peep into, on the island all your own. Wonderful what a great world it was!

Followed summer, and the cowslips gone, the wild roses faintly fragrant through the haze. There was a field of hay, the foxgloves stood looking down. In a little cove, the sun was on the pale granite where you bathed, and the shadow was in the rocks. Before the mist came stealing, you went home through the ripening oats, the glare of the sea fading from the high air as the fog-horn started to moo on the other island. And then the sea-fog went, it was autumn, the oatsheaves lying prone, the great moon, another island, rose golden out of the sea, and rising higher, the world of the sea was white.

So autumn ended with rain, and winter came, dark skies and dampness and rain, but rarely frost. The island, your island, cowered dark, holding away from you. You could feel, down in the wet, sombre hollows, the resentful spirit coiled upon itself like a wet dog coiled in gloom, or a snake that is neither asleep nor awake. Then in the night, when the wind left off blowing in great gusts and volleys, as at sea, you felt that your island was a universe, infinite and old as the darkness; not an island at all, but an infinite dark world where all the souls from all the other bygone nights lived on, and the infinite distance was near.

Strangely, from your little island in space, you were gone forth into the dark, great realms of time, where all the souls that never die veer and swoop on their vast, strange errands. The little earthly island has dwindled, like a jumping-off place, into nothingness, for you have jumped off, you know not how, into the dark wide mystery of time, where the past is vastly alive, and the future is not separated off.

This is the danger of becoming an islander. When, in the city, you wear your white spats and dodge the traffic with the fear of death down your spine, then you are quite safe from the terrors of infinite time. The moment is your little islet in time, it is the spatial universe that careers round you.

But once isolate yourself on a little island in the sea of space, and the moment begins to heave and expand in great circles, the solid earth is gone, and your slippery, naked dark soul finds herself out in the timeless world, where the chariots of the so-called dead dash down the old streets of centuries, and souls crowd on the footways that we, in the moment, call bygone years. The souls of all the dead are alive again, and pulsating actively around you. You are out in the other infinity.

Something of this happened to our islander. Mysterious
'feelings' came upon him that he wasn't used to; strange
awareness of old, far-gone men, and other influences; men
of Gaul, with big moustaches, who had been on his
island, and had vanished from the face of it, but not out
of the air of night. They were there still, hurtling their
big, violent, unseen bodies through the night. And there
were priests with golden knives and mistletoe; then other
priests with a crucifix; then pirates with murder on the sea.

Our islander was uneasy. He didn't believe, in the day-
time, in any of this nonsense. But at night it just was so.
He had reduced himself to a single point in space, and, a
point being that which has neither length nor breadth, he
had to step off it into somewhere else. Just as you must
step into the sea, if the waters wash your foothold away,
so he had, at night, to step off into the other world of
undying time.

He was uncannily aware, as he lay in the dark, that the
blackthorn grove that seemed a bit uncanny even in the
realm of space and day, at night was crying with old men
of an invisible race, around the altar stone. What was a
ruin under the hornbeam trees by day, was a moaning of
blood-stained priests with crucifixes, on the ineffable
night. What was a cave and a hidden beach between coarse
rocks, became in the invisible dark the purple-lipped
imprecation of pirates.

To escape any more of this sort of awareness, our islander daily concentrated upon his material island. Why
should it not be the Happy Island at last? Why not the
last small isle of the Hesperides, the perfect place, all filled
with his own gracious, blossom-like spirit? A minute
world of pure perfection, made by man himself.

He began, as we begin all our attempts to regain Paradise, by spending money. The old, semi-feudal dwelling-
house he restored, let in more light, put clear lovely
carpets on the floor, clear, flower-petal curtains at the
sullen windows, and wines in the cellars of rock. He
brought over a buxom housekeeper from the world, and

a soft-spoken, much-experienced butler. These two were to be islanders.

In the farmhouse he put a bailiff, with two farmhands. There were Jersey cows, tinkling a slow bell, among the gorse. There was a call to meals at midday, and the peaceful smoking of chimneys at evening, when rest descended.

A jaunty sailing-boat with a motor accessory rode in the shelter in the bay, just below the row of three white cottages. There was also a little yawl, and two row-boats drawn up on the sand. A fishing-net was drying on its supports, a boatload of new white planks stood criss-cross, a woman was going to the well with a bucket.

In the end cottage lived the skipper of the yacht, and his wife and son. He was a man from the other, large island, at home on this sea. Every fine day he went out fishing, with his son, every fair day there was fresh fish in the island.

In the middle cottage lived an old man and wife, a very faithful couple. The old man was a carpenter, and man of many jobs. He was always working, always the sound of his plane or his saw; lost in his work, he was another kind of islander.

In the third cottage was a mason, a widower with a son and two daughters. With the help of his boy, this man dug ditches and built fences, raised buttresses and erected a new outbuilding, and hewed stone from the little quarry. One daughter worked at the big house.

It was a quiet, busy little world. When the islander brought you over as his guest, you met first the dark-bearded, thin, smiling skipper, Arnold, then his boy Charles. At the house, the smooth-lipped butler who had lived all over the world valeted you and created that curious creamy-smooth, disarming sense of luxury around you which only a perfect and rather untrustworthy servant can create. He disarmed you and had you at his mercy. The buxom housekeeper smiled and treated you with the subtly respectful familiarity that is only dealt out to the true gentry. And the rosy maid threw a glance at you, as if you were very wonderful, coming from the great outer world. Then you met the smiling but watchful bailiff, who came from Cornwall, and the shy farm-hand from Berkshire, with his clean wife and two little children: then the rather sulky farm-hand from Suffolk. The mason, a Kent man, would talk to you by the yard if you let him. Only the old carpenter was gruff and elsewhere absorbed.

Well then, it was a little world to itself, and everybody feeling very safe, and being very nice to you, as if you were really something special. But it was the islander's world, not yours. He was the Master. The special smile, the special attention was to the Master. They all knew how well off they were. So the islander was no longer Mr So-and-so. To everyone on the island, even to you yourself, he was 'the Master'.

Well, it was ideal. The Master was no tyrant. Ah, no! He was a delicate, sensitive, handsome master, who wanted everything perfect and everybody happy. Himself, of course, to be the fount of this happiness and perfection.

But in his way, he was a poet. He treated his guests royally, his servants liberally. Yet he was shrewd, and very wise. He never came the boss over his people. Yet he kept his eye on everything, like a shrewd, blue-eyed young Hermes. And it was amazing what a lot of knowledge he had at hand. Amazing what he knew about Jersey cows, and cheese-making, ditching and fencing, flowers and gardening, ships and the sailing of ships. He was a fount of knowledge about everything, and this knowledge he imparted to his people in an odd, half-ironical, half-portentous fashion, as if he really belonged to the quaint, half-real world of the gods.

They listened to him with their hats in their hands. He loved white clothes; or creamy white; and cloaks, and broad hats. So, in fine weather, the bailiff would see the elegant tall figure in creamy-white serge coming like some bird over the fallow, to look at the weeding of the turnips. Then there would be a doffing of hats, and a few minutes of whimsical, shrewd, wise talk, to which the bailiff answered admiringly, and the farm-hands listened in silent wonder, leaning on their hoes. The bailiff was almost tender, to the Master.

Or, on a windy morning, he would stand with his cloak blowing in the sticky sea-wind, on the edge of the ditch that was being dug to drain a little swamp, talking in the teeth of the wind to the man below, who looked up at him with steady and inscrutable eyes.

Or at evening in the rain he would be seen hurrying across the yard, the broad hat turned against the rain. And the farm-wife would hurriedly exclaim: 'The Master! Get up, John, and clear him a place on the sofa.' And then the door opened, and it was a cry of: 'Why, of all things, if it isn't the Master! Why, have ye turned out then, of a night like this, to come across to the like of we?' And the bailiff took his cloak, and the farm-wife his hat, the two farm-hands drew their chairs to the back, he sat on the sofa and took a child up near him. He was wonderful with children, talked to them simply wonderful, made you think of Our Saviour Himself, said the woman.

He was always greeted with smiles, and the same peculiar deference, as if he were a higher, but also frailer being. They handled him almost tenderly, and almost with adulation. But when he left, or when they spoke of him, they had often a subtle, mocking smile on their faces. There was no need to be afraid of 'the Master'. Just let him have his own way. Only the old carpenter was sometimes sincerely rude to him; so he didn't care for the old man.

It is doubtful whether any of them really like him, man to man, or even woman to man. But then it is doubtful if he really liked any of them, as man to man, or man to woman. He wanted them to be happy, and the little world to be perfect. But anyone who wants the world to be perfect must be careful not to have real likes or dislikes. A general goodwill is all you can afford.

The sad fact is, alas, that general goodwill is always felt

as something of an insult, by the mere object of it; and so it breeds a quite special brand of malice. Surely general goodwill is a form of egoism, that it should have such a result!

Our islander, however, had his own resources. He spent long hours in his library, for he was compiling a book of references to all the flowers mentioned in the Greek and Latin authors. He was not a great classical scholar; the usual public-school equipment. But there are such excellent translations nowadays. And it was so lovely, tracing flower after flower as it blossomed in the ancient world.

So the first year on the island passed by. A great deal had been done. Now the bills flooded in, and the Master, conscientious in all things, began to study them. The study left him pale and breathless. He was not a rich man. He knew he had been making a hole in his capital to get the island into running order. When he came to look, however, there was hardly anything left but hole. Thousands and thousands of pounds had the island swallowed into nothingness.

But surely the bulk of the spending was over! Surely the island would now begin to be self-supporting, even if it made no profit! Surely he was safe. He paid a good many of the bills, and took a little heart. But he had had a shock, and the next year, the coming year, there must be economy, frugality. He told his people so in simple and touching language. And they said: 'Why, surely! Surely!'

So, while the wind blew and the rain lashed outside, he would sit in his library with the bailiff over a pipe and pot of beer, discussing farm projects. He lifted his narrow, handsome face, and his blue eyes became dreamy. '*What* a wind!' It blew like cannon-shots. He thought of his island, lashed with foam, and inaccessible, and he exulted. . . . No, he must not lose it. He turned back to the farm projects with the zest of genius, and his hands flicked white emphasis, while the bailiff intoned: 'Yes, sir! Yes, sir! You're right, Master!'

But the man was hardly listening. He was looking at the

Master's blue lawn shirt and curious pink tie with the fiery red stone, at the enamel sleeve-links, and at the ring with the peculiar scarab. The brown searching eyes of the man of the soil glanced repeatedly over the fine, immaculate figure of the Master, with a sort of slow, calculating wonder. But if he happened to catch the Master's bright, exalted glance, his own eye lit up with a careful cordiality and deference, as he bowed his head slightly.

Thus between them they decided what crops should be sown, what fertilisers should be used in different places, which breed of pigs should be imported, and which line of turkeys. That is to say, the bailiff, by continually cautiously agreeing with the Master, kept out of it, and let the young man have his own way.

The Master knew what he was talking about. He was brilliant at grasping the gist of a book, and knowing how to apply his knowledge. On the whole, his ideas were sound. The bailiff even knew it. But in the man of the soil there was no answering enthusiasm. The brown eyes smiled their cordial deference, but the thin lips never changed. The Master pursed his own flexible mouth in a boyish versatility, as he cleverly sketched in his ideas to the other man, and the bailiff made eyes of admiration, but in his heart he was not attending, he was only watching the Master as he would have watched a queer, caged animal, quite without sympathy, not implicated.

So, it was settled, and the Master rang for Elvery, the butler, to bring a sandwich. He, the Master, was pleased. The butler saw it and came back with anchovy and ham sandwiches, and a newly opened bottle of vermouth. There was always a newly opened bottle of something.

It was the same with the mason. The Master and he discussed the drainage of a bit of land, and more pipes were ordered, more special bricks, more this, more that.

Fine weather came at last; there was a little lull in the hard work on the island. The Master went for a short cruise in his yacht. It was not really a yacht, just a little bit of a thing. They sailed along the coast of the main-

land, and put in at the ports. At every port some friend
turned up, the butler made elegant little meals in the
cabin. Then the Master was invited to villas and hotels,
his people disembarked him as if he were a prince.

And oh, how expensive it turned out to be! He had to
telegraph to the bank for money. And he went home
again to economise.

The marsh-marigolds were blazing in the little swamp
where the ditches were being dug for drainage. He almost
regretted, now, the work in hand. The yellow beauties
would not blaze again.

Harvest came, and a bumper crop. There must be a
harvest-home supper. The long barn was now completely
restored and added to. The carpenter had made long
tables. Lanterns hung from the beams of the high-pitched
roof. All the people of the island assembled. The bailiff
presided. It was a gay scene.

Towards the end of the supper the Master, in a velvet
jacket, appeared with his guests. Then the bailiff rose and
proposed 'The Master! Long life and health to the Master!' All the people drank the health with great enthusiasm and cheering. The Master replied with a little speech:
They were on an island in a little world of their own. It
depended on them all to make this world a world of
true happiness and content. Each must do his part. He
hoped he himself did what he could, for his heart was in
his island, and with the people of his island.

The butler responded: As long as the island had such a
Master, it could not help but be a little heaven for all
the people on it. This was seconded with virile warmth
by the bailiff and the mason, the skipper was beside himself. Then there was dancing, the old carpenter was
fiddler.

But under all this, things were not well. The very next
morning came the farm-boy to say that a cow had fallen
over the cliff. The Master went to look. He peered over
the not very high declivity, and saw her lying dead on a
green ledge under a bit of late-flowering broom. A beauti-

ful, expensive creature, already looking swollen. But what a fool, to fall so unnecessarily!

It was a question of getting several men to haul her up the bank, and then of skinning and burying her. No one would eat the meat. How repulsive it all was!

This was symbolic of the island. As sure as the spirits rose in the human breast, with a movement of joy, an invisible hand struck malevolently out of the silence. There must not be any joy, nor even any quiet peace. A man broke a leg, another was crippled with rheumatic fever. The pigs had some strange disease. A storm drove the yacht on a rock. The mason hated the butler, and refused to let his daughter serve at the house.

Out of the very air came a stony, heavy malevolence. The island itself seemed malicious. It would go on being hurtful and evil for weeks at a time. Then suddenly again one morning it would be fair, lovely as a morning in Paradise, everything beautiful and flowing. And everybody would begin to feel a great relief, and a hope for happiness.

Then as soon as the Master was opened out in spirit like an open flower, some ugly blow would fall. Somebody would send him an anonymous note, accusing some other person on the island. Somebody else would come hinting things against one of his servants.

'Some folks think they've got an easy job out here, with all the pickings they make!' the mason's daughter screamed at the suave butler, in the Master's hearing. He pretended not to hear.

'My man says this island is surely one of the lean kine of Egypt, it would swallow a sight of money, and you'd never get anything back out of it,' confided the farmhand's wife to one of the Master's visitors.

The people were not contented. They were not islanders. 'We feel we're not doing right by the children,' said those who had children. 'We feel we're not doing right by ourselves,' said those who had no children. And the various families came to hate one another.

Yet the island was so lovely. When there was a scent of honeysuckle and the moon brightly flickering down on the sea, then even the grumblers felt a strange nostalgia for it. It set you yearning, with a wild yearning; perhaps for the past, to be far back in the mysterious past of the island, when the blood had a different throb. Strange floods of passion came over you, strange violent lusts and imaginations of cruelty. The blood and the passion and the lust which the island had known. Uncanny dreams, half-dreams, half-evocated yearnings.

The Master himself began to be a little afraid of his island. He felt here strange, violent feelings he had never felt before, and lustful desires that he had been quite free from. He knew quite well now that his people didn't love him at all. He knew that their spirits were secretly against him, malicious, jeering, envious, and lurking to down him. He became just as wary and secretive with regard to them.

But it was too much. At the end of the second year, several departures took place. The housekeeper went. The Master always blamed self-important women most. The mason said he wasn't going to be monkeyed about any more, so he took his departure, with his family. The rheumatic farm-hand left.

And then the year's bills came in, the Master made up his accounts. In spite of good crops, the assets were ridiculous, against the spending. The island had again lost, not hundreds but thousands of pounds. It was incredible. But you simply couldn't believe it! Where had it all gone?

The Master spent gloomy nights and days going through accounts in the library. He was thorough. It became evident, now the housekeeper had gone, that she had swindled him. Probably everybody was swindling him. But he hated to think it, so he put the thought away.

He emerged, however, pale and hollow-eyed from his balancing of unbalanceable accounts, looking as if something had kicked him in the stomach. It was pitiable. But the money had gone, and there was an end of it. Another great hole in his capital. How could people be so heartless?

It couldn't go on, that was evident. He would soon be bankrupt. He had to give regretful notice to his butler. He was afraid to find out how much his butler had swindled him. Because the man was such a wonderful butler, after all. And the farm bailiff had to go. The Master had no regrets in that quarter. The losses on the farm had almost embittered him.

The third year was spent in rigid cutting down of expenses. The island was still mysterious and fascinating. But it was also treacherous and cruel, secretly, fathomlessly malevolent. In spite of all its fair show of white blossom and bluebells, and the lovely dignity of foxgloves bending their rose-red bells, it was your implacable enemy.

With reduced staff, reduced wages, reduced splendour, the third year went by. But it was fighting against hope. The farm still lost a good deal. And once more there was a hole in that remnant of capital. Another hole in that which was already a mere remnant round the old holes. The island was mysterious in this also: it seemed to pick the very money out of your pocket, as if it were an octopus with invisible arms stealing from you in every direction.

Yet the Master still loved it. But with a touch of rancour now.

He spent, however, the second half of the fourth year intensely working on the mainland, to be rid of it. And it was amazing how difficult he found it, to dispose of an island. He had thought that everybody was pining for such an island as his; but not at all. Nobody would pay any price for it. And he wanted now to get rid of it, as a man who wants a divorce at any cost.

It was not till the middle of the fifth year that he transferred it, at a considerable loss to himself, to an hotel company who were willing to speculate in it. They were to turn it into a handy honeymoon-and-golf island!

There, take that, island which didn't know when it was well off. Now be a honeymoon-and-golf island!

2

The islander had to move. But he was not going to the mainland. Oh, no! He moved to the smaller island, which still belonged to him. And he took with him the faithful old carpenter and wife, the couple he never really cared for; also a widow and daughter, who had kept house for him the last year; also an orphan lad, to help the old man.

The small island was very small; but being a hump of rock in the sea, it was bigger than it looked. There was a little track among the rocks and bushes, winding and scrambling up and down the islet, so that it took you twenty minutes to do the circuit. It was more than you would have expected.

Still, it was an island. The islander moved himself, with all his books, into the commonplace six-roomed house up to which you had to scramble from the rocky landing-place. There were also two joined-together cottages. The old carpenter lived in one, with his wife and the lad, the widow and daughter lived in the other.

At last all was in order. The Master's books filled two rooms. It was already autumn, Orion lifting out of the sea. And in the dark nights, the Master could see the lights on his late island, where the hotel company were entertaining guests who would advertise the new resort for honeymoon-golfers.

On his lump of rock, however, the Master was still master. He explored the crannies, the odd hand-breadths of grassy level, the steep little cliffs where the last hare-bells hung and the seeds of summer were brown above the sea, lonely and untouched. He peered down the old well. He examined the stone pen where the pig had been kept. Himself, he had a goat.

Yes, it was an island. Always, always underneath among the rocks the Celtic sea sucked and washed and smote its feathery greyness. How many different noises of the sea!

Deep explosions, rumblings, strange long sighs and whistling noises; then voices, real voices of people clamouring
as if they were in a market, under the waters: and again,
the far-off ringing of a bell, surely an actual bell! Then a
tremendous trilling noise, very long and alarming, and an
undertone of hoarse gasping.

On this island there were no human ghosts, no ghosts
of any ancient race. The sea and the spume and the
weather had washed them all out, washed them out so
there was only the sound of the sea itself, its own ghost,
myriad-voiced, communing and plotting and shouting all
winter long. And only the smell of the sea, with a few
bristly bushes of gorse and coarse tufts of heather, among
the grey, pellucid rocks, in the grey, more-pellucid air.
The coldness, the greyness, even the soft, creeping fog of
the sea, and the islet of rock humped up in it all, like the
last point in space.

Green star Sirius stood over the sea's rim. The island
was a shadow. Out at sea a ship showed small lights. Below, in the rocky cove, the row-boat and the motor-boat
were safe. A light shone in the carpenter's kitchen. That
was all.

Save, of course, that the lamp was lit in the house,
where the widow was preparing supper, her daughter helping. The islander went in to his meal. Here he was no
longer the Master, he was an islander again and he had
peace. The old carpenter, the widow and daughter were
all faithfulness itself. The old man worked while ever
there was light to see, because he had a passion for work.
The widow and her quiet, rather delicate daughter of
thirty-three worked for the Master, because they loved
looking after him, and they were infinitely grateful for the
haven he provided them. But they didn't call him 'the
Master'. They gave him his name: 'Mr Cathcart, sir!'
softly and reverently. And he spoke back to them also
softly, gently, like people far from the world, afraid to
make a noise.

The island was no longer a 'world'. It was a sort of

refuge. The islander no longer struggled for anything. He had no need. It was as if he and his few dependants were a small flock of sea-birds alighted on this rock, as they travelled through space, and keeping together without a word. The silent mystery of travelling birds.

He spent most of his day in his study. His book was coming along. The widow's daughter could type out his manuscript for him, she was not uneducated. It was the one strange sound on the island, the typewriter. But soon even its spattering fitted in with the sea's noises, and the wind's.

The months went by. The islander worked away in his study, the people of the island went quietly about their concerns. The goat had a little black kid with yellow eyes. There were mackerel in the sea. The old man went fishing in the row-boat with the lad, when the weather was calm enough; they went off in the motor-boat to the biggest island for the post. And they brought supplies, never a penny wasted. And the days went by, and the nights, without desire, without ennui.

The strange stillness from all desire was a kind of wonder to the islander. He didn't want anything. His soul at last was still in him, his spirit was like a dim-lit cave under water, where strange sea-foliage expands upon the watery atmosphere, and scarcely sways, and a mute fish shadowily slips in and slips away again. All still and soft and uncrying, yet alive as rooted seaweed is alive.

The islander said to himself: 'Is this happiness?' He said to himself: 'I am turned into a dream. I feel nothing, or I don't know what I feel. Yet it seems to me I am happy.'

Only he had to have something upon which his mental activity could work. So he spent long, silent hours in his study, working not very fast, nor very importantly, letting the writing spin softly from him as if it were drowsy gossamer. He no longer fretted whether it were good or not, what he produced. He slowly, softly spun it like gossamer, and if it were to melt away as gossamer in autumn melts, he would not mind. It was only the soft evanescence of gossamy things which now seemed to him permanent. The very mist of eternity was in them. Whereas stone buildings, cathedrals for example, seemed to him to howl with temporary resistance, knowing they must fall at last; the tension of their long endurance seemed to howl forth from them all the time.

Sometimes he went to the mainland and to the city. Then he went elegantly, dressed in the latest style, to his club. He sat in a stall at the theatre, he shopped in Bond Street. He discussed terms for publishing his book. But over his face was that gossamy look of having dropped out of the race of progress, which made the vulgar city people feel they had won it over him, and made him glad to go back to his island.

He didn't mind if he never published his book. The years were blending into a soft mist, from which nothing obtruded. Spring came. There was never a primrose on his island, but he found a winter-aconite. There were two little sprayed bushes of blackthorn, and some wind-flowers. He began to make a list of the flowers of his islet, and that was absorbing. He noted a wild currant bush and watched for the elder flowers on a stunted little tree, then for the first yellow rags of the broom, and wild roses. Bladder campion, orchids, stitchwort, celandine, he was prouder of them than if they had been people on his island. When he came across the golden saxifrage, so inconspicuous in a damp corner, he crouched over it in a trance, he knew not for how long, looking at it. Yet it was nothing to look at. As the widow's daughter found, when he showed it to her.

He had said to her in real triumph:

'I found the golden saxifrage this morning.'

The name sounded splendid. She looked at him with fascinated brown eyes, in which was a hollow ache that frightened him a little.

'Did you, sir? Is it a nice flower?'

He pursed his lips and tilted his brows.

'Well – not showy exactly. I'll show it you if you like.'
'I should like to see it.'

She was so quiet, so wistful. But he sensed in her a
persistency which made him uneasy. She said she was so
happy: really happy. She followed him quietly, like a
shadow, on the rocky track where there was never room
for two people to walk side by side. He went first, and
could feel her there, immediately behind him, following
so submissively, gloating on him from behind.

It was a kind of pity for her which made him become
her lover: though he never realised the extent of the power
she had gained over him, and how *she* willed it. But the
moment he had fallen, a jangling feeling came upon him,
that it was all wrong. He felt a nervous dislike of her. He
had not wanted it. And it seemed to him, as far as her
physical self went, she had not wanted it either. It was
just her will. He went away, and climbed at the risk of
his neck down to a ledge near the sea. There he sat for
hours, gazing all jangled at the sea, and saying miserably
to himself: 'We didn't want it. We didn't really want it.'

It was the automatism of sex that had caught him again.
Not that he hated sex. He deemed it, as the Chinese do,
one of the great life-mysteries. But it had become mechanical, automatic, and he wanted to escape that. Automatic
sex shattered him, and filled him with a sort of death. He
thought he had come through, to a new stillness of desire-
lessness. Perhaps beyond that there was a new fresh deli-
cacy of desire, an unentered frail communion of two
people meeting on untrodden ground.

Be that as it might, this was not it. This was nothing
new or fresh. It was automatic, and driven from the will.
Even she, in her true self, hadn't wanted it. It was automatic in her.

When he came home, very late, and saw her face white
with fear and apprehension of his feeling against her, he
pitied her, and spoke to her delicately, reassuringly. But
he kept himself remote from her.

She gave no sign. She served him with the same silence,

the same hidden hunger to serve him, to be near where he was. He felt her love following him with strange, awful persistency. She claimed nothing. Yet now, when he met her bright, brown, curiously vacant eyes, he saw in them the mute question. The question came direct at him with a force and a power of will he never realised.

So he succumbed, and asked her again.

'Not,' she said, 'if it will make you hate me.'

'Why should it?' he replied, nettled. 'Of course not.'

'You know I would do anything on earth for you.'

It was only afterwards, in his exasperation, he remembered what she said, and was more exasperated. Why should she pretend to do this for *him*? Why not herself? But in his exasperation, he drove himself deeper in. In order to achieve some sort of satisfaction, which he never did achieve, he abandoned himself to her. Everybody on the island knew. But he did not care.

Then even what desire he had left him, and he felt only shattered. He felt that only with her will had she wanted him. Now he was shattered and full of self-contempt. His island was smirched and spoiled. He had lost his place in the rare, desireless levels of Time to which he had at last arrived, and he had fallen right back. If only it had been true, delicate desire between them, and a delicate meeting on the third rare place where a man might meet a woman, when they were both true to the frail, sensitive, crocus-flame of desire in them. But it had been no such thing: automatic, an act of will, not of true desire, it left him feeling humiliated.

He went away from the islet, in spite of her mute reproach. And he wandered about the continent, vainly seeking a place where he could stay. He was out of key; he did not fit in the world any more.

There came a letter from Flora — her name was Flora — to say she was afraid she was going to have a child. He sat down as if he were shot, and he remained sitting. But he replied to her: 'Why be afraid? If it is so, it is so, and we should rather be pleased than afraid.'

At this very moment, it happened there was an auction of islands. He got the maps, and studied them. And at the auction he bought, for very little money, another island. It was just a few acres of rock away in the north on the outer fringe of the isles. It was low, it rose low out of the great ocean. There was not a building, not even a tree on it. Only northern sea-turf, a pool of rain-water, a bit of sedge, rock and sea-birds. Nothing else. Under the weeping western sky.

He made a trip to visit his new possession. For several days, owing to the seas, he could not approach it. Then, in a light sea-mist, he landed, and saw it hazy, low, stretching apparently a long way. But it was illusion. He walked over the wet springy turf, and dark-grey sheep tossed away from him, spectral, bleating hoarsely. And he came to the dark pool with the sedge. Then on in the dampness, to the grey sea sucking angrily among the rocks.

This was indeed an island.

So he went home to Flora. She looked at him with guilty fear, but also with a triumphant brightness in her uncanny eyes. And again he was gentle, he reassured her, even he wanted her again, with that curious desire that was almost like toothache. So he took her to the mainland, and they were married, since she was going to have his child.

They returned to the island. She still brought his meals, her own along with them. She sat and ate with him. He would have it so. The widowed mother preferred to stay in the kitchen. And Flora slept in the guest-room of his house, mistress of his house.

His desire, whatever it was, died in him with nauseous finality. The child would still be months coming. His island was hateful to him, vulgar, a suburb. He himself had lost all his finer distinction. The weeks passed in a sort of prison, in humiliation. Yet he stuck it out, till the child was born. But he was meditating escape. Flora did not even know.

A nurse appeared, and ate at table with them. The

doctor came sometimes, and, if the sea were rough, he too had to stay. He was cheery over his whisky.

They might have been a young couple in Golders Green.

The daughter was born at last. The father looked at the baby, and felt depressed, almost more than he could bear. The millstone was tied round his neck. But he tried not to show what he felt. And Flora did not know. She still smiled with a kind of half-witted triumph in her joy, as she got well again. Then she began to look at him with those aching, suggestive, somehow impudent eyes. She adored him so.

This he could not stand. He told her that he had to go away for a time. She wept, but she thought she had got him. He told her he had settled the best part of his property on her, and wrote down for her what income it would produce. She hardly listened, only looked at him with those heavy, adoring, impudent eyes. He gave her a cheque-book, with the amount of her credit duly entered. This did arouse her interest. And he told her, if she got tired of the island, she could choose her home wherever she wished.

She followed him with those aching, persistent brown eyes, when he left, and he never even saw her weep.

He went straight north, to prepare his third island.

3

The third island was soon made habitable. With cement and the big pebbles from the shingle beach, two men built him a hut, and roofed it with corrugated iron. A boat brought over a bed and table, and three chairs, with a good cupboard, and a few books. He laid in a supply of coal and paraffin and food – he wanted so little.

The house stood near the flat shingle bay where he landed, and where he pulled up his light boat. On a sunny day in August the men sailed away and left him. The sea was still and pale blue. On the horizon he saw the small mail-steamer slowly passing northwards, as if she were walking. She served the outer isles twice a week. He could row out to her if need be, in calm weather, and he could signal her from a flagstaff behind his cottage.

Half a dozen sheep still remained on the island, as company; and he had a cat to rub against his legs. While the sweet, sunny days of the northern autumn lasted, he would walk among the rocks, and over the springy turf of his small domain, always coming to the ceaseless, restless sea. He looked at every leaf, that might be different from another, and he watched the endless expansion and contraction of the water-tossed seaweed. He had never a tree, not even a bit of heather to guard. Only the turf, and tiny turf-plants, and the sedge by the pool, the seaweed in the ocean. He was glad. He didn't want trees or bushes. They stood up like people, too assertive. His bare, low-pitched island in the pale blue sea was all he wanted.

He no longer worked at his book. The interest had gone. He liked to sit on the low elevation of his island, and see the sea; nothing but the pale, quiet sea. And to feel his mind turn soft and hazy, like the hazy ocean. Sometimes, like a mirage, he would see the shadow of land rise hovering to northwards. It was a big island beyond. But quite without substance.

He was soon almost startled when he perceived the steamer on the near horizon, and his heart contracted with fear, lest it were going to pause and molest him. Anxiously he watched it go, and not till it was out of sight did he feel truly relieved, himself again. The tension of waiting for human approach was cruel. He did not want to be approached. He did not want to hear voices. He was shocked by the sound of his own voice, if he inadvertently spoke to his cat. He rebuked himself for having broken the great silence. And he was irritated when his cat would look up at him and mew faintly, plaintively. He frowned at her. And she knew. She was becoming wild, lurking in the rocks, perhaps fishing.

But what he disliked most was when one of the lumps of sheep opened its mouth and baa-ed its hoarse, raucous baa. He watched it, and it looked to him hideous and gross. He came to dislike the sheep very much.

He wanted only to hear the whispering sound of the sea, and the sharp cries of the gulls, cries that came out of another world to him. And best of all, the great silence.

He decided to get rid of the sheep when the boat came. They were accustomed to him now, and stood and stared at him with yellow or colourless eyes, in an insolence that was almost cold ridicule. There was a suggestion of cold indecency about them. He disliked them very much. And when they jumped with staccato jumps off the rocks, and their hoofs made the dry, sharp hit, and the fleece flopped on their square backs, he found them repulsive, degrading.

The fine weather passed, and it rained all day. He lay a great deal on his bed, listening to the water trickling from his roof into the zinc water-butt, looking through the open door at the rain, the dark rocks, the hidden sea. Many gulls were on the island now: many sea-birds of all sorts. It was another world of life. Many of the birds he had never seen before. His old impulse came over him, to send for a book, to know their names. In a flicker of the old passion, to know the name of everything he saw, he even decided to row out to the steamer. The names of these birds! He must know their names, otherwise he had not got them, they were not quite alive to him.

But the desire left him, and he merely watched the birds as they wheeled or walked around him, watched them vaguely, without discrimination. All interest had left him. Only there was one gull, a big, handsome fellow, who would walk back and forth, back and forth in front of the open door of the cabin, as if he had some mission there. He was big, and pearl-grey, and his roundnesses were as smooth and lovely as a pearl. Only the folded wings had shut black pinions, and on the closed black feathers were three very distinct white dots, making a pattern. The islander wondered very much, why this bit of trimming on the bird out of the far, cold seas. And as the gull walked back and forth, back and forth in front of the cabin, strutting on pale-dusky gold feet, holding up his pale yellow beak, that was curved at the tip, with curious alien importance, the man wondered over him. He was portentous, he had a meaning.

Then the bird came no more. The island, which had been full of sea-birds, the flash of wings, the sound and cut of wings and sharp eerie cries in the air, began to be deserted again. No longer they sat like living eggs on the rocks and turf, moving their heads, but scarcely rising into flight round his feet. No longer they ran across the turf among the sheep, and lifted themselves upon low wings. The host had gone. But some remained, always.

The days shortened, and the world grew eerie. One day the boat came: as if suddenly, swooping down. The islander found it a violation. It was torture to talk to those two men, in their homely clumsy clothes. The air of familiarity around them was very repugnant to him. Himself, he was neatly dressed, his cabin was neat and tidy. He resented any intrusion, the clumsy homeliness, the heavy-footedness of the two fishermen was really repulsive to him.

The letters they had brought he left lying unopened in a little box. In one of them was his money. But he could not bear to open even that one. Any kind of contact was repulsive to him. Even to read his name on an envelope. He hid the letters away.

And the hustle and horror of getting the sheep caught and tied and put in the ship made him loathe with profound repulsion the whole of the animal creation. What repulsive god invented animals and evil-smelling men? To his nostrils, the fishermen and the sheep alike smelled foul; an uncleanness on the fresh earth.

He was still nerve-racked and tortured when the ship at last lifted sail and was drawing away, over the still sea. And sometimes, days after, he would start with repulsion, thinking he heard the munching of sheep.

The dark days of winter drew on. Sometimes there was no real day at all. He felt ill, as if he were dissolving, as if dissolution had already set in inside him. Everything was twilight, outside, and in his mind and soul. Once, when he went to the door, he saw black heads of men swimming in his bay. For some moments he swooned unconscious. It was the shock, the horror of unexpected human approach. The horror in the twilight! And not till the shock had undermined him and left him disembodied, did he realise that the black heads where the heads of seals swimming in. A sick relief came over him. But he was barely conscious, after the shock. Later on, he sat and wept with gratitude, because they were not men. But he never realised that he wept. He was too dim. Like some strange, ethereal animal, he no longer realised what he was doing.

Only he still derived his single satisfaction from being alone, absolutely alone, with the space soaking into him. The grey sea alone, and the footing of his sea-washed island. No other contact. Nothing human to bring its horror into contact with him. Only space, damp, twilit, sea-washed space! This was the bread of his soul.

For this reason, he was almost glad when there was a storm, or when the sea was high. Then nothing could get at him. Nothing could come through to him from the outer world. True, the terrific violence of the wind made him suffer badly. At the same time, it swept the world utterly out of existence for him. He always liked the sea to be heavily rolling and tearing. Then no boat could get at him. It was like eternal ramparts round his island.

He kept no track of time, and no longer thought of opening a book. The print, the printed letters, so like the depravity of speech, looked obscene. He tore the brass label from his stove. He obliterated any bit of lettering in his cabin.

His cat had disappeared. He was rather glad. He shivered at the thin obtrusive call. She had lived in the coalshed. And each morning he had put her a dish of porridge, the same as he ate. He washed her saucer with repulsion. He did not like her writhing about. But he fed her scrupulously. Then one day she did not come for her porridge; she always mewed for it. She did not come again.

He prowled about his island in the rain, in a big oil-skin coat, not knowing what he was looking at, nor what he went out to see. Time had ceased to pass. He stood for long spaces, gazing from a white, sharp face, with those keen, far-off blue eyes of his, gazing fiercely and almost cruelly at the dark sea under the dark sky. And if he saw the labouring sail of a fishing-boat away on the cold waters, a strange malevolent anger passed over his features.

Sometimes he was ill. He knew he was ill, because he staggered as he walked, and easily fell down. Then he paused to think what it was. And he went to his stores and took out dried milk and malt, and ate that. Then he forgot again. He ceased to register his own feelings.

The days were beginning to lengthen. All winter the weather had been comparatively mild, but with much rain, much rain. He had forgotten the sun. Suddenly, however, the air was very cold, and he began to shiver. A fear came over him. The sky was level and grey, and never a star appeared at night. It was very cold. More birds began to arrive. The island was freezing. With trembling hands he made a fire in his grate. The cold frightened him.

And now it continued, day after day, a dull, deathly cold. Occasional crumblings of snow were in the air. The days were greyly longer, but no change in the cold. Frozen grey daylight. The birds passed away, flying away. Some he saw lying frozen. It was as if all life were drawing away, contracting away from the north, contracting southwards. 'Soon,' he said to himself, 'it will be all gone, and in all these regions nothing will be alive.' He felt a cruel satisfaction in the thought.

Then one night there seemed to be a relief; he slept better, did not tremble half-awake, and writhe so much, half-conscious. He had become so used to the quaking and writhing of his body, he hardly noticed it. But when for once it slept deep, he noticed that.

He woke in the morning to a curious whiteness. His window was muffled. It had snowed. He got up and opened his door, and shuddered. Ugh! How cold! All white, with a dark leaden sea, and black rocks curiously speckled with white. The foam was no longer pure. It seemed dirty. And the sea ate at the whiteness of the corpse-like land. Crumbles of snow were silting down the dead air.

On the ground the snow was a foot deep, white and smooth and soft, windless. He took a shovel to clear round his house and shed. The pallor of morning darkened. There was a strange rumbling of far-off thunder in the frozen air, and through the newly-falling snow, a dim flash of lightning. Snow now fell steadily down in the motionless obscurity.

He went out for a few minutes. But it was difficult. He stumbled and fell in the snow, which burned his face. Weak, faint, he toiled home. And when he recovered, took the trouble to make hot milk.

It snowed all the time. In the afternoon again there was a muffled rumbling of thunder, and flashes of lightning blinking reddish through the falling snow. Uneasy, he went to bed and lay staring fixedly at nothingness.

Morning seemed never to come. An eternity long he lay and waited for one alleviating pallor on the night. And at last it seemed the air was paler. His house was a cell faintly illuminated with white light. He realised the snow was walled outside his window. He got up, in the dead cold. When he opened his door, the motionless snow stopped him in a wall as high as his breast. Looking over the top of it, he felt the dead wind slowly driving, saw the snow-powder lift and travel like a funeral train. The blackish sea churned and champed, seeming to bite at the snow, impotent. The sky was grey, but luminous.

He began to work in a frenzy, to get at his boat. If he was to be shut in, it must be by his own choice, not by the mechanical power of the elements. He must get to the sea. He must be able to get at his boat.

But he was weak, and at times the snow overcame him. It fell on him, and he lay buried and lifeless. Yet every time he struggled alive before it was too late, and fell upon the snow with the energy of fever. Exhausted, he would not give in. He crept indoors and made coffee and bacon. Long since he had cooked so much. Then he went at the snow once more. He must conquer the snow, this new, white brute force which had accumulated against him.

He worked in the awful, dead wind, pushing the snow aside, pressing it with his shovel. It was cold, freezing hard in the wind, even when the sun came out for a while, and showed him his white, lifeless surroundings, the black sea rolling sullen, flecked with dull spume, away to the horizons. Yet the sun had power on his face. It was March.

He reached the boat. He pushed the snow away, then sat down under the lee of the boat, looking at the sea, which swirled nearly to his feet, in the high tide. Curiously natural the pebbles looked, in a world gone all uncanny. The sun shone no more. Snow was falling in hard crumbs, that vanished as if by a miracle as they touched the hard blackness of the sea. Hoarse waves rang in the shingle, rushing up at the snow. The wet rocks were brutally black. And all the time the myriad swooping crumbs of snow, demonish, touched the dark sea and disappeared.

During the night there was a great storm. It seemed to him he could hear the vast mass of snow striking all the world with a ceaseless thud; and over it all, the wind roared in strange hollow volleys, in between which came a jump of blindfold lightning, then the low roll of thunder heavier than the wind. When at last the dawn faintly discoloured the dark, the storm had more or less subsided, but a steady wind drove on. The snow was up to the top of his door.

Sullenly, he worked to dig himself out. And he managed through sheer persistency to get out. He was in the tail of a great drift, many feet high. When he got through, the frozen snow was not more than two feet deep. But his island was gone. Its shape was all changed, great heaping white hills rose where no hills had been, inaccessible, and they fumed like volcanoes, but with snow-powder. He was sickened and overcome.

His boat was in another, smaller drift. But he had not the strength to clear it. He looked at it helplessly. The shovel slipped from his hands, and he sank in the snow, to forget. In the snow itself, the sea resounded.

Something brought him to. He crept to his house. He was almost without feeling. Yet he managed to warm himself, just that part of him which leaned in snow-sleep over the coal fire. Then again he made hot milk. After which, carefully, he built up the fire.

The wind dropped. Was it night again? In the silence, it seemed he could hear the panther-like dropping of infinite snow. Thunder rumbled nearer, crackled quick after the bleared reddened lightning. He lay in bed in a kind of stupor. The elements! The elements! His mind repeated the word dumbly. You can't win against the elements.

How long it went on, he never knew. Once, like a wraith, he got out and climbed to the top of a white hill on his unrecognisable island. The sun was hot. 'It is summer,' he said to himself, 'and the time of leaves.' He looked stupidly over the whiteness of his foreign island, over the waste of the lifeless sea. He pretended to imagine he saw the wink of a sail. Because he knew too well there would never again be a sail on that stark sea.

As he looked, the sky mysteriously darkened and chilled. From far off came the mutter of the unsatisfied thunder, and he knew it was the signal of the snow rolling over the sea. He turned, and felt its breath on him.

WILLIAM SANSOM

Episode at Gastein

Ludwig de Broda bowed as he passed the new young woman with her orange hair, her pensive grace. He bowed not stiffly, as his more military ancestors would have done, but with the ease of a new world, a world not of private halls but of the less formal lounges of hotels. His face he kept grave, it was unwise to smile too soon. And his eyes seemed after their first deep search scarcely to notice her – like the eyes on the ends of a snail's horns they withdrew their intrusion and stared seriously beyond her. Hers fluttered, there was recognition of his bow in her short glance of understanding, long enough only for this to be established: then they lowered, and with it slightly her head, as if this too were a bow, a half-inclination of the head, for it never retrieved itself.

He passed on, not pausing, a modern middle-aged man in a modern suit, with no trace of former graces but a certain recession of manner. He went in to dinner. He dined alone at his table in the white and gold, hugely mirrored dining-hall.

After dinner he walked back through the lounge, noted where the young woman sat taking her coffee, called a waiter to send a tray of coffee for himself to the adjoining table, and went into the toilet room to wash his hands, to comb his well-combed hair, but really for a minute to wait. It was more tactful for his coffee to be established at the table first, it would appear that the table was his habitually and not chosen intrusively to be near hers.

He judged his time patiently so that, when he walked out

across the red carpet and past the gilded marble pillars, the silver coffee-jug already winked its welcome opposite his chair. He pretended not to notice her. He sat down, poured and stirred his coffee, chose from a new pigskin case a cigar, lit this, and stretched himself at last at ease to look round the lounge. When his eyes met hers he allowed himself a most perceptible start. He coughed, bowed again from his chair, and looked with pained disappointment at his cigar.

'I trust the Fräulein will not be disturbed by this ... smoke ...?'

She seemed not to have noticed his arrival. He repeated his question. She started, noticed him with surprise, smiled and looked at the cigar as if it were a naughty but charming child:

'No, no. I don't mind at all.'

'It would be no trouble to move. ...'

'Please – not on my account.'

'You are very kind ... perhaps I could offer you ...'

But she had looked away again. She closed the interchange calmly. She did not bother to pretend to fumble with her bag. Not even to look in a direction pointedly away from his table – she simply stared straight ahead, hardly at the hotel lounge at all, perhaps seeing nothing, simply effacing herself. But de Broda had reached an age when he was no longer nervous of a snub in these matters. Once he had been most fearful of this, now he was tired and more settled – for what could it matter? – and he leaned without hesitation towards her. For propriety's sake he did not turn his full face, he leaned towards her sideways like a puppet that could not rotate:

'You're staying here for long?'

She seemed not to hear. He coughed – to offer her the excuse of really not having heard – and repeated the question. Again she started, it seemed she awoke from a slight, wide-eyed sleep, and turned to him apologetically:

'I beg your pardon?'

'Forgive me – I asked only, is the Fräulein staying long? For the cure?'

'Oh – I see.' She expressed relief – it was quite as if a hand had fluttered to her heart and she had sighed. Now she could allow herself to smile easily:

'For two weeks. No, not for the cure – for a little holiday.'

'How strange! That is exactly my own position – we must be the only two unemployed by the waters.'

'You forget the ski-run.'

'Ah yes – I'm afraid I do forget that. And when I don't forget, I regret it.'

'Oh?'

'Our country teems with ski-resorts. A good thing, among other things we need visitors. But it's out of character with this old place, it spoils the – the atmosphere.'

She jutted her lower lip – he could see where the lip rouge ended and wetter pink of the real lip began. She gave a small toss of her orange hair – he noticed that it was really orange, not dyed. She grudged at him:

'Atmosphere! It's very little use having atmosphere if you haven't any money. Think of the townsfolk.'

'And vice versa. What's the use of money if there's no one to play music?'

'Music?'

'Music. Poetry. I mean again atmosphere. The music of this curious *fin de siècle*, these hideous hotels, these rustic promenades, this engineering of the waters – everything that with the years ... is growing so much charm!'

'You do not find it oppressive?'

'No. Let me explain. ...'

And he explained. And for an hour they talked. They agreed to walk together the next morning, he would show her something of the quality of his beloved Gastein. So the meeting was consummated, the first act was done, the game was on – with honour on both sides. Both discreet – she the withdrawer seducing, he the seducer withdrawn.

These two, then, met at Gastein in Austria – Bad Gastein to the woman, who took things as they were; and Wildbad Gastein to de Broda, who spent much melancholy time sensing things as they had been.

Wildbad was the old name, Wild Bath, and indeed the old mountain spa must have looked ferocious in earlier days. But still today, for added reasons, it is none the less disquieting. Still the wild rocky torrent falls five hundred feet from the plateau above the basin beneath. It steams and bubbles and whirls perpendicular between the dark stone cliffs of a horrendous ravine, stone cliffs that echo and magnify the awful rush of the waters with a resonance as black as the walls themselves and the sombre mountain firs that rise wet and shadowy up each side. A wild and giddying place – and now two bridges have been built over the narrow ravine, each staring straight down on to the roaring water and the long-drop deadly flat pool beneath, each with a balustrade that feels too shallow to hold a man back.

But that is not all. For part of the water jets from inside the rock itself, and this water is hot, it steams, its white radioactive steam clouds up with the spray of the cold torrent to mist an inferno of iron winches, lock-gates, great timbers and writhing waist-thick iron pipes that climb all about the gorge – such atrocious emblems appear and vanish in the hot mist like heavy instruments of torture. Meanwhile, man came to look on. And man built up and down the walls of the cliff-sides a range of violent hotels, monster edifices whose thousand windows skyscraper not only upwards but downwards too – for their main floors open behind on to mountain streets that strike about their middles. It is as though the walls of New York were placed at a vertiginous angle above no street but a hollow staircase of water: or as if the giddy buildings of Monte Carlo were transported, paler but still unsteady, high into the mountain snows. The hotels bear such names as Grand Hôtel de l'Europe, Elizabethpark Hotel, Germania – an aristocratic fusion from the *fin de siècle* playgrounds. It is from the gilded interiors of such engines of enchanting taste that men look out on to the chasm and its tortuous mists.

De Broda loved the place. He was now forty years of age, a bachelor whose parents were dead, alone in a world that had greatly changed since his youth. He had himself never known the splendours of the Austro-Hungarian Empire, but remnants of the Double Eagle were impressed on his heart and he was never far from a melancholy sense sweet enough, and of a strange anticipatory nature, of those things past. He was well enough supplied with money – he had inherited houses in Vienna and land in green Styria – and he had time to spare to stay now and then in one of the older hotels at Gastein.

Recently a new experience had befallen him – he had found himself saying his name over a shop-counter and feeling the name belonged to someone else. That is, he himself had no name, and his name made the vague shape of a person in his mind – someone he had known, and rather despised, who had been close to him but nevertheless remained a stranger, something of a shadowed enemy. He tried the name again, running it over his lips – but it had obviously nothing whatever to do with the flesh and bone and mind and blood that tried to believe it fitted. He thought then of the names of friends, of people he admired – each one of them, with the concrete personalities they evoked, he could imagine bearing his own name. So I am a stranger to myself, he concluded. And then: 'Of course, this is a common experience. At one time or another, we all wake up to our names. They represent the past figure of ourselves, a sort of shadowy film actor we never quite liked, of whose acting we were rather ashamed. They represent the worst in ourselves, our knowing nasty second selves.'

But though he reasoned thus, de Broda was left with the unreasonable feeling that really – though really, too, he knew this was nonsense – he had no longer a name. Everyone else but he had a name. And this feeling, illogical but nevertheless lingering strong, emphasized for him his lack of a bloodmark in the world – his parentless, childless state wandering in winter the nearly empty halls of this summer spa. He felt spectral.

For the previous three years he had had it on his mind to marry: that is to say, to make a sensible effort to find a woman who would measure up to his melancholy and upon whom in return he longed to lavish all the affection frustrated and stored inside him. Such a lady he found difficult to find. Some were too frivolous, some were too severe: some liked him too much, many did not like him at all. He discounted the possibility of falling in love, it semed too late: although he saw it was possible, it was impossible to foresee. But with masculine conceit and male vigour he did not discount the possibility that a quite young girl might find him attractive – and lately he had conceived the notion that, given youth and a fair intelligence, such a young person might be malleable in his sensitive fingers, she could be moulded in time into the form of a perfect consort. An ambitious plan, one with risks – but possible. And the prettier the woman, de Broda said to himself as he planned his dream, the better.

So he had kept his eyes open. And now they had noticed with interest and some intention the figure of this good-looking young woman with the orange hair, the pensive grace. She could not have been more than twenty-five years old.

For her part, Fräulein Laure Perfuss also had hopes for a profitable holiday. She was just twenty-six years old; and though she had felt on her twenty-fifth birthday a sense of having arrived at a never-to-be-experienced-again barrier of the years – the decimal system is engraved deeply in our hearts – now that she was twenty-six a different foreboding, almost a panic momentum towards the terrible age of thirty, had seized her. To be thirty – and unmarried! Laure was on the look-out for a husband: or, let us be fair, she was inclined to observe the gentlemen she met with a more deeply considerative, a more long-range eye.

And there were other reasons for this. Unlike de Broda, but like most Austrians of upper caste, she had come down in the world. Her family had lost money and their home: now she herself lived in one room high up in a cold old mansion high up the Mariahilfer Strasse – her mother had long ago returned to their native Tyrol. She herself was too much now of a Viennese to leave. She worked in a high-class Konditorei – and though her wages were small, this was the one reliable pleasure of her life. Although she stood on the service side of a counter piled with trays of cakes and cellophaned sweets, it still meant for her a real connection with the old life. To that same shop she had been brought as a child by her mother. She remembered the silk blinds, tasselled, and the colour of pale creamed coffee; silver trays of sweets flashing their softness and sugar – montelimar, dragees, pralines, a hundred cellophaned marvels; most of all the polished wooden order of the yellow parquet floor and the great brass-trimmed counter and the tables with their smooth cane chairs – no gilt or plush nor coloured fabrication here, only the smooth polished woods everywhere and the cakes and the silver-trayed sweets. Now, when Fräulein Laure served her customers in the middle of the morning, when the smell of coffee and scents of fur and perfume excited the air, when noise and a brisk draught of the street entered with the glass door's opening – she remembered autumns long past, when fresh from treading the yellow leaves outside, her own buttoned gaiters had swung under those same tables: and she remembered with pleasure, with no regret. Although she was on the wrong side of the counter, she could still smell the actuality of the sweet smells, she still walked among the elegancies of the room.

But – though one of the happiest states of life is to like one's work – she knew this could not go on. She was a woman, she feared the shelf. She had fallen in and out of love. Several times she had been near to marriage: but a certain hope had always held her back. Her young men, also poor, might have made excellent husbands. But they would not have provided excellent homes. Laure was simply holding on for her prince on his white steed. However, he had not come. And now she was twenty-six and already in the mirror of her mind heading hard for thirty.

In the circumstances, Bad Gastein was not the best choice for a holiday. The great old spa was threequarters empty, the hotel the same – but the short holiday was a gift from an aunt with romantic memories of the grand days, and Gastein had been almost a condition. As it was, this man whose card she now had in her bag, Herr de Broda, was the only unattached, the only nearly young man staying in the hotel. She assessed him carefully. He was handsome. She saw a white-skinned, dark-haired man – there was a bloom on his skin like polished bone. His hair grew thickly, it was tough and its wave oiled down, it was shaved low at the back of his neck, even beneath his collar. His dark eyebrows met to make less a satanic than a thoughtful appearance – for his eyes were large, soft, southern. Jewish or half Italian – his family had been shipowners in Fiume. He was reserved and spoke with a laboured weariness. The 'poetic type', she decided. In his way he was charming, really quite charming. And well mannered. And well-off.

That evening she sat at her dressing-table and thoughtfully ran the sharp edge of his card against the flesh of her middle finger. She looked down at her clear-varnished nails holding the white card: then up at her face in the mirror. She tossed her orange hair and stared. Sometimes she had idled – a little fearfully – with the idea of a rich protector. Since the war several girls she knew had affianced themselves thus – and it had not seemed to make much change in them. She stared in the mirror at her face, beautiful and saddened by such thoughts. *Her* face! How tragic that it should be given away! *Tragic.* Yes, even in marriage.

The next day they walked together in the snow. It was fine January weather. The U-shaped valley lay before them many miles below, and they set out for the winding König Karol Promenade, skirting the side of the mountain along the right-hand side of the U. Above, firs rose in tiers. Their herring-bone branches glittered like marquisite. Far below, with coloured villages mapped on what seemed a flat white play-board, the valley: on foggy days from these promenades, when the valley was hidden, one felt one was looking out to sea.

But now no sea – everywhere soft snow. And soundless – their footsteps soft, the sudden shush sound of a passing sleigh, bells from below muffled, and in the immense false spring sky, blue as spring, a wide smiling sense that all occasional cries were welcomed upwards and like birds embraced in the sunlit echo of the upper air.

De Broda was well-slept, bathed, fresh, clean. Into the warmth of his big fur coat he took deep breaths of cold magical air. He felt fine. But he felt no 'countryman' feeling: he felt no temptation to become rougher, more rustic in the way of his walk. He felt, exquisitely, that he was a townsman sipping the weather, the scenery: he was a metropolitan tasting from within his warm elegance the country air. And beside him, in her green cape and her white fur hat, walked this pleasing graceful girl from Vienna. Her orange hair cut sharply against the white snow. What was it like? He wondered – then laughed deep inside his coat, for it was like nothing else but a patch of horse-urine in the snow. Or, should he try to say, the orange-iron mark of a mountain spring?

He said instead: 'And in Vienna, Fräulein Perfuss – do you live still with your family? Or have you your own – but these are hard days to find a flat. . . .'

'I live alone.'

'A career girl? What times we move in!'

'I work a little.'

'Let me guess – the arts? No? Then I have it – you design dresses! That cloak . . . !'

'Wrong again.'

She laughed – it was a carefully light careless laugh – and put her hand up to shade her eyes pretending to look out over the valley. She could tell him about that job much later.

'You're very inquisitive,' she laughed.

He spread his hands: 'Inquisitive? No. Interested – yes! Perhaps because I hope we are going to be very good friends – it's most natural to be interested.'

'In that case I shall listen to you first. Talk to me about yourself. Tell me about the things you like.'

He was only too glad. Her education could commence immediately.

He halted abruptly in the snowy track and pointed. 'I like that,' he said.

They were just below the great façade of the Germania, golden-buff in the snow. Its terraces descended to the path, the bark-balustraded woodland promenade on which they stood. Over the near hedge of snow, on the nearest terrace, rose a small wrought-iron kiosk. Icicles hung from its summer roof. It looked like a prettily iced cake. 'You can smell the lilac,' he said.

She looked up at him and sniffed: 'Lilac?' she asked. Her eyes narrowed, peering for the joke.

'I mean, you can feel the gardens as they are in summer. But – winter has stolen the scent of lilac, time the scent of patchouli.'

'It looks pretty draughty to me,' she said.

He laughed. But he continued. His voice lingered about the ironwork, then rose up to the great hotel above. He spoke of the dresses of the ladies in the Emperor's day, of the carriages, all the wealth of leisurely fashion before the Wars. She listened, staring at the little kiosk with its eagle emblem. She found him dull. But he was careful to picture in the scene the things she might like – muffs, gloves, fans, jewellery – and once or twice she caught his mood, she felt a pleasing sorrowful pang.

They stood and looked back over the valley to where the

hub of the spa bridged its ravine like a many-windowed Bridge of Sighs. There had been a heavy fall of snow; all around, on each separate object – a small bush, a balustrade, a rustic fence – the fall had moulded a strange snow-shape, fat and round and always benevolent. De Broda went on to tell his Fräulein Perfuss of the many famous people of the near past who had visited the spa, and who by virtue of merely their uniforms and their figuration in a more ample age, had taken on a distant charm. He told her of Bismarck. He told her how the Emperor himself had come to open the small mountain-railway station – there was a plaque there commemorating the event.

By now Laure gave him all her attention. She was interested – at the way he spoke and possibly by what he said. For his part, de Broda felt his usual satisfaction on speaking of these things. When he spoke of them his imagination widened and they came even closer. But usually he discussed them – now he found he was teaching, he was feeding words and scenes to the upturned and – yes! – interested face by his side. He felt himself grow physically bigger.

They walked slowly back. The crisp air, the altitude, the wintry sunlight enlivened them. The very orderliness of the place, within the soft disorder of snow, was pleasing. They passed a Kurhaus, a Pediküre-salon – this was a spa for the aged, well conducted, comfortable and safe. Down past the old Straubinger Hotel, grey-green and cream against the snow: past Stone and Blyth, the English tailors: past false pink marble, past a stucco Greek mask and grapes, past a stone stag's head – each framed by the white snow: past the entrance of the old Wandelbahn, the long glazed gallery – how thoughtful! – for walking in wet weather: and suddenly de Broda stopped. By the entrance of a hotel he had found a new treasure – something he had never seen before. Excitedly, he drew Laure's attention to it.

It was a miniature copper Chinese pavilion screwed to the wall. In the tarnished copper frame of the pavilion old and dusty charts were set, and dials and needles. It was called, in retrained lettering, Lambrecht's Wettertelegraf and Thermo-Hygroscop. What slow mystery was enacted here! What an air of the diligent, hush-voiced laboratory! De Broda was delighted. Again simply the sense of something of an older decade – irrespective of aesthetic worth – claimed him. He began to speak at length thrilledly. He invented a myth to suit its solemn inauguration on that wall years ago, he described with wit the wonder, almost the terror this strange little pavilion had evoked among an ailing aristocracy of the time. '*That's* progress!' 'But what is the pen writing, what then is it writing?' 'Chinese, madam,' the General had answered.

He suddenly found he was talking to himself. Laure had moved a foot or two aside and was peering, as decently as she could, at a group of film photographs advertising the nearby cinema.

Separately, at six o'clock, they lay in their thermal baths, thinking.

'Not so good,' de Broda thought. 'A waste of time. Films!' He gave a vicious whisk to the black hoselength lurking like an eel with him in the grave-deep bath.

Along the quiet corridor, up some stairs, and down another corridor, Laure too lay naked in deep warm water.

'Wettertelegraf!' she pouted to her legs floating white, dead, detached. 'Really!' She patted the china tassel of the bellrope with a pettish groan. '*What* does he expect a girl to ...'

'She ought to understand,' he said aloud, 'that there are other interests in life than, than ...' He heard his voice echoing round the tiles. It sounded like someone else intoning at him. Instinct drifted his hand across the most intimate nakedness.

'Why doesn't he behave like a normal man? Why doesn't he say something like ... like what normal men say?' She switched herself round frowning, clutching the bath-steps for support, and looked up at the brass-bound clock in the wall. Five minutes more. Five minutes to lie warm and think. She looked down her long white body and watched her hair float up like the feelers of a pale anemone.

So they lay in their big private baths and gave themselves to the warm healing water. Neither needed healing. But in such tiled seclusion, in the little tall rooms with their ample graves of water, and with the high black windows above showing the white beat of the snow outside, demonstrating as an aquarium feature all the coldness of the Austrian mountain night outside against the warmth within – in such clean tiled seclusion and such large warm water not only the body but also the mind was healed.

'Come, come,' de Broda thought. 'Don't let's be intolerant. Don't le's be hurried. It was only a lapse – why, in any case, shouldn't she like the films? A young girl has her interests. There are very good films, too. Sometimes. She was really most charming... that is, earlier....' And alone there his lips parted in a wide smile as he remembered the pleasant feelings he had, the expanded sense of himself, before the unfortunate matter of the Wettertelegraf. Then he kicked his foot right out of the water in self-reproach. 'Vanity!' he said sternly. He stared suddenly hard at his big toe sticking up as from a separate body. There were several long black hairs streaming down beneath the nail. 'Why!' he thought in wonder, 'I've never noticed *those* before.'

Laure grew warmer and more comfortable. 'Still, I like a man to be different. He's different, all right.' She grimaced. Then, suddenly startled by all the water round her, wondered: 'Should I put my head under?' She decided not. Relieved, she thought: 'He's really rather *charming*. He'd be a credit. I can just see him at the head of the table, a party for just six....' And her mind crept about silver candlesticks, a glitter of glasses, and the form of de Broda across the polished table with his polished manners so ably discoursing – he inclined a little forward to the lady seated on his right. That lady too inclined forward, her eyes never leaving his face. . . . Laure rose with an abrupt splash and began soaping herself severely. 'As for *her* . . .' she muttered decisively.

'I wonder,' de Broda mused, 'what her body's like?' He thought hard, suspended now on the water on his stomach, only his chin jutting on to one of the marble steps and supporting all. It proved difficult to imagine a strange woman's body: a known one was always substituted. 'Anyway, she's beautiful.'

'But I suppose,' she thought, 'I suppose he's hairs all over. . . .'

And he who liked most kinds said ponderously to himself, 'She's just my type.'

'Laure!' She giggled to herself as she made an untranslatable pun.

During the next few days they saw much of each other. They went for sleigh-rides up and down the mountain tracks. The sleighs were trimmed with brass and curved ironwork, their high seats were padded with green plush – and as they carved their soft-belled way through the steep alleys, as they passed fir-trees with fretted branches moulded by snow to look themselves like huge fir-cones, as they mounted to Rudolfshöhe or descended past a curtain of icicles to the lower rocks, all was romantic all most *altoesterreichisch*. The sleigh-drivers wore moss-green hats or hats of Styrian black and emerald. But once – much to de Broda's disgust – one of them wore an old leather flying-bonnet. De Broda had noticed this the moment they approached the line of sleighs waiting for hire. And he had shuffled about in the snow for a few minutes, hoping someone else would take the man. But no – and Laure had looked at him suspiciously as he made false conversation. He was about to try to explain to her – and suddenly found this impossible. It would sound like so much whimsy. Such refinements are only communicable between people of similar taste. And he had, in fact, too

good a sense of humour to persist – so they had hired
the man. The drive was nevertheless spoilt. He could not
take his eyes off that flying-bonnet.

However, that morning produced its great compensa-
tion. They descended at one of the largest of the enormous hotels. There in the immense empty lounge they had
ordered glasses of the bubbling spa water itself – for it
was too late for coffee. Cold water after the brisk cold
drive! They had laughed. And for some reason he had
mentioned – perhaps à *propos* of the desolate air of an
out-of-season hotel – the works of Thomas Mann. She had
read them. And she had read much else. To his surprise
he found she had developed quite a reasonable taste in
literature. He found with joy that at last they had one
taste in common.

But why? Then he thought of a girl's life, of her gentle
bringing up, of the hours of careful seclusion imposed on
her. He did not think of the hours of seclusion imposed
on a working girl, hours in a room alone with an empty
purse. However, in a way and not knowing it, he was right.
For without her early education, Laure might have preferred to books the little radio, or hour-long experiments
with her own face in the mirror.

Thenceforward they talked a lot about books. Once, de
Broda found himself wondering: If she has read so much,
if her imagination is thus so livened – why does she not
respond more easily to the other things I talk about? The
senses of time? Myths of the past? Could I – after all –
be phrasing these things badly? He could not believe so.
But then he did not know that books for Laure were in
the first place a last resort. When she was out and about
– and especially now on her holiday – her desire was for
action and life. Though she understood much of de Broda's
discourse, she was impatient of it. She listened with half
an ear. She wanted to escape sentiments that in her reading she had only half-experienced, for in its way the grey
page was a prison.

Still, they had a subject in common. It greased their

passage. As the days went on, they became more intimate. However – it was not all easy. There was the afternoon, for instance, when it snowed again. Even the quiet air of Gastein grew quieter. Sounds underfoot were muffled by the old snow, and the new fall filled the air with a dizzy kinematic flicker. One looked up, and the white sky was black with flakes forever dropping: one looked at the black firs and the dark plastered houses and the flakes fell white: it was the sight of so much falling without sound that added to the soundlessness. In such air they walked a little – snow mounted and melted in Laure's orange hair, on the brim of de Broda's hat. To avoid getting wet through they turned into a hotel. The light was fading. It was time for coffee.

Out of the soundlessness of the snow – through the double swing-doors into steamheat and light and suddenly voices from everywhere!

'It's not!'

'It is!'

'Der Bobby!'

'Bobby! In Gastein!'

And for a moment it seemed an endless number of people in high spirits and smart clothes crowded round de Broda. He was startled, confused – and then annoyed. These were old friends from Vienna, friends from ten years ago when he had led – despite the times, perhaps because of the times – a gayer and more frivolous life. Before the worm had crept in – before he had reached that point in early middle years when a tiredness, a certain intolerant familiarity with life had claimed him. One could not call this a false tiredness; but it was disproportionate; and perhaps a little later on it would melt with the tolerance of years and he would regain some of his easier, earlier, priceless, worthless joys.

But now he had the worm. And greeted by this group of light people he felt angry, embarrassed and ashamed. Indeed, the latter he might be allowed – for this little lot were not the best kind of company. They might have been

gay, but they made a strident flashy exhibition of themselves too. They talked, among the quiet coffee-drinkers,
at the tops of their voices: in their actions they pirouetted
and gestured with too great an ease – their absolute indifference to the room was a conscious insult; a boordom.

'But Bobby – you must come with us!'

'Here – this table by the piano?'

'Egon's going to play!'

'Oh – the Bobby ... how serious! ... this way to the
museum, please!'

De Broda had so many to shake hands with that he
had time to plan his retreat. With his back to Laure –
whom he had not introduced – he made his face into a
mask of theirs and winked at them. He winked that he
wanted to be alone with his little piece. Ah, they thought,
the Bobby! The old Bobby! And instantly they acknow-
ledged the formality of the occasion – it was the only
convention they bowed to. They nodded knowingly and
left him.

De Broda led Laure over to the furthest end of the
room. He felt ashamed that he had denied his real personality, thus he was awkward.

'Awful people,' he apologized. 'I'm so sorry.'

'But they seemed quite gay.'

'I used to know them once – a long time ago.'

They ordered coffee. Near them hung a picture of a fat
German Count – a famous and ferocious General – seated
on a horse. He was in full hunting-dress, and from his
magnificent eminence on the great stallion he held proudly
in his hand a single desolate dead hare. It was entitled:
'Jagd'.

De Broda tried to find some aesthetic quality in the
picture, found none, and was driven to talking again of
the atmosphere of period it now described. Laure listened,
but listlessly. Meanwhile the other party had grouped
themselves round the piano, and the Hungarian Egon – a
small round dapper man with a black moustache, an oiled
and energetic man – had begun to play the piano. The

others hummed, then broke into song. It was a tango: 'Küss' mich heut' portugiesisch'. One or two of the other people in the lounge looked round and smiled. An old man shook his head, but benevolently behind his paper. Plainly the room was not so insulted as de Broda had thought. Laure's eyes gleamed a growing delight.

Suddenly she turned to him: 'Why don't we go over there?'

'But Laure ...!'

'So little happens here – they look fun. *Do* let's!'

He felt sad and funless, clumsily and drily a spoiler of fun. He felt how much older he was. Yet persisted:

'Look, Laure – those are silly people. They're not worth while. I don't want you to know them.'

'But they're your friends?'

'Of a kind – of an old vintage, gone sour.'

'I'm not so sure who's sour.' She paused. 'Why don't you want *me* to meet them? Why *me*?'

He made an earnest expression, he made a grave, thoughtful face of care for her:

'Because, Laure, I take *you* seriously.'

It should have worked. But it didn't. It was a mistake. It gave Laure exactly the confirmation of his interest in her that she had wanted. He had never said anything like that before, and the spoken word, however often it is spoken, is important.

Power is an ugly word. Let us say it gave her a feeling of certainty, and with this of exhilaration.

'Oh how sweet!' she smiled. And then giggled. '... Bobby dear!'

He was still looking shocked when she put her finger to her lips and, standing up, asked him to excuse her. She went as if to the ladies' room. But on the way she passed the piano, just as 'Kiss me today in a Portugese way' was coming to an end. Not stopping, she smiled at them un-reservedly and sang out the last two bars. They clapped. And she was out through the swing-doors.

So that when after a few minutes she returned they felt

they knew her and implored her to sing more with them. She did, and for a long time she stood and chatted and laughed and sang.

De Broda was left alone with the German Count and his hare. He stared up at the picture and fumed.

But later, lying in his warm appeaseful bath, he forgave her. After all, she didn't know the crowd in question. And it showed she was lively. A girl should have her fun. It was indeed, he concluded happily, a very rare combination – an intelligent girl, an *intellectual* girl with a liking for liveliness. But he thanked heaven the party had already driven off back to Vienna.

Two days later, up towards the Villa Cäcilie, a young man ski-ed straight into them.

They all fell down.

But no one was hurt. The young man had come fast round the bend, had tried to check as he saw them, had struck a patch of ice, but then in fact had fallen and come only slithering into them on his behind. De Broda had thrown Laure back into the snow and himself across her. Now, surprised and covered with white patches, they all sat in the snow and felt themselves. Only Laure laughed.

The young man – he was plainly a visitor, he wore no local fawn or green but a dark blue ski-suit and a long peaked cap – was most apologetic. He asked repeatedly if they were not hurt? He showed not only politeness but real concern. De Broda was mollified. He laughed, shaking the snow off his coat, and assured the young man that no harm was done. He felt rather pleased that he had thrown himself in protection across Laure.

That evening the young man called at their hotel. He held some tickets in his hand. He was dressed in American clothes, but moved with European gestures of courtesy.

'I can't forgive myself for this morning's accident ... it was really so foolish of me,' he said to de Broda. 'Please let me make some slight recompense – there is a gala dance tomorrow at the . . .'

'But, my dear fellow, don't for a moment think—'

'I would be honoured if your daught—if the Fräulein and yourself would be my guests.'

He turned for the first time to Laure.

'You must persuade him, Fräulein!'

Of course de Broda had not missed that suppressed 'daughter'. His instant reaction was to accept, to show how young he was, to show he could dance as gaily as anyone else. But reactions have their own reactions: and irritated by the youthful parade forced upon him, and moved also by his underlying dislike of dancing – he protested that he himself did not enjoy such evenings at a holiday resort. He inferred that they could be better had in the metropolis.

It was half-past seven, the cleaned and rested hour after the bath. De Broda, comfortable and thus the more generous, gestured towards Laure. 'But naturally,' he said, 'if Fräulein Perfuss would like to go—'

The young man said nothing; but he looked at Laure with a polite questioning smile. Consideratively, as though this kind of invitation occurred nightly at Gastein, Laure said: 'Well – let's see, tomorrow night. No, I'm not doing anything. I don't think – yes. I'd be delighted to accompany you.'

'Excellent!'

Then the young man out of politeness, without much emphasis, tried again to persuade de Broda.

'No, no, no. I wouldn't think of it. You two enjoy yourselves.' He held his hand up to ward off finally all protestation. Then: 'But I must introduce you – Fräulein Perfuss. And my name is de Broda.'

'Peter Hörnli. Enchanted.'

'Hörnli?'

'From Zürich.'

'Ah. And how are you finding our Austria?'

After a while the young man left. They agreed he

seemed a nice enough young fellow. De Broda felt pleased
and strangely possessive. It showed him, really for the
first time, how intimate they had become in these few
days. He knew, and it pleased him to know, that he could
let her go off for an evening without fear. Besides, the
chap was just a young Swiss.

Laure seemed to have appreciated his action. She grew
even more charming during the next few days. She had
enjoyed the dance very much, she said. It was a change.
Herr Hörnli had proved a most pleasant companion.

Then one evening, two days later, de Broda took her up
above Gastein to dinner in an inn on the Böckstein plateau. Plateau? It was another valley, another great U above
the Gastein U. In Gastein one could think there was
nothing higher, in Gastein one had touched the sky. But
lo! a five minutes' walk up the mountainside that enclosed
the great valley – and there one was on the ground floor
of another valley again enclosed by horseshoe mountains!
One felt this stepped ascent might go on forever, it was
like entering a hall of mirrors. In such discovery there is
magic. Laure and de Broda, as they stepped up on to
Böckstein, felt as if they had entered a dream. And that
evening was indeed enchanted.

First, the magic of discovering such a valley – as mysteriously exciting as a strange garden discovered in childhood, a garden through a gate in a wall, a garden that one
feels, in the instant one finds it, will disappear the next
day never to be found again. Secondly, the snow had
ceased to fall, and a clear crescent moon stood high in the
sky, casting blue light everywhere: icicles in fir-trees
flashed this light, and one saw how people had first thought
of putting tinsel on Christmas trees. They went into an
inn and ate trout freshly fished from the rocky river: trout
cooked in butter from the cream of the valley, herbed from
the valley, and followed down by a bottle of one of the
valley's cold clear rain-gold wines. Coffee, imported on a
tired schilling, was hell. But then out into the moonlight,
out cleansing the mouth with the smell of snow, and a

wine-warmed walk to another inn just across the way. In there, a live merriment prevailed; it was the weekly zither-abend. Two squat coarse men with faces of the mountains, gnome-faces with close eyes and great noses, plucked at the little stringed boards before them. Their fingers were broad and swollen, too big for the finely-laid strings. Yet they plucked, plucked with curiosity – as if this were a strange cabalistic game and the zithers magic boards – and out sang the heavy little mountain waltzes.

More wine, and de Broda found himself linking arms and leaning close against a warm, flushed, happy Laure. Sometimes everybody in the room sang and thumped the tables, and Laure and de Broda sang too. They were closer, easier, more comfortable with each other than ever before. In that white room, clean as a dairy, and among the villagers in their sober suits and their drunken orderli-ness – they had touched an atmosphere removed a hundred miles from the grave majesty of Gastein. By some miracle of ventilation, the smoke of cigars vanished instantly; much wine was drunk, yet none spilled; it was unusual and dreamlike to see so many swaying wine-filled bodies and to hear such boisterous music in so orderly, so white and scrubbed a room. But this was no place of Swiss prettiness, it was heavy and solid.

De Broda was enjoying himself. He felt relaxed and blank-minded and light-headed. Occasionally he tried to pull himself – as he called it – together. How could the hour be improved? Once, he remembered that Count Czernin's shooting-box stood along the valley: and he began to speak of this. But he soon stopped.

Suddenly Laure put her arm round his neck and kissed him.

It was at the end of a song which she had been hum-ming to herself, smiling down at the wine-flask. The song ended with three long waltz-beats. On each chord she gave him a long decided kiss on the lips.

De Broda was surprised to find himself not at all as-tonished. It seemed the most normal thing. Not, indeed, that it was unusual for a couple to kiss at a time of music and wine. Nor, very naturally, was it unexciting. No, it was exciting. But still – normal, as though it had been ordained, as though it might already have happened before.

As the songs were sung, as the wine-flasks emptied, they kissed again. De Broda, for once speechless, murmured only her name. Laure said nothing. She was by no means drunk: but there was about her a carelessness and a flushed bright enchantment. She seemed full of secret thoughts – secrets that made her blush and smile into herself. Now and then she held her head back from de Broda and looked at him carefully, her lips parted in peculiar interest, half-closed eyes seeming to measure him.

They left, and arm in arm walked down the snowy hill-road. At the escarpment edge Gastein came into view, they were just above the huddled high roofs – it looked a strange metropolis huddled in the moonlit gorge. Nearby the waterfall drummed. They left the road and stamped through moss-mounds of snow to the bridge over the fall. There they stood and gazed with wonder and with fear at the spectacle beneath.

Wide in front the moonlit valley – white and wide, with the mountainsides tinselling their firs into blue-black distance. But just beneath only darkness and the cold roar of ceaseless water. Sound echoed from the rock walls round them, such a weight of water has a machine roar, the light wooden bridge itself seemed to drum with the sound. De Broda put his arm round Laure. They stood close together moved by the great beauty around them, close too against the beautiful greatness of the fearful thing below them.

The cold air exhilarated, it was sparkling clear and mixed wonderfully with the warm wine-fumes. A great joy seemed to swell within de Broda's breast, he bent closer to her profile, so sadly, so beautifully incised in the moonlight – and with a blessed sense of release the words of a proposal rose to his lips.

'Laure, dearest Laure. . . .' he whispered.

She turned to him.

And then suddenly the long elegant worm inside rose, the delicate worm bit him. As it bit, his lips made themselves thinner, he felt his eyes focus clearer. 'No,' murmured the cold emotionless worm. 'No. Don't be overtaken by events. You did not decide to do this yet. You decided to take exactly your own time, choose your hour, seek your setting. In another couple of days, you said.'

'Laure,' de Broda said, 'let's go.'

The next morning he came down late, enquired for Laure, and was told she had already left for a walk. It had become their custom to spend their mornings together, and he was a little irritated. However, he blamed himself for rising so late, put on his coat and went out.

It was a beautiful morning. He decided to descend the steep paths by the waterfall itself, and found himself in strange country. Great conduit pipes like sleeping boas wandered among the snow and jagged rocks; rusted winches and lock-gates draped their curtains of icicle: such a vast old machinery astounded, and steam from the hot spring rose all around against the snow. Down there, deep in the gorge, the roar of the torrent drowned all other sound. De Broda was fascinated; but not for more than a quarter-hour. Normally he enjoyed a solitary walk, normally he was delighted to escape companionship. But not that day. He began to find himself uneasy for Laure's company.

She did not appear at luncheon.

He spent the afternoon wandering from hotel to hotel in the hope of seeing her. He ended the afternoon with a book, and went up to his bath early.

But once more the comfort of those waters put him at his ease, and it was in good temper that he descended to dine.

For a number of reasons – because until the previous night they had not been on intimate but only on familiar terms, because also de Broda had been taking his time and had wished to maintain some independence, and moreover because the very size of the great mirrored and pillared dining-hall suggested a propriety that linked each table privately with each guest – they had not dined at the same table. So, since that evening Laure came down late, they did not meet until after dinner.

De Broda was careful to seem unconcerned. He waved an invitation to her from his coffee-table – the distance of manners between the lounge and the dining-room, in fact no more than an inch of curtained glass door, might have been a mile – and Laure smiled her way over.

He did not ask her anything, but entered instantly into a discourse upon his own day:

'. . . one might have been on a harbour quay, such extra-ordinary machinery for controlling the water, and on each side the hotel walls, like wharves . . .'

'Really?'

'. . . and far, far above, against the sky, our bridge . . .'

'Our bridge?'

'I mean, the bridge we stood on last night.'

'Oh, my dear, of *course*.'

A pause. De Broda risked a tender look. He felt truly tender: only his mind, his mind layered with experience, made it a risk.

Laure smiled brightly back. There was something inside her bubbling to come out. Suddenly it came:

'You know,' she said – and her lips dropped as though she ought not to say it – 'at least you don't know, you'd never *guess* where *I*'ve been today!'

Desperate to control himself, de Broda made a blank, bored face that in other circumstances might have looked plain rude. But Laure was too concerned to notice.

'I daren't tell you,' she said. 'I daren't!'

He managed a smile: 'Then you must keep it a dead secret. No! Not a word!'

Laure's mouth hung still half-open. She stopped, astonished. Then a look of such disappointment came into her eyes that even de Broda saw he was being too cruel.

He leaned closer, and making a play of conspiracy, whispered: 'A secret – but let *me* into it.'

She took a deep breath:

'I've been ski-ing!'

It was so much a reverse of all he wished for that he forgot himself.

'Ski-ing! Why? Who on earth with?'

'Oh . . .'

She pretended nonchalance:

'Herr Hörnli.'

'Who . . .? Oh, that young Swiss?'

'Yes. He passed the hotel earlyish – long before you were up. (How's the head, by the way?) We talked a few minutes. Then he said why didn't I ski, and he would teach me. It was such a beautiful morning I went.'

De Broda regained himself with a pale smile: 'So you went up and I went down.'

'Can't say I didn't go down once or twice too,' she giggled. De Broda laughed uneasily.

'But you enjoyed yourself?'

'Mm. It was lovely.'

And she went on to tell him all about it. She told him how fine the air was, what fun it had been, where they had lunched, how they had tobogganed home.

'It was difficult again at first,' she finished. 'But I'll soon get used to it.'

De Broda had been thinking – in the tolerance of his chair and the coffee and the lovely brightnesses of her smile and her hair – thinking how after all a day out must have made a refreshing change. But at her last words he properly flinched:

'Get *used* to it?'

'Yes. I'm going to concentrate.'

'But Laure – you've only four days left!'

'That's exactly it. Only four days. I'll have to work hard.'

'You're going ski-ing every day?'

'Oh yes.'

'But Laure – our walks together, we were going . . .'

'Ludwig dear – *please*. You know I was supposed to be having a holiday. It's as much for my health as anything. After being cooped up in that . . . in Vienna. I really owe it to myself.'

'Then I won't be seeing much of you.'

'Oh, Ludwig – yes. In the evenings.'

'It's not much.'

'So you don't want to see me in the evening?'

'You know I didn't mean that.'

'But you *said* so.'

'No. Please, Laure dearest – how can I put it – I meant . . .'

And for a few minutes they lightly quarrelled. De Broda grew more flustered and more apologetic. With fine petulant logic she undressed all his well-meaning. De Broda found himself physically sweating and gasping a little for breath.

Laure relaxed. And de Broda was so much relieved that together they spent a quiet pleasant evening.

Yet every so often de Broda remembered the kisses of the night before, and glanced at her curiously. How could she seem to forget so quickly? How retreat so easily to her earlier distance from him? Retreating to lead him on? It didn't feel like it.

The wine? Perhaps. But he thought not. And he contented himself by shaking inside his polite face a worldly wise head. 'Women!' his wisdom said. It explained nothing. It excused everything. 'Women – they're unpredictable!' he repeated, and felt much better.

Had he been alone, that is truly alone, he would have delighted in the great blue winter weather and enjoyed a long walk on the white mountainside. But he was less alone than lonesome. So the next day found him impatient of the mountains and simply drifting about the small centre of Gastein itself. He knew he was alone until the evening, the whole day was free – but he could make no decision. In fact, what he had to do was simply wait until she returned. Until that time life had no moment. It was much the same, though much magnified, as the empty endless day before a long anticipated treat, before a ball.

So he wandered round the hotels and cure-houses and the little shops. Gastein is small. One can wander from end to end in ten minutes. And back. And back again. Neither the antlers on the Villa Solitude nor the wild bulk of the Grand Hôtel de l'Europe nor the glass canopy of the art nouveau fashion arcade, nor the damask and great brass hatpegs of the Mozart any longer entranced him. Finally he thumped the snow off his boots, entered enormous swing-doors, took a chair in an immense empty lounge and ordered a glass of active water.

The waiter – one waiter for a hundred empty chairs – approached and receded soundlessly on thick carpet. He came and went like a figure projected, magnified and then minimized, on a screen of empty air. All one side of the lounge was glass. A long way away rose a splendid view of the mountains. But inside at the tables one felt more the glass than the view – which lay back removed like a picture. Glassy cold light like water filled every corner of the lounge. Nowhere the comfort of a dark warm shadow.

Far away, through pillars and down marble steps, the majestic door occasionally revolved, a hushed conversation whispered at the desk with its shaded light, and some other lonely traveller passed on quiet carpets into tall corridors and away. Occasionally a bell buzzed somewhere: one expected, somehow, a sort of answer to this discreet summons: but none was heard.

De Broda's little bottle of water bubbled silently. But it made the only movement, and a fierce one, in the room. He himself sat absolutely still. He was engraved in the solitude – any movement would ricochet painfully in such quiet. The noise of movement would stamp too severely, then echo, then vanish to reinforce the vacuum: its shape of movement would jitter slyly in mirrors all around. For

there were many mirrors – the great hall was built at a
time when opulence mattered more than taste. Many styles
were mixed – gilt, marbles, mirrors, plushes, brasses fought
for stately precedence. It was indistinguishable from the
hotel hall of a capital railway terminus anywhere. And in
it de Broda began to feel as lonely as a waiting traveller.
Of course, he was one.

He sighed to his glass of water. He looked round for a
paper: there was none. He looked round to see if, finally,
the great room was empty: it was. He looked down at his
fingers – it might be an idea to manicure his nails: but
they were already done. He thought he would run over
whatever papers might be in his wallet, and he felt in his
pocket: but it was not there. He remembered, as one can
know with instant certainty the difference between a lost
and left wallet – leaving it in the hotel. But in this he was
nearly saved. For a moment he became anxious. Ordering
a drink without money! Would they think—? How would
he convince them? But wearily the moment subsided, he
had remembered how well known he was.

And minute by minute the loneliness grew – he could
quite easily have called for a paper, but his mood and the
silence forbade it – and that strange feeling of 'having no
name' returned. Ludwig de Broda, he said it to himself,
Ludwig de Broda. It seemed absurd – or less than that,
meaningless. He looked down at his paunch. There was
certainly someone there, a slimmish someone who kept
unbuttoned the lowest button on his waistcoat, and that
someone was, as he knew, himself. But was it Ludwig de
Broda? No.

That Ludwig de Broda was a nothing. A little fearfully,
the man in the chair tried to substantiate him. He racked
his mind for scenes where de Broda had figured. The film,
not in monotone as so often in a dream, but in full colour
as flesh and clothes flashed across his mind. De Broda
waving goodbye to a girl from the deck of a steamer leaving Budapest: de Broda in the Dolomites, a small lung-
fresh figure alone with a huge view: and for no particular

reason de Broda in a narrow alley in Vienna, and again at some party, and in a room full of flowers lifting the hem of a housemaid's skirt, and so on.

He watched this de Broda in flashes through his life – until he entered the last ten years, the years of aestheticism. And now as he watched that figure of himself in picture galleries, or watching the Belvedere die in the winter sun, or standing in a railway terminus evoking its rampant days – now the character of the figure converged with his own actuality in the sort of railway hotel lounge where he was sitting and he grew more apprehensive as still it stayed separate. It seemed always to be someone else. He tried to shake the thought away, he sat up and concentrated on what was around him.

It was, of course, the hall of a railway terminus. That had dovetailed nicely: so then he shook the terminus away, and made himself see that he was in Bad Gastein and nowhere else. But rather than bringing him to his senses, this instead reinforced the abysmal sense of loss into which he had drifted. For now again, examining a frieze of plaster amorini, feeling the long dusted drift of the great tasselled curtains, realizing the brass double eagle worked into the fender by the great fireplace – he was again back in the past century. And, whatever melancholy pleasures he derived from the paradise past, he suffered three distinct and almost material losses whenever he thought of it.

First, the appalling notion that he had just missed all that – not by any acceptable stretch of time, such as a hundred years – but by a single generation. He had just missed it – and this easily led to a feeling that it had been purposely done to him, that he had been left out.

Secondly, there was the suspicion that *life then had been all right*. As in our personal memories we usually tend to isolate and picture not times of distress but scenes of happiness or elation – how equally natural is it to conjure up and exaggerate the best of a whole period of the past! He saw in the decade of that brass double eagle only amplitude and finesse. It made today worse. So – *he had been robbed,* he was lost in the daylight present.

And thirdly, thinking of the *fin de siècle,* he had an impression always of people in groups, never single. The group of the family – when homes were spacious and by whole households lived in. And the larger groups of occasion: the full house of the opera, the fashionable drives of the Ringstrasse seemed to have been peopled not by individuals about their own pursuits but by a gathering of people framed in a picture of united purpose. And in the country, or in such a hotel as that in which he now sat, he saw large groups at the tables, parties of people always, and always at some height of laughter or private festival. Now, of course, there were no groups, there was neither fulness nor purpose. *There was only loneliness.*

But already it was one o'clock. An hour for luncheon, and it would be two o'clock. The long hours until he would see Laure again were lessening. He cheered up a little.

After his bath, the day over, fresh and expectant, he was delighted to find Laure down in the lounge early.

Her orange head was bent over a writing-desk. When he went over to her she looked up happily. Her face still held the flush of the snows, she had the cool radiant certainty of a woman who has just descended from the bedroom mirror. She looked up and smiled:

'I'm just writing home – to plead for another two days.'

'Good! Excellent!'

'What they'll say I don't know! Still, I'll risk it. You didn't know I worked in a shop, did you?'

'Well ... no ... you never told me. ...'

Interesting. But de Broda was too pleased by this sudden present of a longer stay to pay much attention to it. Vaguely he thought of her as the manageress, the director of the shop: though he would in fact have scarcely been troubled by the knowledge of her more humble position.

It was not unusual. Besides, his snobberies were of a different kind.

'It's a cake-shop,' she said. And with a flourish of signature, 'There! Either the mine goes up or it doesn't.'

She was in high spirits. They spent a pleasant half-hour together and then parted to dine. During dinner, exhilarated by her company after the lonely hours, he decided to make his proposal that evening. He was quite sure he was infatuated, he suspected it might be love. He considered where his words might best be said – over a bottle of wine in the Mozart? On the Wilhelm Promenade, with the great snowbound valley beneath? Mm. Or – or in a double-bath, perhaps? He chuckled. Then he thought of the high bridge over the waterfall. That was plainly the answer.

After dinner they had coffee together. Then, after some twenty minutes, Laure took out a mirror, patted her hair and said: 'Nine o'clock! I must go.'

Unconcerned her fingers smoothed the button on a gold lipstick case and the little red knob slid out. She raised it to her lips. For a moment de Broda could say nothing. He sat quite still, only his eyes widened in dread. Then he blurted:

'Going? Going? Going where ...?'

'I have an appointment.'

'But – but I thought we were going to spend ... you said ...'

'Did I? But we made no arrangement.'

She was still looking in the mirror. Her fingers moved too steadily, her face showed too little expression – it was plain she avoided looking at him.

He leaned forward, grasped the arm of her chair:

'You said we could spend the evenings together. When we talked about your ski-ing. And tonight – tonight's very important. ...'

'Oh? How?'

'Well ...'

'But look, Herr de Broda – or should I say Bobby ...?'

Now she did look at him, her teeth and the little mirror's teeth smiling bright malice, and the red lipstick point like a sweet poison in between:

'... look, we're not exactly living together, are we? And you never never said: Fräulein Laure, I beg you to enchant me with your company between the hours of nine and twelve o'clock tonight! No no! Nothing like that from Bobby! As a matter of fact, I'm going out to dance.'

'Laure!'

'Bobby!' she mimicked.

He got angry. He decided to put his foot down once and for all.

'Who are you going out with?'

She frowned:

'That sounds rather a demand. Really, Ludwig!'

He gripped the arm of her chair harder and leant his pale face earnestly towards her. A touch of rose fevered his cheekbones. He said very softly:

'Tell me!'

She laughed, a little frightened: 'Well – if you *must* know, it's Peter.'

'Peter?' His voice rose. '*What* Peter?'

'Peter Hörnli.'

He raised his eyebrows – his one joined eyebrow. Then drawled, more comfortably: 'Oh him – the ski-boy.'

Her voice was sharp. 'And what's wrong with that?'

'Nothing.'

Then he leant closer towards her, he lost his anger, he spoke earnestly and sincerely:

'Laure dear. Don't go. I've got – so much to tell you. Laure – Laure darling.... I love you. I want you, Laure – I want you to be my wife.'

The lipstick dropped away. Her hardness dropped away. Her eyes softened, but she still frowned.

She just said: 'Oh.'

'Laure – put him off. I wanted to tell you – to ask you later. When we were walking somewhere ... not here.

397

But now I've had to . . . Laure,' he took a deep and terrible breath, 'will you be my wife?'

She said nothing. Only her eyes searched his face anxiously, as though she were looking not for love but for a sign of illness – and carefully her hand was placing the lipstick on the table.

He went on, talking quickly. 'Laure – it's only Hörnli. You can easily leave a note. Do, darling, write one now, we can go out the other way – he's calling for you, I suppose?'

Slowly she said: 'But Ludwig – Ludwig – I – I can't marry you.'

His mouth pursed into a smile, as at some little puzzle he shook his head.

'No,' she said. 'I'm already engaged.'

She put her hand softly over his. It was no touch, it was a compress.

'Yes,' she said. 'To Peter Hörnli.'

His hand loosened on the arm of her chair. He looked simply puzzled.

'I'm so sorry, Ludwig.'

There was a small commotion by the inner swing-doors: a stamping of snow, beating of gloves.

'There he is already – Ludwig, you don't want to meet . . . no . . . of course. No – I must go.'

She rose and left him. She did not look back.

De Broda sat quite still. More than anything – he was seized with wonder. He simply could not understand. An old feeling overwhelmed him – of being in class and not knowing the lesson. Blankly and almost casually, as if there was no hope of solving the problem, as if that Hörnli were a puzzle of white numerals on a blackboard, he tried to examine him. Standing there by the swing-doors he looked young – unbelievably young. Could he then be not a boy but a man? De Broda had imagined him as eighteen or so. But he remembered how as one grows older ages in both directions become muddled – and saw he might be at least twenty-five, more. And his haircut – like an

American advertisement. He was still in his ski-trousers, yet with some sort of belted loose coat: these were clothes de Broda could not understand, they came from another world. In fact, the New World – over his gestures, which were properly German-Swiss, there ran a veneer of American posture, frank agilities of the collegiate, laconicisms of the film. To de Broda's older culture such mannerisms were still confounding, though he had seen them extend through many European cities. But he deduced from them neither the levelling of false emotions nor the destruction of class patronage that at their best they represented – he deduced simply bad boorish manners. He saw only the bravo-me of it. It was alien to his heart.

So that now watching this Hörnli greeting Laure – with a strange nonchalant ease as if there were time only for the broadest smile, a large effusion all at once for they must be getting on, getting places – he was even more astounded that Laure should take such a man seriously. That brash boy with his easy smile? That cock-a-hoop young nothing? That figure of all unsubtlety, swaggerer of dance-halls, that sportsman?

That sportsman put on his hat at a gay angle and wheeled Laure, laughing Laure, through the swing-doors and out. Slim-hipped, loose-shouldered, his back covered Laure like the curtain of a play, and then that too was gone and the vestibule left empty.

For some minutes de Broda was unable to gather himself. He had not moved, his face hung almost in a smile. It was unbelievable. Then slowly he rose and walked up the stairs to his room.

He went to the mirror. He looked at his face. It looked no different. At forty he saw the face of thirty, the age-marks over the well-known shape he treated as no more than a mist on the mirror. He looked down at his hands – his slender, washed, workless fingers that could speak subtleties unknown to mouths. Further down – to the suit he wore, to its civil suavity, its politely traditional cut. To his shoes, sober and elegant. And up to the mind behind his face – a mind tutored in graces of good taste, a mind of knowledge and sometimes wit but always of culture and taste. Vain, he thought. Quite a few faults, of course. But really – how *could* she?

It all seemed so absurd. There in his bedroom, alone, he gave a shrug to his shoulders and smiled. Then suddenly – half-way between the mirror and the bed – he stopped dead. Half-way across the bedroom carpet, isolated on that carpet, the full realization of what had happened fell upon him. Its appalling echo rang round the room, sang in his empty ears. She had refused him! She had left him! She had preferred someone else to *him*! Nothing he could ever do would revise it. To him, *him*, she had preferred that boy. . . .

He grasped for his overcoat and left that room quickly. But at the head of the stairs paused – ashamed to be seen by the people in the lounge below. Then his shoulders straightened and he descended, went quickly through and out into the snow. It was a clear night, the snow glowed white everywhere. Sometimes a lighted window showed a yellow square, festive and telling of warmth within. But de Broda saw nothing, he did not know where he was walking. Through his mind there raced backwards the perspective of events – too clearly he saw the answers to questions he had chosen to ignore. The episode with that party from Vienna – of course that was what she really wanted: and her abrupt interest in the ski-run: and, most bitter of all, the way she had kissed him on that magic evening in the zither-tavern – he saw how this was no more than a kind of overflow of her exhilaration with Hörnli, it had been a gesture of gaiety embracing not him but the idea of love.

The snow made no noise beneath his slow trudging boots: he felt that love for him had passed forever. Past the mauve light of a Kurhaus, past a man hacking ice from a wooden sledge – the white road leading uphill looked as uneventful and empty as his own life would henceforth be. At least the road twisted, and it rose higher to some

horizon . . . but his life? Nothing appeared there – only a
level road, unposted, with neither turning nor end nor anything ever to happen on it. As he watched his dark boots
on their lonely procession, as if they covered no flesh of
his but were boots of a warder taking him along that road,
he lost the last of his spirit. He felt old and finished.

He saw sadly that those two together told no more
than an old and simple tale – youth to youth. They shared
together energies and vitalities he would never know again.
And they shared together a spirit of the times, an accept-
ance of the present that he would never understand, a
modern spirit strange as a foreign language. A thousand
small utterances of day-to-day life separated him from
that bounceful, youthful spirit: they would not think
twice of, say, the look of a bottle of medicine – whereas
he would long for the scrolled designs of older ointments;
they would drive to Grinzing on a motor-bicycle and love
it: they would accept, accept, accept – yes, they would
enter into things. How simple – yet how strange! How
strange that however one might groom oneself, however
fine a taste and a culture and a manner and all urbanity
one might achieve – and however young one still felt and
even almost looked – one could never be accepted exactly
as a fellow-being by youth.

The dark firs rose above him like bird-giants, their
branches ridged like feathers, their topmost tufts sly as
little heads. Ice on the road gleamed its cold. What might
have been a magical winter's night looked only forlorn –
it was a scene only of cold desolation. The wide valley
stretched below, like something seen not now but in a
long and snowbound time ago. De Broda lifted his eyes
from his boots and looked curiously around him. He found
these very boots had led him near to where that high
bridge hung across the ravine and its rocky torrent.

Then two things happened. Small matters – but the
kind that grow large in a grieving mind. Over the crest
of the hill a motor came whirring its chains on the ice.
It bore down towards de Broda. Quite normally he had to

step to the side to let it pass. It passed, and, with its lights and air of company, disappeared. De Broda stood in the thick snow at the side of the road – again alone on a lonely road – and felt the motor had pushed him there with personal intent, with a jeer.

And then, when he had moved on a step, suddenly the door of a villa opened. It was a villa standing alone and the door lay along a short path. But quite visibly in its rectangle of yellow light stood the figure of a woman. She leaned forward slightly, she seemed to be peering out on to the snow, perhaps on to the road, perhaps at him. Quite suddenly, she closed the door again: and all was again dark.

De Broda turned away and hurried towards the bridge.

His mind was quite made up. He hurried with his head butting forward, with his mind in fact bowed towards the bridge and away from all light and sound and people.

But not all sound: for there came towards him the dark shuddering murmur – at first only a vibration through the snow – of the waterfall. He hurried faster to meet it. Ice caked under his heels. He slipped, he lurched as he ran. He passed into the belt of firs that with their wet dark leaves guarded that place. Then his hands gripped wide on the wooden balustrade, he looked down. It was suddenly quite dark, a cloud passed over the moon.

Foam splashed white somewhere deep in the darkness, it was difficult to see where, it was like looking down to the bottom of a well. The rock face fell vertically, stone echoed a watery roar through darkness all around; yet there grew down the sides, on every ledge, less like trees than something poisonous, the firs – dark-draped ladies suckled by rock and spray and shadows. Their arms dripped water. Sound of water echoed everywhere. Water flooded with the nightmare sound of a vast dam breaking, rearing its black smooth mass like a wall to pour down forever over everything.

De Broda stood there gritting his teeth, the muscles in his arms clenched ready. The sound below, the feel of flat water beneath hummed dragging at his mind, he leaned nearer the desirable, the terrible — then suddenly sobbed and flung himself on the ground. Breathing with fear, very slowly and carefully he crept off the little bridge on his knees.

He lurched up and stumbled into the surety of the trees: then stopped, and still breathing hard, looked back. The sound had receded, the bridge without its fall looked sure and graceful, a rustic affair among snowy firs. Without questioning himself, instantly bold again, he sneered at it within himself and began to return: but as the roaring sound grew he stopped, tried another step — then his heart altogether failed him, he turned and walked quickly away. Yet he refused to feel defeated. Vertigo, he thought. And quite natural. A matter difficult to imagine, easy to experience.

He reached the road, and heard voices. Two people were leaving the villa whose door he had seen open. Their voices came clearly across on the frosty air, he was instantly on his guard. Perhaps it had not been vertigo? Perhaps he had been simply afraid to finish what he had in mind? The doubt grew as those voices approached. He walked quicker to be ahead of them — not to be seen aimless, slinking off the road. The voices receded, he felt bolder. His figure straightened, he felt they could still see him, but they were safer and further away. He'd show them — an abrupt blood of revenge rose and gritted his teeth. And with it came a sudden idea that turned his footsteps fast down towards his hotel. Water, he thought, there was water without vertigo, the place was running with water! Revenge then, on the waters, on the voices. Revenge the proud way, a Roman revenge!

Immediately he was in he ordered the bath and went to his washstand for a razor. He could even smile as he remembered that of course there was only a safety razor. And the man's face engraved on the little packet of blades bore an expression hardly adequate to the situation. He tore the face off the packet and extracted several blue-black, carefully greased little blades from their envelopes. He wondered how many to take and then took two – with some idea of two wrists. He put the blades in his dressing-gown pocket and left for the bathroom.

The maid had already filled the bath. The water lay quite still. But it steamed slightly from its surface, it had a presence of movement like an animal asleep. When de Broda shut and bolted the thick white door he was alone with it, he was insulated from the passage and all sound and all people: such near-marine doors fit exactly.

Casually, almost as though he were in fact going to shave – for he moved slow under the weight of self-pity and revenge – he placed the two little blades down on the floor-edge of the bath. He took off his dressing-gown and approached the steps naked. The water in those square pools lies below the level of the floor, there are steps and a steadying hand-rail down into it: and thus de Broda had time, approaching the head of the steps, exactly to feel himself naked. He felt unprotected. He had a moment to realise that people must come eventually and find him thus. He paused in shame. He looked back along the tiles to his dressing-gown. But he had brought no under-clothes in, it would mean drenching that gown. It was unthinkable. He turned again to the steps. So they'd find him naked? Well, the more shame on them, the more revenge.

And then down into the warm still water, down into the green receiver among the white clean tiles.

First to soak, to get heat into the veins. He lay back floating with his shoulders resting on the marble step. The bath was wide, the sense of luxuriance pleased him. This was fitting. He took a wrist from the water and examined it curiously. He had never noted it so closely before; so hairless, such soft flesh: he saw how blue veins crossed above the tendons – so many brittle tendons, like the thin bones in a chicken's leg, with veins crossing them like soft blue bridges. He tried to remember where the pulse was, remembered not to use his thumb, found it; and found his other hand holding his own wrist delicately as though it were someone else's. He had been five minutes in the bath. He turned to the razor-blades.

It was difficult to pick them off the tile. They lay flatly, they were sharp, he did not want to cut his thumb so he got one up with his finger-nails, his nails pincered it up like a magnet picking a weight of steel.

He held the little blade carefully. He remembered sharpening pencils with such double-edge blades, how they were greased and could slip back into the hand – and he pressed the ball of his thumb hard into the little range of slots to fasten his grip. That was in his right hand. Easing himself up to sit steadily on the step, he raised his left wrist. He turned the underside of the wrist upwards – he felt for a moment he was looking at a wristwatch – and his eye wandered over the blade and saw the second one resting on the bath-side. He saw that instinctively thinking of two wrists he had brought two blades. That was unnecessary, absurd – but it produced another problem. Which to cut first? Now that the right hand held the blade, and thus the left wrist should be the first to be cut – would not the left and weaker wrist be too weakened by the cut to manage the blade for the right? Perhaps the left hand should cut first – the stronger right one would withstand the wound better? Very carefully, careful not to cut himself, he exchanged the little blade between his fingers and thumbs.

But now holding it in his left hand – and feeling thus insecure, for the left was not used to such precise movement – a further trouble showed itself. It was very important to be both exact and quick: but that meant changing over the blade quickly and cutting fast with the right hand before it was weakened. Would it be shocked numb for those vital seconds? He thought – and then saw that after all his instinct had been right, there was no reason why he should not hold a second blade ready in the right hand. It would avoid the delicate change. He turned and, again very carefully, pincered the second blade off the tiles. Precariously holding the left hand away from his body, he nearly slipped. And that made him suddenly think: what if the shock made the right-hand fingers open and that blade dropped away down in the water?

He shook his head impatiently. That had to be risked. Main thing was to get on with it. Against his real will – which wished, since they were his own wrists, to cut carefully and tenderly – he told himself to do it quickly, to hold both hands in front in the air and then – slash quickly. With the movement of drumsticks. Like a man with butterpats. Quickly. One-two. He stretched out his hands, turned the right wrist inwards, held his breath and waited.

Waited for what?

A word of command.

From whom?

For the first time he realized that word must come from himself and no one else: he was absolutely alone with his own will.

The steam rose lightly on the water's surface, no more than a snaking of mist on the bath green. The snow pawed silently on the black window above. Movement everywhere – but no sound. He felt no longer alone, but in a crowd of movers making no sound but restlessly waiting. And supposed he would make no sound either, razorblades made no sound. Suddenly he saw himself sliding down after it was done, a splashing of water, the dark blood clouding round him in the water. He grew greatly afraid.

Afraid of what? Because he had to make his own hands move to do it? Was he afraid of decision? No, not him! He looked closely at the skin on his wrist, soft and so tenderly his own. He saw how his finger-pads were soaked in the steamy air and ridged like fresh-waved white sand, like dead skin. Abruptly then a new thought came from nowhere, a thought suddenly from the world lost outside the bathroom. Something whispered to him that Hörnli was a Swiss. A Swiss would own Swiss francs. And Swiss francs were very valuable. And he saw instantly for the first time what precisely he wanted to see – that the Swiss francs rather than Hörnli were what Laure wanted. Not the young man's potency but the potency of money! Only that.... He understood well what a hard currency meant. So what was he so troubled about? *He* was not preferred, this was something quite different.... With abounding relief he lowered a little his hands. He let out his tense breath. And lay there feeling for the first time the old pleasant warmth of the bath.

But a doubt was there. He held hard on to this new bright belief, but deeper in his brain a dark and troublesome doubt assembled like a cloud. He held hard, he concentrated on the idea of Swiss francs. His chin came out – and abruptly and proudly a new thought came. He decided to find out. He would go against all his principles – he would go out dancing with them, to a beer cellar with them, and by God he would go up in the ski-lift! Yes, and he'd even ski! He'd stay with them at all their games and find out!

Then – he saw himself up at the ski-station. He saw clearly. He watched as the minute passed and he saw what would happen pass like a bright film through the minute....

He saw himself up there by the hut, dressed for snow. He saw exactly how he was dressed, and how it was a bright and sunlit day, and how he was buckling on his skis among a merry crowd of people buckling on theirs. Much colour against the snow, much excitement: the air was crisp and the crowd of them were ready for the day's sport. Laure and Hörnli were not yet there. He himself had gone up early. He wanted to be there ready for them. And he was cunning enough to know that he needed practice, he needed quite a time on the nursery slopes. He was out of practice by a good many years.

But people were moving off, the white slopes were a dapple of gnome colour – people as small as children, suddenly a child as big in perspective as a grown-up, all dressed the same, it was difficult to make out ... and he balanced himself up on his sticks and walked sliding easily off.

But as soon as a slope came he was down. He had difficulty getting up. One ski slid one way, the back of the other caught in the snow and remained sticking up helplessly. Yet he managed to struggle upright. Then off for a few metres . . . and down again. This time worse.

He struggled with all his strength. His hat fell off. A child of five swerved easily past him. He was dreadfully knotted. But, sweating now, he did finally force himself up. He went veering on. Knees together, feet wider and wider, all awkwardness, no figure of a man. And collapsed again. Voices shouted: 'Achtung! Achtung!' And through his snow-filled eyes he seemed to see voices swear as they swerved past him. He was just in the way. Painfully again he tried to get up. He got up. But he was facing the wrong way. Then to turn. Putting that one leg awkwardly up and round. But in mid-turn the other leg slid away – and once more he was down in a baffled mess. He was finished. He knew he would never get out of this, never get back to land. He was right back in the first days of learning, humiliated and tired and useless. . . .

He sat up panting, a clown-figure tangled and snow-drenched. And just then he heard his name: 'Ludwig!' He listened and looked vaguely up back the slope and an echo came, a laughing echo: 'Bobby! Bobby! Bobby!'

Up above he saw Laure and Hörnli pointing at him and waving and laughing. Then together, as they saw him looking at them, they prised on their sticks and came sweeping down the slope.

Together, as though they were linked, they passed where he was and smiled and called good-naturedly: 'Ludwig – Enjoy yourself! Goodbye . . . goodbye . . .!' And they were past.

He watched them, the pair, sure as a couple can be, ski-ing beautifully down the long white slope, then up another, over again and across the wide snowfield, always smaller, further, smaller — until together they passed away over the mountainside and were gone.

De Broda sat absolutely still in the hot water, a little razor-blade held in each hand like the parts of a child's broken toy. And slowly two tears, two big single tears, dropped from his eyes, dribbled over his cheeks, and fell into the other water beneath.

GRAHAM GREENE

May We Borrow
Your Husband?

I

I never heard her called anything else but Poopy, either
by her husband or by the two men who became their
friends. Perhaps I was a little in love with her (absurd
though that may seem at my age) because I found that I
resented the name. It was unsuited to someone so young
and so open – too open; she belonged to the age of trust
just as I belonged to the age of cynicism. 'Good old
Poopy' – I even heard her called that by the elder of
the two interior-decorators (who had known her no
longer than I had): a sobriquet which might have been
good enough for some vague bedraggled woman of
middle-age who drank a bit too much but who was useful
to drag around as a kind of blind – and those two certainly needed a blind. I once asked the girl her real name,
but all she said was, 'Everyone calls me Poopy' as though
that finished it, and I was afraid of appearing too square
if I pursued the question further – too middle-aged perhaps as well, so though I hate the name whenever I write
it down, Poopy she has to remain: I have no other.

I had been at Antibes working on a book of mine, a
biography of the seventeenth-century poet, the Earl of
Rochester, for more than a month before Poopy and her
husband arrived. I had come there as soon as the full
season was over, to a small ugly hotel by the sea not far
from the ramparts, and I was able to watch the season

depart with the leaves in the Boulevard Général Leclerc. At first, even before the trees had begun to drop, the foreign cars were on the move homeward. A few weeks earlier, I had counted fourteen nationalities, including Morocco, Turkey, Sweden and Luxembourg, between the sea and the Place de Gaulle, to which I walked every day for the English papers. Now all the foreign number-plates had gone, except for the Belgian and the German and an occasional English one, and, of course, the ubiquitous number-plates of the State of Monaco. The cold weather had come early and Antibes catches only the morning sun – good enough for breakfast on the terrace, but it was safer to lunch indoors or the shadow overtook the coffee. A cold and solitary Algerian was always there, leaning over the ramparts, looking for something, perhaps safety.

It was the time of year I liked best, when Juan les Pins becomes as squalid as a closed fun-fair with Lunar Park boarded up and cards marked 'Fermeture Annuelle' outside the Pam-Pam and Maxim's, and the Concours International Amateur de Striptease at the Vieux Colombiers is over for another season. Then Antibes comes into its own as a small country town with the Auberge de Provence full of local people and old men sit indoors drinking beer or pastis at the *glacier* in the Place de Gaulle. The small garden, which forms a roundabout on the ramparts, looks a little sad with the short stout palms bowing their brown fronds; the sun in the morning shines without any glare, and the few white sails move gently on the unblinding sea.

You can always trust the English to stay on longer than others into the autumn. We have a blind faith in the southern sun and we are taken by surprise when the wind blows icily over the Mediterranean. Then a bickering war develops with the hotel-keeper over the heating on the third floor, and the tiles strike cold underfoot. For a man who has reached the age when all he wants is some good wine and some good cheese and a little work, it is the best season of all. I know how I resented the arrival of the interior-decorators just at the moment when I had hoped to be the only foreigner left, and I prayed that they were birds of passage. They arrived before lunch in a scarlet Sprite – a car much too young for them, and they wore elegant sports-clothes more suited to spring at the Cap. The elder man was nearing fifty and the grey hair that waved over his ears was too uniform to be true: the younger had passed thirty and was as black as the other was grey. I knew their names were Stephen and Tony before they even reached the reception desk, for they had clear, penetrating yet superficial voices, like their gaze, which had quickly lighted on me where I sat with a Ricard on the terrace and registered that I had nothing of interest for them, and passed on. They were not arrogant: it was simply that they were more concerned with each other, and yet perhaps, like a married couple of some years' standing, not very profoundly.

I soon knew a great deal about them. They had rooms side by side in my passage, though I doubt if both rooms were often occupied, for I used to hear voices from one room or the other most evenings when I went to bed. Do I seem too curious about other people's affairs? But in my own defence I have to say that the events of this sad little comedy were forced by all the participants on my attention. The balcony where I worked every morning on my life of Rochester overhung the terrace where the interior-decorators took their coffee, and even when they occupied a table out of sight those clear elocutionary voices mounted up to me. I didn't want to hear them; I wanted to work. Rochester's relations with the actress, Mrs Barry, were my concern at the moment, but it is almost impossible in a foreign land not to listen to one's own tongue. French I could have accepted as a kind of background noise, but I could not fail to overhear English.

'My dear, guess who's written to me now?'
'Alec?'

'No, Mrs Clarenty.'

'What does the old hag want?'

'She objects to the mural in her bedroom.'

'But, Stephen, it's divine. Alec's never done anything better. The dead faun . . .'

'I think she wants something more nubile and less necrophilous.'

'The old lecher.'

They were certainly hardy, those two. Every morning around eleven they went bathing off the little rocky peninsula opposite the hotel – they had the autumnal Mediterranean, so far as the eye could see, entirely to themselves. As they walked briskly back in their elegant bikinis, or sometimes ran a little way for warmth, I had the impression that they took their baths less for pleasure than for exercise – to preserve the slim legs, the flat stomachs, the narrow hips for more recondite and Etruscan pastimes.

Idle they were not. They drove the Sprite to Cagnes, Vence, St Paul, to any village where an antique store was to be rifled, and they brought back with them objects of olive wood, spurious old lanterns, painted religious figures which in the shop would have seemed to me ugly or banal, but which I suspect already fitted in their imaginations some scheme of decoration the reverse of commonplace. Not that their minds were altogether on their profession. They relaxed.

I encountered them one evening in a little sailors' bar in the old port of Nice. Curiosity this time had led me in pursuit, for I had seen the scarlet Sprite standing outside the bar. They were entertaining a boy of about eighteen who, from his clothes, I imagine worked as a hand on the boat to Corsica which was at the moment in harbour. They both looked very sharply at me when I entered, as though they were thinking, 'Have we misjudged him?' I drank a glass of beer and left, and the younger said 'Good evening' as I passed the table. After that we had to greet each other every day in the hotel. It was as though I had been admitted to an intimacy.

Time for a few days was hanging as heavily on my hands as on Lord Rochester's. He was staying at Mrs Fourcard's baths in Leather Lane, receiving mercury treatment for the pox, and I was awaiting a whole section of my notes which I had inadvertently left in London. I couldn't release him till they came, and my sole distraction for a few days was those two. As they packed themselves into the Sprite of an afternoon or an evening I liked to guess from their clothes the nature of their excursion. Always elegant, they were yet successful, by the mere exchange of one *tricot* for another, in indicating their mood: they were just as well dressed in the sailors' bar, but a shade more simply; when dealing with a Lesbian antique dealer at St Paul, there was a masculine dash about their handkerchiefs. Once they disappeared altogether for the inside of a week in what I took to be their oldest clothes, and when they returned the older man had a contusion on his right cheek. They told me they had been over to Corsica. Had they enjoyed it? I asked.

'Quite barbaric,' the young man, Tony, said, but not, I thought, in praise.

He saw me looking at Stephen's cheek and he added quickly, 'We had an accident in the mountains.'

It was two days after that, just at sunset, that Poopy arrived with her husband. I was back at work on Rochester, sitting in an overcoat on my balcony, when a taxi drove up – I recognised the driver as someone who plied regularly from Nice airport. What I noticed first, because the passengers were still hidden, was the luggage, which was bright blue and of an astonishing newness. Even the initials – rather absurdly PT – shone like newly-minted coins. There were a large suitcase and a hat-box, all of the same cerulean hue, and after that a respectable old leather case totally unsuited to air travel, the kind one inherits from a father, with half a label still left from Shepheard's Hotel or the Valley of the Kings. Then the passengers emerged and I saw Poopy for the first time. Down below, the interior-decorators were watching too, and drinking Dubonnet.

She was a very tall girl, perhaps five feet nine, very slim, very young, with hair the colour of conkers, and her costume was as new as her luggage. She said, 'Finalmente,' looking at the undistinguished façade with an air of rapture – or perhaps it was only the shape of her eyes. When I saw the young man I felt certain they were just married; it wouldn't have surprised me if confetti had fallen out from the seams of their clothes. They were like a photograph in the *Tatler*; they had camera smiles for each other and an underlying nervousness. I was sure they had come straight from the reception, and that it had been a smart one, after a proper church wedding.

They made a very handsome couple as they hesitated a moment before going up the steps to the reception. The long beam of the Phare de la Garoupe brushed the water behind them, and the floodlighting went suddenly on outside the hotel as if the manager had been waiting for their arrival to turn it up. The two decorators sat there without drinking, and I noticed that the elder one had covered the contusion on his cheek with a very clean white handkerchief. They were not, of course, looking at the girl, but at the boy. He was over six feet tall and as slim as the girl, with a face that might have been cut on a coin, completely handsome and completely dead – but perhaps that was only an effect of his nerves. His clothes, too, I thought, had been bought for the occasion, the sports-jacket with a double slit and the grey trousers cut a little narrowly to show off the long legs. It seemed to me that they were both too young to marry – I doubt if they had accumulated forty-five years between them – and I had a wild impulse to lean over the balcony and warn them away – 'Not this hotel. Any hotel but this.' Perhaps I could have told them that the heating was insufficient or the hot water erratic or the food terrible, not that the English care much about food, but of course they would have paid me no attention – they were so obviously 'booked', and what an ageing lunatic I should have appeared in their eyes. ('One of those eccentric English types one finds abroad' – I could imagine the letter home.) This was the first time I wanted to interfere, and I didn't know them at all. The second time it was already too late, but I think I shall always regret that I did not give way to that madness ...

It had been the silence and attentiveness of those two down below which had frightened me, and the patch of white handkerchief hiding the shameful contusion. For the first time I heard the hated name: 'Shall we see the room, Poopy, or have a drink first?'

They decided to see the room, and the two glasses of Dubonnet clicked again into action.

I think she had more idea of how a honeymoon should be conducted than he had, because they were not seen again that night.

2

I was late for breakfast on the terrace, but I noticed that Stephen and Tony were lingering longer than usual. Perhaps they had decided at last that it was too cold for a bathe; I had the impression, however, that they were lying in wait. They had never been so friendly to me before, and I wondered whether perhaps they regarded me as a kind of cover, with my distressingly normal appearance. My table for some reason that day had been shifted and was out of the sun, so Stephen suggested that I should join theirs: they would be off in a moment, after one more cup ... The contusion was much less noticeable today, but I think he had been applying powder.

'You staying here long?' I asked them, conscious of how clumsily I constructed a conversation compared with their easy prattle.

'We had meant to leave tomorrow,' Stephen said, 'but last night we changed our minds.'

'Last night?'

'It was such a beautiful day, wasn't it? "Oh," I said

to Tony, "surely we can leave poor dreary old London a little longer?" It has an awful staying power – like a railway sandwich.'

'Are your clients so patient?'

'My dear, the clients? You never in your life saw such atrocities as we get from Brompton Square and like venues. It's always the same. People who pay others to decorate for them have ghastly taste themselves.'

'You do the world a service then. Think what we might suffer without you. In Brompton Square.'

Tony giggled. 'I don't know how we'd stand it if we hadn't our private jokes. For example, in Mrs Clarenty's case, we've installed what we call the Loo of Lucullus.'

'She was enchanted,' Stephen said.

'The most obscene vegetable forms. It reminded me of a harvest festival.'

They suddenly became very silent and attentive, watching somebody over my shoulder. I looked back. It was Poopy, all by herself. She stood there, waiting for the boy to show her which table she could take, like a new girl at school who doesn't know the rules. She even seemed to be wearing a school uniform: very tight trousers, slit at the ankle – but she hadn't realized that the summer term was over. She had dressed up like that, I felt certain, so as not to be noticed, in order to hide herself, but there were only two other women on the terrace and they were both wearing sensible tweed skirts. She looked at them nostalgically as the waiter led her past our table to one nearer the sea. Her long legs moved awkwardly in the pants as though they felt exposed.

'The young bride,' Tony said.

'Deserted already,' Stephen said with extreme satisfaction.

'Her name is Poopy Travis, you know.'

'It's an extraordinary name to choose. She couldn't have been *christened* that way, unless they found a very liberal vicar.'

'He is called Peter. Of an undefined occupation. Not

Army, I think, do you?'

'Oh no, not Army. Something to do with land perhaps – there's an agreeable *herbal* smell about him.'

'You seem to know nearly all there is to know,' I said.

'We looked at their police *carnet* before dinner.'

'I have an idea,' Tony said, 'that PT hardly represents their activities last night.' He looked across the tables at the girl with an expression extraordinarily like hatred.

'We were both taken,' Stephen said, 'by the air of innocence. One felt he was more used to horses.'

'He mistook the yearnings of the rider's crotch for something quite different.'

Perhaps they hoped to shock me, but I don't think it was that. I really believe they were in a state of extreme sexual excitement; they had received a *coup de foudre* last night on the terrace and were quite incapable of disguising their feelings. I was an excuse to talk, to speculate about the desired object. The sailor had been a stop-gap; this was the real thing. I was inclined to be amused, for what could this absurd pair hope to gain from a young man newly married to the girl who now sat there patiently waiting, wearing her beauty like an old sweater she had forgotten to change? But that was a bad simile to use: she would have been afraid to wear an old sweater, except secretly, by herself, in the playroom. She had no idea that she was one of those who can afford to disregard the fashion of their clothes. She caught my eye and, because I was so obviously English, I suppose, gave me half a timid smile. Perhaps I too would have received the *coup de foudre* if I had not been thirty years older and twice married.

Tony detected the smile. 'A regular body-snatcher,' he said. My breakfast and the young man arrived at the same moment before I had time to reply. As he passed the table I could feel the tension.

'*Cuir de Russie*,' Stephen said, quivering a nostril. 'A mistake of inexperience.'

The youth caught the words as he went past and

turned with an astonished look to see who had spoken, and they both smiled insolently back at him as though they really believed they had the power to take him over ...

For the first time I felt disquiet.

3

Something was not going well; that was sadly obvious. The girl nearly always came down to breakfast ahead of her husband – I have an idea he spent a long time bathing and shaving and applying his *Cuir de Russie*. When he joined her he would give her a courteous brotherly kiss as though they had not spent the night together in the same bed. She began to have those shadows under the eyes which come from lack of sleep – for I couldn't believe that they were 'the lineaments of gratified desire'. Sometimes from my balcony I saw them returning from a walk – nothing, except perhaps a pair of horses, could have been more handsome. His gentleness towards her might have reassured her mother, but it made a man impatient to see him squiring her across the undangerous road, holding open doors, following a pace behind her like the husband of a princess. I longed to see some outbreak of irritation caused by the sense of satiety, but they never semed to be in conversation when they returned from their walk, and at table I caught only the kind of phrases people use who are dining together for the sake of politeness. And yet I could swear that she loved him, even by the way she avoided watching him. There was nothing avid or starved about her; she stole her quick glances when she was quite certain that his attention was absorbed elsewhere – they were tender, anxious perhaps, quite undemanding. If one inquired after him when he wasn't there, she glowed with the pleasure of using his name. 'Oh, Peter overslept this morning.' 'Peter cut himself. He's staunching the blood now.' 'Peter's mislaid his tie. He thinks the floor-waiter has purloined it.' Certainly she loved him; I was far less certain of what his feelings were.

And you must imagine how all the time those other two were closing in. It was like a mediaeval siege: they dug their trenches and threw up their earthworks. The difference was that the besieged didn't notice what they were at – at any rate, the girl didn't; I don't know about him. I longed to warn her, but what could I have said that wouldn't have shocked her or angered her? I believe the two would have changed their floor if that would have helped to bring them closer to the fortress; they probably discussed the move together and decided against it as too overt.

Because they knew that I could do nothing against them, they regarded me almost in the rôle of an ally. After all, I might be useful one day in distracting the girl's attention – and I suppose they were not quite mistaken in that; they could tell from the way I looked at her how interested I was, and they probably calculated that my interests might in the long run coincide with theirs. It didn't occur to them that, perhaps, I was a man with scruples. If one really wanted a thing scruples were obviously, in their eyes, out of place. There was a tortoise-shell star mirror at St Paul they were plotting to obtain for half the price demanded (I think there was an old mother who looked after the shop when her daughter was away at a *boîte* for women of a certain taste); naturally, therefore, when I looked at the girl, as they saw me so often do, they considered I would be ready to join in any 'reasonable' scheme.

'When I looked at the girl' – I realize that I have made no real attempt to describe her. In writing a biography one can, of course, just insert a portrait and the affair is done: I have the prints of Lady Rochester and Mrs Barry in front of me now. But speaking as a professional novelist (for biography and reminiscence are both new forms to me), one describes a woman not so much that the reader should see her in all the cramping detail of colour and shape (how often Dickens's elaborate portraits seem like directions to the illustrator which might well

have been left out of the finished book), but to convey
an emotion. Let the reader make his own image of a
wife, a mistress, some passer-by 'sweet and kind' (the
poet required no other descriptive words), if he has a
fancy to. If I were to describe the girl (I can't bring myself at this moment to write her hateful name), it would
be not to convey the colour of her hair, the shape of her
mouth, but to express the pleasure and the pain with
which I recall her – I, the writer, the observer, the sub-
sidiary character, what you will. But if I didn't bother to
convey them to her, why should I bother to convey them
to you, *hypocrite lecteur*?

How quickly those two tunnelled. I don't think it was
more than four mornings after the arrival that, when I
came down to breakfast, I found they had moved their
table next to the girl's and were entertaining her in her
husband's absence. They did it very well; it was the first
time I had seen her relaxed and happy – and she was
happy because she was talking about Peter. Peter was
agent for his father, somewhere in Hampshire – there
were three thousand acres to manage. Yes, he was fond
of riding and so was she. It all tumbled out – the kind of
life she dreamed of having when she returned home.
Stephen just dropped in a word now and then of a
rather old-fashioned courteous interest, to keep her going.
Apparently he had once decorated some hall in their
neighbourhood and knew the names of some people Peter
knew – Winstanley, I think – and that gave her immense confidence.

'He's one of Peter's best friends,' she said, and the
two flickered their eyes at each other like lizards' tongues.

'Come and join us, William,' Stephen said, but only
when he had noticed that I was within earshot. 'You know
Mrs Travis?'

How could I refuse to sit at their table? And yet in
doing so I seemed to become an ally.

'Not *the* William Harris?' the girl asked. It was a
phrase which I hated, and yet she transformed even that,

with her air of innocence. For she had a capacity to make everything new: Antibes became a discovery and we were the first foreigners to have made it. When she said, 'Of course, I'm afraid I haven't actually *read* any of your books,' I heard the over-familiar remark for the first time; it even seemed to me a proof of her honesty – I nearly wrote her virginal honesty. 'You must know an awful lot about people,' she said, and again I read into the banality of the remark an appeal – for help against whom, those two or the husband who at the moment appeared on the terrace? He had the same nervous air as she, even the same shadows under the lids, so that they might have been taken by a stranger, as I wrote before, for brother and sister. He hesitated a moment when he saw all of us there and she called across to him, 'Come and meet these nice people, darling.' He didn't look any too pleased, but he sat glumly down and asked whether the coffee was still hot.

'I'll order some more, darling. They know the Winstanleys, and this is *the* William Harris.'

He looked at me blankly; I think he was wondering if I had anything to do with tweeds.

'I hear you like horses,' Stephen said, 'and I was wondering whether you and your wife could come to lunch with us at Cagnes on Saturday. That's tomorrow, isn't it? There's a very good racecourse at Cagnes ...'

'I don't know,' he said dubiously, looking to his wife for a clue.

'But, darling, of course we must go. You'd love it.'

His face cleared instantly. I really believe he had been troubled by a social scruple: the question whether one accepts invitations on a honeymoon. 'It's very good of you,' he said, 'Mr ...'

'Let's start as we mean to go on. I'm Stephen and this is Tony.'

'I'm Peter.' He added a trifle gloomily, 'And this is Poopy.'

'Tony, you take Poopy in the Sprite, and Peter and I

will go by *autobus*.' (I had the impression, and I think Tony had too, that Stephen had gained a point.)

'You'll come too, Mr Harris?' the girl asked, using my surname as though she wished to emphasize the difference between me and them.

'I'm afraid I can't. I'm working against time.'

I watched them that evening from my balcony as they returned from Cagnes and, hearing the way they all laughed together, I thought, 'The enemy are within the citadel: it's only a question of time.' A lot of time, because they proceeded very carefully, those two. There was no question of a quick grab which I suspect had caused the contusion in Corsica.

4

It became a regular habit with the two of them to entertain the girl during her solitary breakfast before her husband arrived. I never sat at their table again, but scraps of the conversation would come over to me, and it seemed to me that she was never quite so cheerful again. Even the sense of novelty had gone. I heard her say once, 'There's so little to do here,' and it struck me as an odd observation for a honeymooner to make.

Then one evening I found her in tears outside the Musée Grimaldi. I had been fetching my papers, and, as my habit was, I made a round by the Place Nationale with the pillar erected in 1819 to celebrate – a remarkable paradox – the loyalty of Antibes to the monarchy and her resistance to 'les Troupes Etrangères' who were seeking to re-establish the monarchy. Then, according to rule, I went on by the market and the old port and Lou-Lou's restaurant up the ramp towards the cathedral and the Musée, and there in the grey evening light, before the street-lamps came on, I found her crying under the cliff of the château.

I noticed too late what she was at or I wouldn't have said, 'Good evening, Mrs Travis.' She jumped a little as she turned and dropped her handkerchief, and when I picked it up I found it soaked with tears – it was like holding a small drowned animal in my hand. I said, 'I'm sorry,' meaning that I was sorry to have startled her, but she took it in quite another sense. She said, 'Oh, I'm being silly, that's all. It's just a mood. Everybody has moods, don't they?'

'Where's Peter?'

'He's in the museum with Stephen and Tony looking at the Picassos. I don't understand them a bit.'

'That's nothing to be ashamed of. Lots of people don't.'

'But Peter doesn't understand them either. I know he doesn't. He's just pretending to be interested.'

'Oh well . . .'

'And it's not that either. I pretended for a time too, to please Stephen. But he's pretending just to get away from me.'

'You are imagining things.'

Punctually at five o'clock the *phare* lit up, but it was still too light to see the beam.

I said, 'The museum will be closing now.'

'Walk back with me to the hotel.'

'Wouldn't you like to wait for Peter?'

'I don't smell, do I?' she asked miserably.

'Well, there's a trace of Arpège. I've always liked Arpège.'

'How terribly experienced you sound.'

'Not really. It's just that my first wife used to buy Arpège.'

We began walking back, and the mistral bit our ears and gave her an excuse when the time came for the reddened eyes.

She said, 'I think Antibes so sad and grey.'

'I thought you enjoyed it here.'

'Oh, for a day or two.'

'Why not go home?'

'It would look odd, wouldn't it, returning early from a honeymoon?'

'Or go on to Rome – or somewhere. You can get a plane

to most places from Nice.'

'It wouldn't make any difference' she said. 'It's not the place that's wrong, it's me.'

'I don't understand.'

'He's not happy with me. It's as simple as that.'

She stopped opposite one of the little rock houses by the ramparts. Washing hung down over the street below and there was a cold-looking canary in a cage.

'You said yourself ... a mood ...'

'It's not his fault,' she said. 'It's me. I expect it seems very stupid to you, but I never slept with anyone before I married.' She gulped miserably at the canary.

'And Peter?'

'He's terribly sensitive,' she said, and added quickly, 'That's a good quality. I wouldn't have fallen in love with him if he hadn't been.'

'If I were you, I'd take him home – as quickly as possible.' I couldn't help the words sounding sinister, but she hardly heard them. She was listening to the voices that came nearer down the ramparts – to Stephen's gay laugh. 'They're very sweet,' she said. 'I'm glad he's found friends.'

How could I say that they were seducing Peter before her eyes? And in any case wasn't her mistake already irretrievable? Those were two of the questions which haunted the hours, dreary for a solitary man, of the middle afternoon when work is finished and the exhilaration of the wine at lunch, and the time for the first drink has not yet come and the winter heating is at its feeblest. Had she no idea of the nature of the young man she had married? Had he taken her on as a blind or as a last desperate throw for normality? I couldn't bring myself to believe that. There was a sort of innocence about the boy which seemed to justify her love, and I preferred to think that he was not yet fully formed, that he had married honestly and it was only now that he found himself on the brink of a different experience. And yet if that were the case the comedy was all the crueller. Would everything have gone normally well if some conjunction of the planets had not crossed their honeymoon with that hungry pair of hunters?

I longed to speak out, and in the end I did speak, but not, so it happened, to her. I was going to my room and the door of one of theirs was open and I heard again Stephen's laugh – a kind of laugh which is sometimes with unintentional irony called infectious; it maddened me. I knocked and went in. Tony was stretched on a double bed and Stephen was 'doing' his hair, holding a brush in each hand and meticulously arranging the grey waves on either side. The dressing-table had as many pots on it as a woman's.

'You really mean he told you that?' Tony was saying. 'Why, how are you, William? Come in. Our young friend has been confiding in Stephen. Such really fascinating things.'

'Which of your young friends?' I asked.

'Why, Peter, of course. Who else? The secrets of married life.'

'I thought it might have been your sailor.'

'Naughty!' Tony said. 'But *touché* too, of course.'

'I wish you'd leave Peter alone.'

'I don't think he'd like that,' Stephen said. 'You can see that he hasn't quite the right tastes for this sort of honeymoon.'

'Now you happen to like women, William,' Tony said. 'Why not go after the girl? It's a grand opportunity. She's not getting what I believe is vulgarly called her greens.' Of the two he was easily the more brutal. I wanted to hit him, but this is not the century for that kind of romantic gesture, and anyway he was stretched out flat upon the bed. I said feebly enough – I ought to have known better than to have entered into a debate with those two – 'She happens to be in love with him.'

'I think Tony is right and she would find more satisfaction with you, William dear,' Stephen said, giving a last flick to the hair over his right ear – the contusion was quite gone now. 'From what Peter has said to me, I think you'd be doing a favour to both of them.'

'Tell him what Peter said, Stephen.'

'He said that from the very first there was a kind of hungry femininity about her which he found frightening and repulsive. Poor boy – he was really trapped into this business of marriage. His father wanted heirs – he breeds horses too, and then her mother – there's quite a lot of lucre with that lot. I don't think he had any idea of – of the Shape of Things to Come.' Stephen shuddered into the glass and then regarded himself with satisfaction.

Even today I have to believe for my own peace of mind that the young man had not really said those monstrous things. I believe, and hope, that the words were put into his mouth by that cunning dramatiser, but there is little comfort in the thought, for Stephen's inventions were always true to character. He even saw through my apparent indifference to the girl and realized that Tony and he had gone too far; it wouldn't suit their purpose, if I were driven to the wrong kind of action, or if, by their crudities, I lost my interest in Poopy.

'Of course,' Stephen said, 'I'm exaggerating. Undoubtedly he felt a bit amorous before it came to the point. His father would describe her, I suppose, as a fine filly.'

'What do you plan to do with him?' I asked. 'Do you toss up, or does one of you take the head and the other the tail?'

Tony laughed. 'Good old William. What a clinical mind you have.'

'And suppose,' I said, 'I went to her and recounted this nice conversation?'

'My dear, she wouldn't even understand. She's incredibly innocent.'

'Isn't he?'

'I doubt it – knowing our friend Colin Winstanley. But it's still a moot point. He hasn't given himself away yet.'

'We are planning to put it to the test one day soon,' Stephen said.

'A drive in the country,' Tony said. 'The strain's telling on him, you can see that. He's even afraid to take a siesta for fear of unwanted attentions.'

'Haven't you *any* mercy?' It was an absurd old-fashioned word to use to those two sophisticates. I felt more than ever square. 'Doesn't it occur to you that you may ruin her life – for the sake of your little game?'

'We can depend on you, William,' Tony said, 'to give her creature comforts.'

Stephen said, 'It's no game. You should realize we are saving *him*. Think of the life that he would lead – with all those soft contours lapping him around.' He added, 'Women always remind me of a damp salad – you know, those faded bits of greenery positively swimming ...'

'Every man to his taste,' Tony said. 'But Peter's not cut out for that sort of life. He's very sensitive,' he said, using the girl's own words. There wasn't any more I could think of to say.

5

You will notice that I play a very unheroic part in this comedy. I could have gone direct, I suppose, to the girl and given her a little lecture on the facts of life, beginning gently with the régime of an English public school – he had worn a scarf of old-boy colours, until Tony had said to him one day at breakfast that he thought the puce stripe was an error of judgment. Or perhaps I could have protested to the boy himself, but, if Stephen had spoken the truth and he was under a severe nervous strain, my intervention would hardly have helped to ease it. There was no move I could make. I had just to sit there and watch while they made the moves carefully and adroitly towards the climax.

It came three days later at breakfast when, as usual, she was sitting alone with them, while her husband was upstairs with his lotions. They had never been more charming or more entertaining. As I arrived at my table they were giving her a really funny description of a house in

Kensington that they had decorated for a dowager duchess who was passionately interested in the Napoleonic wars. There was an ashtray, I remember, made out of a horse's hoof, guaranteed – so the dealer said – by Apsley House to have belonged to a grey ridden by Wellington at the Battle of Waterloo; there was an umbrella stand made out of a shell-case found on the field of Austerlitz; a fire-escape made of a scaling ladder from Badajoz. She had lost half that sense of strain listening to them. She had forgotten her rolls and coffee; Stephen had her complete attention. I wanted to say to her, 'You little owl.' I wouldn't have been insulting her – she *had* got rather large eyes.

And then Stephen produced the master-plan. I could tell it was coming by the way his hands stiffened on his coffee-cup, by the way Tony lowered his eyes and appeared to be praying over his *croissant*. 'We were wondering, Poopy – may we borrow your husband?' I have never heard words spoken with more elaborate casualness.

She laughed. She hadn't noticed a thing. 'Borrow my husband?'

'There's a little village in the mountains behind Monte Carlo – Peille it's called – and I've heard rumours of a devastatingly lovely old bureau there – not for sale, of course, but Tony and I, we have our winning ways.'

'I've noticed that,' she said, 'myself.'

Stephen for an instant was disconcerted, but she meant nothing by it, except perhaps a compliment.

'We were thinking of having lunch at Peille and passing the whole day on the road so as to take a look at the scenery. The only trouble is there's no room in the Sprite for more than three, but Peter was saying the other day that you wanted some time to have a hair-do, so we thought ...'

I had the impression that he was talking far too much to be convincing, but there wasn't any need for him to worry: she saw nothing at all. 'I think it's a marvellous idea,' she said. 'You know, he needs a little holiday from

me. He's had hardly a moment to himself since I came
up the aisle.' She was magnificently sensible, and perhaps
even relieved. Poor girl. She needed a little holiday, too.

'It's going to be excruciatingly uncomfortable. He'll
have to sit on Tony's knee.'

'I don't suppose he'll mind that.'

'And, of course, we can't guarantee the quality of food
en route.'

For the first time I saw Stephen as a stupid man. Was
there a shade of hope in that?

In the long run, of the two, notwithstanding his bru-
tality, Tony had the better brain. Before Stephen had
time to speak once more, Tony raised his eyes from the
croissant and said decisively, 'That's fine. All's settled,
and we'll deliver him back in one piece by dinner-time.'

He looked challengingly across at me. 'Of course, we
hate to leave you alone for lunch, but I am sure William
will look after you.'

'William?' she asked, and I hated the way she looked at
me as if I didn't exist. 'Oh, you mean Mr Harris?'

I invited her to have lunch with me at Lou-Lou's in
the old port – I couldn't very well do anything else – and
at that moment the laggard Peter came out on to the terrace. She said quickly, 'I don't want to interrupt your
work ...'

'I don't believe in starvation,' I said. 'It has to be
interrupted for meals.'

Peter had cut himself again shaving and had a large
blob of cottonwool stuck on his chin: it reminded me of
Stephen's contusion. I had the impression, while he stood
there waiting for someone to say something to him, that
he knew all about the conversation; it had been carefully
rehearsed by all three, the parts allotted, the unconcerned
manner practised well beforehand, even the bit about the
food ... Now somebody had missed a cue, so I spoke.

'I've asked your wife to lunch at Lou-Lou's,' I said. 'I
hope you don't mind.'

I would have been amused by the expression of quick

431

relief on all three faces if I had found it possible to be amused by anything at all in the situation.

6

'And you didn't marry again after she left?'

'By that time I was getting too old to marry.'

'Picasso does it.'

'Oh, I'm not quite as old as Picasso.'

The silly conversation went on against a background of fishing-nets draped over a wallpaper with a design of wine-bottles – interior decoration again. Sometimes I longed for a room which had simply grown that way like the lines on a human face. The fish soup steamed away between us, smelling of garlic. We were the only guests there. Perhaps it was the solitude, perhaps it was the directness of her question, perhaps it was only the effect of the *rosé*, but quite suddenly I had the comforting sense that we were intimate friends. 'There's always work,' I said, 'and wine and a good cheese.'

'I couldn't be that philosophical if I lost Peter.'

'That's not likely to happen, is it?'

'I think I'd die,' she said, 'like someone in Christina Rossetti.'

'I thought nobody of your generation read her.'

If I had been twenty years older, perhaps, I could have explained that nothing is quite as bad as that, that at the end of what is called 'the sexual life' the only love which has lasted is the love that has accepted everything, every disappointment, every failure and every betrayal, which has accepted even the sad fact that in the end there is no desire so deep as the simple desire for companionship.

She wouldn't have believed me. She said, 'I used to weep like anything at that poem about "Passing Away". Do you write sad things?'

'The biography I am writing now is sad enough. Two people tied together by love and yet one of them incapable of fidelity. The man dead of old age, burnt-out, at less

than forty, and a fashionable preacher lurking by the bedside to snatch his soul. No privacy even for a dying
man: the bishop wrote a book about it.'

An Englishman who kept a chandler's shop in the old
port was talking at the bar, and two old women who
were part of the family knitted at the end of the room.
A dog trotted in and looked at us and went away again
with its tail curled.

'How long ago did all that happen?'

'Nearly three hundred years.'

'It sounded quite contemporary. Only now it would
be the man from the *Mirror* and not a bishop.'

'That's why I wanted to write it. I'm not really interested in the past. I don't like costume-pieces.'

Winning someone's confidence is rather like the way
some men set about seducing a woman; they circle a
long way from their true purpose, they try to interest
and amuse until finally the moment comes to strike. It
came, so I wrongly thought, when I was adding up the
bill. She said, 'I wonder where Peter is at this moment,'
and I was quick to reply, 'What's going wrong between
the two of you?'

She said, 'Let's go.'

'I've to wait for my change.'

It was always easier to get served at Lou-Lou's than
to pay the bill. At that moment everyone always had a
habit of disappearing: the old woman (her knitting
abandoned on the table), the aunt who helped to serve,
Lou-Lou herself, her husband in his blue sweater. If the
dog hadn't gone already he would have left at that
moment.

I said, 'You forget – you told me that he wasn't happy.'

'Please, please find someone and let's go.'

So I disinterred Lou-Lou's aunt from the kitchen and
paid. When we left, everyone seemed to be back again,
even the dog.

Outside I asked her whether she wanted to return to
the hotel.

'Not just yet – but I'm keeping you from your work.'

'I never work after drinking. That's why I like to start early. It brings the first drink nearer.'

She said that she had seen nothing of Antibes but the ramparts and the beach and the lighthouse, so I walked her around the small narrow backstreets where the washing hung out of the windows as in Naples and there were glimpses of small rooms overflowing with children and grandchildren; stone scrolls were carved over the ancient doorways of what had once been noblemen's houses; the pavements were blocked by barrels of wine and the streets by children playing at ball. In a low room on a ground floor a man sat painting the horrible ceramics which would later go to Vallauris to be sold to tourists in Picasso's old stamping-ground – spotted pink frogs and mauve fish and pigs with slits for coins.

She said, 'Let's go back to the sea.' So we returned to a patch of hot sun on the bastion, and again I was tempted to tell her what I feared, but the thought that she might watch me with the blankness of ignorance deterred me. She sat on the wall and her long legs in the tight black trousers dangled down like Christmas stockings. She said, 'I'm not sorry that I married Peter,' and I was reminded of a song Edith Piaf sings, '*Je ne regrette rien*'. It is typical of such a phrase that it is always sung or spoken with defiance.

I could only say again, 'You ought to take him home,' but I wondered what would have happened if I had said, 'You are married to a man who only likes men and he's off now picnicking with his boy friends. I'm thirty years older than you, but at least I have always preferred women and I've fallen in love with you and we could still have a few good years together before the time comes when you want to leave me for a younger man.' All I said was, 'He probably misses the country – and the riding.'

'I wish you were right, but it's really worse than that.'

Had she, after all, realized the nature of her problem? I waited for her to explain her meaning. It was a little like a novel which hesitates on the verge between comedy and tragedy. If she recognized the situation it would be a tragedy; if she were ignorant it was a comedy, even a farce – a situation between an immature girl too innocent to understand and a man too old to have the courage to explain. I suppose I have a taste for tragedy. I hoped for that.

She said, 'We didn't really know each other much before we came here. You know, weekend parties and the odd theatre – and riding, of course.'

I wasn't sure where her remarks tended. I said, 'These occasions are nearly always a strain. You are picked out of ordinary life and dumped together after an elaborate ceremony – almost like two animals shut in a cage who haven't seen each other before.'

'And now he sees me he doesn't like me.'

'You are exaggerating.'

'No.' She added, with anxiety, 'I won't shock you, will I, if I tell you things? There's nobody else I can talk to.'

'After fifty years I'm guaranteed shockproof.'

'We haven't made love – properly, once, since we came here.'

'What do you mean – properly?'

'He starts, but he doesn't finish; nothing happens.'

I said uncomfortably, 'Rochester wrote about that. A poem called "The Imperfect Enjoyment".' I don't know why I gave her this shady piece of literary information; perhaps, like a psycho-analyst, I wanted her not to feel alone with her problem. 'It can happen to anybody.'

'But it's not his fault,' she said. 'It's mine. I know it is. He just doesn't like my body.'

'Surely it's a bit late to discover that.'

'He'd never seen me naked till I came here,' she said with the candour of a girl to her doctor – that was all I meant to her, I felt sure.

'There are nearly always first-night nerves. And then if a man worries (you must realize how much it hurts his pride) he can get stuck in the situation for days – weeks

435

even.' I began to tell her about a mistress I once had –
we stayed together a very long time and yet for two
weeks at the beginning I could do nothing at all. 'I was
too anxious to succeed.'

'That's different. You didn't hate the sight of her.'

'You are making such a lot of so little.'

'That's what he tries to do,' she said with sudden
school-girl coarseness and giggled miserably.

'We went away for a week and changed the scene, and
everything after that was all right. For ten days it had
been a flop and for ten years afterwards we were happy.
Very happy. But worry can get established in a room, in
the colour of the curtains – it can hang itself up on coat-
hangers; you find it smoking away in the ashtray marked
Pernod, and when you look at the bed it pokes its head
out from underneath like the toes of a pair of shoes.'
Again I repeated the only charm I could think of. 'Take
him home.'

'It wouldn't make any difference. He's disappointed,
that's all it is.' She looked down at her long black legs;
I followed the course of her eyes because I was finding now
that I really wanted her and she said with sincere conviction, 'I'm just not pretty enough when I'm undressed.'

'You are talking real nonsense. You don't know what
nonsense you are talking.'

'Oh no, I'm not. You see – it started all right, but then
he touched me' – she put her hands on her breasts – 'and
it all went wrong. I always knew they weren't much good.
At school we used to have dormitory inspection – it was
awful. Everybody could grow them big except me. I'm no
Jayne Mansfield, I can tell you.' She gave again that
mirthless giggle. 'I remember one of the girls told me to
sleep with a pillow on top – they said they'd struggle for
release and what they needed was exercise. But of course
it didn't work. I doubt if the idea was very scientific.' She
added, 'I remember it was awfully hot at night like that.'

'Peter doesn't strike me,' I said cautiously, 'as a man
who would want a Jayne Mansfield.'

'But you understand, don't you, that, if he finds me ugly, it's all so hopeless.'

I wanted to agree with her – perhaps this reason which she had thought up would be less distressing than the truth, and soon enough there would be someone to cure her distrust. I had noticed before that it is often the lovely women who have the least confidence in their looks, but all the same I couldn't pretend to her that I understood it her way. I said, 'You must trust me. There's nothing at all wrong with you and that's why I'm talking to you the way I am.'

'You are very sweet,' she said, and her eyes passed over me rather as the beam from the lighthouse which at night went past the Musée Grimaldi and after a certain time returned and brushed all our windows indifferently on the hotel front. She continued, 'He said they'd be back by cocktail-time.'

'If you want a rest first' – for a little time we had been close, but now again we were getting further and further away. If I pressed her now she might in the end be happy – does conventional morality demand that a girl remains tied as she was tied? They'd been married in church; she was probably a good Christian, and I knew the ecclesiastical rules: at this moment of her life she could be free of him, the marriage could be annulled, but in a day or two it was only too probable that the same rules would say, 'He's managed well enough, you are married for life.'

And yet I couldn't press her. Wasn't I after all assuming far too much? Perhaps it was only a question of first-night nerves; perhaps in a little while the three of them would be back, silent, embarrassed, and Tony in his turn would have a contusion on his cheek. I would have been very glad to see it there; egotism fades a little with the passions which engender it, and I would have been content, I think, just to see her happy.

So we returned to the hotel, not saying much, and she went to her room and I to mine. It was in the end a comedy and not a tragedy, a farce even, which is why I have given this scrap of reminiscence a farcical title.

7

I was woken from my middle-aged siesta by the telephone. For a moment, surprised by the darkness, I couldn't find the light-switch. Scrambling for it, I knocked over my bedside lamp – the telephone went on ringing, and I tried to pick up the holder and knocked over a tooth-glass in which I had given myself a whisky. The little illuminated dial of my watch gleamed up at me marking 8.30 The telephone continued to ring. I got the receiver off, but this time it was the ashtray which fell over. I couldn't get the cord to extend up to my ear, so I shouted in the direction of the telephone, 'Hullo!'

A tiny sound came up from the floor which I interpreted as 'Is that William?'

I shouted, 'Hold on,' and now that I was properly awake I realized the light-switch was just over my head (in London it was placed over the bedside table). Little petulant noises came up from the floor as I put on the light, like the creaking of crickets.

'Who's that?' I said rather angrily, and then I recognized Tony's voice.

'William, whatever's the matter?'

'Nothing's the matter. Where are you?'

'But there was quite an enormous crash. It hurt my eardrum.'

'An ashtray,' I said.

'Do you usually hurl ashtrays around?'

'I was asleep.'

'At 8.30? William! William!'

I said, 'Where are you?'

'A little bar in what Mrs Clarenty would call Monty.'

'You promised to be back by dinner,' I said.

'That's why I'm telephoning you. I'm being *responsible*, William. Do you mind telling Poopy that we'll be a little late? Give her dinner. Talk to her as only you know how. We'll be back by ten.'

'Has there been an accident?'

'I could hear him chuckling up the phone. 'Oh, I wouldn't call it an accident.'

'Why doesn't Peter call her himself?'

'He says he's not in the mood.'

'But what shall I tell her?' The telephone went dead.

I got out of bed and dressed and then I called her room. She answered very quickly; I think she must have been sitting by the telephone. I relayed the message, asked her to meet me in the bar, and rang off before I had to face answering any questions.

But I found it was not so difficult to cover up; she was immensely relieved that somebody had telephoned. She had sat there in her room from half-past seven onwards thinking of all the dangerous turns and ravines on the Grande Corniche, and when I rang she was half afraid that it might be the police or a hospital. Only after she had drunk two dry Martinis and laughed quite a lot at her fears did she say, 'I wonder why Tony rang you and not Peter me?'

I said (I had been working the answer out), 'I gather he suddenly had an urgent appointment – in the loo.'

It was as though I had said something enormously witty.

'Do you think they are a bit tight?' she asked.

'I wouldn't wonder.'

'Darling Peter,' she said, 'he deserved the day off,' and I couldn't help wondering in what direction his merit lay.

'Do you want another Martini?'

'I'd better not,' she said, 'you've made me tight too.'

I had become tired of the thin cold *rosé*, so we had a bottle of real wine at dinner and she drank her full share and talked about literature. She had, it seemed, a nostalgia for Dornford Yates, had graduated in the sixth form as far as Hugh Walpole, and now she talked respectfully about Sir Charles Snow, who she obviously thought had been knighted, like Sir Hugh, for his services to literature.

I must have been deeply in love or I would have found her innocence almost unbearable – or perhaps I was a little tight as well. All the same, it was to interrupt her flow of critical judgments that I asked her what her real name was and she replied, 'Everyone calls me Poopy.' I remembered the PT stamped on her bags, but the only real names that I could think of at the moment were Patricia and Prunella. 'Then I shall simply call you You,' I said.

After dinner I had brandy and she had a kümmel. It was past 10.30 and still the three had not returned, but she didn't seem to be worrying any more about them. She sat on the floor of the bar beside me and every now and then the waiter looked in to see if he could turn off the lights. She leant against me with her hand on my knee and she said such things as 'It must be wonderful to be a writer', and in the glow of brandy and tenderness I didn't mind them a bit. I even began to tell her again about the Earl of Rochester. What did I care about Dornford Yates, Hugh Walpole or Sir Charles Snow? I was even in the mood to recite to her, hopelessly inapposite to the situation though the lines were:

> Then talk not of Inconstancy,
>   False Hearts, and broken Vows;
> If I, by Miracle, can be
> This live-long Minute true to thee,
>   'Tis all that Heav'n allows

when the noise – what a noise! – of the Sprite approaching brought us both to our feet. It was only too true that all that heaven allowed was the time in the bar at Antibes.

Tony was singing; we heard him all the way up the Boulevard Général Leclerc; Stephen was driving with the greatest caution, most of the time in second gear, and Peter, as we saw when we came out on to the terrace, was sitting on Tony's knee – nestling would be a better description – and joining in the refrain. All I could make out was

'Round and white
  On a winter's night,
The hope of the Queen's Navee.'

If they hadn't seen us on the steps I think they would have driven past the hotel without noticing.

'You *are* tight,' the girl said with pleasure. Tony put his arm round her and ran her up to the top of the steps. 'Be careful,' she said, 'William's made me tight too.'

'Good old William.'

Stephen climbed carefully out of the car and sank down on the nearest chair.

'All well?' I asked, not knowing what I meant.

'The children have been very happy,' he said, 'and very, very relaxed.'

'Got to go to the loo,' Peter said (the cue was in the wrong place), and made for the stairs. The girl gave him a helping hand and I heard him say, 'Wonderful day. Wonderful scenery, wonderful...' She turned at the top of the stairs and swept us with her smile, gay, reassured, happy. As on the first night, when they had hesitated about the cocktail, they didn't come down again. There was a long silence and then Tony chuckled. 'You seem to have had a wonderful day,' I said.

'Dear William, we've done a very good action. You've never seen him so *détendu*.'

Stephen sat saying nothing; I had the impression that today hadn't gone quite so well for him. Can people ever hunt quite equally in couples or is there always a loser? The too-grey waves of hair were as immaculate as ever, there was no contusion on the cheek, but I had the impression that the fear of the future had cast a long shadow.

'I suppose you mean you got him drunk?'

'Not with alcohol,' Tony said. 'We aren't vulgar seducers, are we, Stephen?' But Stephen made no reply.

'Then what was your good action?'

'*Le pauvre petit Pierre*. He was in such a state. He had quite convinced himself — or perhaps she had convinced

441

him – that he was *impuissant*.'

'You seem to be making a lot of progress in French.'

'It sounds more delicate in French.'

'And with your help he found he wasn't?'

'After a little virginal timidity. Or near virginal. School hadn't left him quite unmoved. Poor Poopy. She just hadn't known the right way to go about things. My dear, he had a superb virility. Where are you going, Stephen?'

'I'm going to bed,' Stephen said flatly, and went up the steps alone. Tony looked after him, I thought with a kind of tender regret, a very light and superficial sorrow. 'His rheumatism came back very badly this afternoon,' he said. 'Poor Stephen.'

I thought it was well then to go to bed before I should become 'Poor William' too. Tony's charity tonight was all-embracing.

8

It was the first morning for a long time that I found myself alone on the terrace for breakfast. The women in tweed skirts had been gone for some days, and I had never before known 'the young men' to be absent. It was easy enough, while I waited for my coffee, to speculate about the likely reasons. There was, for example, the rheumatism ... though I couldn't quite picture Tony in the character of a bedside companion. It was even remotely possible that they felt some shame and were unwilling to be confronted by their victim. As for the victim, I wondered sadly what painful revelation the night would certainly have brought. I blamed myself more than ever for not speaking in time. Surely she would have learned the truth more gently from me than from some tipsy uncontrolled outburst of her husband. All the same – such egoists are we in our passions – I was glad to be there in attendance ... to staunch the tears ... to take her tenderly in my arms, comfort her ... oh, I had quite a romantic day-dream on the terrace before she came down the steps and I saw that she had never had less need of a comforter.

She was just as I had seen her the first night: shy, excited, gay, with a long and happy future established in her eyes. 'William,' she said, 'can I sit at your table? Do you mind?'

'Of course not.'

'You've been so patient with me all the time I was in the doldrums. I've talked an awful lot of nonsense to you. I know you told me it was nonsense, but I didn't believe you and you were right all the time.'

I couldn't have interrupted her even if I had tried. She was a Venus at the prow sailing through sparkling seas. She said, 'Everything's all right. Everything. Last night – he loves me, William. He really does. He's not a bit disappointed with me. He was just tired and strained, that's all. He needed a day off alone – *détendu*.' She was even picking up Tony's French expressions second-hand. 'I'm afraid of nothing now, nothing at all. Isn't it strange how black life seemed only two days ago? I really believe if it hadn't been for you I'd have thrown in my hand. How lucky I was to meet you and the others too. They're such wonderful friends for Peter. We are all going home next week – and we've made a lovely plot together. Tony's going to come down almost immediately we get back and decorate our house. Yesterday, driving in the country, they had a wonderful discussion about it. You won't know our house when you see it – oh, I forgot, you never *have* seen it, have you? You must come down when it's all finished – with Stephen.'

'Isn't Stephen going to help?' I just managed to slip in.

'Oh, he's too busy at the moment, Tony says, with Mrs Clarenty. Do you like riding? Tony does. He adores horses, but he has so little chance in London. It will be wonderful for Peter – to have someone like that because, after all, I can't be riding with Peter all day long, there will be a lot of things to do in the house, especially now, when I'm not accustomed. It's wonderful to think that Peter won't have to be lonely. He says there are going to be Etruscan murals in the bathroom – whatever Etruscan means; the drawing-room *basically* will be eggshell green and the dining-room walls Pompeian red. They really did an awful lot of work yesterday afternoon – I mean in their heads, while we were glooming around. I said to Peter, "As things are going now we'd better be prepared for a nursery," but Peter said Tony was content to leave all that side to me. Then there are the stables: they were an old coach-house once, and Tony feels we could restore a lot of the ancient character and there's a lamp he bought in St Paul which will just fit . . . it's endless the things there are to be done – a good six months' work, so Tony says, but luckily he can leave Mrs Clarenty to Stephen and concentrate on us. Peter asked him about the garden, but he's not a specialist in gardens. He said, "Everyone to his own métier", and he's quite content if I bring in a man who knows all about roses.

'He knows Colin Winstanley too, of course, so there'll be quite a band of us. It's a pity the house won't be all ready for Christmas, but Peter says he's certain to have wonderful ideas for a really original tree. Peter thinks . . .'

She went on and on like that; perhaps I ought to have interrupted her even then; perhaps I should have tried to explain to her why her dream wouldn't last. Instead, I sat there silent, and presently I went to my room and packed – there was still one hotel open in the abandoned fun-fair of Juan between Maxim's and the boarded-up Striptease.

If I had stayed . . . who knows whether he could have kept on pretending for a second night? But I was just as bad for her as he was. If he had the wrong hormones, I had the wrong age. I didn't see any of them again before I left. She and Peter and Tony were out somewhere in the Sprite, and Stephen – so the receptionist told me – was lying late in bed with his rheumatism.

I planned a note for her, explaining rather feebly my departure, but when I came to write it I realized I had still no other name with which to address her than Poopy.

444

WILLIAM TREVOR

The Grass Widows

The headmaster of a great English public school visited every summer a village in County Galway for the sake of the fishing in a number of nearby rivers. For more than forty years this stern, successful man had brought his wife to the Slieve Gashal Hotel, a place, so he said, he had come to love. A smiling man called Mr Doyle had been for all the headmaster's experience of the hotel its obliging proprietor: Mr Doyle had related stories to the headmaster late at night in the hotel bar, after the headmaster's wife had retired to bed; they had discussed together the fruitfulness of the local rivers, although in truth Mr Doyle had never held a rod in his life. 'You feel another person,' the headmaster had told generations of his pupils, 'among blue mountains, in the quiet little hotel.' On walks through the school grounds with a senior boy on either side of him he had spoken of the soft peace of the riverside and of the unrivalled glory of being alone with one's mind. He talked to his boys of Mr Doyle and his unassuming ways, and of the little village that was a one-horse place and none the worse for that, and of the good plain food that came from the Slieve Gashal's kitchen.

To Jackson Major the headmaster enthused during all the year that Jackson Major was head boy of the famous school, and Jackson Major did not ever forget the paradise that then had formed in his mind. 'I know a place,' he said to his fiancée long after he had left the school, 'that's perfect for our honeymoon.' He told her about the heathery hills that the headmaster had recalled for him, and the lakes and rivers and the one-horse little village in which, near a bridge, stood the ivy-covered bulk of the Slieve Gashal Hotel. 'Lovely, darling,' murmured the bride-to-be of Jackson Major, thinking at the time of a clock in the shape of a human hand that someone had given them and which would naturally have to be changed for something else. She'd been hoping that he would suggest Majorca for their honeymoon, but if he wished to go to this other place she didn't intend to make a fuss. 'Idyllic for a honeymoon,' the headmaster had once remarked to Jackson Major, and Jackson Major had not forgotten. *Steady but unimaginative* were words that had been written of him on a school report.

The headmaster, a square, bald man with a head that might have been carved from oak, a man who wore rimless spectacles and whose name was Angusthorpe, discovered when he arrived at the Slieve Gashal Hotel in the summer of 1968 that in the intervening year a tragedy had occurred. It had become the custom of Mr Angusthorpe to book his fortnight's holiday by saying simply to Mr Doyle: 'Till next year then', an anticipation that Mr. Doyle would translate into commercial terms, reserving the same room for the headmaster and his wife in twelve months' time. No letters changed hands during the year, no confirmation of the booking was ever necessary: Mr Angusthorpe and his wife arrived each summer after the trials of the school term, knowing that their room would be waiting for them, with sweet-peas in a vase in the window, and Mr Doyle full of welcome in the hall. 'He died in Woolworth's in Galway,' said Mr Doyle's son in the summer of 1968. 'He was buying a shirt at the time.'

Afterwards, Mr Angusthorpe said to his wife that when Mr Doyle's son spoke those words he knew that nothing was ever going to be the same again. Mr Doyle's son, known locally as Scut Doyle, went on speaking while the headmaster and his small wife, grey-haired, and bespectacled also, stood in the hall. He told them that he had inherited the Slieve Gashal and that for all his adult life

446

he had been employed in the accounts department of a paper-mill in Dublin. 'I thought at first I'd sell the place up,' he informed the Angusthorpes, 'and then I thought maybe I'd attempt to make a go of it. "Will we have a shot at it?" I said to the wife, and, God bless her, she said why wouldn't I?' While he spoke, the subject of his last remarks appeared behind him in the hall, a woman whose appearance did not at all impress Mr Angusthorpe. She was pale-faced and fat and, so Mr Angusthorpe afterwards suggested to his wife, sullen. She stood silently by her husband, whose appearance did not impress Mr Angusthorpe either, since the new proprietor of the Slieve Gashal, a man with shaking hands and cocky black moustache, did not appear to have shaved himself that day. 'One or other of them, if not both,' said Mr Angusthorpe afterwards, 'smelt of drink.'

The Angusthorpes were led to their room by a girl whose age Mr Angusthorpe estimated to be thirteen. 'What's become of Joseph?' he asked her as they mounted the stairs, referring to an old porter who had always in the past been spick and span in a uniform, but the child seemed not to understand the question, for she offered it no reply. In the room there were no sweet-peas, and although they had entered by a door that was familiar to them, the room itself was greatly altered: it was, to begin with, only half the size it had been before. 'Great heavens!' exclaimed Mr Angusthorpe, striking a wall with his fist and finding it to be a partition. 'He had the carpenters in,' the child said.

Mr Angusthorpe, in a natural fury, descended the stairs and shouted in the hall. 'Mr Doyle!' he called out in his peremptory headmaster's voice. 'Mr Doyle! Mr Doyle!'

Doyle emerged from the back regions of the hotel, with a cigarette in his mouth. There were feathers on his clothes, and he held in his right hand a half-plucked chicken. In explanation he said that he had been giving his wife a hand. She was not herself, he confided to Mr Angusthorpe, on account of it being her bad time of the month.

'Our room,' protested Mr Angusthorpe. 'We can't possibly sleep in a tiny space like that. You've cut the room in half, Mr Doyle.'

Doyle nodded. All the bedrooms in the hotel, he told Mr Angusthorpe, had been divided, since they were uneconomical otherwise. He had spent four hundred and ten pounds having new doorways made and putting on new wallpaper. He began to go into the details of this expense, plucking feathers from the chicken as he stood there. Mr Angusthorpe coldly remarked that he had not booked a room in which you couldn't swing a cat.

'Excuse me, sir,' interrupted Doyle. 'You booked a room a year ago: you did not reserve a specific room. D'you know what I mean, Mr Angusthorpe? I have no note that you specified with my father to have the exact room again.'

'It was an understood thing between us—'

'My father unfortunately died.'

Mr Angusthorpe regarded the man, disliking him intensely. It occurred to him that he had never in his life carried on a conversation with a hotel proprietor who held in his right hand a half-plucked chicken and whose clothes had feathers on them. His inclination was to turn on his heel and march with his wife from the unsatisfactory hotel, telling, if need be, this unprepossessing individual to go to hell. Mr Angusthorpe thought of doing that, but then he wondered where he and his wife could go. Hotels in the area were notoriously full at this time of year, in the middle of the fishing season.

'I must get on with this for the dinner,' said Doyle, 'or the wife will be having me guts for garters.' He winked at Mr Angusthorpe, flicking a quantity of cigarette ash from the pale flesh of the chicken. He left Mr Angusthorpe standing there.

The child had remained with Mrs Angusthorpe while the headmaster had sought an explanation downstairs. She had stood silently by the door until Mrs Angusthorpe, fearing a violent reaction on the part of her husband if he discovered the child present when he returned, suggested that she should go away. But the child had taken no notice of that and Mrs Angusthorpe, being unable to think of anything else to say, had asked her at what time of year old Mr Doyle had died. 'The funeral was ten miles long, missus,' replied the child. 'Me father wasn't sober till the Monday.' Mr Angusthorpe, returning, asked the child sharply why she was lingering and the child explained that she was waiting to be tipped. Mr Angusthorpe gave her a threepenny-piece.

In the partitioned room, which now had a pink wallpaper on the walls and an elaborate frieze from which flowers of different colours cascaded down the four corners, the Angusthorpes surveyed their predicament. Mr Angusthorpe told his wife the details of his interview with Doyle, and when he had talked for twenty minutes he came more definitely to the conclusion that the best thing they could do would be to remain for the moment. The rivers could hardly have altered, he was thinking, and that the hotel was now more than inadequate was a consequence that would affect his wife more than it would affect him. In the past she had been wont to spend her days going for a brief walk in the morning and returning to the pleasant little dining-room for a solitary lunch, and then sleeping or reading until it was time for a cup of tea, after which she would again take a brief walk. She was usually sitting by the fire in the lounge when he returned from his day's excursion. Perhaps all that would be less attractive now, Mr Angusthorpe thought, but there was little he could do about it and it was naturally only fair that they should at least remain for a day or two.

That night the dinner was well below the standard of the dinners they had in the past enjoyed in the Slieve Gashal. Mrs Angusthorpe was unable to consume her soup because there were quite large pieces of bone and gristle in it. The headmaster laughed over his prawn cocktail because, he said, it tasted of absolutely nothing at all. He had recovered from his initial shock and was now determined that the hotel must be regarded as a joke. He eyed his wife's plate of untouched soup, saying it was better to make the best of things. Chicken and potatoes and mashed turnip were placed before them by a nervous woman in the uniform of a waitress. Turnip made Mrs Angusthorpe sick in the stomach, even the sight of it: at another time in their life her husband might have remembered and ordered the vegetable from the table, but what he was more intent upon now was discovering if the Slieve Gashal still possessed a passable hock, which surprisingly it did. After a few glasses, he said:

'We'll not come next year, of course. While I'm out with the rod, my dear, you might scout around for another hotel.'

They never brought their car with them, the headmaster's theory being that the car was something they wished to escape from. Often she had thought it might be nice to have a car at the Slieve Gashal so that she could drive around the countryside during the day, but she saw his argument and had never pressed her view. Now, it seemed, he was suggesting that she should scout about for another hotel on foot.

'No, no,' he said. 'There is an excellent bus service in Ireland.' He spoke with a trace of sarcasm, as though she should have known that no matter what else he expected of her, he did not expect her to tramp about the roads looking for another hotel. He gave a little laugh, leaving the matter vaguely with her, his eyes like the eyes of a fish behind his rimless spectacles. Boys had feared him and disliked him too, some even had hated him; yet others had been full of a respect that seemed at times like adoration. As she struggled with her watery turnips she could sense that his mind was quite made up: he intended to remain for the full fortnight in the changed hotel because the lure of the riverside possessed him too strongly to consider an alternative.

'I might find a place we could move to,' she said. 'I mean, in a day or so.'

'They'll all be full, my dear.' He laughed without

humour in his laugh, not amused by anything. 'We must simply grin and bear it. The chicken,' he added, 'might well have been worse.'

'Excuse me,' Mrs Angusthorpe said, and quickly rose from the table and left the dining-room. From a tape-recorder somewhere dance music began to play.

'Is the wife all right?' Doyle asked Mr Angusthorpe, coming up and sitting down in the chair she had vacated. He had read in a hotelier's journal that tourists enjoyed a friendly atmosphere and the personal attention of the pro-prietor.

'We've had a long day,' responded the headmaster genially enough.

'Ah well, of course you have.'

The dining-room was full, indicating that business was still brisk in the hotel. Mr Angusthorpe had noted a fami-liar face or two and had made dignified salutations. These people would surely have walked out if the hotel was impossible in all respects.

'At her time of the month,' Doyle was saying, 'the wife gets as fatigued as an old horse. Like your own one, she's gone up to her bed already.'

'My wife—'

'Ah, I wasn't suggesting Mrs Angusthorpe was that way at all. They have fatigue in common tonight, sir, that's all I meant.'

Doyle appeared to be drunk. There was a bleariness about his eyes that suggested inebriation to Mr Angus-thorpe and his shaking hands might well be taken as a sign of repeated over-indulgence.

'She wakes up at two a.m. as lively as a bird,' said Doyle. 'She's keen for a hug and a pat—'

'Quite so,' interrupted Mr Angusthorpe quickly. He looked unpleasantly at his unwelcome companion. He al-lowed his full opinion of the man to pervade his glance.

'Well, I'll be seeing you,' said Doyle, rising and seeming to be undismayed. 'I'll tell the wife you were asking for her,' he added with a billowing laugh, before moving on to another table.

Shortly after that, Mr Angusthorpe left the dining-room, having resolved that he would not relate this conversation to his wife. He would avoid Doyle in the future, he promised himself, and when by chance they did meet he would make it clear that he did not care to hear his comments on any subject. It was a pity that the old man had died and that all this nastiness had grown up in his place, but there was nothing whatsoever that might be done about it and at least the weather looked good. He entered the bar and dropped into conversation with a man he had met several times before, a solicitor from Dublin, a bachelor called Gorman.

'I was caught the same way,' Mr Gorman said, 'only everywhere else is full. It's the end of the Slieve Gashal, you know: the food's inedible.'

He went on to relate a series of dishes that had already been served during his stay, the most memorable of which appeared to be a rabbit stew that had had a smell of ammonia. 'There's margarine every time instead of butter, and some queer type of marmalade in the morning: it has a taste of tin to it. The same mashed turnip,' said Gorman, 'is the only vegetable he offers.'

The headmaster changed the subject, asking how the rivers were. The fishing was better than ever he'd known it, Mr Gorman reported, and he retailed experiences to prove the claim. 'Isn't it all that matters in the long run?' suggested Mr Gorman, and Mr Angusthorpe readily agreed that it was. He would refrain from repeating to his wife the information about the marmalade that tasted of tin, or the absence of variation where vegetables were concerned. He left the bar at nine o'clock, determined to slip quietly into bed without disturbing her.

In the middle of that night, at midnight precisely, the Angusthorpes were awakened simultaneously by a noise from the room beyond the new partition.

'Put a pillow down, darling,' a male voice was saying as clearly as if its possessor stood in the room beside the Angusthorpes' bed.

'Couldn't we wait until another time?' a woman pleaded in reply. 'I don't see what good a pillow will do.'

'It'll lift you up a bit,' the man explained. 'It said in the book to put a pillow down if there was difficulty.'

'I don't see—'

'It'll make entry easier,' said the man. 'It's a well-known thing.'

Mrs Angusthorpe switched on her bedside light and saw that her husband was pretending to be asleep. 'I'm going to rap on the wall,' she whispered. 'It's disgusting, listening to this.'

'I think I'm going down,' said the man.

'My God,' whispered Mr Angusthorpe, opening his eyes. 'It's Jackson Major.'

At breakfast, Mrs Angusthorpe ate margarine on her toast and the marmalade that had a taste of tin. She did not say anything. She watched her husband cutting into a fried egg on a plate that bore the marks of the waitress's two thumbs. Eventually he placed his knife and fork together on the plate and left them there.

For hours they had lain awake, listening to the conversation beyond the inadequate partition. The newly wed wife of Jackson Major had wept and said that Jackson had better divorce her at once. She had designated the hotel they were in as a frightful place, fit only for Irish tinkers. 'That filthy meal!' the wife of Jackson Major had cried emotionally. 'That awful drunk man!' And Jackson Major had apologised and had mentioned Mr Angusthorpe by name, wondering what on earth his old headmaster could ever have seen in such an establishment. 'Let's try again,' he had suggested, and the Angusthorpes had listened to a repetition of Mrs Jackson's unhappy tears. 'How can you rap on the wall?' Mr Angusthorpe had angrily whispered.

'How can we even admit that conversation can be heard? Jackson was head boy.'

'In the circumstances,' said Mrs Angusthorpe at breakfast, breaking the long silence, 'it would be better to leave.'

He knew it would be. He knew that on top of everything else the unfortunate fact that Jackson Major was in the room beyond the partition and would sooner or later discover that the partition was far from soundproof could be exceedingly embarrassing in view of what had taken place during the night. There was, as well, the fact that he had enthused so eloquently to Jackson Major about the hotel that Jackson Major had clearly, on his word alone, brought his bride there. He had even said, he recalled, that the Slieve Gashal would be ideal for a honeymoon. Mr Angusthorpe considered all that, yet could not forget his forty years' experience of the surrounding rivers, or the information of Mr Gorman that the rivers this year were better than ever.

'We could whisper,' he suggested in what was itself a whisper. 'We could whisper in our room so that they wouldn't know you can hear.'

'Whisper?' she said. She shook her head.

She remembered days in the rain, walking about the one-horse village with nothing whatsoever to do except to walk about, or lie on her bed reading detective stories. She remembered listening to his reports of his day and feeling sleepy listening to them. She remembered thinking, once or twice, that it had never occurred to him that what was just a change and a rest for her could not at all be compared to the excitements he derived from his days on the river-bank, alone with his mind. He was a great, successful man, big and square and commanding, with the cold eyes of the fish he sought in mountain rivers. He had made a firm impression on generations of boys, and on parents and governors, and often on a more general public, yet he had never been able to give her children. She had needed children because she was, compared with him, an unimportant kind of person.

She thought of him in Chapel, gesturing at six hundred boys from the pulpit, in his surplice and red academic hood, releasing words from his throat that were as cold as ice and cleverly made sense. She thought of a time he had expelled two boys, when he had sat with her in their drawing-room waiting for a bell to ring. When the chiming had ceased he had risen and gone without a word from the room, his oaken face pale with suppressed emotion. She knew he saw in the crime of the two boys a failure on his part, yet he never mentioned it to her. He had expelled the boys in public, castigating them with bitterness in his tone, hating them and hating himself, yet rising above his shame at having failed with them: dignity was his greatest ally.

She sat with him once a week at the high table in the dining-hall, surrounded by his prefects, who politely chatted to her. She remembered Jackson Major, a tall boy with short black hair who would endlessly discuss with her husband a web of school affairs. 'The best head boy I remember,' her husband's voice said again, coming back to her over a number of years: 'I made no mistake with Jackson.' Jackson Major had set a half-mile record that remained unbroken to this day. There had been a complaint from some child's mother, she recalled, who claimed that her son had been, by Jackson Major, too severely caned. *We must not forget*, her husband had written to that mother, *that your son almost caused another boy to lose an eye. It was for that carelessness that he was punished. He bears no resentment: boys seldom do.*

Yet now this revered, feared, and clever man was suggesting that they should whisper for a fortnight in their bedroom, so that the couple next door might not feel embarrassment, so that he himself might remain in a particularly uncomfortable hotel in order to fish. It seemed to Mrs Angusthorpe that there were limits to the role he had laid down for her and which for all her married life she had ungrudgingly accepted. She hadn't minded being bored for this fortnight every year, but now he was asking more than that she should continue to feel bored; he was asking her to endure food that made her sick, and to conduct absurd conversations in their bedroom.

'No,' she said, 'we could not whisper.'

'I meant it only for kindness. Kindness to them, you see—'

'You have compensations here. I have none, you know.'

He looked sharply at her, as at an erring new boy who had not yet learnt the ways of school.

'I think we should leave at once,' she said. 'After breakfast.'

That suggestion, he pointed out to her, was nonsensical. They had booked a room in the hotel: they were obliged to pay for it. He was exhausted, he added, after a particularly trying term.

'It's what I'd like,' she said.

He spread margarine on his toast and added to it some of the marmalade. 'We must not be selfish,' he said, suggesting that both of them were on the point of being selfish and that together they must prevent themselves.

'I'd be happier,' she began, but he swiftly interrupted her, reminding her that his holiday had been spoilt enough already and that he for his part was intent on making the best of things. 'Let's simply enjoy what we can,' he said, 'without making a fuss about it.'

At that moment Jackson Major and his wife, a pretty, pale-haired girl called Daphne, entered the dining-room. They stood at the door, endeavouring to catch the eye of a waitress, not sure about where to sit. Mrs Jackson indicated a table that was occupied by two men, reminding her husband that they had sat at it last night for dinner. Jackson Major looked towards it and looked impatiently away, seeming annoyed with his wife for bothering to draw his attention to a table at which they clearly could not sit. It was then, while still annoyed, that he noticed the Angusthorpes.

Mrs Angusthorpe saw him murmuring to his wife. He

led their way to their table, and Mrs Angusthorpe observed that his wife moved less eagerly than he.

'How marvellous, sir,' Jackson Major said, shaking his headmaster by the hand. Except for a neat moustache, he had hardly changed at all, Mrs Angusthorpe noticed; a little fatter in the face, perhaps, and the small pimples that had marked his chin as a schoolboy had now cleared up completely. He introduced his wife to the headmaster, and then he turned to Mrs Angusthorpe and asked her how she was. Forgetfully, he omitted to introduce his wife to her, but she, in spite of that, smiled and nodded at his wife.

'I'm afraid it's gone down awfully, Jackson,' Mr Angusthorpe said. 'The hotel's changed hands, you know. We weren't aware ourselves.'

'It seems quite comfortable, sir,' Jackson Major said, sitting down and indicating that his wife should do the same.

'The food was nice before,' said Mrs Angusthorpe. 'It's really awful now.'

'Oh, I wouldn't say awful, dear,' Mr Angusthorpe corrected her. 'One becomes used to a hotel,' he explained to Jackson Major. 'Any change is rather noticeable.'

'We had a perfectly ghastly dinner,' Daphne Jackson said.

'Still,' said Mr Angusthorpe, as though she had not spoken, 'we'll not return another year. My wife is going to scout around for a better place. You've brought your rod, Jackson?'

'Well, yes, I did. I thought that maybe if Daphne felt tired I might once or twice try out your famous rivers, sir.'

Mrs Angusthorpe saw Mrs Jackson glance in surprise at her new husband, and she deduced that Mrs Jackson hadn't been aware that a fishing-rod had comprised part of her husband's luggage.

'Capital,' cried Mr Angusthorpe, while the waitress took the Jacksons' order for breakfast. 'You could scout round together,' he said, addressing the two women at once, 'while I show Jackson what's what.'

457

'It's most kind of you, sir,' Jackson Major said, 'but I think, you know—"

'Capital,' cried Mr Angusthorpe again, his eyes swivelling from face to face, forbidding defiance. He laughed his humourless laugh and he poured himself more tea. 'I told you, dear,' he said to Mrs Angusthorpe. 'There's always a silver lining.'

In the hall of the Slieve Gashal Doyle took a metal stand from beneath the reception desk and busied himself arranging picture postcards on it. His wife had bought the stand in Galway, getting it at a reduced price because it was broken. He was at the moment offended with his wife because of her attitude when he had entered the hotel kitchen an hour ago with a number of ribs of beef. 'Did you drop that meat?' she had said in a hard voice, looking up from the table where she was making bread. 'Is that dirt on the suet?' He had replied that he'd been obliged to cross the village street hurriedly, to avoid a man on a bicycle. 'You dropped the meat on the road,' she accused. 'D'you want to poison the bloody lot of them?' Feeling hard done by, he had left the kitchen.

While he continued to work with the postcards, Mr Angusthorpe and Jackson Major passed before him with their fishing-rods. 'We'll be frying tonight,' he observed jollily, wagging his head at their two rods. They did not reply: weren't they the queer-looking eejits, he thought, with their sporty clothes and the two tweed hats covered with artificial flies. 'I'll bring it up, sir,' Jackson Major was saying, 'at the Old Boys' Dinner in the autumn.' It was ridiculous, Doyle reflected, going to all that trouble to catch a few fish when all you had to do was to go out at night and shine a torch into the water. 'Would you be interested in postcards, gentlemen?' he inquired, but so absorbed were Mr Angusthorpe and Jackson Major in their conversation that again neither of them made a reply.

Some time later, Daphne Jackson descended the stairs of

the hotel. Doyle watched her, admiring her slender legs and the flowered dress she was wearing. A light blue cardigan hung casually from her shoulders, its sleeves not occupied by her arms. Wouldn't it be great, he thought, to be married to a young body like that? He imagined her in a bedroom, taking off her cardigan and then her dress. She stood in her underclothes; swiftly she lifted them from her body.

'Would you be interested in postcards at all?' inquired Doyle. 'I have the local views here.'

Daphne smiled at him. Without much interest, she examined the cards on the stand, and then she moved towards the entrance door.

'There's a lovely dinner we have for you today,' said Doyle. 'Ribs of beef that I'm just after handing over to the wife. As tender as an infant.'

He held the door open for her, talking all the time, since he knew they liked to be talked to. He asked her if she was going for a walk and told her that a walk would give her a healthy appetite. The day would keep good, he promised; he had read it in the paper.

'Thank you,' she said.

She walked through a sunny morning that did little to raise her spirits. Outside the hotel there was a large expanse of green grass, bounded on one side by the short village street. She crossed an area of the grass and then passed the butcher's shop in which earlier Doyle had purchased the ribs of beef. She glanced in and the butcher smiled and waved at her, as though he knew her well. She smiled shyly back. Outside a small public house a man was mending a bicycle, which was upturned on the pavement: a child pushing a pram spoke to the man and he spoke to her. Farther on, past a row of cottages, a woman pumped water into a bucket from a green pump at the road's edge, and beyond it, coming towards her slowly, she recognised the figure of Mrs Angusthorpe.

'So we are grass widows,' said Mrs Angusthorpe when she had arrived at a point at which it was suitable to speak.

'Yes.'

'I'm afraid it's our fault, for being here. My husband's, I mean, and mine.'

'My husband could have declined to go fishing.'

The words were sour. They were sour and icy, Mrs Angusthorpe thought, matching her own mood. On her brief walk she had that morning disliked her husband more than ever she had disliked him before, and there was venom in her now. Once upon a time he might at least have heard her desires with what could even have been taken for understanding. He would not have acted upon her desires, since it was not in his nature to do so, but he would not have been guilty, either, of announcing in so obviously false a way that they should enjoy what they could and not make a fuss. There had been a semblance of chivalry in the attitude from which, at the beginning of their marriage, he had briefly regarded her; but forty-seven years had efficiently disposed of that garnish of politeness. A week or so ago a boy at the school had been casual with her, but the headmaster, hearing her report of the matter, had denied that what she stated could ever have occurred: he had moulded the boy in question, he pointed out, he had taken a special interest in the boy because he recognised in him qualities that were admirable: she was touchy, the headmaster said, increasingly touchy these days. She remembered in the first year of their marriage a way he had of patiently leaning back in his chair, puffing at the pipe he affected in those days and listening to her, seeming actually to weigh her arguments against his own. It was a long time now since he had weighed an argument of hers, or even devoted a moment of passing consideration to it. It was a long time since he could possibly have been concerned as to whether or not she found the food in a hotel unpalatable. She was angry when she thought of it this morning, not because she was unused to these circumstances of her life but because, quite suddenly, she had seen her state of resignation as an insult to the woman she once, too long ago, had been.

'I would really like to talk to you,' Mrs Angusthorpe said, to Daphne Jackson's surprise. 'It might be worth your while to stroll back to that hotel with me.'

On her short, angry walk she had realised, too, that once she had greatly disliked Jackson Major because he reminded her in some ways of her husband. A priggish youth, she had recalled, a tedious bore of a boy who had shown her husband a ridiculous respect while also fearing and resembling him. On her walk she had remembered the day he had broken the half-mile record, standing in the sports field in his running clothes, deprecating his effort because he knew his headmaster would wish him to act like that. What good was winning a half-mile race if he upset his wife the first time he found himself in a bedroom with her?

'I remember your husband as a boy,' said Mrs Angusthorpe. 'He set an athletic record which has not yet been broken.'

'Yes, he told me.'

'He had trouble with his chin. Pimples that wouldn't go away. I see all that's been overcome.'

'Well, yes—'

'And trouble also because he beat a boy too hard. The mother wrote, enclosing the opinion of a doctor.'

Daphne frowned. She ceased to walk. She stared at Mrs Angusthorpe.

'Oh yes,' said Mrs Angusthorpe.

They passed the butcher's shop, from the doorway of which the butcher now addressed them. The weather was good, the butcher said: it was a suitable time for a holiday. Mrs Angusthorpe smiled at him and bowed. Daphne, frowning still, passed on.

'You're right,' Mrs Angusthorpe said next, 'when you say that your husband could have declined to go fishing.'

'I think he felt—'

'Odd, I thought, to have a fishing-rod with him in the first place. Odd on a honeymoon.'

They entered the hotel. Doyle came forward to greet them. 'Ah, so you've palled up?' he said. 'Isn't that grand?'

'We could have a sherry,' Mrs Angusthorpe suggested, 'in the bar.'

'Of course you could,' said Doyle. 'Won't your two husbands be pegging away at the old fish for the entire day?'

'They promised to be back for lunch,' Daphne said quickly, her voice seeming to herself to be unduly weak. She cleared her throat and remarked to Doyle that the village was pretty. She didn't really wish to sit in the hotel bar drinking sherry with the wife of her husband's headmaster. It was all ridiculous, she thought, on a honeymoon.

'Go down into the bar,' said Doyle, 'and I'll be down myself in a minute.'

Mrs Angusthorpe seized with the fingers of her left hand the flowered material of Daphne's dress. 'The bar's down here,' she said, leading the way without releasing her hold.

They sat at a table on which there were a number of absorbent mats which advertised brands of beer. Doyle brought them two glasses of sherry, which Mrs Angusthorpe ordered him to put down to her husband's account. 'Shout out when you're in need of a refill,' he invited. 'I'll be up in the hall.'

'The partition between our bedrooms is far from soundproof,' said Mrs Angusthorpe when Doyle had gone. 'We were awakened in the night.'

'Awakened?'

'As if you were in the room beside us, we heard a conversation.'

'My God!'

'Yes.'

Blood rushed to Daphne Jackson's face. She was aware of an unpleasant sensation in her stomach. She turned her head away. Mrs Angusthorpe said:

'People don't speak out. All my married life, for instance, I haven't spoken out. My dear, you're far too good for Jackson Major.'

It seemed to Daphne, who had been Daphne Jackson

for less than twenty-four hours, that the wife of her husband's headmaster was insane. She gulped at the glass of sherry before her, unable to prevent herself from vividly recalling the awfulness of the night before in the small bedroom. He had come at her as she was taking off her blouse. His right hand had shot beneath her underclothes, pressing at her and gripping her. All during their inedible dinner he had been urging her to drink whisky and wine, and drinking quantities of both himself. In bed he had suddenly become calmer, remembering instructions read in a book.

'Pack a suitcase,' said Mrs Angusthorpe, 'and go.'

The words belonged to a nightmare and Daphne was aware of wishing that she was asleep and dreaming. The memory of tension on her wedding day, and of guests standing around in sunshine in a London garden, and then the flight by plane, were elements that confused her mind as she listened to this small woman. The tension had been with her as she walked towards the altar and had been with her, too, in her parents' garden. Nor had it eased when she escaped with her husband on a Viscount: it might even have increased on the flight and on the train to Galway, and then in the hired car that had carried her to the small village. It had certainly increased while she attempted to eat stringy chicken at a late hour in the dining-room, while her husband smiled at her and talked about intoxicants. The reason he had talked so much about whisky and wine, she now concluded, was because he'd been aware of the tension that was coiled within her.

'You have made a mistake,' came the voice of Mrs Angusthorpe, 'but even now it is not too late to rectify it. Do not accept it, reject your error, Mrs Jackson.'

Doyle came into the bar and brought to them, without their demanding it, more sherry in two new glasses. Daphne heard him remarking that the brand of sherry was very popular in these parts. It was Spanish sherry, he said, since he would stock nothing else. He talked about Spain and Spaniards, saying that at the time of the Spanish

463

Armada Spanish sailors had been wrecked around the nearby coast.

'I love my husband,' Daphne said when Doyle had gone again.

She had met her husband in the Hurlingham Club. He had partnered her in tennis and they had danced together at a charity dance. She'd listened while he talked one evening, telling her that the one thing he regretted was that he hadn't played golf as a child. Golf was a game, he'd said, that must be started when young if one was ever to achieve championship distinction. With tennis that wasn't quite so important, but it was, of course, as well to start tennis early also. She had thought he was rather nice. There was something about his distant manner that attracted her; there was a touch of arrogance in the way he didn't look at her when he spoke. She'd make him look at her, she vowed.

'My dear,' said Mrs Angusthorpe, 'I've seen the seamy side of Jackson Major. The more I think of him the more I can recall. He forced his way up that school, snatching at chances that weren't his to take, putting himself first, like he did in the half-mile race. There was cruelty in Jackson Major's eye, and ruthlessness and dullness. Like my husband, he has no sense of humour.'

'Mrs Angusthorpe, I really can't listen to all this. I was married yesterday to a man I'm in love with. It'll be all right—'

'Why will it be all right?'

'Because,' snapped Daphne Jackson with sudden spirit, 'I shall ask my husband as soon as he returns to take me at once from this horrible hotel. My marriage does not at all concern you, Mrs Angusthorpe.'

'They are talking now on a riverside, whispering maybe so as not to disturb their prey. They are murmuring about the past, of achievements on the sports field and marches undertaken by a cadet force. While you and I are having a different kind of talk.'

'What our husbands are saying to one another, Mrs Angusthorpe, may well make more sense.'

'What they are not saying is that two women in the bar of this hotel are unhappy. They have forgotten about the two women: they are more relaxed and contented than ever they are with us.'

Mrs Angusthorpe, beady-eyed as she spoke, saw the effect of her words reflected in the uneasy face of the woman beside her. She felt herself carried away by this small triumph, she experienced a headiness that was blissful. She saw in her mind another scene, imagining herself, over lunch, telling her husband about the simple thing that had happened. She would watch him sitting there in all his dignity: she would wait until he was about to pass a forkful of food to his mouth and then she would say: 'Jackson Major's wife has left him already.' And she would smile at him.

'You walked across the dining-room at breakfast,' said Mrs Angusthorpe. 'An instinct warned me then that you'd made an error.'

'I haven't made an error. I've told you, Mrs Angusthorpe—'

'Time will erode the polish of politeness. One day soon you'll see amusement in his eyes when you offer an opinion.'

'Please stop, Mrs Angusthorpe. I must go away if you continue like this—'

' "This man's a bore," you'll suddenly say to yourself, and look at him amazed.'

'Mrs Angusthorpe—'

'Amazed that you could ever have let it happen.'

'Oh God, please stop,' cried Daphne, tears coming suddenly from her eyes, her hands rushing to her cheeks.

'Don't be a silly girl,' whispered Mrs Angusthorpe, grasping the arm of her companion and tightening her fingers on it until Daphne felt pain. She thought as she felt it that Mrs Angusthorpe was a poisonous woman. She struggled to keep back further tears, she tried to wrench her arm away.

'I'll tell the man Doyle to order you a car,' said Mrs Angusthorpe. 'It'll take you into Galway. I'll lend you money, Mrs Jackson. By one o'clock tonight you could be sitting in your bed at home, eating from a tray that your mother brought you. A divorce will come through and one day you'll meet a man who'll love you with a tenderness.'

'My husband loves me, Mrs Angusthorpe—'

'Your husband should marry a woman who's keen on horses or golf, a woman who might take a whip to him, being ten years older than himself. My dear, you're like me: you're a delicate person.'

'Please let go my arm. You've no right to talk to me like this—'

'He is my husband's creature, my husband moulded him. The best head boy he'd ever known, he said to me.'

Daphne, calmer now, did not say anything. She felt the pressure on her arm being removed. She stared ahead of her, at a round mat on the table that advertised Celebration Ale. Without wishing to and perhaps, she thought, because she was so upset, she saw herself suddenly as Mrs Angusthorpe had suggested, sitting up in her own bedroom with a tray of food on her knees and her mother standing beside her, saying it was all right. 'I suddenly realised,' she heard herself saying. 'He took me to this awful hotel, where his old headmaster was. He gave me wine and whisky, and then in bed I thought I might be sick.' Her mother replied to her, telling her that it wasn't a disgrace, and her father came in later and told her not to worry. It was better not to be unhappy, her father said: it was better to have courage now.

'Let me tell Doyle to order a car at once.' Mrs Angusthorpe was on her feet, eagerness in her eyes and voice. Her cheeks were flushed from sherry and excitement.

'You're quite outrageous,' said Daphne Jackson.

She left the bar and in the hall Doyle again desired her as she passed. He spoke to her, telling her he'd already

ordered a few more bottles of that sherry so that she and
Mrs Angusthorpe could sip a little as often as they liked.
It was sherry, he repeated, that was very popular in the
locality. She nodded and mounted the stairs, not hearing
much of what he said, feeling that as she pushed one leg in
front of another her whole body would open and tears
would gush from everywhere. Why did she have to put up
with talk like that on the first morning of her honeymoon?
Why had he casually gone out fishing with his old headmaster? Why had he brought her to this terrible place and
then made her drink so that the tension would leave her
body? She sobbed on the stairs, causing Doyle to frown
and feel concerned for her.

'Are you all right?' Jackson Major asked, standing in the
doorway of their room, looking to where she sat, by the
window. He closed the door and went to her. 'You've been
all right?' he said.

She nodded, smiling a little. She spoke in a low voice:
she said she thought it possible that conversations might be
heard through the partition wall. She pointed to the wall
she spoke of. 'It's only a partition,' she said.

He touched it and agreed, but gave it as his opinion that
little could be heard through it since they themselves had
not heard the people on the other side of it. Partitions
nowadays, he pronounced, were constructed always of
soundproof material.

'Let's have a drink before lunch,' she said.

In the hour that had elapsed since she had left Mrs
Angusthorpe in the bar she had changed her stockings and
her dress. She had washed her face in cold water and had
put lipstick and powder on it. She had brushed her suède
shoes with a rubber brush.

'All right,' he said. 'We'll have a little drink.'

He kissed her. On the way down he told her about the
morning's fishing and the conversations he had had with

his old headmaster. Not asking her what she'd like, he ordered both of them gin and tonic in the bar.

'I know her better than you do, sir,' Doyle said, bringing her a glass of sherry, but Jackson Major didn't appear to realise what had happened, being still engrossed in the retailing of the conversations he had had with his old headmaster.

'I want to leave this hotel,' she said. 'At once, darling, after lunch.'

'Daphne—'

'I do.'

She didn't say that Mrs Angusthorpe had urged her to leave him, nor that the Angusthorpes had lain awake during the night, hearing what there was to hear. She simply said she didn't at all like the idea of spending her honeymoon in a hotel which also contained his late headmaster and the headmaster's wife. 'They remember you as a boy,' she said. 'For some reason it makes me edgy. And anyway it's such a nasty hotel.'

She leaned back after that speech, glad that she'd been able to make it as she'd planned to make it. They would move on after lunch, paying whatever money must necessarily be paid. They would find a pleasant room in a pleasant hotel and the tension inside her would gradually relax. In the Hurlingham Club she had made this tall man look at her when he spoke to her, she had made him regard her and find her attractive, as she found him. They had said to one another that they had fallen in love, he had asked her to marry him, and she had happily agreed: there was nothing the matter.

'My dear, it would be quite impossible,' he said.

'Impossible?'

'At this time of year, in the middle of the season? Hotel rooms are gold dust, my dear. Angusthorpe was saying as much. His wife's a good sort, you know—'

'I want to leave here.'

He laughed good-humouredly. He gestured with his hands, suggesting his helplessness.

I cannot stay here,' she said.

'You're tired, Daphne.'

'I cannot stay here for a fortnight with the Angus-thorpes. She's a woman who goes on all the time; there's something the matter with her. While you go fishing—'

'Darling, I had to go this morning. I felt it polite to go. If you like, I'll not go out again at all.'

'I've told you what I'd like.'

'Oh, for God's sake!' He turned away from her. She said:

'I thought you would say yes at once.'

'How the hell can I say yes when we've booked a room for the next fortnight and we're duty-bound to pay for it? Do you really think we can just walk up to that man and say we don't like his hotel and the people he has staying here?'

'We could make some excuse. We could pretend—'

'Pretend? Pretend, Daphne?'

'Some illness. We could say my mother's ill,' she hurriedly said. 'Or some aunt who doesn't even exist. We could hire a car and drive around the coast—'

'Daphne—'

'Why not?'

'For a start, I haven't my driving licence with me.'

'I have.'

'I doubt it, Daphne.'

She thought, and then she agreed that she hadn't. 'We could go to Dublin,' she said with a fresh burst of urgency. 'Dublin's a lovely place, people say. We could stay in Dublin and—'

'My dear, this is a tourist country. Millions of tourists come here every summer. Do you really believe we'd find decent accommodation in Dublin in the middle of the season?'

'It wouldn't have to be decent. Some little clean hotel—'

'Added to which, Daphne, I must honestly tell you that I have no wish to go gallivanting on my honeymoon. Nor do I care for the notion of telling lies about the illness of people who are not ill, or do not even exist.'

'I'll tell the lies. I'll talk to Mr Doyle directly after lunch. I'll talk to him now.' She stood up. He shook his head, reaching for the hand that was nearer to him.

'What's the matter?' he asked.

Slowly she sat down again.

'Oh, darling,' she said.

'We must be sensible, Daphne. We can't just go gallivanting off—'

'Why do you keep on about gallivanting? What's it matter whether we're gallivanting or not so long as we're enjoying ourselves?'

'Daphne—'

'I'm asking you to do something to please me.'

Jackson Major, about to reply, changed his mind. He smiled at his bride. After a pause, he said:

'If you really want to, Daphne—'

'Well, I do. I think perhaps it'll be awkward here with the Angusthorpes. And it's not what we expected.'

'It's just a question,' said Jackson Major, 'of what we could possibly do. I've asked for my mail to be forwarded here and, as I say, I really believe it would be a case of out of the frying-pan into nothing at all. It might prove horribly difficult.'

She closed her eyes and sat for a moment in silence. Then she opened them and, being unable to think of anything else to say, she said:

'I'm sorry.'

He sighed, shrugging his shoulders slightly. He took her hand again. 'You do see, darling?' Before she could reply he added: 'I'm sorry I was angry with you. I didn't mean to be: I'm very sorry.'

He kissed her on the cheek that was near to him. He took her hand. 'Now tell me,' he said, 'about everything that's worrying you.'

She repeated, without more detail, what she had said already, but this time the sentences she spoke did not sound like complaints. He listened to her, sitting back and not interrupting, and then they conversed about all she had said. He agreed that it was a pity about the hotel and explained to her that what had happened, apparently, was that the old proprietor had died during the previous year. It was unfortunate too, he quite agreed, that the Angusthorpes should be here at the same time as they were because it would, of course, have been so much nicer to have been on their own. If she was worried about the partition in their room he would ask that their room should be changed for another one. He hadn't known when she'd mentioned the partition before that it was the Angusthorpes who were on the other side of it. It would be better, really, not to be in the next room to the Angusthorpes since Angusthorpe had once been his headmaster, and he was certain that Doyle would understand a thing like that and agree to change them over, even if it meant greasing Doyle's palm. 'I imagine he'd fall in with anything,' said Jackson Major, 'for a bob or two.'

They finished their drinks and she followed him to the dining-room. There were no thoughts in her mind: no voice, neither her own nor Mrs Angusthorpe's, spoke. For a reason she could not understand and didn't want to bother to understand, the tension within her had snapped and was no longer there. The desire she had felt for tears when she'd walked away from Mrs Angusthorpe was far from her now; she felt a weariness, as though an ordeal was over and she had survived it. She didn't know why she felt like that. All she knew was that he had listened to her: he had been patient and understanding, allowing her to say all that was in her mind and then being reassuring. It was not his fault that the hotel had turned out so unfortunately. Nor was it his fault that a bullying old man had sought him out as a fishing companion. He couldn't help it if his desire for her brought out a clumsiness in him. He was a man, she thought: he was not the same as she was: she must meet him half-way. He had said he was sorry for being angry with her.

In the hall they met the Angusthorpes on their way to the dining-room also.

471

'I'm sorry if I upset you,' Mrs Angusthorpe said to her, touching her arm to hold her back for a moment. 'I'm afraid my temper ran away with me.'

The two men went ahead, involved in a new conversation. 'We might try that little tributary this afternoon,' the headmaster was suggesting.

'I sat there afterwards, seeing how horrid it must have been for you,' Mrs Angusthorpe said. 'I was angry at the prospect of an unpleasant fortnight. I took it out on you.'

'Don't worry about it.'

'One should keep one's anger to oneself. I feel embarrassed now,' said Mrs Angusthorpe. 'I'm not the sort of person—'

'Please don't worry,' murmured Daphne, trying hard to keep the tiredness that possessed her out of her voice. She could sleep, she was thinking, for a week.

'I don't know why I talked like that.'

'You were angry—'

'Yes,' said Mrs Angusthorpe.

She stood still, not looking at Daphne and seeming not to wish to enter the dining-room. Some people went by, talking and laughing. Mr Gorman, the solicitor from Dublin, addressed her, but she did not acknowledge his greeting.

'I think we must go in now, Mrs Angusthorpe,' Daphne said.

In her weariness she smiled at Mrs Angusthorpe, suddenly sorry for her because she had so wretched a marriage that it caused her to become emotional with strangers.

'It was just,' said Mrs Angusthorpe, pausing uncertainly in the middle of her sentence and then continuing, 'I felt that perhaps I should say something. I felt, Mrs Jackson—'

'Let's just forget it,' interrupted Daphne, sensing with alarm that Mrs Angusthorpe was about to begin all over again, in spite of her protestations.

'What?'

'I think we must forget it all.'

Daphne smiled again, to reassure the woman who'd been

outrageous because her temper had run away with her. She wanted to tell her that just now in the bar she herself had had a small outburst and that in the end she had seen the absurdity of certain suggestions she had made. She wanted to say that her husband had asked her what the matter was and then had said he was sorry. She wanted to explain, presumptuously perhaps, that there must be give and take in marriage, that a bed of roses was something that couldn't be shared. She wanted to say that the tension she'd felt was no longer there, but she couldn't find the energy for saying it.

'Forget it?' said Mrs Angusthorpe. 'Yes, I suppose so. There are things that shouldn't be talked about.'

'It's not that really,' objected Daphne softly. 'It's just that I think you jumped to a lot of wrong conclusions.'

'I had an instinct,' began Mrs Angusthorpe with all her previous eagerness and urgency. 'I saw you at breakfast time, an innocent girl. I couldn't help remembering.'

'It's different for us,' said Daphne, feeling embarrassed to have to converse again in this intimate vein. 'At heart my husband's patient with me. And understanding too: he listens to me.'

'Of course,' agreed Mrs Angusthorpe, slowly nodding her head and moving at last towards the dining-room.